**S0-ABA-569**

**"Lily is a masterpiece!"**       *—Romantic Times*

# FORBIDDEN ECSTASY

"I am sorry for what I said," he murmured against her hair. "Forgive me, Lily. I misjudged you. I would never hurt you."

"Let me go, Devon. You must."

"Say you forgive me. I was angry, and those words—they were not well said. If I hurt you, I'm sorry." She stayed rigid, fists tight against his chest. "But I wanted you so much. I still do. I can't stop thinking about you, Lily. You've taken over my mind."

Her heart was racing. She ought to hate this painless but unbreakable embrace, but she didn't. "Don't say these things to me. Nothing's changed. It's impossible."

"Why is it?" One hand began to stroke the slim length of her back. "You liked it before, when we kissed. Let me kiss you again, just once. Let me, Lily."

**"This one is a keeper!"**       *—Rendezvous*

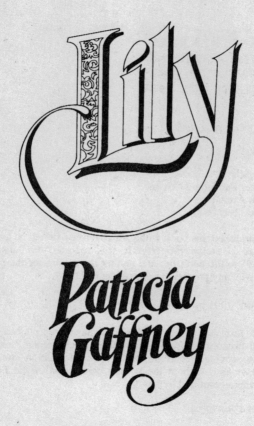

Lily

Patricia Gaffney

LEISURE BOOKS     NEW YORK CITY

*This book is for Alicia Condon,*
*past whom nothing gets.*
*Thanks for ferreting out all my facile shortcuts*
*and making me tell the truth.*

A LEISURE BOOK®

April 2000

Published by
Dorchester Publishing Co., Inc.
276 Fifth Avenue
New York, NY 10001

ISBN 0-8439-4772-1

The name "Leisure Books" and the stylized "L" with design are trademarks of Dorchester Publishing Co., Inc.

Printed in the United States of America.

# One

"Judas!"

Lily whipped her hand away from the red-hot handle of the roasting spit and flapped her fingers in the smoky air. "Ow, ow, ow," she yelped—softly, so her guests couldn't hear. Gripping her wrist, she squeezed her watering eyes shut as a blade of intense irritation sliced through her, so sharp it almost eclipsed the pain. It was at times like this when she wished she knew more swear words.

The roast pork was black, ruined; even the grease in the pan was only a dried-up charcoal glaze. Fanny, of course, was nowhere in sight; her twelve-year-old maid-of-all-work must have gone home as soon as she'd put the meat on the spit, no doubt expecting it to turn itself. Maid-of-*no*-work was a likelier title, fumed Lily. But what in God's name was she going to feed them now?

She wrapped the wet dishclout around her right thumb and wiped her eyes on her sleeve. There was no

need to check the larder. She did anyway, but a miracle
had not occurred since this morning: two eggs and a jar
of lemon pickle were still the only edible contents.
Uninvited houseguests had a way of depleting a girl's
pantry, especially if it was nearly empty to begin with.
Now after three dinners, two suppers, and innumerable
teas, Lily's pocketbook was empty, too.

Nothing for it but to tell them. Who knew, they might
even treat *her* to a meal for once. She unwrapped her
thumb and blew on the raised welt, smoothed her hair
back in its unruly red knot, straightened her shoulders,
and started up the worn basement steps to her first-floor
sitting room.

In the doorway she paused, and a quick flood of the
old vexation spurted through her. Roger Soames sat
beside the fire in her father's old chair, slippered feet on
the fender, reading the Lyme Regis *Monitor* and sipping
from a glass of canary wine. The *last* glass of canary
wine, she thought crossly; she hoped he enjoyed it, for
there would be no more. She wondered how Reverend
Soames's fire-and-brimstone God managed to overlook
his fondness for spirits—then chastised herself for
judging him. And yet she couldn't like him, even if he
was her . . . well, she wasn't exactly sure what he was.
He was her father's third cousin, but whether that made
him her fourth cousin or her third once removed or
something else altogether, she didn't know. What mattered was that he was her last male relative, the executor of her father's estate—if a legacy mostly of debts
could be called an "estate"—and, for thirteen more
months, her legal guardian.

She was even less clear on her relationship to Lewis,
Soames's son, who was sitting at her little writing desk
and scribbling something with a quill. A sermon? A new
tract on pious, godfearing behavior? Again she scolded
herself: she had absolutely no right to make fun of him.
Soames might or might not be a religious hypocrite, she
hadn't finally made up her mind on that score, but son

Lewis was a genuine believer, a truly devout man. Curious, then, that she couldn't quite bring herself to like him, either.

Reverend Soames glanced up from his newspaper. "Ah, Lily. Dinner is ready?"

"Cousin," she faltered, unable to call him "Roger" even though he'd invited her to, "I'm most awfully sorry, but there's been an accident. In the kitchen. Dinner's ruined," she confessed, spreading her hands.

A gleam of annoyance flared in his cold gray eyes before he masked it with an understanding smile. "Never mind, child. Come in, come, it's time we talked."

How could it be? thought Lily, almost in desperation. They'd been talking for two days! Before that she hadn't even known she *had* two cousins from Exeter, much less a legal guardian. And now she was being worried, tormented, and bullied into marrying a man she didn't care for, didn't even know. Had she been too polite? How many ways were there to say "no?"

She moved farther into the room reluctantly, hands in the pockets of her shabby morning gown, nervously fingering the shillings in change she'd gotten back from the coal man this morning. "If it's about Lewis and me—"

Soames stood up. He was a large, blocky man with a square face, big square hands, square shoulders. His body looked hard, as if carved out of a block of wood. No, not carved—*chopped*, with a hatchet or an ax. But his clothes were beautifully tailored and expensive, an anomaly that said much, in Lily's opinion, for the sincerity of his commitment to the poor and unfortunate. He wore his iron-gray hair parted in the middle, folded into little sausage curls over his ears, and tied in back in a queue. His thick neck and wide, bluish jaw gave him a bovine look. He even had square teeth.

"Maidenly shyness is an estimable quality," he announced, cutting her off in the fluid, booming tone that she could imagine sent sinners to their knees—or scrabbling in their pockets for donations. "And natural reserve is a trait to be nurtured and admired in a young Christian female. I respect you for it. But wisdom and humility are even higher virtues, and the young soul must aspire to them as well before the gates of heaven crack open for her. Come, my dear, it's time to pray." He stretched both huge, hair-covered hands out to her and bowed his head.

Blister it! Lily shot a glance at Lewis, who was getting up from behind the desk and moving toward them, presumably to join in the praying. Rebellion stirred sluggishly in her bosom, like a soldier roused from sleep before an uneven battle. She kept her hands at her sides. "Cousin Roger, I'm afraid that somehow I've misled you—all inadvertently, I promise. You do me great honor by proposing this marriage between Lewis and me"—here she turned what she hoped was a humble, appealing smile on her younger cousin—"but it just can't be."

"Why?"

Soames had snapped the word out. Was his infuriating equanimity finally deserting him? Would they both throw politeness away now and speak their minds?

"Because the match is unsuitable," she said.

"Why?"

Now they were getting to it. But politeness was too ingrained a habit to relinquish so easily. "Because I'm not worthy of it. Lewis is my superior in every way, but most particularly in the—the spiritual way. He deserves a wife who can complement and encourage that part of him. A woman closer to his equal, one who—"

"Lily, Lily," Soames cut in, shaking his big head disappointedly. "You speak of what Lewis 'needs' as if you knew the answer better than God. But what do *you* need?"

*Money*, she answered immediately, but inaudibly. Just

enough to get by on until she was twenty-one and came into her minuscule "inheritance." Then she could live in impoverished independence forever, if she chose to, and not marry anyone at all!

"You can't answer, I see. But I know what it is you need."

"Do you?" For the first time a tiny note of irreverence crept into her voice. She heard it, and vowed not to repeat it. *Burn no bridges* had been one of her father's maxims, one of his few practical ones. If she allowed fatigue and exasperation to snap her self-control, the goal would be lost. And the goal was to get these men out of her house in such a gracious, ladylike way they would hardly even know they'd been dismissed. She wanted them gone, but she needed their goodwill.

"What you need, Lily, is guidance. Something you've had precious little of in your short life, I fear. Your father set a shocking example. When your willfulness causes me to lose patience with you, I think of the life you've led; then my annoyance vanishes and I forgive you."

Lily's fingers curled into her palms. Condescending ass! And how dare he speak of her father that way?

"From now on, I intend to be your guardian in every sense of the word, but most particularly in the spiritual."

Again she fought for control. "I thank you for that. You're very kind, and I'm sure my soul can use . . . all the guidance it can get. I've no objection at all to any instruction you think is best. But as for me marrying Lewis, really, it's simply not possible. We hardly know each other, we've only just met—"

"Permit me to claim a higher wisdom in this matter than you, my dear child. But we've wasted enough time talking. I have a large flock of souls to attend to, men and women who depend on me for moral and spiritual leadership. I can't stay here past tomorrow."

She tried not to look jubilant.

"There's no sense in delaying the marriage. You'll come with us to my home in Exeter tomorrow—you've only a month left on the lease of this house, after all. In three weeks the banns can be announced, and then the wedding can take place. In my home. Naturally I'll officiate. You and Lewis will live with my wife and me, at least for a while, until you're—"

"Cousin, please—you mistake me! I have not agreed to this!"

The look of arrogant benevolence faltered, but only for a moment. "Think, Lily," Soames said softly, smoothly. "What else can you do? You have no means to support yourself, and thus no alternative."

*You smug, hypocritical, self-righteous* . . . She steadied herself, clasped demure hands, and looked at the floor. "You're right, of course. But I had hoped that you might see another way to help me. My needs are small, I require very little. And I know you to be a generous man. If you would make me a modest loan, in your capacity as executor and under any terms agreeable to you, and only until my father's small bequest comes to—"

"Ha!"

She looked up sharply. She thought she saw cynical recognition in his eyes—as if he'd decided his new-found cousin wasn't so very different from him after all—but it was gone in an instant.

"My generosity is not being tested now," he told her. "We're discussing the will of the Lord."

She blinked to disguise her annoyance. This was too unfair! "But surely the Lord's will in matters like this is a puzzle to men, an ambiguous thing."

"Often it is. Not in this case."

"But why? Why?"

"Because I saw it in a vision. The Lord vouchsafed to me an image of His will at work, and I saw with great clarity the wisdom and perfect order of your union with Lewis. Come, we'll pray."

He reached for her hands and drew them forcibly away from her sides. He gave one to Lewis and then dropped to his knees. Lewis followed, and Lily found herself forced to kneel between them on the thin rug in front of the fireplace. Soames's grip on her burned hand was torture, but when she tried to pull away he only held tighter.

"Almighty God, we beseech Thee! Look down upon Thy pitiful servant, Lily Trehearne, and grant her the wisdom to know Thy will and the humility to accept it. Make known to her the awesome folly of her pride and the sin of her arrogance, and in Thy infinite mercy grant her pardon. Reveal to this woman, this most unworthy of Thy daughters, the wages of sin and the penalty for selfishness."

There was more, much more, but she shut her ears to it. Finally he stopped. She stole another glance at Lewis. His head was bowed, eyes shut tight; like his father, he seemed to be offering up a private prayer. What was in his mind? she wondered dismally, examining his set, expressionless face and stubborn mouth. He was a big, hulking man, like his father; the resemblance between them was unmistakable, although Lewis wore his hair short in the manner of a workingman—a laborer for the Lord. In the brief time she'd known him he'd hardly spoken directly to her, and then only to second his father's pronouncements. She understood that he was as much in favor of this ridiculous marriage as Soames, and yet he'd shown no personal interest in her whatsoever, either as a friend or as a woman. Why were they so set on this union? Lily's father had left her a pathetically small living—it couldn't be for her money. Might Soames really have had a vision? She supposed such things were possible, and yet . . . somehow she didn't believe it.

The small of her back had begun to ache; the muscles between her shoulder blades felt as if they were on fire. Soames's huge hand tightened around hers. She winced, but took heart—he must be about to get up.

But no. "Oh Lord, who art the fountainhead and the giver of strength—" he resumed, and the litany of her transgressions began all over again.

From time to time he would stop, and on each occasion hope would soar in her that this time he'd really finished; but always he started up again, with an undaunted energy that distressed and demoralized her. She heard the clock on the mantel strike two times, and finally she couldn't bear it any longer. The bones in her knees felt in danger of fracturing if she knelt on them for one more minute. And she was afraid she was going to cry. At the end of one of Soames's protracted silences, before he could get out anything more than "Hear us, almighty G—" she jerked her hands out of both men's damp grasps and clambered stiffly to her feet.

"Please, I beg your pardon, but it's useless!" She cradled her smarting hand against her bosom, fighting back tears of pain and frustration and embarrassment. They were looking up at her with identical disbelieving expressions; she took an awkward step back to distance herself from them. "I'm sorry, but it's impossible. I cannot marry you, Lewis—I don't care for you and you don't care for me. Please try to understand, I mean no disrespect to either of you, and—and certainly not to God. But the vision was yours, Cousin Roger, not mine, and all our prayers can't change that." They got up slowly, still staring at her, and she felt compelled to keep talking. "Surely as men of God you believe that matrimony is a holy state, not one to be entered into lightly. And don't you agree that a man and woman ought to have as much in common as possible before they take such an important step? But Lewis and I, apart from esteem, I hope, and mutually—"

"Lewis, go out of the room and leave Lily and me alone."

Lily's eyes widened. Even Lewis looked surprised. But after a second's hesitation he obeyed, and closed the door behind him.

Soames faced her. She felt the full force of his personality and tried not to quake. The image of David and Goliath flitted through her mind; religious metaphors rarely occurred to her, but this was certainly the day for them. She watched her cousin's great box of a chest expand, and focused her eyes on the diamond and gold stickpin nestled incongruously in the frothy folds of his stock. The extravagance of it made him seem more human, less like the living voice of God, and she knew she would need to hold on to that sensibility to survive in the battle of wills that was coming.

But when he finally spoke his voice was pitched low and conversationally. It made his words all the more chilling. "You must marry Lewis, Lily. It is the will of God. If you refuse, I will take steps to see that you regret it. In this life."

Lily knew a threat when she heard one. "What will you do?" she asked, keeping her hands still when they wanted to flutter to her throat.

"I give you one last chance. Will you marry my son?"

"Please—"

"Will you marry him?"

She drew a nervous breath and managed somehow not to flinch from his dark, penetrating stare. "I cannot," she said quietly.

Without looking away, he reached into the pocket of his waistcoat. A hundred lurid possibilities occurred to her before he withdrew a flat leather purse. When he opened it and took out all the bills inside, she spoke up hastily.

"I will not take money, you can't bribe me."

He smiled coldly and turned away, bending over the fireplace grate. He stirred the smoldering coals to life with the poker and then, while she gaped in astonishment, he dropped the thick wad of money on top. It caught fire instantly.

"Stop, what are you—? Your money! Reverend Soames, what have you done?" Aghast, she darted closer. The bills in the middle hadn't ignited yet, maybe she could save them! But he prodded with the poker and they flared up in a quick, bright blaze. Then there was nothing left, not even smoke. And she could only gaze at him with her mouth open.

"Lewis!"

Almost immediately the door to the hall opened and her younger cousin came through. "Yes, Father?"

"Go and get the constable. Lily's stolen all my money, over seventy pounds."

"Judas!"

Lewis didn't move; he looked as shocked as Lily felt. "But—Father, how can this be? Are you sure?"

"I know it was she. I left my pocketbook on the mantel this morning. It's empty—look. No one's been here, it couldn't be anyone else." Lily and Lewis began talking at once. "Go!" thundered Soames, silencing them. Lewis went out.

This is a dream, thought Lily. She heard the front door open and close and thought, This can't be happening.

He moved to stand between her and the door. "Now is the time to change your mind. If you do, I'll simply tell the constable I was mistaken."

"You can't do this!"

"Otherwise I'll tell him to put you in the stocks. He'll do it, immediately, on the strength of my word. After you're tried, you'll be lucky if they transport you or send you to prison; more likely they'll hang you."

"Is *this* God's will?" she cried, fury overcoming her fright if only for a second. "You must be mad!"

"It is God's will. Repent, Lily Treharne. Pride and

vanity are sins for which you will rightly suffer in hell for eternity." His eyes burned and flecks of saliva flew from his mouth when he spoke. "Repent! Fall to your knees and beg almighty God's forgiveness." Before she could move he seized her shoulders and forced her to kneel again. On his knees beside her, hanging onto her flailing hands, he started to pray.

The words sounded mad now, the voice rabid. She pulled and hauled at his hands, but he wouldn't release her. Thoughts gone, acting on instinct, she bit him on the back of one giant paw. He yelled an irreligious oath and let go. She got one foot on the floor and sprang up, but his fingers snaked out and captured her ankle. He gave a vicious tug and she fell backwards, almost on top of him. When she cried out, he put a hand over her mouth. Once again she used her teeth. He jerked away and she twisted, shoving at him with both hands, thrusting against his chest with all her strength. The push caught him off balance; he fell sideways with a thud as some part of him struck the fireplace. Lily saw her chance, staggered to her feet, and ran for the door.

She stopped to look back, amazed because he wasn't following. She saw him sprawled across the hearth, motionless and open-eyed. The left side of his head ran bright red with blood.

She screamed.

The impulse to run again was all but irresistible. She conquered it and crept across the room, forcing herself to crouch beside him. She reached out to touch his neck, but her hand shook so badly she had to steady it by clamping down on her wrist with the other. She found his pulse, strong but unsteady, and after that her own heart seemed to start beating again.

His legs were tangled under his heavy body in an unnatural-looking way. She pulled them straight, appalled at their leaden inertness. He was breathing, she saw, but his face was gray. She shook him lightly by the shoulders. "Cousin! Reverend Soames!" No response. Would he recover? Would he die? Either way, they would think she had tried to kill him.

She stood up, hugging herself to control the shaking. What should she do? A constable was on his way to her house. She would tell him what had happened, of course. Surely he wouldn't believe she'd tried to murder her cousin. Would he? If only she had close friends or family here, people who knew her and could speak up for her! She dashed at tears that began to spill down her cheeks. "Oh, dear God," she said out loud in a strangled voice, feeling the prickly edge of panic nudge deep inside. Once more she bent over her cousin's body. "Please, please, please—" Four violent knocks thundered against the street door, and she jolted upright.

"Open up!" A man's voice, gruff and imperious. But they couldn't get in until she let them—the door was locked on the inside. She backed out of the room, eyes still on Soames as if even now he might leap up and grab her. In the dark hall she stopped, listening to the knocking grow louder, angrier. An image of the faces of the men behind the door froze her in place. "This is the constable! Open the door in the name of the law!"

Lily spun around, lifted her skirts, and ran.

Down the basement steps and across the kitchen floor to the service door, shoes clattering a panicky rhythm on the flagstones. Outside, she hurried through her tiny back garden to the alley. The fringe of her shawl caught on the gate hinge; she had to stop and untangle it, choking back a scream of frustration. A knot of children broke off their game of catch-Meg-on-a-snag to stare at her as she brushed past. "Miss Trehearne—" said one, a little black-haired boy who had never seen his pretty new neighbor without a smile. But she kept on and didn't look back.

Out of their sight, she broke into a run. The dark maze of alleys here near the harbor was completely unfamiliar to her; within minutes she was lost. Dogs barked and snapped, following her, chasing her out of their territory. Men stared; she hurried on with her head down. At last she came out into a wide, traveled street that she recognized. The afternoon sun in her eyes was a shock. She lifted her shawl to cover her hair and set off, away from the water, looking straight ahead and stepping smartly as if her destination were imminent and important. Her heart pounded hurtfully, almost deafening her.

She saw a fat carriage up ahead, in front of an inn. When she was almost abreast of it, she saw that it was the mail coach. The white-haired driver flung a last bundle on top and slammed his boot against the wooden fender.

"Wait!"

He paused and looked at her.

"Have you room for one more fare?"

"Aye, if ye've no baggage."

"No, none." Suddenly she went limp. And no money! But then she remembered, and reached into the pocket of her gown. "I've got three and a half shillings. How far can you take me?"

He scratched his beard and squinted. "Three an' a half? Reckon that's about Bridgwater."

"Bridgwater. Is that in Somerset?"

"Aye." He blew a gusty, surprised laugh. "It's mayhap halfway between here an' Bristol, where I'm bound."

She hesitated no longer. "I'll go, then." Handing him the coins, she stepped back. He opened the door, pulled down the step, put her in with a hand on her elbow, and slammed the door behind her. In the dimness she had an impression of men moving over to make room. Then she was sitting by the window, smoothing down her skirts and staring out at the brick building opposite. The coach gave a jerk and they were on their way.

"Will you take a cup of tea and a biscuit, lovey, while you wait?"

Lily pretended to consider it. "Oh . . . I don't think so, thanks very much. I had my dinner about an hour ago."

Mrs. Bickle, the landlady of the White Cow, gave her a nod and a smile and bustled off to see to her other customers. Lily leaned back against the settle. She'd eaten a piece of bread and butter early this morning, nothing since, and if she hadn't folded her arms across her stomach Mrs. Bickle would have heard it growl. Why hadn't she kept something back from the coachman, if only a few pennies? Too late now.

One of the men from the mail coach was staring at her. He'd been doing it for the past hour; she'd hoped this quick stopover in Chard would jar him out of his infatuation. Apparently it hadn't. She twisted around to look out the window, away from his rapt but surreptitious peering, just as another coach bumped and rattled into the inn yard. Because there was nothing else to do, she watched the passengers alight. Only after they were all out and straggling toward the door did it occur to her that one or more of them might be looking for her. A sliver of fear cut through her then, leaving her skin prickly and her palms damp. But the five travelers who entered the common room were so obviously not enforcers of the law—in fact, one or two looked quite the opposite—that she relaxed.

They found seats among the other company, and Mrs. Bickle called for the potboy to help her with the new crush. Two of the latecomers, a woman and a young man, sat down at a table near Lily's bench. She studied them idly, struck by the dourness of their very similar countenances. Mother and son? Aunt and nephew? Whatever they were, they looked as if nothing good had ever happened to them in their lives. Or if it had, they would steadfastly refuse to admit it. But they were neat, clean, respectably dressed—poverty wasn't the cause of their discontent.

Her thoughts were interrupted as Mrs. Bickle bustled

over to the man and woman. "You'll be wanting a bit of tea, won't you, loveys? Poor dears, you've half a day's journey still before Penzance, at the least."

Lily's admiration for Mrs. Bickle's professionalism rose several notches: the pinched-face pair across the way were the least likely "loveys" she'd ever seen. The woman was stout, with wide shoulders and no visible neck. Two pure white streaks in her dark hair began at the temples and blazed all the way back into a tight, fat chignon, a style that made Lily think of a skunk. Or a snake. Even the landlady's exuberant friendliness couldn't coax a smile out of her.

"We don't go to Penzance," she snapped, "we go to Trewyth and will be there by midnight. Now we'll have scones with our tea, not biscuits, and take care they're hot or I won't pay."

The young man, a black-eyed, hulking replica of his companion, looked across at Lily, and she glanced away, pretending she hadn't been eavesdropping. It was obscurely comforting to know that she hadn't misjudged them, that they were at least as unpleasant as she'd thought.

She put her head back against the high settle and tried to think what to do. She'd never heard of Bridgwater, and in a few hours she would be there. She was literally penniless, and in all probability she was wanted by the law, at least for stealing, probably for assault, perhaps even murder. She had no family, not even close friends —the rather vagabond existence she'd led with her father for the last ten years had prevented her from making lasting attachments. Mrs. Troublefield was the closest thing she had to a friend, but an hour ago Lily had left Lyme Regis and her kindly next-door neighbor behind.

The wisdom of that act troubled her again, as it had at least a dozen times since she'd climbed into the mail coach. If she'd stayed, they *might* have believed her. She was a respectable woman, had never been in any kind of trouble. Her father had occasionally made himself known to local law-keepers for minor infractions, but surely they wouldn't have held that against her. But it was too late now. Running away had insured the appearance of guilt, and there was nothing to do but make the best of things. But how? How was she going to. . . .

Her thoughts tapered off. She kept her eyes unfocused on the middle distance while the tail end of a conversation brought her to rigid attention.

". . . afraid I wouldn't know of anyone who'd suit you just now," Mrs. Bickle was saying. "But why would you be wantin' to hire servants from so far away? Are there not girls much closer to home who would do? If your master's house is in Cornwall, why don't you look—"

"Because the estate is isolated, and it's hard to find any but slovenly country girls who'll stay past a month or two. The master's particular and won't put up with sluts. It was only an idea," the sour-faced woman added ungraciously. "I thought to ask, though I didn't really expect you to know anyone who would do."

Mrs. Bickle's smile finally wavered, and her curtsey was the merest bob of the knees before she turned and left the room.

She was hardly out the door when Lily stood up and followed her.

She found the landlady in the inn's private parlor, pouring tea for an old man who was reading the newspaper in front of a coal fire. When she saw Lily, her smile came back. "The privy's behind the house, dear, just through this—"

"Mrs. Bickle, I have a favor to ask you. I have no money, nor am I likely to get any soon, so I won't pretend that what I need is only to be a loan. I want to write a letter. It—it's rather urgent. I don't need a stamp, just pen and ink, and perhaps an envelope if you—"

"Is it a piece of paper and a quill you want?"

"I—yes."

"Well, for goodness sake." She looked relieved that it wasn't more. "Come over here, lamb." She went to a writing desk in the corner of the parlor. "Can you see in the murk? I can light a candle if you want it."

"No, this is fine. Thank you so much, I can't tell you—"

"Nonsense, help yourself and take as long as you like." She gave Lily two bracing pats on the arm and went out.

She sat down. The paper was plain but surprisingly good—an unhoped-for piece of luck. She found the newest-looking quill and dipped it in the well inset in the desktop. After a minute's thought, she began to write.

"Lily Tr—" She stopped short, amazed at the stupidity of what she'd almost done. What would her name be, then? T-r what? A tiny smile pulled at her lips and she set the pen to paper again. "Lily Troublefield has been in my employ for the last year and a half. During that time she has shown herself to be a biddable, honest, and able girl in the capacity of maid-of-all-work in my household. She leaves my employ because"—she paused again and tapped the quill against her lips thoughtfully—"because I am about to embark on a year-long journey on the European Continent, and Lily is unwilling to continue in service away from home for so long a time. I know her to be of good character and cheerful disposition; she is naturally industrious and uncommonly intelligent for a girl of her class. My recommendation of Lily is unqualified."

Had she overdone it? Probably, but she couldn't help liking the "uncommonly intelligent" part. With a self-conscious flourish, she signed the paper, "Dow. Lady Estelle Clairton-Davies, Marchioness of Frome."

There really was such a person—she owned a coun-

try house outside Lyme, and once Lily had seen her
rather grand coach-and-four waiting beside a jeweler's
shop in the town. But she'd skillfully gotten rid of her
ladyship by shipping her off to Europe, so the likelihood
of anyone writing to her to verify the truthfulness of this
reference was small—a risk worth taking. She sprin-
kled silver sand across the paper, waited a moment and
blew it away, folded the letter, and tucked it into an
envelope. It looked too crisp, too clean. She massaged it
between her fingers for a few seconds, folded it in half,
unfolded it, folded it again. Better. She slid it into her
pocket and stood up.

How did she look? Her dark-blue dress of cotton
cambric was shabby enough, but was it too fine none-
theless for the likes of a humble maid-of-all-work?
Perhaps, but then again, perhaps not for one who had
worked in the home of so illustrious a personage as the
Marchioness of Frome. It didn't matter, she had nothing
else. And there were other ways to convince the prune-
faced lady from Cornwall that she was a maid. She
squared her shoulders and started for the common
room.

She wasn't there. Lily searched the room frantically
with her eyes. She wasn't there!

"Did you write your letter, dearie?"

"The lady in the black coat, she came in the coach
after ours and there was a man with her, younger—"

"They've gone out, love. The Penzance coach is just
leaving. You can catch her if you—"

She broke off when Lily spun around and dashed for
the door. Halfway through it, she remembered to stop
and call back over her shoulder, "Thank you for the
paper! Good-bye!" The startled landlady lifted a hand to
wave, but Lily had disappeared.

The young man was already handing the woman into
the coach. "Oh, Mrs.—madam! Excuse me!" she cried,
breaking into a run across the rutted dirt yard. She
reached them out of breath. The hostile looks they

turned on her had a diminishing effect on her confidence. She took a breath and plunged in.

"Beggin' your pardon, mistress, but I chanced t' overhair what you were sayin' t' the landlady just naow, an' I was after wonderin' if you'd be thinkin' o' meself for housemaid, like. I've a wonderful good character from me last lady, so she told me, an' I'm a nate an' tidy parson by nature an' would wark tremendous hard for you. Would you be wantin' t' see me character?"

Well, it was *sort* of Irish, or at least more Irish than anything else. She hoped. Without waiting for the woman's answer, she took out the envelope and thrust it into her hands, smiling a big, respectful smile. The woman returned it with a suspicious scowl, but Lily decided it was her natural expression and not meant personally. Yet.

She shrugged one massive shoulder with irritation and opened the envelope. Lily waited, praying the ink was dry. She hazarded a glance at the man. They had to be mother and son; the resemblance was too strong to be accounted for by any other relationship. But he was smiling, something she hadn't seen his mother do. It wasn't a nice smile.

The mother finished reading and looked up. She had small black eyes, slightly protruding, and narrowed to slits now with skepticism. Lily spoke quickly. "Is it a good one, then? I'm not much for raidin'," she said with a little embarrassed laugh, "but me mistess did say 'twould sarve me well when th' time came." When the *toime* came, I should've said, she fretted, wondering if the accent was such a good idea after all. Her father was an Irishman, but he'd lost most of his lilt after all the years lived in England. But sometimes, when he'd drunk too much whiskey, he would lapse into an exaggerated brogue, and it was her imperfect memory of that accent that Lily was relying on now to see her through this interview.

"If it's true, it'll serve."

She widened her eyes in innocent protest. "Oh, ma'am, it's true, be Jaysus, as God is me witness—"

"Hold your tongue! Would you take the Lord's name to my face? How dare you!" Her scowl blackened and her bulldog eyes snapped with indignation. "If you come into my service, that sort of talk won't be tolerated. What kind of household did this great lady of Frome manage, then? A godless one, I'm bound, if you're the result."

"Oh, no, ma'am, don't be thinkin' it! It's a daycent garul I am, truly, only sometimes me tongue gets away from me. It's because o' me dear departed father." She made it rhyme with "lather." "He were a good man at heart, but a terrible blasphemer. Naow when I'm in distress, like, out pops the very wards I used t' scold 'im about."

"So you're in distress, are you?"

"I—" She thought fast. "Not *distress*, as you might say, but more like anxious. I was after stoppin' in Axminster t' visit me old friend Fanny, her as works as housemaid for th' pastor's wife, an' while we was traipsin' around the market fair in th' taown, me pocket was picked! Pure an' clane, an' turned outside-in like a pilla case. Well, ma'am, it shortened me holiday considerably, you can understand, an' put me in nade of anither post sooner than I was plannin'. Would you be thinkin' of hirin' me, naow?"

The fat coachman came around in front of the horses and glowered at them. "You'll have to get up now, I can't be waiting any longer."

Lily turned winsome eyes to her prospective employer. But that lady was not to be persuaded by winsome eyes, nor hurried by an impatient coachman. "If I gave you a job, you'd start in the scullery. It's three shillings a month, and you must buy your own cap and aprons. You'd work hard and have Sunday mornings off—to go to church, not Mass—as well as an afternoon a month for yourself. I'm Mrs. Howe, housekeeper to a viscount; Devon Darkwell is his name, Lord Sandown. Is that your only dress?"

"I—yes, ma'am."

"It'll do for now, I suppose. Can you pay coach fare to Trewyth?"

"I can't!"

"Then that'll have to come out o' your wage as well." She tapped the edge of the envelope in the V between her thumb and forefinger and peered at Lily consideringly. "You don't look that strong."

"I am, though. You'd be—"

"And if I ever hear a sacrilegious word out o' your mouth again, I'll box your ears and send you packing."

"You won't, I prom—"

"Get in, then, and be quick. You're keeping everyone in the coach waiting."

# Two

Despite worry and nerves and the great question mark her immediate future had become, Lily slept fitfully much of the way to Cornwall. Exhaustion overwhelmed anxiety; and oblivion, she discovered, served a dual purpose: it allowed her to keep her atrociously inept Irish accent to herself a little longer—what a bird-witted idea *that* had been—and it gave her a respite from the sullen, unnerving silences of the Howes—mother and son, as she'd surmised. Early on in the journey she'd made tentative inquiries about her new situation, but with paltry success. Their destination was a place called Darkstone Manor, and Mrs. Howe spoke in short, belligerent sentences of "the master" and "his lordship," but beyond that Lily could get little from either of them about her new employer. The smell of the sea grew stronger as they went, and yet she had no idea where they were or even toward which Cornish coast, Channel or Atlantic, they were traveling.

It was after midnight and the moon had set by the
time they reached Trewyth; all Lily could make of the
silent village was that it was small and clean. She
climbed from the public coach, limbs stiff from fatigue
and inactivity, and waited, shivering a little in the misty
chill, while the driver threw the Howes' baggage down
from the top. They had rather a lot of it, she noted,
considering they'd only been away for three days while
Mrs. Howe visited her sister in Bruton. Lily heard the
sound of hooves and turned to see another coach, a
handsome black private carriage in need of a wash,
clattering toward them down the unpaved street. Lord
Sandown's equipage, she assumed, sent to carry them
the rest of the way to the manor house. She felt weary
beyond thought. As she climbed into the carriage she
wondered how long it would take, and whether she had
strength enough to go another mile before she collapsed.

But in a mercifully short while their new vehicle
turned in at high stone lodge gates bordering a wooded
park and moved sedately down a twisting gravel drive.
She forgot her fatigue and peered out the window
curiously, but there was little to see except the black
shapes of trees passing almost within arm's reach of the
carriage on either side. The salt tang of the sea was
stronger now in the windless midnight hush. She
thought she could make out a light up ahead, but the
road bent sharply and she lost sight of it.

"There'll be room for you in Lowdy Rostarn's bed in
the attic," Mrs. Howe said suddenly. "Go on up directly
and straight to sleep, no talking. Well?"

"Yes, ma'am," Lily said hurriedly. She wasn't used to
taking orders and hadn't spoken up quickly enough.

Mrs. Howe had her plump hand on the door handle.
In the next minute the carriage stopped and she flung
the door open, lowered the step herself, and got out, not
waiting for assistance.

"After you," said the son, whose name was Trayer, and despite the darkness Lily sensed an impudent grin on his lips.

She stepped to the ground, and stood in the gravel half-circle before the brooding black bulk of an enormous house. Three and a half stories of Cornish granite hovered above her like a dark, wide-winged hawk, obliterating starlight in the southern sky. *Darkstone*. She whispered the name, motionless before its austere immenseness. There might be towers at the far corners, but in the blackness she couldn't be sure. She grew dizzy gazing up at the invisible demarcation between roof and night sky. From somewhere, everywhere, the sound of water on rock was a steady, sibilant hiss. As she watched, lightless cliffs of sheer stone wall seemed to stretch and expand at the edges of her vision, as if to surround her. Fatigue, she scoffed, pulling her thin shawl tighter. Nevertheless, the impression lingered.

Torchlight wavered on worn stone steps leading to the entrance, a scarred and iron-belted oak door with a huge ring for a handle. The Howes were seeing to their bags again. Unthinking, drawn to the light, Lily moved toward the door. She'd put her foot on the first step when she heard the fast, angry crunch of stones behind her.

Mrs. Howe caught her by the elbow and spun her around. "Ignorant trull! Insolent little baggage! Where do you think you're going?"

"I—I forgot myself, I didn't think—"

"Forgot yourself!" For a wild second Lily thought the housekeeper would strike her. But with a powerful effort she reined in her temper and pointed toward the east end of the house. "The servants' steps are there, around that corner. Mayhap her grand ladyship in Lyme lets servant girls use her front door, but there's none o' that here. You'd best learn your place quick, Lily Troublefield, or I'll make you sorry."

"Yes, ma'am. I beg your pardon." She made her voice

contrite, but inside she burned with indignation. Head bowed, leaving Trayer and the coachman to see to the luggage, she followed Mrs. Howe along a flagstone walk that led around the house to a small courtyard and stone basement steps. The housekeeper opened the door at the bottom and swept inside; Lily went more slowly, feeling her way in the dark. She was in a corridor; at its far end a dim light glowed, and Howe trudged toward it stolidly. It proved to come from the kitchen, an enormous, echoing chamber whose far wall was taken up entirely by the biggest brick hearth Lily had ever seen.

"Dorcas!"

A girl, a wan wisp of a child no older than twelve or thirteen, jerked herself awake on a stool next to the hearth. "Ooh, ma'am, ee're back, I weren't sleepin'!" she said in a nervous gush, scrambling off the stool.

"Let the lamp burn out, didn't you? Ignorant girl! Nothing but the candle to greet us, and I *told* you what time we'd be back. Get upstairs; I'll deal with you in the morning."

Dorcas mumbled, "Ais, ma'am," looking terrified. She was small, dull-haired, and gray-skinned, with a sore on her lip. Scurrying out, she threw Lily only one quick, curious glance.

"You'll help Dorcas in there tomorrow," Howe announced, shrugging a massive shoulder toward a door that led to the dark scullery. "Have that grate cleaned and the fire lit before Mrs. Belt comes in— that's the cook. She starts the breakfast at five. Now get off to bed." She took Lily by the elbow and hustled her back out into the dim corridor. "The servants' stairs are at the end o' this hall, straight ahead. Lowdy's room's in the attic, the first door on the left. Go on, now." Lily was halfway down the hall when Mrs. Howe called out, "And get a cap for that hair by tomorrow or I'll cut it off!"

Feeling her way in the deepening dark, Lily had to fight back tears. She muttered, "Damn," as her elbow

struck the wainscot with a sharp crack. She found the
steps by stumbling up the first one, barely catching
herself before her chin hit the fourth. *"Damn,"* she said
again, holding onto the wall—then stopped, arrested by
a sound somewhere above her. A voice? Yes, loud and
angry, a man's voice—and now a terrific muffled thud.

She climbed the last stair to the first-floor landing and
stood still, peering around the corner down the length
of a wide, high-ceilinged hall. She made out a door at
the far end, broad and grand, and realized it must be the
great front door Mrs. Howe had forbidden her to use.
Another hall bisected this one halfway to the door; the
voices—two now, one raging, one placating—came
from the right. She saw two huge shadows lunge in the
writhing light from candles in a sconce along the wall,
and would have retreated to the dark staircase behind
her—but then the first voice came again. The words
were garbled, unintelligible, but underneath anger Lily
heard the bare, wrenching sound of a wild anguish. The
rawness of it pierced something inside her—she found
she couldn't move. Flattening her back against the wall,
she held her breath and waited.

"Jesus God, Cobb, she took him. Why? Why did she
take him?"

Devon Darkwell, Viscount Sandown, the master of
Darkstone Manor, shook off his steward's grip and
lurched drunkenly into the relative brightness of the
entry hall. Swaying, he stood under the wide, unlit
chandelier and drank four swallows of brandy from the
crystal decanter in his hand. French brandy, his brother's smuggled finest; it went down as smooth as warm
silk. But tonight something was wrong with it. He'd
been drinking steadily since early afternoon and he
wasn't drunk yet. Or not drunk enough.

Arthur Cobb reached out with his good arm—the
other ended in a handless stub at the cuff of his
coat—and muttered, "'Ere, now, all's well, ee've no call
t' be swingin' this about. I'll just take—"

Devon jerked away, irritated, and then stared down in bloodshot perplexity at the silver hunting pistol lying in his palm. He couldn't remember taking it out of his desk drawer. The sight of it exhumed the macabre remains of his vicious meditation. "I wish she weren't dead," he rasped, hollow-eyed. "If she weren't dead, I could kill her."

His black-bearded steward stiffened, and reached once more for the gun. Devon's hand clenched around it harder and he bared his teeth, intent on the chaos of bitterness and violence inside him—when a sound, a soft intake of breath, diverted him. He whirled, facing the darkness, and saw the pale outline of a face, receding.

"Stop!" The face halted for a second, then retreated again. "Stop, I said!" He took three unsteady steps forward. Was it a woman? "You there, come here," he commanded. A moment passed. Then the figure approached, unwillingness obvious in every lagging footfall, and he saw that it was a woman, a girl, with dark hair and light eyes. He'd never seen her before.

She stopped again, and something told Devon she would come no farther now. He fumbled the pistol into his jacket pocket and moved toward her, snatching a candle from the wall bracket as he went. "Who are you?" he demanded when he reached her. He held the candle high and peered at her.

Lily clutched her hands together, quelling the impulse to fling them up like a shield between herself and this staring giant of a man who smelled of drink and looked capable of anything. His straight brown hair hung to his collar, wild and disheveled; his coat was rumpled, his white stock untied and wine-stained. He had a dangerous face, and the expression in his bleak blue eyes frightened her. Gathering her nerve, she said, "I'm Lily," in a quiet voice, and waited for whatever would happen next.

Devon's stare narrowed. She was tall and slender in

her dark gown. A pale, gentle face. Green eyes, or maybe
gray. Her mouth looked soft; a forgiving mouth. He
couldn't tell what color her hair was. While he watched,
some of the fury in him abated, seemed to shrivel under
the steadiness of her level gaze. "Are you?" he said, and
was surprised to hear something close to composure in
his tone. "Yes, I can see the resemblance." He wanted to
touch her, to find out if her white cheek was as soft as it
looked. *Lily.* But he had a bottle in one hand, a candle in
the other. "What are you doing in my house, Lily?" She
could tell him anything, he thought, anything at all:
what he wanted was to hear her voice again.

Lily realized she wasn't afraid. There was no anger in
the man's face now, only pain, and a whimsical politeness. "I'm your new housemaid, sir," she explained
softly. And then, appalled, she watched his face change
again, slowly, this time to cold contempt.

Devon stepped back. "Of course," he said, lips twisting in a nasty smile. He let the candle thud to the floor
and reached into his pocket. The girl's frightened gasp
pleased him. Behind him, Cobb muttered something; he
broke off when Devon whirled and jerked the pistol up
and out with both hands. Squinting, he squeezed the
trigger and fired.

The great glass chandelier in the foyer dropped like a
boulder and struck the bare wood floor with a deafening
crash. Lily screamed, twisting away from a spray of
flying crystal. The master spun back around. She saw his
face, black with some inscrutable emotion, and shrank
back. He took a step toward her, at the same moment
the man named Cobb plucked the gun out of his hand.

Devon snarled; Cobb braced himself. But instead of
attacking, Devon fell back against the wall, striking his
shoulders with a rough thud. He uttered curses in a soft,
passionless monotone. His hand shook when he raised
the brandy decanter to his lips.

Cobb turned away, toward Lily. "Get upstairs, girl,"
he advised in a low voice.

"Why?" Devon wiped his mouth with his sleeve and
fixed her with a sardonic eye. "She's the bleeding *maid*,
isn't she? Let her clean up the mess."

Her knees wouldn't stop trembling. She looked back
and forth between the two men in confusion, unsure if
the master was serious or not.

"Go on," Cobb repeated stolidly. "Where be your
room?"

"I—I'm to sleep with someone called Lowdy."

"Go up, then. Say naught o' this to Lowdy or anyone,
d'you hear? Keep it to yourself."

"Yes, I will," she promised. But she saw skepticism in
the man's black stare.

She threw a last glance at Devon Darkwell. He had
slid to the floor. His forearms hung heavily between his
knees; the empty decanter dangled from his fingers. He
was staring into space, head against the wall, and there
was nothing in his hard eyes now except emptiness. Lily
picked up her skirts and ran.


"My real name's Loveday. Loveday Rostarn. Pretty,
edn it? People've called me Lowdy all my life, though, so
I reckon I'm stuck wi' it. Is that all ee d' have t' sleep in,
an?"

Lily glanced down at her worn shift. "Aye, this is it."

"Well, they d' say winter's over, though hereabouts
you can't be sartin till summer. An' 'ave ee no clawthes
but that dress yonder, an' no other shoes? How did ee
come t' such a press?"

"I—it—everything was stolen, at a fair. All me money
an' every stitch I owned." It was almost impossible to
speak Irish to Lowdy Rostarn; Lily's brain was too tied
up trying to understand what Lowdy was saying to her
in Cornish. What a pair they were going to make!

"Ee d' look all done in, poor lamb. Blaw out the
candle an' crawl in. Mrs. 'Owe d' give out but one candle
a week t' each maid's room, Sundays, so we've four
nights t' go on that bit o' nub. But tes dark as a blatherin'

sack wi' no moon t'night. Are ee hungry? I 'ad a pennorth o' broken biscuits, but I et 'em."

"I was before; I think I'm just numb now." Lily took a last look around at the distempered walls and bare floorboards, the sparse, ill-assorted furniture, the spotted mirror and chipped washbasin. The room was cold now—what must it be like in February? She imagined waking up shivering, finding ice on the water in the jug, the face flannel frozen solid. She blew out the candle and crept between the sheets of the cast-off iron four-poster—two-poster now; the other two had been cut down so the bed could be wedged sideways under the eaves. Everything smelled of damp and mildew and rot. The mattress was lumpy and ridiculously thin. Lowdy pushed half of the hard pillow over for Lily to share. She murmured, "Thank you," and thought about her new bedmate.

For herself, Lily would probably not have welcomed a pathetic-looking intruder to her small room and smaller bed in the wee hours of the morning. But Lowdy had seemed genuinely glad for the company, causing Lily to wonder if domestic life in this great mansion of a place was lonely sometimes for a young girl. Lowdy was seventeen, and had worked here for two years. She was short-legged, small-breasted, and wide-hipped, and her solid little body looked strong, much stronger than Lily's. She had pretty black hair, cut short, and a sensible face. But a chipped front tooth appeared whenever she smiled, which was often, and then she looked playful and a little sly. Her thick Cornish accent was completely unfamiliar to Lily, almost Slavic-sounding if she let her mind wander and didn't concentrate. Luckily the girl spoke slowly, with a phlegmatic deliberateness that usually allowed Lily to decipher the meaning of one sentence before she started another.

"What's it like to work here?" Lily whispered in the darkness. But what she wanted to know was what "the master" was like, and if the scene she'd just witnessed

downstairs was typical or an aberration. Lowdy was a
heavy sleeper, however, and knew nothing of gunshots
and crashing chandeliers; and since Lily had promised
the man named Cobb that she would say nothing of the
incident, she could see no way to ask the question
directly.

"Oh, no worser'n any an' betterer'n most." Lowdy
yawned and settled on her side. "Tes Mrs. 'Owe you d'
want t' be watchin' out for. Her's as mean as a splatty ol'
pig, I'd as lief bait a bull as cross 'er."

"What does she do?"

"She hits, is what. Enid, the girl last but one afore ee,
she smoted 'er onct so rough-like, she breaked 'er arm.
An' Sidony, the scullery maid as was 'ere in September
month two years past—before me, but I heard of
it—she falled down the dairy step and near died.
Naught was said above-stairs, but below they all knowed
it were 'Owe. An' the maid no more'n a cheeil at the
time, a little small tiddler o' thirteen."

Lily lay still, appalled. Tales got spread in tight-knit
households, she told herself; gossip blossomed and
grew. Surely Lowdy was exaggerating.

"An' ee did ought t' stay clear o' Trayer as well, for
what he does is worser'n hittin'."

That had the ring of truth. She heard Lowdy yawn
again and spoke quickly, before her sleepy informant
could drift off. "What's the master like? To—work for, I
mean. Mrs. Howe said he's very particular about the
maids."

Lowdy snorted. "Phaw, tes a cabby lie. Master bain't
in mind we're alive, has eyes for naught but 'is work."

"His work?"

"Ais, 'im's a great squire, owns a mine an' land an'
sheep an' what-not. Mrs. 'Owe d' say such a thing about
'im bein' *particular* t' make up for losin' so many girls.
She can't keep 'em, is what."

"Why do you stay, Lowdy?"

"Pick me liver, where would I go?"

"Don't you have family?"

"Naw. Hired on 'ere at me first fair, right out o' orph'nage."

They were both quiet for a time. Lily thought Lowdy had fallen asleep, and spoke softly in case she had. "Is the master ever a violent man?"

"Master? Nay. Nay, 'im's just grim-like. Scarcely ever speaks, not t' us, not t' anyone. His wife runned off an' left 'im, I heard. She'm dead now."

"When, Lowdy? How long ago?"

"Don't know. Afore me. He d' have a brother, the *young* master, but 'e lives somewheres else. In Devon wi' their mother, I b'lieve. Only comes 'ere when there's smugglin' afoot—an' they d' say 'e's comin' tomorrow. He'm a free-trader an' d' captain 'is own ship."

This Lily definitely did not believe. As she lay pondering her next question, Lowdy began to snore.

She closed her own eyes and shifted on the hard, uncomfortable mattress. At least there weren't any bugs. The casement window must face the sea, for in the new quiet she could hear its secretive whispering. She tried to put her thoughts in order, but memories butted and shuffled against each other and it was impossible. In her mind's eye she saw her cousin sipping canary wine beside the fire, his great heavy legs braced against the fender. She saw the faces of the children she'd fled past in the alley. She saw Trayer Howe's crude and patient staring. His mother's black, spiteful eyes, and the two white streaks blazing in her dark hair.

Then Devon Darkwell's bitter, hard-edged face filled her mind. The odd gentleness that had suffused it when he'd asked, "What are you doing in my house, Lily?" Later, he'd called her *the bleeding maid*. Would he remember her if they met again? If she went away from this place tomorrow, she knew she would never forget *him*.

# Three

At four-thirty the next morning, half-awake and nearly numb with exhaustion, Lily splashed cold water on her face and fumbled into her clothes in the chilly pitch dark. She found the uncarpeted back stairs by almost falling down them, and negotiated the three narrow flights to the basement by holding onto the wall. Dorcas was already busy in the lamp-lit kitchen. She told Lily to lay the fire in the kitchen hearth—in tones that suggested she'd never told anyone to do anything in her young life—and then two more upstairs because it was cold this morning, in the dining room and the master's library. Lily swept the kitchen hearth clean, fetched coal in the scuttle, and set to work.

"Don't ee want t' clean the basket first off?" Dorcas said timidly, coming up behind her. "Ee did ought to, miss, for Mrs. 'Owe d' say we must, for every fire, each morning."

"Oh yes, I—I forgot." Lily sat back on her heels and contemplated the sooty, fire-blackened grate. She and her father had been through lean times, but they'd never been so poor that they hadn't kept at least one servant. Thus she could make and light a fire easily enough, but she had never cleaned a grate. "How, um . . . Dorcas, how do I . . ."

"Don't ee know how?" Her listless eyes widened in amazement.

"I was parlormaid in my last post, you see, so I didn't have to." A ridiculous excuse, but all she could think of on short notice.

Dorcas's face reflected awe and disbelief in equal measure. Nevertheless, she showed Lily how to brush, black-lead, and polish the grate and the fire tools, and burnish the steel parts with emery paper. It was a filthy, tedious job, time-consuming and physically taxing, and as she went from one fireplace to the next and then the next, the reason for doing it became more and more elusive. What was the point? she wanted to know by the time she reached the third. You got it perfect, you lit a fire, and you ruined it. Why not do it every *other* day—even once a week?

There was, of course, no one to whom she could put that futile question. But it would occur to her again in other contexts as the morning wore on. Why was it necessary to scrub the stone floor in the scullery every day before breakfast? What was the point of whitening the area steps each morning? Did all the brass door fixtures really need a *daily* polishing?

By seven-thirty she was shaking with hunger, and as weary as if she'd done a full day's work. But breakfast in the servants' hall was only a hasty meal of cheese and dough cakes left over from last night's supper, washed down with a mug of beer. Every bite was delicious; she savored each one as if it might be her last. Mrs. Howe sat at the head of the long wooden table—over which a painted sign on the wall proclaimed, "Cleanliness Comes Next to Godliness"—and her stern presence set the tone for what little, almost furtive conversation there was. Stringer, the butler, presided at the foot, silent and uninvolved. Between them were the other household servants—cook, master's valet, parlormaid, housemaids, kitchen and scullery maids, a groom and two stable lads, coachman, three footmen, dairy and laundry maids—all arranged in some subtle hierarchical order too obscure for Lily to comprehend.

She understood that she was at the nether end of it, though. The advantage of this was that hardly anyone spoke to her, so her Irish brogue could languish all but unheard a little longer. The only one who paid any attention to her was the groom, a roguish-looking fellow with bright orange hair. His name was Galen MacLeaf, and according to him there wasn't a man in Cornwall who had a more cunning hand with horseflesh. Or, his blue eyes seemed to twinkle, with the ladies. Lily found his flirting outrageous and inoffensive. He was small and wiry, with beautiful hands and a cast in one eye—a defect that didn't diminish his attractiveness, even enhanced it somehow. He was a charmer. Listening to his exaggerated boasts, she had almost begun to enjoy herself when she happened to glance across the table at Lowdy. Gone was her new roommate's sweet, friendly expression, replaced by anger and unmistakable jealousy. After that, Lily kept her eyes on her plate and her mouth shut.

More chores in the kitchen occupied the rest of the morning. She received shy orders from Dorcas and less shy ones from the cook, Mrs. Belt, an arrow-faced, white-haired woman. Close to noon, Mrs. Howe found Lily toiling in the scullery and informed her, with a brittle anger out of proportion to the offense, that she hadn't cleaned the grate in the library properly and must do it again. Weak and weary, she returned with her heavy firebox and set to work.

Lowdy found her there a quarter of an hour later.

"Lord, look at ee, your face'm darkerer'n Lady Alice's blackamoor footman. 'Ere, take this."

Lily took the wadded-up handkerchief Lowdy held out and dragged it across her cheeks, dismayed at the quantity of greasy black ash that came away. "Who's Lady Alice?" she muttered, wiping her arms, which were black to the elbow.

"Master's lady friend, comes t' visit wi' his mother onct in a while. 'Ere, take this too."

"Oh, Lowdy." It was a cap, gray from washing, strings bedraggled. "I'll pay you back when I can, I promise I will."

"Phaw. Come on downstairs now, afore master gets back." A housemaid's duties above-stairs, Lily had learned, had to be finished before dinner, so that no one "above" would have to set eyes on anything as disagreeable as a humble cleaning servant after one o'clock in the afternoon. "'Owe d' say you're t' scrub the area steps again, didn't do it right first time, an' then come back in 'ere an' finish." She watched Lily put the cap on and tuck her dark red hair under it. "Ee d' have pretty hair," she said wistfully, fingering her own short, dark locks.

Lily remembered how Galen MacLeaf had flirted with her this morning at breakfast. "That's what my young man's always after tellin' me," she said impulsively— and suddenly remembering she was supposed to be Irish.

"'Ave ee got un, an?"

"Aye, we're betrothed."

Lowdy's big, chip-toothed smile lit up her face. "Well, now," she said, guiding Lily out of the room with a soft hand. "Well, now, edn that grand?"

Dinner was another dour, silent meal, and afterward Lily wasn't sure she had the strength to get up. It had become impossible to think of what was happening to her even remotely as an adventure. She was plagued and haunted by the idea of lying down somewhere, anywhere, and closing her eyes just for a few minutes. Every muscle pleaded for a rest; the skin on her palms was raw, her fingernails blackened and torn. Food no longer had the power to restore her, so profound was her fatigue. But there were still steps to be whitened, and after that birds to be plucked, peas to be shelled, pots to be scrubbed, and a hundred miscellaneous chores to be done for any servant who was superior to her—which was all of them. The single bright moment in the awful, exhausting day came when it was finally over and she was allowed to have a bath, in the last big tub of hot wash water in the laundry house. She made the most of it, washing her hair and taking as long as she possibly could, knowing it would be her only all-over wash for the week.

When supper finally came—a bowl of watery soup and a pilchard on a chunk of bread—she'd lost her appetite and had to force the salty fish down. Even then, bedtime had to wait. The servants gathered in the hall for an hour every evening, to talk and do mending or other personal tasks. Lowdy told her in a whisper that she couldn't go up yet even if all her chores were done, for Mrs. Howe had to lead them first in evening prayers, and those didn't begin until nine o'clock. Lily fell asleep waiting, slumped in a hard chair at the table, her chin on her chest.

"Rose is sick," Mrs. Belt said one morning a week later, pointing at two covered trays on the kitchen table. "Take these up to the master an' the young master, then come right back an' help me with this sourbread."

"You mean—to their rooms?"

"No, to your room. Then call 'em an' make 'em come up there an' eat it."

She flushed. The cook was famous for her sarcasm, and Lily was frequently the butt of it. She picked up the trays and hurried out.

As she climbed the two flights of stairs to the second floor—*gentry* stairs; she'd never been allowed on them before—she felt a flutter of trepidation, and scolded herself for it. She had not seen the master since the night of her arrival. But he would not be drunk and raving at half past eight in the morning—so how foolish, how absurd, how silly of her to be nervous. That was what she told herself all the way down the hall to the door of the room she'd been told belonged to the younger Mr. Darkwell. Putting one tray down on a table beside the door, she rapped out a timid knock.

"Yes!"

"Breakfast, sir." *Sar*, I should have said, she worried as she straightened her cap.

"Yes, bring it!"

Was she just supposed to walk in, then? He'd sounded impatient. She opened the door and went in.

And stopped dead. Mouth open, eyes wide. Shocked, but unable to look away from the riveting sight of the young master's bare backside. He glanced at her reflection in the wardrobe mirror, in front of which he was standing and shaving his chin. "On the bed is fine," he tossed over his naked shoulder.

It took half a minute for the words to penetrate. They did so at the same moment he turned completely around to face her, perplexed by her hesitation. Some sound escaped her involuntarily. Certainly not a scream, and not really a squeal either, she would later assure herself repeatedly, merely a—sound. Then she did the only thing she could think of, which was to set the tray down on the nearest flat surface—the bed, fortunately—pivoted in the opposite direction from nude Mr. Darkwell, and scampered out. Just before the door closed, she heard him start to guffaw.

She stood in the silent hall looking straight ahead, face flaming, reliving it all. The irony wasn't lost on her that for almost a week she'd been hoping to catch a glimpse of the young master, without success—and now that she'd gotten more than a glimpse, she had no idea what his face looked like. She tried hard to find what had just occurred as amusing as he did, a laugh on herself if nothing else. Or an educational experience, for she'd never seen a naked man before. But it wasn't possible to feel anything except nervousness and anxiety, because the joke or the lesson wasn't over yet. She had one more tray to deliver. What if, at this very moment, the *master* was at exactly the same stage in his morning toilette as his brother? Why this would be even more unnerving, she wasn't sure. It just would.

On the way back down the hall to the other side of the staircase, she succeeded in pulling herself together. She was behaving like a child. Still, it took courage to bring back a shy fist and knock on the door. No answer. Another knock, hardly audible even to her. She shook herself impatiently and gave a good rap.

"Come in!"

She jumped, rattling cups and spoons. With eyes closed, she pushed the door open and stood still.

"Well?"

She opened one eye and hazarded a quick survey of the room. And went weak in the knees with relief, for the master was sitting at his desk, fully dressed in somber black, and glaring at her from behind a pair of steel spectacles.

"Oh, good mornin', sar," she gushed, flashing what she hoped was a friendly smile. He didn't answer. His room, she saw with a corner of her attention, was sparsely furnished and absolutely devoid of clutter. She set the tray down on the bed, its rumpled sheets the only untidy element in the neat whole—which must be why the sight of it unsettled her so much—and turned to go.

"Not there, *here.*" He pointed at the top of his desk, above the papers he was scribbling on. He looked very formal, she thought, sitting in his own bedroom in coat and waistcoat and white ruffled shirt, back straight and shoulders rigid.

"Oh, o' course, sar." She curtsied rather awkwardly, picked up the tray again, and brought it to him. When she set it down with a bit of a clatter, his scowl deepened. Thinking to redeem herself, she reached for the teapot, to pour his first cup out for him. His arm went out at the same moment and their hands collided. The teapot overturned for an instant before he righted it.

"Bloody hell!" He whipped off his glasses, stood up, and kept on swearing, flicking his scalded fingers in the air to cool them.

His straight brown hair was neat today, Lily thought distractedly, and tied back in a queue. He had a proud face, the bones fine and jutting. An expressive face, she saw, but closed now, and cautious, lips tight, blue-green eyes cloaked. But the bitterness of his expression came from two deep vertical lines slashing down from his cheekbones to the corners of his lips. Although his tall, broad-shouldered body looked tough and ruthless, she noticed that he moved with a careful, silent litheness that hinted at enormous self-control—as if he must keep some unpredictable emotion in check.

She bit her lips in dismay. "Oh, sar, I'm that sorry! It's a great clumsy beast I am, not warth shootin' for me hide. Is the pain terrible?"

Devon recognized her then. He even remembered her name. He saw the same kindness in her serious gray-green eyes that he'd noticed that night, and felt the same pull to her. And then the identical angry retreat. "You're Irish," he said stiffly.

She searched his face for incredulity, but saw only a frown. "Aye, I am." The words were hard to say; she was conscious of a sharp reluctance to use her inexpert brogue on this man. Why? Because he was shrewd, and he would see through it quickly—but it wasn't only that.

What, then? She didn't want to lie to him, she realized with a shock.

"Are you afraid of me?"

"No." And that was the surprising truth.

Her answer dissatisfied him; he wasn't interested in the trust of this girl, this housemaid. But he said, "Good," with his bitter smile. "Gunshots are a rarity here, and I'm quite harmless."

"O' course, sar," she murmured.

He thought he heard skepticism, and raised one dark brow. Her dress was shabby, he noted, her shoes old and broken, her maid's cap disreputable. For all that, she didn't much resemble a servant. Something about her face. Her skin, perhaps? Too smooth and white, too . . . healthy. Or her eyes, clear gray-green and fine, with a look in them that hinted there was more going on in her head than serving him breakfast.

He swung away from her abruptly. "Well? Haven't you anything to do?"

"I do, yes—"

"Then go about your business." The irritation in his tone startled even him.

Lily drew in her breath. She gazed at him for another second, then crossed to the door and closed it softly behind her.

Devon sat down at his desk and took a sip of tepid tea. A dozen thoughts curled and turned in his mind, like restless fish caught in a drift net. One kept surfacing again and again, no doubt because among them it was his only remote certainty: The girl called Lily was anything but a maid.

# Four

Clayton Darkwell jerked on the bell rope a second time, and almost immediately a breathless parlormaid trotted into the library. "Coffee!" ordered the young master. "Right away, and in a very large pot." The girl bobbed a curtsey and scurried back out the door. "Well? What are you looking at?"

Devon watched his brother collapse on the sofa and cover his eyes with one hand. "When you don't come home until dawn," he said dryly, "it's always a relief to know you've not been up to anything more foolish than getting blind drunk." *What hypocrisy*, he thought with an unamused half-smile. A week ago he himself had gotten worse than blind drunk, coldly and deliberately. The fifth anniversary of his wife's death had seemed as good a time as any to pull out a pistol and start shooting up his house.

Clay pinched the bridge of his nose and groaned. "I swear it was the rum at John Poltrane's. And he'd even paid duty on the swill. But I beat him out of twenty guineas at loo, so there's some justice." Devon didn't return his pained but cocky grin. "Well, I don't see what you've got to be self-righteous about. I saw your light on when I stumbled in, after all. The only difference between us is that I drink with my friends and you drink alone."

His brother's already shuttered face hardened a little more, and Clay looked down, regretting his words. "You should have come with us," he resumed a moment later, lightly. "Afterward we went to the Hornet's Nest." Devon steepled his fingers under his chin and grunted without interest. "There's a new girl there, Dev, she's really something to see. I think she weighs more than I do. Her name's Eulalia. I'm not joking!" He laughed delightedly when Devon finally begrudged a ghost of a smile. "Come with us the next time, why don't you? John and Simon always ask about you. You'd enjoy yourself, I swear you would."

Lord Sandown got up from behind the paper-strewn library table and walked to a pair of French doors set between shelves of books in the rear wall. He threw the doors open, and immediately the muted sound of the sea filled the room. A cloud of sandpipers piped derisively over a glassy-calm Channel. "No, I don't think so," he said, standing stiff and straight against the bright glitter of the day.

The girl came in with Clay's coffee. Devon waited for her to go, and for Clay to stretch out full length on the sofa with a cup and saucer propped on his stomach. "Have you given any more thought to what we were discussing earlier?" Clay's wary expression prompted Devon to lift a sardonic brow. "I see you haven't."

"I've been busy."

The brow arched higher.

"Damn it, Dev, I'm too young to bury myself in a mine!"

"I haven't asked you to go down and work in it. Just to manage it."

"I'm too young for that, too."

"But not too young to risk your stupid neck ferrying contraband brandy."

Clay pulled his knees up and crossed his arms over his chest. "For God's sake, let's not start this again. This is a fight neither of us ever wins."

Devon let his breath out slowly. "No, I don't want to quarrel, either." Because if he did, if he pushed his brother too far, Clay would simply leave and conduct his idiotic free-trading enterprise from some other hidden port along the coast. At least having Clay here allowed him to exert a small amount of influence. But not much.

Clay tried to sound reasonable. "What I do isn't a bit dangerous, I promise you. My men are skilled and loyal, and my sloop's the fastest in the Channel." He grinned his charming, boyish grin. "And, God, Dev, I'm having such a damned good time."

"I wonder how good a time you'll have when they hang you."

"Ah, but they'll never catch me."

"You're a fool, Clay. You're waiting right now for the bloody moon to wane, aren't you?"

"No," he denied, but guiltily. "I've come to visit you, my only brother."

Devon snorted. "If you needed the money, it might make some kind of sense."

"Perhaps I don't need it, but there are plenty of people hereabouts who do," Clay said with dignity.

"Oh, yes, I'd forgotten—you do it for *charity*."

"Yes, as a matter of fact, I do. Partly, anyway. Oh, hell," he admitted, laughing, "I do it for the excitement."

"And the glory."

"Well, now, it's true, women do tell me I'm a hell of a fellow these days."

Devon's patience snapped. "God damn it, you're twenty-three years old! This is a childish, stupid business, and someday soon they're going to catch you—it's just a question of time."

"No, they won't. The Revenue cutters move like old cows in the water, you ought to see them. They'll never outrun the *Spider*. And I've got her hidden where—"

"For God's sake, don't tell me," Devon broke in. "I don't want to know." He shook his head in slow disgust. "They'll catch you on land, then, where you're weakest. The Excise men are everywhere these days, and so are their paid informers. You can't trust anyone. How do you convert the contraband into money for the pockets of the poor? That's where they'll catch you," he warned, stabbing a stiff, angry finger in Clay's direction, "in the midst of that process. Half the countryside knows about you already; all the Revenue officers are waiting for is proof."

"They won't get it on land, either," Clay returned confidently. "I've got a man who handles that end of things for me."

"Who? No—don't tell me." He smiled in spite of himself when Clay broke into a laugh. After a pause he asked reluctantly, "Can you trust him, this . . . middleman?"

"Yes, of course. Absolutely. Listen, don't worry about me, Dev, it's a waste of time."

Devon leaned against the doorpost. "I wish you would give it up. Come and work for me. I'll *give* you the damn mine if you want it."

Clay made a face. "Tell that to Francis Morgan."

"He works for me. He could work for you."

"Not bloody likely. We can't stand each other."

"Yes, I know. What I've never understood is why."

"He's a prissy-arsed fop."

"Not really. But what would it matter if he were? There's more to it than that."

"This is a pointless conversation. Besides, you said you were going to sell him a partnership."

"That's only in the talking stage. If you would run the mine I'd give it to you tomorrow, all of it."

Clay stood and stretched. "But as you just pointed out, I don't need the money."

His brother's face went stony. "A man needs to work."

"You work *too* hard," Clay shot back, weary of being on the defensive. "You carry it to the other extreme. You never go anywhere, never leave Darkstone. When was the last time you went up to the house in London? You haven't visited Mother in Devonshire since last Christmas. It's not as if the place would fall to ruin without you—Cobb could run things perfectly well if you went away for a while." He stuck his hands in his pockets when Devon made no answer. "I know why you stay here," he said stubbornly. "You're just like Father."

"Am I?" Devon said without inflection. "In what way?"

"You stay here because of the sea. Mother says he needed it to steady him. It's what kept him sane."

Devon turned his head slowly, staring out across the terraced garden toward the jagged cliff's edge and the flat brightness of water and sky beyond. He did need the sea. A modest goal, sanity. Not a great deal to ask out of life.

"Speaking of Mother," Clay said too brightly, a little too quickly, "she's threatening to descend on you soon. And this time she's bringing Alice."

Devon heaved a sigh and folded his arms.

"Why don't you just marry the girl and put them both out of their misery?"

"Why don't *you* marry her?"

"Me?" Clay looked horrified. "You have to marry first, you're older." Then, remembering, he colored and looked down.

Devon's jaw tightened, but he kept his tone light and

even. "Sorry, but I've already had a wife. If you're waiting for me to take another, you'll die an old man before you get one for yourself."

"Then we'll die together, two rickety old bachelors. We could do worse."

"I expect we could." A fleeting warmth kindled in his wintry eyes, and Clay returned it with a quick, affectionate smile.

A movement in the doorway caught their attention. "Come in, Cobb," Devon called to the tall, black-bearded man who hesitated in the threshold.

"Didn't want t' disturb you."

"Not at all, Clay and I were finished anyway."

"How are you, Cobb?" asked Clay, nodding a welcome to his brother's lanky steward.

"Brave and well, sir, I thank you."

"Can you ride over to Luxulyan with me today?" Devon asked. "I'd like you to look at Audie Trevithick's fold. He's selling off half his rams."

"I can." Cobb shifted his feet, massaging his broad-brimmed hat between the fingers of his only hand. "Thur's trouble at Ross Menethorp's," he said.

"What sort of trouble?"

"His sheep broke through his north hedge last night. Two dozen went over the cliff; his dog saved the rest."

"Was he drunk?"

"I can't be sure o' that."

"I see. I'll speak to him this morning."

"That's as you please. The oast house is in need o' repairs, Fletcher says. In the rain last week, the roof tiles—"

"Good morning, Devon."

Devon turned. "Francis—I thought we weren't going to meet until dinnertime. Is something wrong at the mine?"

Francis Morgan moved into the room, his ebony walking stick tilted over one shoulder. "No, no. In fact, the pump engine in the new seam is working perfectly now, if I say so myself. It was the bearings, exactly as I told you. No, I wanted to speak to you about the ticketing tonight in Truro. Oh—hello, Clay, didn't see you there.''

Clay made no effort to rise. "Francis," he drawled, staring up at the tall, elegant figure of his brother's mine agent. He took in the man's polished boots, foam-white cravat, and powdered periwig; then, with a faintly disdainful lowering of the eyes, he went back to his newspaper.

"Is there a problem?" asked Devon, coming toward Francis.

"I hope not, but I'd like to talk to you about a strategy I've got in mind once the bidding starts."

"Wait a moment. Cobb, are we through for now?"

"Ais, I suppose. I'll go wi' you to Menethorp's if you want. Would ten o'clock suit you?"

"That's fine, yes. I'll meet you at the gate."

"Wait, Cobb, I'll go with you." Clay got up from the sofa. "See you later, Dev." To Francis Morgan he gave a curt nod, and the mine agent returned it in kind.

Clay and Cobb strolled toward the stables together in a comfortable silence. They separated there, and Cobb walked on toward the oast house. Clay went inside the barn and called out for the groom. "MacLeaf! Are you in here? Galen, my boy, are you at home?" At a noise in the wide stable doors behind him, he turned.

It was Lily.

She flushed when she made out who he was in the sudden dimness, and his knowing grin did nothing to lessen her embarrassment. Remembering her foolishness in his bedroom this morning made her cheeks burn. She was relieved when MacLeaf came out of his tiny cubbyhole beside the harness room and greeted Clay, drawing the young master's attention away from herself. She longed to leave, but the message she'd been entrusted by Lowdy to deliver to the stableman was of great moment—at least to Lowdy. It was also one that must be delivered in private. So she backed up against the nearest stall and tried to make herself invisible while young Mr. Darkwell told MacLeaf to fetch Tamar, his horse.

While she waited, she studied him covertly. Although they shared certain features, the Darkwell brothers were not really at all alike, she decided. It wasn't only that the young master was shorter and slighter, his soft hair a lighter shade of brown; the chief difference was one of demeanor. Clayton's face was open and uncomplicated, his bearing casual, even indolent. Devon Darkwell, on the other hand, was stiff and controlled, moody, humorless, anything but indolent. His face was the opposite of open. Something as bitter as acid had etched the deep lines on either side of his mouth, and behind his beautiful eyes she had once glimpsed desolation.

When Clay sauntered over and smiled at her, she realized she'd been staring. "Morning," he said pleasantly. "Again."

"Good morning, sar." She dropped a belated curtsey.

"I see you've recovered from the shock."

She knew she was blushing again, and it annoyed her. "It's bearin' up I am," she answered crisply.

That made him grin. "What's your name?"

"Lily Troublefield."

Clay laughed, and was enchanted when she smiled back at him, as if to share the joke. "Where do you come from, Lily Troublefield?"

"From Lyme Regis. That is, from Kildare originally, but not in a great many years."

"Kildare, you say?"

"Yes, sar." He looked as if he had something to say about that—or worse, *ask*—and she spoke up hurriedly to divert him. "Is that your horse? He's a right beauty, isn't he?"

It worked; Clay turned away from her to watch MacLeaf saddle his proud gray three-year-old. "He is that. I mean to run him at Epsom next month."

"In the one-and-a-quarter?"

"Probably. Either that or the mile-and-a-half."

"He'll want to watch out for the turn at Tattenham Corner, won't he? And the descent after it can be a trial for a young horse. But he looks like a goer to me." She remembered herself. "Sure and he's a foine animal, I'm thinkin'."

Clay was staring at her in open surprise. With the bit halfway into the animal's mouth, MacLeaf's hands went still and he turned to look at her, too.

Lily cleared her throat self-consciously. "Me father was after bein' a racin' man. Used to take me about to some of the meetings, Doncaster and Newmarket and . . . such."

"A racing man?"

"Well, more a bettin' man, as you might say. He was especially good at losin'," she admitted candidly. "But once his two-year-old filly won the sweepstake purse at the St. Leger. Twenty-five guineas, that was." She smiled, recalling it. She'd tried to talk him into paying off some of his debts with the winnings, but with no success—he'd treated his friends to a two-day celebration and spent every penny of it in a Parkhill tavern.

Clay and MacLeaf exchanged looks. The stableman led the horse outside to the hard-packed yard. Disdaining the mounting block, Clay leaped to his back. He turned in the saddle to look back at Lily, who stood in the doorway watching him. "I'm going up to Tattersall's in August, Miss Lily Troublefield. Would you care to come along and help me pick out a pair of fine, strong hunters?"

She laughed. "Ask me closer to the time, Mr. Darkwell; I can never be plannin' so far in advance."

"I might just do that." With a grin and a wink, he

turned his horse and nudged it into a jaunty trot and then, very quickly, an elegant canter.

MacLeaf came toward her, grinning his gap-toothed grin. She smiled back at him. Sometimes she had trouble deciding which of his eyes to focus on when she spoke to him. Usually his right eye slanted off a bit to the side; but as soon as she'd fix him with a stare to his left, as often as not that one would go sliding off and the right one would seem to straighten itself out. It was a most disconcerting thing, and sometimes she wondered if he could possibly be doing it on purpose.

"How are you going along, Galen?" she asked amiably.

"Oh, well-a-fine, thank ee for asking. An' you, Miss Lily?"

"I'm very brave. I've a message for you from Lowdy."

He made a great business of looking disappointed. "Tedn from your fair self, an?"

She lifted a shoulder playfully. "Lowdy says she can meet you tonight after supper beside the lake, but only for an hour."

His expressive face lit up. "You d' tell 'er I'll be there." Then he remembered that he was a rake. "Will you be there with 'er, Miss Lily?" he inquired with a waggish leer.

"No indeed, I won't, Mr. MacLeaf."

"Ah, too bad. We should've been a rare boiling, us three." He rested his hand on the wall behind her and leaned close in a most familiar way. "What's that owl-faced cook makin' me for dinner today, my heart?"

She smiled blandly. She'd have enjoyed flirting with Galen MacLeaf if Lowdy hadn't liked him so much. "Veal cutlets for Mrs. Howe in her room, hashed mackerel and potatoes for the rest of us in the hall."

"The devil you say!"

She laughed out loud at his comical expression. Over his shoulder, she caught sight of two men approaching from the house. One was Francis Morgan; the other was the master.

Some instinct made her jump sideways, away from MacLeaf's arm-barrier against the stable door. It occurred to her afterward that the sudden movement had a guilty look about it. The men walked past. Francis Morgan kept talking and didn't see her. But the master's austere gaze raked her with a look that, in her agitation, Lily took for scorn. There wasn't a doubt in her mind that Devon Darkwell thought she'd been trysting with the stableman.

What surprised her was the urgency of the impulse she felt to go after him and set him straight. Of course she did no such thing. She interrupted MacLeaf in the middle of a sentence and excused herself, explaining that the housekeeper would scold her if she stayed away any longer. Then she hurried back to the house. That afternoon, Mrs. Howe set her to washing the scullery walls as a punishment for being late.

# Five

"By Jakes, it's hot!" Lowdy thumped her heels and fists against the mattress in sweaty irritation and leapt out of bed. "Thur bain't a whiff o' breeze blawin' in th' whole blighted county, I'm bound. Lord's my life, I hate June."

Lily wiped away the perspiration under her nose and groaned agreement, too enervated to speak. She was sitting up in bed, slouched against the headrail, weary but loath to lie down because the damp sheets smelled of mildew and stuck to her skin. Through the open window came the chime of the clock in the library two floors below, counting out midnight.

Lowdy went to kneel on the chair under the window, elbows on the sill, and stared up at the face of the full moon. "Do ee think Galen's lookin' up right now," she mused dreamily, "seein' the selfsame moon I'm starin' at?"

Lily tried to picture it, and couldn't help wondering

which eye he would be staring at it with. "I expect he's been fast asleep these two hours or more. As you and I should be." She'd stopped struggling with an Irish accent for Lowdy's benefit days ago; the story she'd made up to account for using it in the first place—that she'd been running away from an abusive uncle and had hoped she would sound more like an experienced housemaid if she said she was Irish—hadn't sounded very believable in her own ears, but Lowdy had never questioned it.

Her stomach growled. Across the room, Lowdy heard. "Lily!" she exclaimed, plain face alight. "I'm just now rememberin'—I filched us a red apple from the resters in the stillroom this mornin'!"

"Glory be to God, Lowdy, hurry and get it before I faint dead away," Lily urged dramatically.

The maid found the stolen treat in her apron and brought it to the bed. A month ago Lily would have gone proudly to the stocks without a murmur before she'd have taken a farthing from her worst enemy. Now Lowdy's near-daily pilfering of a piece of fruit or a chunk of bread seemed a logical, cold-blooded act of survival, something to feel no more guilt over than a soldier might for shooting back at his foes. She sank her teeth into her carefully apportioned half of apple, savoring the tart spurt of juice in her mouth and making small sighing sounds of satisfaction. "I'm beginning to think they taste better stolen," she sighed, her eyes closed in pure pleasure.

"Tes a fact, they do," Lowdy confirmed with her mouth full.

"But still, you're taking an awful chance. If Mrs. Howe ever caught you, I'm sure you'd lose your place."

"Don't ee worry an inch, she ain't going to catch me. Did ee talk to 'er today, an? About your 'advance?'"

"Yes."

"And did 'er turn you down, like I said?"

"Yes."

"Hah."

Lily drooped against the pillow, remembering her meeting with Mrs. Howe this afternoon. She'd chosen the time herself, hoping the housekeeper would be at her most agreeable after a supper of cold salmon, broiled neck of mutton with capers, and fresh peas in lemon sauce—a cut above the barley soup and liver pudding that had been the fare in the servants' hall. "What do you want?" Mrs. Howe had asked in her ungracious way, ensconced in her comfortable sitting room.

Lily made her request—a small advance on the salary she would begin to earn once her debts were finally paid off, so that she could start setting a little something by of her own. As Lowdy had gloomily foreseen, she might as well have saved her breath.

"Think you're too good for the rest of us, don't you? Can't wait to get away so you can put on all your fine airs among grander folk, eh?" Her black, bulging eyes snapped with venom. "I'll tell you how you can get away, you ignorant girl. You can earn your wage like the rest of us, the way the almighty God intended—with the sweat o' your brow and the labor o' your own two hands. 'He that maketh haste to be rich shall not be innocent.'" A crafty smile crawled across her unkind face after that pronouncement. "Why, I'll even help you. I'll let you have extra chores, if that's what you want. You can start with the rugs on the first floor. At the end of each day, after all your other work's done, you can roll one up, drag it outside, hang it on a line, and beat it until it's clean and fresh. I'll inspect it afterward, naturally, and pay you a half-penny for each one if I'm satisfied."

"Half a penny! But—I couldn't even lift one of the carpets by myself!"

"That's your lookout. And don't be thinking you'll ask any o' the other girls to help; this would be your work, no one else's. Now, take my offer or not, it's the best you'll get. What do you say? Be quick—there's chores to do."

She'd had to blink back tears of frustration. "You know I can't!"

"Have done, then. Stop wasting my time and get back to work. And remember that it's the duty of servants to perform the will of God from the heart, 'not with eyeservice as men-pleasers, but with fear and trembling, as unto Christ.'"

"Splatty ol' pig," Lowdy said matter-of-factly, swallowing the last bit of apple and licking her fingers. "I telled you not t' waste time wi' that one."

"She doesn't like me, Lowdy."

"She don't like anybody."

"No, but—I truly think she hates me."

Lowdy made a face, but didn't dispute it.

Lily plucked at the coverlet, feeling the familiar weight of frustration. She'd been at Darkstone for weeks now, but she was no closer to a solution to her predicament. Her first month's wages had come to nothing, and now she was in debt not only to Mrs. Howe but to Lowdy as well, for soap, tooth powder, cap, and aprons. She ought to write to Mrs. Troublefield, her neighbor in Lyme, and ask for news. She needed to know what had become of Roger Soames, to find out if he was alive or dead and, if the former, what state of mind he might be in regarding herself. Had he set the authorities to search for her? Did he still claim she was a thief? Or, by some miracle, had he come to his senses and forgiven her out of Christian charity for her part in the fiasco that had brought her to this place?

That last seemed unlikely. But Lily was an optimist; she would not dismiss the possibility out of hand. Still, she hesitated to find out by writing to Mrs. Troublefield, because she hated to involve that kind woman by putting her in a position, if someday she should be questioned, of having to lie for Lily's sake and say she didn't know where she'd gone. For the dozenth time she berated herself for running away. Time was her only ally now, and all she could do was cling to a childlike hope that someday, somehow, things would be all right again.

"Ugh," Lowdy grunted suddenly, sitting up in the bed. "The devil 'imself 'ud melt like tallow grease in this oven. Lily."

"What?"

"Let's go swimmin'."

"We can't."

"Why not? Not in the sea, in the lake. Pirate's Mere, 'aven't ee ever been there? Nobody'd see, we'd sneak out quiet-like as mouses."

"It's too dangerous—if anyone caught us we'd get sacked." But even so, she couldn't help imagining it, how cool and lovely a swim would be.

"Well, you d' come or not, Miss Scairty-face, but I'm goin'." And she threw off her dingy nightrail and began to pull her dress on over her head. "I ain't wearin' shift nor stays, neither. Ooh, how cool an' clean I mean t' be ten minutes from now. I'll come back an' tell all how it was, Lily, make it like ee didn't miss nothing."

"Oh, all right," Lily grumbled, climbing off the bed and fumbling in the dark for her own dress. "But if we're caught, it'll be your fault."

"We won't get catched. We'll sneak out master's lib'ry door and scuttle down the cliff steps all unknown. Now, hurry!"

Darkstone Manor faced north, away from the sea, at the top of a broad, green headland. Terraced gardens sloped behind it for a hundred yards before the cliff's edge, gentling the precariousness of the aspect. Along the headland a twisting path wound away for a mile in either direction. At the bottom of steep steps leading to the sea, another path curved to the right and rose again, skirting a dark pine wood before it came out at the top of an inland body of water—Pirate's Mere. It was a natural oddity, its shallow waters divided from the sea by a wide bar of white sand. Tonight it was dark and still and tranquil, in contrast to the surging, whitecapped Channel so close by. Lily and Lowdy undressed beside a line of high black boulders bisecting the narrow beach.

"You bain't goin' in in your shift, surely."

Lily glanced across at Lowdy's sturdy nakedness. She frowned. "You're not wearing anything at all?"

"Phaw, sink me if I will! What was ee plannin' t' wear tomorrow for shift, an? 'Twouldn't ever dry by time. Come, Lily, quit your moolin' an' let's go in."

Lily hesitated a few more seconds, considering. She drew off her worn and patched chemise slowly, cautiously, not quite knowing what to expect. She'd never been naked out-of-doors before. But nothing happened: dozens of heads didn't pop up from the thick woods behind to shout, "Cover yourself!" as she'd half anticipated. And the soft night air on her skin was delicious. Looking down at her own white breasts and belly and thighs, she shivered with an illicit thrill; she'd thought the stealing of apples an exciting sin, but it paled to paltry insignificance next to naked midnight bathing.

She stepped with great care over smooth stones and soft sand toward the mere's edge—she'd never been barefoot outdoors, either. Gentle lapping waves wet her toes; she moved farther in warily. "Come in all at onct," Lowdy advised from fifteen feet out. "Tes warm-like and lovely in no time."

"But I can't swim."

"Neither can I; I'm standin' on my two feet."

Emboldened, Lily waded in to her waist, her breath sucked in at the unexpected chill. But in seconds it felt warm and luscious, and she bent her knees and let the water rise to her shoulders. "Oh, it's wonderful, it's glorious!" she laughed, splashing her arms. She paddled over to Lowdy, where the water was deeper. The muddy bottom felt cold and squishy between her toes. "Oh, you can float," she said enviously.

"Anybody can float."

"Not me." Nevertheless, she lay back and kicked her legs, enjoying the startling chill on her scalp when her head touched the water, and tried to imitate Lowdy's restful-looking posture on the pool's surface. She sank.

"Pull air in your chest and keep still," Lowdy instructed once Lily had resurfaced and stopped coughing. "Stay calm-like, that's the knack."

After a few more tries, Lily mastered the art of floating on her back. She stared up at the lustrous pearl of the full moon, her arms and legs spread, breathing shallowly, and savored the acquisition of this newest skill, musing that at times like these it was *almost* possible to categorize her present circumstances as an adventure. If she could see an end to this interlude, this interruption of what she still regarded hopefully as her real life, she might even be able to enjoy it, once in a while. But in truth, she could see no end. Still, she clung to her natural optimism: instead of dwelling on the hopelessness of things, she started a water fight with Lowdy.

"What was that?"

Devon paused in the act of drying off his legs with his shirt and listened. "What? I don't hear anything." He dragged on his breeches—then stopped again, fingers going still over the buttons. "I hear it now. It sounded like a scream." He threw his shirt in the sand and strode off in the direction of the sound—a high-pitched, woman's cry. It came again, and he quickened his pace. Clay stumbled after him, fastening his breeches and shrugging into his wet shirt as he went. The light of the full moon brightened the sandy track edging the pool on the inland side. When he was a dozen feet from a humpbacked line of boulders trailing from the woods to the water and blocking the track, Devon halted. Clay nearly collided into his back.

Lily and Lowdy waded out of the water through the thick sand, heading for their clothes, still laughing. At the very moment they realized they'd come out on the wrong side of the boulders, they saw the men. Lowdy let out a screech and darted forward. Lily followed, unthinking—and went weak when she discovered there was nowhere to run: the high rocks ran straight into the woods, and in front of them was an impenetrable tangle of marram grass and wild rhododendron. They should have fled back into the water!

Too late now. To retreat would be to expose their naked bodies all over again. Clutching her arms across her chest, Lily stood beside Lowdy in front of the tallest boulder, her back turned toward the two Messrs. Darkwell, and waited for them to go away.

They didn't.

"God's my life," breathed Clay, "'tis a pair of mermaids." He shot Devon a hopeful glance. "I don't suppose you'd be interested in speaking to them, would you? It's a couple of the housemaids, you know; I recognize the tall one, she's—"

"I know who she is."

"Oh." That surprised him. "Well, I'm only thinking, this being such an auspicious meeting, two of them and two of us, almost like fate if you—" he broke off, startled when, without a word, Devon left him and began to walk toward the two women huddling in front of the black rock "—believe in that sort of thing," Clay trailed off to himself, and strode out after him.

Impossible, thought Lily, hearing them come; they cannot mean to speak to us! She made a futile physical effort to become smaller. The nearer they drew, the more potent was her desire to crawl into the face of the granite boulder and vanish. Lowdy began to giggle in the most annoying way; she wanted to box her ears.

Now the two men were standing directly behind them; she knew it because the very air seemed to have changed. She imagined she could hear them breathing. Even so, she jumped when a voice drawled, almost in her ear, "Good evening, ladies." She recognized that amused, good-natured cockiness and knew it was the young master who had spoken. But it was his brother whose presence she sensed most keenly, whose cold, blue-green gaze she thought she could feel like an icy brand on the bare skin of her back.

"Good evenin' t' you," Lowdy threw back over her shoulder with another silly, coquettish giggle.

"What an unexpected pleasure, meeting you lovely ladies like this. My brother and I were wondering if you would care to join us for a short stroll around the lake. We might even take another . . . dip together, if you're of a mind. Hmm? Does that interest you the least little bit?"

Lowdy said yes. Lily's eyes went wide with shock and incredulity. But Lowdy had said yes and Lily hadn't misheard, for now she was bobbing her head and laughing that same idiotic, infuriating giggle that made Lily want to take her by the shoulders and shake her until her crooked teeth rattled.

"Well, now, that's fine," said Clay, laughing too. "What about you?" he inquired, again in Lily's ear.

"No! Please, just go away."

Every muscle in her body jerked when Devon Darkwell said in a low, compelling tone, one she somehow apprehended more in her body than her ears, "Yes, I think that would be best." His brother glanced at him uncertainly. Devon made himself clear. "Leave us, Clay. You and your friend have a pleasant walk."

Clay finally closed his mouth. His astonishment was greater than his disappointment. Lowdy turned around and faced him without a blush; he took her hand automatically, hardly looking at her. "I can't remember," he marveled over his shoulder as he led her away, stark naked and giggling, "the last time you pulled rank on me, Dev."

Then he was gone, and Lily was alone with Viscount Sandown.

Devon roughly shoved to the back of his mind the question of what the hell he thought he was doing; if he considered that for half a minute, he would walk away from this girl without a backward look. He didn't want to walk away. Or stop looking.

What he wanted was to touch her. The dress she'd worn that day in his room hadn't even hinted at the loveliness of the woman underneath the faded blue cotton. He watched his hand go out, then pause in the air an inch or two from her shoulder. His arm cast a shadow across her pale back, darkening the thick stream of hair that hung down past her shoulders. The moonlight silvered her skin and made it look indescribably soft. He saw her white-fingered grip on her upper arms, and wondered fleetingly if she was frightened. He wanted to hear her voice again. "Will you turn around?" he said quietly.

She shook her head.

"No?" he prompted.

"No."

"But you must. Have you never heard of the *droit du seigneur?*" he murmured with uncharacteristic whimsy, mostly to himself.

Without a thought, Lily snapped out, "That was a Norman, not a Cornish custom, and anyway, it died out six hundred years ago."

Devon's hovering hand jerked away. "How do you know that?" he asked in amazement.

She bit her tongue. "Please, please, I cannot talk to you like this!"

"Why? Are you embarrassed?" She looked like a warm marble goddess to him, tall and straight and slender, and he had an urge to touch each fragile vertebra with his fingertips, moving down so slowly, past her narrow waist to her sleek, saucy buttocks. "You're much too beautiful to be embarrassed." On an impulse he said, "Meet me tonight, later. Come to my room." Instantly he regretted his words.

Lily was so overwrought she wanted to weep. "No, I can't, I can't. You've mistaken me, my lord, I'm not— like Lowdy."

"Your friend?"

She nodded.

"No indeed," he agreed in a murmur, "you're not at all like Lowdy." Regret drifted away. And now it was impossible not to touch her; his earlier scruples vanished—she was only a maid, after all. But when he pushed her wet hair aside and slid his fingers along the delicate ridge of her backbone, she gave a soft gasp and dropped her head; he could feel light tremors quaking through her, from her shoulders to her long, white thighs.

"You must let me go," Lily pleaded in a strained whisper.

"I'm not detaining you."

"Please. You don't understand."

What he understood was that she needed subtler handling. With deep reluctance, he let his hand fall away; when it grazed her hip, she shuddered again and went poker-stiff. "Meet me tomorrow, then," he suggested in a whisper. "In the afternoon. We'll go for a walk."

She said the first thing that came into her head. "I have to scrub the stillroom floor tomorrow afternoon."

He ventured a smile. "I commend your industry. But I think you might manage to postpone that particular chore, don't you? Four o'clock, inside the park gates."

Lily took a deep breath. "A walk?"

He nodded solemnly. "A walk."

"And if I come, will you go away now?"

"Are you bargaining with me?" When she made no answer, he conceded gravely, "Yes, I will go away."

"Very well, then. I—I will meet you."

"I'm much relieved." Did she think he would have accepted a refusal?

There was a lengthy pause.

"Well?" Lily said finally. She couldn't stand this much longer.

"Ah, I'd forgotten. The bargain." He took a step back, sweeping her with one last glance. With what he considered saintly restraint, he walked away and left her alone.

# Six

But when four o'clock came the next afternoon, Lily was kneeling in a half-inch of caustic suds and scouring the tile floor of the stillroom with a bristle brush. Devon found her there at four-twenty. His irritation was extreme, and derived from two sources: an inability to understand, in the harsh light of day, what could possibly have seemed so urgent last night; and bafflement over the fact that he'd actually gone to meet the chit anyway, had been waiting at the appointed time and place like some lovestruck footboy come a-courting— and she'd had the gall not to show up! Clay was right, he thought sourly; he ought to get out more. The next time his brother went whoring in Truro, he would go with him. Then maybe he wouldn't be so eager to make a fool of himself at home.

Scrubbing away, Lily saw his long black shadow fall across the floor. She jerked up, the brush sliding from her slick fingers. She sat back on her heels and plucked nervously at her skirts. Her petticoat was soaked, but she'd tied the hem of her gown up with ribbons to keep it off the wet tiles. She felt dowdy and disheveled and unattractive. "I couldn't come," she blurted out before he could say anything. "Mrs. Howe says I must finish this and then help the parlor maid with the polishing. I'm sorry. I meant to come but I—couldn't."

"Stand up."

She searched his face. It was more than stern and remote now; it was angry. She hadn't expected that. She scrambled to her feet, wiping her hands on her coarse hessian apron.

"You seem to be laboring under a misconception. You don't work for Mrs. Howe, you work for me. If you intend to continue, you'll learn to follow my orders, not hers—at least not when they contradict mine. Is that clear?"

Her chin went up, her shoulders back. "Yes, my lord, that is perfectly clear."

Watching her try to control her temper, Devon felt some of his own begin to fade. "Good. Then let's begin again. Meet me at the park gates in ten minutes." He raised one eyebrow and waited.

"Yes, my lord." She dropped a sarcastic curtsey.

The brow went higher. But he said no more, only turned on his heel and stalked out.

Lily thought of all the mild, ineffectual curses she knew. They helped to soothe her temper, but did nothing for her nerves. When Mrs. Howe had refused her request for an hour off this afternoon—to post a letter in the village, she'd fabricated—her first reaction had been heartfelt relief: now she wouldn't have to meet the master, it wasn't her fault, and it couldn't even be called cowardice. She'd never imagined that he would actually come here and fetch her. What did he want with her, anyway? A "walk," he said. Ha! Did he take her for an infant? A walk had been the last thing on his mind last night; she had no reason to think things had changed because the sun was shining.

Well, she would soon find out. And regardless of what he expected, a walk was all he was going to get. She would not be defenseless, naked, and vulnerable today, and acute embarrassment would not be a weapon he could use against her. She went outside, untying the strings that held her skirts up as she went, trying to shake out the wrinkles. Useless, of course. And silly, too; if she wanted to attract him—which she didn't—it would take considerably more than an unwrinkled gown. Or considerably less, she amended wryly, knowing it had been her *lack* of clothing that had stirred his interest in her to begin with. No matter—let the master see her in full daylight in her one and only gown, every patch and wrinkle in place; let him see her work-red hands and freckled nose, her bedraggled hair tucked up into Lowdy's ancient gray cap. That should cool his interest quickly enough, and then her life could go back to what she was forced these days to call normal. She straightened her cap with a combative jerk and strode off toward the deer park.

Devon saw her coming from a good distance away. She was taller than average, and she had an unusual long-legged stride, graceful and purposeful at the same time. He knew the exact moment she saw him because she shortened her steps, self-conscious, and looked away as if something fascinating had caught her attention at the side of the path. Her profile was lovely, and his ill humor dissipated a little more as he considered that perhaps he hadn't lost his mind after all, or not completely, when he'd insisted on this assignation. When she reached him, she stopped a good six feet away and bobbed another curtsey—this one perfunctory, not sarcastic—murmuring, "My lord," in an undertone.

"Stop my-lording me," he snapped. "No one calls me that except my valet and my housekeeper."

"Why?"

"Because it makes them feel important."

Nervous, Lily fought a strong impulse to laugh. "I meant, why does no one call you 'my lord?'"

"Because I don't wish them to."

He looked so very lordlike, his voice matching the frostiness of his turquoise eyes glaring down the length of his bony, arrogant nose, that this time she did laugh. But she instantly sobered when he scowled at her, unamused.

"Why is it you're not the least bit Irish today, I wonder? Nor last night either, as I recall."

*Stupid, stupid*, she berated herself, ruing for at least the hundredth time the foolish scheme that had caused her nothing but trouble. Even though she'd half expected something like this from him, the suddenness of the question addled her. Stalling, she started to walk, and he went along the path beside her, hands clasped behind his back. Hawthorn and wild nut trees bordered the track. A thrush twittered somewhere close by; overhead a lark sang. "Well, you see, sir, I was desperate for a job," she began—truthfully. "When I first saw Mrs. Howe in the inn at Chard, I—I thought she was Irish."

"Mrs. Howe? You thought my housekeeper was *Irish*?"

"Yes—um, *black* Irish. Indeed, sir, I thought she was, and from a distance it seemed to me she even sounded Irish. So I said I was Irish, so that she would like me, and I used my father's accent to try to convince her. He—he *was* Irish," she finished witlessly. She'd thought her explanation to Lowdy had sounded lame, but compared to this one it had the ring of Holy Gospel. But she could hardly tell her employer she was no housemaid at all and that she'd forged her reference! "But everything else is true, sir, I swear, and my last lady did give me an excellent character. I'm a good girl, truly I am, and a very hard worker. You wouldn't turn me off for fibbing a bit to get hired, would you?" She looked up at him through her lashes, head tilted appealingly. He had that eyebrow cocked again, and under it his cool blue gaze was the color of pure skepticism.

"No, not for that," he answered—with menace, it seemed to Lily, and immediately she thought of all the other things he could fire her for. Or send her to gaol for. "Where do you come from?" he asked abruptly, scattering her thoughts again.

"From Lyme Regis. Most recently."

"And before that?"

"Oh, all over. My father was a wandering man."

"Was your mother a wandering woman?"

"She was . . . a reluctant wanderer. She died when I was ten."

"I'm sorry. What's your last name, Lily?"

She mumbled her silly name.

"What?"

"Troublefield," she repeated distinctly, looking him straight in the eye.

He knew she was challenging him, but to what end he wasn't sure. To laugh? To call her a liar? "An honest name," he said carefully. "Not particularly Irish, though, I'd have said."

"No—my father's mother was an O'Herlihy." That at least was true. When a full minute passed and he didn't reply, she began to hope that the subject of her ethnic heritage was closed, finally and forever. They were walking through an overgrown copse of fir and alder trees whose arching branches thwarted the last rays of late-afternoon sun and plunged the path into murky near-darkness. Mr. Darkwell's park was not particularly well kept, Lily noticed. He must be more interested in maintaining his farmlands, cattle herds, and copper mines than in perfecting the accoutrements of a rich squire's manor house. Much about him intrigued her, and there were many questions she wanted to ask—but of course she couldn't. It would be fatal to forget her role and attempt to speak to him on a near-equal footing, as a lady might speak to a gentleman. A housemaid would know her place at all times and never presume to ask the master anything about his private life. But how frustrating—especially since he could ask her anything he liked about *her* private life, and she was expected to answer every question or risk being reprimanded, even fired, for impertinence!

Just then he reached out and took her arm, pulling her down a narrow side trail that branched off the main one. Before the trees closed off the prospect, she caught a glimpse of a man rounding a corner of the main path and coming toward them. "That—wasn't that Mr. Cobb?"

"Yes."

His tone was brusque and quelling; she said no more. Minutes later they came out of the dark wood and into a clearing at the top of a cliff. The salt wind whipping at her skirts smelled fresh and wild. Sea birds cried and swooped above the pale, opal-green water, and far away she could see a pair of fishing boats bobbing like toys on the horizon.

Rough steps carved out of the rocks zigzagged down to a narrow, boulder-strewn beach below. Devon pointed to the largest rock. "Do you see that boulder down there, the one with iron rings in the side?"

Lily shielded her eyes with one hand and squinted. "Yes, I see it."

"It's called the 'drowning rock.' And this is the 'drowning cove.' Years ago, on stormy nights—so the story goes—men from the neighborhood would light lanterns on this spot and wave them at passing ships. If they were in trouble, the ships would make their way in toward what they thought was safe harbor. But the rocks here are invisible and deadly, and the ships broke up and foundered in the surf."

"Wreckers! I've heard of them."

"Any sailor who had the misfortune to survive was tied to that rock down there and left to drown in the rising tide. Meanwhile the wreckers plundered and looted whatever they could salvage from his battered ship."

Lily shivered, imagining it. "I've heard stories like that about the wild Cornish coast, but I never really believed them."

"Why not?"

"Well . . . why tie sailors to a rock and let them drown? Why not murder them straightaway in some quicker, cruder fashion? And couldn't the metal rings have been put there simply to tie up boats?"

He smiled slightly. "You've a cynical nature, I see."

"No, I haven't—sir. I think it's much more cynical to believe that men would treat each other with such cruelty."

He was thinking how pretty she was with her long lashes and fine eyes, a dazzling green now in the soft glow of the sunset behind his shoulder.

When he didn't answer, Lily asked, "Do you believe the story?"

He looked out across the choppy, white-lipped waves, remembering when he and Clay used to play pirate in this cove. They would explore the caves in the cliffside and then pretend to tie each other to the drowning rock when the tide was out, scampering up the stone steps in feigned panic when it returned. Years ago, that had been, when he hadn't had a care in the world.

The girl was waiting for his answer, but suddenly he was tired of talk. He wanted to see what color her hair was in the daylight. Without warning, he plucked her cap off and watched dark red curls tumble down around her shoulders.

Lily was so surprised she put both hands on top of her head—as if he'd just snatched off her wig. "Sir!" she got out before he pulled her, again without asking, into his arms. She strained away automatically, but he held her firmly and kissed her on the mouth. She stood perfectly still.

Devon pulled back, frowning. "I would like to kiss you."

He was a few seconds late with that, she reflected hazily. "I believe you already have."

His frown faded and turned into a wary smile. "I would like to kiss you again."

If he had then said, "May I?" she would have said no. But he didn't ask, and she lost her opportunity to refuse. He moved in more slowly this time, and although she meant to keep herself as stiff as before, soon she found herself softening to him. His lips were warm—that surprised her. They brushed hers with a light, stroking pressure, and when he kissed the corners of her mouth they made a soft, indescribable sound that thrilled her. She pulled back and murmured something in surprise when she felt the wet tip of his tongue slip between her teeth. His big hand moved to the back of her head, holding her steady. She said, "Oh," again, but it wasn't a protest at all. For a few heartbeats she tried to feel detached, to assess her reaction to this new, intimate kind of kissing. Then she forgot. His breath on her cheek was soft and seductive; his closed eyes prompted her to close hers. A delicious warmth began somewhere in the middle of her and then spread, thick and slow like honey, everywhere. Moments passed and she sighed and opened her mouth to him when his lips demanded it, and held on to his hard shoulders when her knees began to wobble.

He broke away so abruptly she almost fell against him. Disoriented, she watched without comprehension while he jerked his arms out of his coat of brown broadcloth and laid it on a soft-looking spot of ground a few feet away. She understood his intention at the moment he reached for her hand. She snatched it away and backed up. Her cap lay on the ground at her feet. She bent to pick it up, then turned her back on him and stared out across the darkening swell of the Channel. Overhead, a single gull screamed repeatedly in mechanical, matter-of-fact fury.

Devon took advantage of the moment to get his breathing under control. As he studied her rigid back, remembering with graphic precision how she had looked last night, wet and naked, he felt his surprise change into annoyance. He'd wasted enough time woo-ing this girl, it seemed to him; they should have arrived by now at the heart of things. He'd brought her here for only one reason—a quick leap up the ladder, as Clay would say. Whether this sudden shyness was real or pretended didn't interest him; what he wanted was to come to an understanding with her, one way or another, quickly.

He circled around her so that she had to look at him. "What is the matter?" he asked without gentleness. "Will you lie with me or not?"

Lily was distraught. She struggled to answer, still reeling from the aftereffects of the kissing, and straining against pride and bruised emotions and a quickening undercurrent of anger. "No, I will not," she managed to say without crying.

Devon stared at her for a full minute, hands on his hips. "Right. Come on, then."

He scooped up his jacket and set off at a fast walk, back through the trees to the path. She followed auto-matically for a moment or two, thinking of nothing. Then she stopped. Anger was bubbling closer to the surface and she started to tremble all over.

Twenty feet ahead, he glanced around. After a few seconds' hesitation, he walked back to her. "Why not?" he demanded, reluctantly.

"I don't even know you!" With a tremendous effort, she reminded herself that she was supposed to be someone like Lowdy. "And I—I have a young man," she tacked on hastily. "He would not like it."

Devon nodded slowly. That made sense. She made a half-turn to put her cap on again, pushing all her glorious hair under it. He was baffled by the regret he felt over what he was about to lose. God, she was a tasty piece. She finished and faced him, greenish eyes downcast. He couldn't resist. "But he doesn't mind kissing, does he?"

"What?"

He caught her up in his arms again. "Your young man won't care if we do this," he whispered, and kissed her hard.

Lily's resistance crumbled at the first touch of his lips. It was as if they had never stopped, as if that interruption had been some perverse mistake they both regretted and were making up for now. She wound her arms around his neck and pressed against him, every sense engrossed and besieged by his mouth and the fervent stroking of his hands on her back. He dragged her cap off again and filled his fingers with her hair, never stopping the kiss, and she moaned her perfect willingness against his lips and into his mouth.

Devon muttered half-coherent words of praise and wonder while he slid his hands down her back to her buttocks. They were exactly as strong and pert and luscious as he'd imagined, and his one regret was that they weren't naked. But that could be remedied. That she had a lover bothered his conscience for less than a second, and after that he started to pull her skirts up in back, drawing them in handfuls over her calves, her knees, her sleek thighs. Lily gasped when she realized what was happening and tried to push him away. He had to drop her skirts and grab her around the waist to hold on to her. He kissed her again, ruthlessly, and rejoiced when he felt her weaken. "Lily, Lily," he whispered, seducing her with the strength of his need. He located the buttons at the front of her gown and started unfastening them. He was half finished when he lost patience and sleeked his hand inside to hold one soft, full breast.

With a light cry, of self-denial as much as alarm, Lily broke away again. She spun around, breathing hard, almost weeping, holding the front of her dress together in two shaky hands.

Devon closed his eyes and listened to the heavy thudding of his heart in his ears, louder than the sea, louder than anything. Philosophically, that's how he must take this second rejection. And it was a rejection, not missishness or flirtation. She was struggling with frustration as much as he was—that alone gave him a little comfort. When she turned around, he felt a most unfamiliar impulse to apologize. He suppressed it easily. But she looked so unhappy. "Do I take it, Lily," he asked lightly, "that in all likelihood you're not going to change your mind?"

She blushed furiously. He was the most *direct* man she had ever known. She only wished that the answer to his question had leapt a little more swiftly to her tongue; but in due course it did, and she replied, "No, sir, I will not change my mind."

"Ah, too bad." His regret was genuine. "I think you might have enjoyed it. I'm quite certain I would have." She blushed again, and that almost made him smile. "In that case, why don't you go back to the house? I'll be along in a few minutes."

All at once she understood. She knew why he'd sent her to the park alone, and why he'd pulled her out of sight before Mr. Cobb could see them—why he wanted her to go back to the manor house now without him. He was ashamed to be seen with her.

The realization rocked her. She felt humiliated on the deepest level, and fought hard not to burst into tears in front of him. But before she could move or speak, she heard hasty footsteps on the path ahead of them. He heard at the same time and turned away to confront the intruder, his body taking on a combative posture.

It was Clay. In another mood, Lily might have found his surprise comical. She felt Devon's embarrassment and shared it, while at the same time a small part of her admitted to a certain spiteful satisfaction because his shameful secret—herself—was out in the open. She watched his face harden, his stance grow even more rigid, as if he were daring his brother to say or even think something jocular about the situation.

But Clay was bursting with other news. He drew Devon aside, out of her hearing, and spoke to him excitedly. Lily made no attempt to listen, but she couldn't help watching. It was clear that they were arguing; Clay was urging something, and Devon was adamantly refusing. She decided she would wait until they were finished, if only so that the master could properly dismiss her.

"If we don't try it tonight, it'll be too late! There're only six of them now; by tomorrow more Revenue men will join them, and then it *will* be impossible."

"It's impossible now. They've got her, Clay, the *Spider*'s theirs. It's just a matter of time—hours, probably—before they confiscate her formally. This had to happen sooner—"

"Not if we take her back tonight! I've got three men already; I can get more, but not in time. If you'll help us, Dev, we could get her back right out from under their noses. I can sail her to France tonight, they'd never even—"

"Let them have the bleeding sloop! For God's sake, it's time you quit this foolishness."

Clay's jaw jutted stubbornly. "No. I won't let her die this way, floated docilely off to London by a bunch of incompetent government bastards. Christ, they'll probably keep her and turn her into one of their own cutters! I'll sink her myself before I'll let them do it!"

"Oh, for—"

"God damn it, if you won't help me, I'll go by myself."

Devon never doubted that he meant it. But suddenly he had an idea. "All right, I'll come." He shrugged off the hand Clay slapped jubilantly against his shoulder. "But on one condition. If we get the damned ship back, you must promise you'll sell her or sink her or whatever the bloody hell you like, but one way or another you'll give her up for good this time. Is it a bargain?"

Clay looked floored; for a moment he couldn't speak. When he could, it was only to curse.

"Do you agree or not?" Devon interrupted, his face and voice ice cold with resolve.

"Damn you," Clay said for the third or fourth time. "All right," he finally sputtered, and allowed himself to be turned around and urged back down the path.

"Good!" Devon pounded him on the back and hustled him along, grinning with anticipation.

Open-mouthed, Lily watched them go. Not once did the master look back. Clearly he had forgotten her existence. She felt cold again, and furious and humiliated. She was tired of feeling humiliated. Following behind slowly, she tried to see the humorous side of the situation, but from her current perspective there wasn't one. Especially when, later that evening, Mrs. Howe made her go without supper for leaving her work.

# Seven

Prayers were over; it was time to go to bed. But Lily hung back when Lowdy paused to wait for her in the hall. "You go up," she told her, "I want to finish this mending. I'll be along in a minute." But when Mrs. Howe ordered her to bed half an hour later, she still couldn't face the thought of lying down on that hot, lumpy mattress and listening to Lowdy's lusty snores for an hour or more. She was tired, but a storm was coming and she felt restless and keyed up.

She bade the housekeeper a brusque good night, but instead of continuing upstairs when she reached the first-floor landing, she moved silently down the pitch-dark hall to the master's library. The French doors were locked. She unlocked them and slipped outside.

The wind was fierce; she caught her cap just before it blew off and stuffed it into the pocket of her gown. Clouds flew past the moon in ragged tatters, fitfully darkening the way and causing her to stumble twice on the path that circled the house to the front drive. She would walk to the main gate and back, she decided; after that, maybe she could sleep.

Halfway to the highroad, though, she began to have second thoughts. Thunder rumbled everywhere, and now the wind was blowing with a rough, indifferent violence that she'd never experienced before. Needle-sharp raindrops stung her face intermittently, warning that the storm that had threatened all evening was finally imminent. But it was the very wildness that drew her on, frightened and thrilled at the same time, farther into the groaning black roar of the night. She pulled her hair out of her face and held it down in one fist; but it scarcely mattered because now the darkness was all but absolute, and seeing the way had become an exercise in futility. The storm's awesome power brought a realization of her personal insignificance, and of the cosmic unimportance of all the things she filled her life with—not a brand new insight, and not altogether unpleasant, for under it lay the safe, prosaic certainty that in half an hour she would be snug in her bed.

The first flare of lightning startled her; in its blue-white blaze she saw the gates ahead, closer than she'd expected. A practical, apprehensive part of her said to turn back now and go home; the stubborn part said the gates were the goal and she would turn back when she reached them. The rain had stopped, for now, but the savage wind still blew her skirts around her legs like sails on a storm-trapped schooner.

She arrived at the gates. As always, they were open, their delicate iron grilles more for ornament than protection nowadays. She reached out to touch one of the crumbling brick-and-mortar posts, both as a personal acknowledgment that she'd reached her goal and for something solid to hold on to. There was no warning; the sound of hoofbeats was muffled complete-ly by the wailing wind. A horse screamed; hooves scrabbled in the air scant inches from her face; a rider fell. She shrank back against the cold stone in utter

darkness, petrified, expecting to be mauled or trampled
in the next moment. But the wind dropped, and in the
relative quiet the clatter of hooves sounded behind her,
diminishing. In the next second a flash of lightning
illuminated the writhing form of a man on the ground,
not six feet from where she stood. She shuffled toward
him in the sudden dark, hands outstretched. Her ankles
touched him at the moment lightning flared again. It
was the master.

"Get the horse! The horse, damn it! Stop him!" He
thought he saw the white flash of petticoats move away
from him in the blackness. He pressed his soaked
handkerchief to the gash in his shoulder again and
growled into the wind, teeth gritted, praying he
wouldn't pass out. The pain lessened as he lay there; he
became conscious that the fall hadn't broken any bones,
that he was in no worse shape than he'd been half a
minute ago. Which wasn't saying a great deal. The gate
post was behind him—he saw it in a fleeting interval of
light—and he shoved himself backward until he was
leaning against it. Somewhere to his right he heard his
horse nicker. Had the girl found him or had he come
back on his own?

Lily had no experience with frightened, lathered
stallions. She found Devon's by serendipity: she walked
into him. It startled them both, and the first thing her
astonished hand reached out for in reflex was his bridle.
He backed up angrily, but somehow she held on, and
after a moment he quieted enough to let her lead him in
what she hoped was the direction of his owner.

She found him eventually. He was still on the ground,
and she was afraid he'd injured himself in the fall. "Are
you hurt?"

"No. Go away."

She stood over him, holding his horse's reins. "But if
you're hurt—"

"I'm all right."

"Let me—"

"Go!"

Instead she dropped to her knees in front of him. "You need help, you're—" She broke off when she saw, in an instant's burst of lightning, the dark stain of blood that had soaked through the entire front of his jacket. She made an anguished sound, more moan than scream, and Devon dropped his head back against the gate post and closed his eyes. So much for getting home unnoticed.

"Help me up."

"I'll get someone to—"

"Damn it! Don't tell me again what you'll do. Help me to stand up—that's the order. Have you got it?"

"Yes, I believe so."

"Good."

Crouching, she half clasped him around the middle and tried to lift him. A low noise in his throat told her she was hurting him. It worked better when he put one arm around her shoulders. They struggled to their feet together, and then she had to lean all her weight against him to keep him upright; otherwise he would have toppled over on her like a ladder. They stood that way for a minute or two, his back to the gate post, her body pressed against him. The wet-leather smell of his buckskin jacket was pungent in her nostrils.

"The horse is gone."

Lily looked behind her. "He must've gone to the sta—" A string of curses cut her off; their vileness stunned her. He was furious.

Then the rain came.

In seconds they were drenched to the skin. Huge, pelting drops struck them with the force of hurled stones, plastering clothes to skin, hair to faces. The wind ripped and tore and howled, battering at them with a ferocity that drove them to cling together, protecting their faces against each other's bodies. Thunder cracked and roared; lightning flared incessantly. Lily felt Devon's hand at the back of her neck, warm on her wet skin, holding her steady. After a wild, endless time, when speaking above the wind and water was impossible, the rain stopped—as abruptly as it had started. But they both knew it would begin again, probably soon.

She pulled away, out of his arms. He was only a black blur against the lighter blackness behind him. "Please, won't you let me go for help?" she asked as calmly as possible, pushing her dripping hair out of her eyes. He just shook his head, and she smothered a few curses of her own. "Can you walk?"

"Of course I can walk."

"Then we should go now, before it starts again. Put your arm around me. Am I allowed to ask where you're hurt?"

He only grunted at first, annoyed by her sarcastic tone, but finally bit out a curt, "Shoulder." She moved to his right, and he got his good arm around her. At least the girl was tall, he thought as they set off at a snail's pace down the lane toward the house, about half a mile away.

Minutes later they had to stop, and again a dozen times after that when the storm recommenced or when his weakness forced him to rest, beside whatever inadequate shelter they happened to be near. His helplessness appalled him; his way of confronting it was to ignore it, and it was Lily who had to call for their frequent pauses. He wouldn't sit down, for fear of not being able to get up again, so she had to prop him against the trunk of the nearest sturdy tree, holding him upright with her full weight against him, while he recovered enough strength to walk on. In a second-long burst of lightning she saw that the wet front of her dress was stained pink now from the contact; she wondered how much blood he had lost, if he would faint soon in the middle of the road, and what she would do if he did.

If she hadn't understood by now that he wanted secrecy, she would have when they drew close to the path that led to his steward's cottage. "Let me fetch Mr.

Cobb," she pleaded. "He can help you better than I can."

"No." Uttering the word required all his strength. He stopped walking and clung to her with both arms, battling a new dizziness that frightened him. It passed, slowly, and when it was gone he felt her slender, small-boned body shaking. "Are you all right?" he murmured, his face buried in her wet hair.

"Yes, of course." She straightened her spine and got a better grip around his waist, willing strength into her weak legs.

If she could have seen his face in the darkness then, she'd have been surprised to note a flicker of a smile. Her tone reminded him of his; it held a mirror up to his own bravado. What a pair they made. "I'm relieved to hear it. Let's not have a race, though; I don't quite feel up to it."

She couldn't help smiling herself at that. "Another time, perhaps," she said, echoing his dryness.

Eventually they reached the house. They got in through the same door by which Lily had left it earlier. The first two floors of the house were unoccupied, so there was no need for silence. But the sudden stillness after the deafening fury of the storm was uncanny; every footfall, each creaky floorboard, sounded like an explosion, and they climbed the long staircase to the second floor as quietly as possible.

In his room, Devon collapsed at the foot of the bed and leaned against the post. In a fog of pain and fatigue, he listened to the scratch of flint and steel and watched as Lily lit two candles at his bedside. In the sudden soft light, he thought she looked like a half-drowned cat. But he must look even worse, because when she turned, holding one candle aloft, her flushed face paled and her eyes widened with alarm.

"God save us," she breathed. He looked like a corpse. His eyes, the only color in his face, were haggard and lifeless, maybe already feverish. The bloodless lips were set against his pain in a tight grimace, and his huddled body, so dogged and stubborn before, looked blunted now, almost insensate. The buckskin jacket was black from his blood, the shirt under it bright red. "Please," she begged, "for God's sake, you must let me fetch a doctor."

She thought he wouldn't respond, that his numbed gaze would be her answer. But finally he roused himself to speak—slowly, conserving his strength. "I think it looks worse than it is. It wouldn't have been my choice, but I'm afraid you're the only one who can help me. I'm sorry."

She stared at him for a few more silent seconds. "Right, then," she said with a briskness she was far from feeling, and set the candle down. Her hands fumbling at his coat were as gentle as she could make them, but his closed eyes and drawn breath made it plain that everything she did hurt him. She got his soaked shirt unbuttoned and started to ease it over his shoulders. He didn't move and made no sound. The sight of his face made her stop, frightened, and turn nearly as white as he. "Are there any scissors in this room?"

"Desk. Drawer."

She got them. Sitting beside him, she cut away the bloody cloth in a long line from his cuff to his collar, and the shirt fell off him. Painlessly. They both sagged a little from relief.

Lily put a hand out to brush the damp hair back from his forehead. "All right?" she murmured. He nodded slowly.

His wound was a gash—from a knife? a cutlass?—in the fleshy part of his shoulder, above the collarbone. It went deep, but, from what she could see, only flesh and muscle had been injured. If the weapon had struck a few inches to the right, it would have severed his jugular vein.

She found the pitcher and basin on his washstand and

carried them back to the bed with an armful of towels. While his fingers clenched again around the wooden post, she soaked away the blood and cleaned the wound as best she could. All that kept her from swooning was willpower, and the knowledge that there really was no one else to help him. He would despise her—she would despise herself—if she passed out at his feet because his wound was ugly and his blood sickened her. And when she came to, she would only have to begin again. So she gritted her teeth and clamped down on the panic and nausea churning in her stomach, and did her work as cleanly and efficiently as she could.

"It ought to be sewn," he said.

She kept her hands busy, her head down.

"Did you hear me?"

She rubbed the wet end of a clean towel lightly across the bloody stains on his broad chest and the hard muscles of his stomach, drying his skin afterward. Her throat tightened. Finally she lifted her eyes. She mouthed the word "Please," but couldn't get out a sound. Her shame was complete when she felt her eyes fill with tears.

Devon rested his temple against the bedpost. "All right," he said on an exhausted sigh. "We'll skip that. Bind it with cloths now, as tightly as you can."

She obeyed in silence, shoulders hunched with dejection, winding clean strips of toweling over his shoulder and under his opposite arm, making a firm bandage. Afterward she helped him to stand up and got him into bed. She pulled his boots off, then his stockings. She ought to strip off his wet breeches. She knew it, but a second later she found herself pulling the covers up to his chest instead. Another unasked-for lesson, she thought grimly, in personal cowardice.

"I'm going to get something for you to eat." Had he heard her? His eyes were closed and he didn't answer. She touched her fingertips to the side of his face and whispered, "You'll be all right now. You're safe. I'll come back soon." Still no response. She slipped out without a sound.

"Where were you?" he demanded the moment she returned, his voice imperious, his eyes too bright.

"I've brought you some soup. It's not hot, I didn't want to light a—"

"Don't leave again without telling me."

"No, I won't," she promised calmly, while a prickle of fear shivered through her. She sat down on the edge of the bed and took the bowl of broth from the tray.

He frowned at the spoon she held to his lips. "I don't want that."

"You need to eat."

"It's brandy I need. Get it."

"Not until you eat your soup." He glared at her. "Come," she wheedled, forcing a smile. "Just a little." She raised her eyebrows and waited, the spoon at his lips, and finally he opened his mouth and started to eat.

He fell asleep before the bowl was half finished. She relaxed slightly, noting that already his face had a little more color. But perhaps that was fever. She pulled a chair close to the bed and sat down. The wind had decreased, but the rain still streamed in torrents. She listened to it slam against the windowpane, thinking she ought to get up and put a blanket over herself. Her clothes were wet through, and tonight would not be a good time to catch a chill. In a minute, she thought wearily; I'll get up in a minute. She fell asleep listening to the pouring rain, and to Devon's deep and steady breathing.

She awoke to find him staring at her. How long had they slept? She had no idea.

"You look terrible."

She wasn't offended; she'd seen him looking better too, after all. "Thank you very much. How do you feel?" She got up and stood over him. His eyes were clearer, the set of his mouth not quite as pained.

He waved the question away. "Listen to me. There's something you have to do. I wish I could do it myself but I can't, and there's no one else." She was surprised when he reached for her wrist and held it tightly. "I want you to find my horse and unsaddle him, put him up. He's probably standing in front of the stables in the rain. He's gentle, in the main; he won't cause you any trouble if you handle him calmly. Put him in his stall and rub him down. Then put his tack away and dry it off. If there's blood anywhere, get rid of it. Do it quietly. MacLeaf's there, and there's another lad who sleeps in the loft. Don't take a light. Can you do that?"

"Yes, I can do it."

His eyes traveled over her slim, straight body, noticing the weary slope of her shoulders, the shapeless dress that still clung damply to her skin. Her face was gray and drawn with fatigue. He wished he was through asking her favors. But he wasn't. "After that, I want you to bury my clothes. Anywhere, but away from the house."

She opened her mouth to ask a question, then closed it. He wouldn't answer anyway. She would do this because it was important to him, and later she would ask herself why that made it important to her.

"When you come back, Lily, I want you to change clothes. Get dry and put on another dress. You'll take— you won't be any help to me if you make yourself ill."

There were many things she could have said to that. Instead she gathered his bloody, discarded garments into her arms. "Will you be all right? I don't know how long I'll be. There's water here in the pitcher if—"

"I'll be all right."

"Are you sure?"

"Yes."

"Well, then. Go to sleep—that's the best thing."

"I will."

"I'll come back soon." Reluctant, oddly unwilling to

leave him, she broke the thread that held their gaze and went away.

Devon stared into the shadow-corners of his room, listening to the retreat of her light footfalls. The wind heaved an angry squall of rain at the window, and he shifted uncomfortably as he imagined her facing the storm again. If he had had any choice he would not have asked her to go; he'd have gone himself or sent someone else. But he had no choice. Why he trusted her was a mystery, and yet he did.

The pain in his shoulder was coming in waves. One came now, and to distract himself he thought of the last time he'd seen her, in the park yesterday, before Clay had interrupted them. She'd wanted to lie with him, but had resisted. That had surprised him; girls of her class were not often so scrupulous. So he'd sent her away, and the look on her face afterward was vivid in his memory even now. She had felt humiliated. Why? What had she expected of him?

The pain receded a little. He put Lily out of his mind and thought of his brother. Bloody ox-headed fool— he'd gotten away without a scratch. His damned ship was somewhere in the Channel by now, far enough south, with any luck, to have missed the storm. And here he lay, half-dead and weak as a new foal, relying on his housemaid to make sure he wasn't arrested for assaulting a riding party of the king's officers. When Clay returned, Devon would have a few things to say to him.

He rubbed his forehead wearily, making a wry face. In point of fact, leaving out the small matter of a bayonet wound, things in St. Remy's Bay had worked out exactly the way he'd wished. No one had gotten killed—as far as he knew. Clay hadn't been recognized and now was probably safe, maybe already on French soil. Best of all, when Clay came home he would have to honor the bargain they'd made, and give up playing at being a free-trader. His smuggling days were over. The fear

Devon had lived with for two years, that his brother would be caught, tried, and hanged—that was over, too. Now Clay would have to get on with some normal kind of life. Whether that meant managing the mine or not would be his decision; Devon wouldn't force that down his throat—couldn't if he'd wanted to. But at least Clay would be safe, and engaged in an occupation that, for a change, wasn't illegal.

The pain returned, a deep, burning ache that brought sweat out all over his body. God, he hoped the girl would bring brandy with her when she came back. A doctor would dose him with laudanum, but he didn't have a doctor. He had Lily Troublefield. He closed his eyes against the throbbing in his shoulder and thought of her. He fell asleep remembering the way she'd kissed him, and how close she had come yesterday to letting him make love to her in the grass.

He was still sleeping when, more than an hour later, Lily returned. She set down her double burden—a bucket of water and a scuttle of coal—and went to Devon on the bed. One of the candles had burned down to nothing and the other was sputtering. She replaced them with new tapers she found in the bedside cabinet and held one high, to see him. He was pale, not flushed, and when she touched him his skin was warm but not hot.

She had become an expert fire-starter in the weeks she'd been at Darkstone; within minutes she had the coals laid and lit in the fireplace grate and a hearty blaze burning. She felt silly—he was fast asleep—but still she couldn't resist a few sharp glances at Devon as she stripped off gown and shift, shoes and stockings. The fire's heat on her skin felt heavenly; she turned before it slowly, warming herself, shaking her wet hair out close to the flames.

What would she put on? There were no extra blankets in sight—and certainly no clothes strewn around this

tidy, austere room that she might appropriate for a
couple of hours. She hesitated a second, then went to
the wardrobe. And paused, hand on the knob, arrested
by the sight of herself in the mirror on the door. It was
the first time she'd seen all of her own naked body since
she'd run away from Lyme. Something was different,
but at first she couldn't tell what it was. Something
about her shape, her . . . Then she knew. She had
muscles she'd never had before, and they gave her body
a new look, a different kind of definition. Subtle, but
definite. She looked strong. That would have dismayed
her—women weren't supposed to be strong!—but after
a few more seconds of narrow-eyed perusal, she decided
she still looked feminine. She still had breasts and hips
and thighs, and none of them looked the least bit manly.
It was all right, then.

She resisted an impulse to turn around and try to see
what Devon Darkwell had found so intriguing two
nights ago on the beach. Instead she opened the wardrobe and pulled out the first thing her hand touched—
his dressing gown, hanging from a hook on the door.
Purple, and the softest silk imaginable. She really
shouldn't—she should choose something less personal
—but even as she thought it she was putting her arms
through the sleeves and tugging the sash tight around
her waist. He used some spice-scented cologne; she
shrugged one shoulder and buried her nose in the soft
material, inhaling a wispy vestige of it, eyes closed.

Time was passing. With a little guilty start, she set
about rinsing the watery bloodstains out of her gown
and shift. Afterward, she dragged two chairs over to the
fire, as close to the flames as she dared, and carefully
laid her wet clothes and stockings over them. They had
to be dry by morning; they simply had to. Reaching
down, she gave the coals another stir with the poker.
Then there was nothing to do but wait.

Fortunately there was one more chair in the room,

the master's leather-upholstered desk chair—the one he'd been sitting in that day she'd brought him his breakfast and then scalded him with hot tea. She pulled the chair over to the bed and sank down in it wearily. The smell of the leather was homey, somehow comforting, and the seat was roomy enough so she could bring her folded legs up onto it. She burrowed in drowsily, arms clasped, forehead pressed against the soft leather wing, and closed her eyes.

# Eight

This was a hallucination. He didn't feel feverish, but what other explanation could there be? A naked goddess was standing in front of his fireplace.

He could see her clearly, in profile, ruffling a wild mane of dark, curly hair over the flames. In that bent-over posture her back made a long, delicate line against the flickering orange blaze, and her pretty white breasts looked lush and ripe. Long arms, long slender legs, ivory-white skin as smooth as marble. Just then she straightened, and turned directly toward him. Her flowing hair covered one proud breast; the other was flushed a rosy pink from the heat. She was slim-hipped but shapely, as strong as Diana, as beautiful as Venus. And he was delirious, for in that moment she reached for her shabby-looking chemise and pulled it over her head, and he recognized her. She was no goddess, she was Lily Troublefield.

She saw his rapt, open-eyed stare as soon as her head cleared the neckline of her shift. She smothered a gasp

of shock and whirled to face the fire. "You were looking!" she accused breathlessly. "Don't look!" She heard
the rustle of covers and threw a glance past her shoulder. He'd pulled the sheet up over his face.

A nervous laugh stuck in her throat. She jerked on her
stockings and then her dress, hazily conscious that the
former were dry, the latter not, and her shift somewhere in between. She took a few hesitant steps toward
the bed, still buttoning her sleeves. "All right," she said
cautiously, pausing six feet away. She watched his
fingers pinch the sheet underneath and slowly pull it
down. It ruffled his hair, his eyelashes, the tip of his
nose. His lips. For a second she saw the same feverish
light in his eyes as before, and then it changed to
amusement. She stared back, entranced. She'd seen
numerous moods flicker in and out of those expressive
turquoise eyes, but never amusement.

Then that was gone too, and the hard look she knew
best came down. "What time is it?"

"I don't know. Early still, five or so. I have to go."

"Go?"

"I have to start my work."

"Why?"

She looked at him blankly.

"Go, then," he conceded with a cranky wave of the
hand, belatedly seeing her point. For a moment he'd
forgotten that it was as important that her life appear to
go on as normal as it was for his.

"What will you do? Someone should help you. Please,
if you would just let me—"

"Don't start in again, Lily. There's no one but you."
Stiff, he tried to sit up straighter; the pain struck hard,
and he swore. "Keep Trayer out of here," he grated
through his teeth.

"How?"

"How the hell do I know?" He squeezed his eyes shut
and clamped down on his temper. "I leave that up to
you. Just keep him out. Keep 'em all out. Tell them I'm

sick, and bring me my breakfast yourself." When he opened his eyes, she was twisting her hands and looking as if he'd asked her to wade across the Channel. "Well? You did it before. What's the matter?"

She sighed, thinking he had no idea how things worked below-stairs, what it meant in the servant hierarchy to bring the master's tray, and how difficult a task he'd given her. Stabling his temperamental stallion was a child's game compared to this!

"Nothing." She went to the head of the bed and reached up for the bell pull. "Wait five minutes and then ring the bell," she told him, putting the tasseled rope in his hand. "Five minutes. *Don't fall asleep.*" She recalled herself. "Sir." She walked to the door and turned back. "What would you like for breakfast?"

"Brandy."

"Anything in addition to that?"

"No." He watched her drop another of her ironic curtseys and slip out the door.

*Anything in addition to that?* What sort of way was that for a housemaid to talk? The girl was educated, but for some reason she wouldn't admit it. He closed his eyes and settled deeper into the pillows, wincing. A more interesting question was, what sort of way was that for a housemaid to *look?* he thought sleepily, remembering her naked before the fire, as lovely and desirable as any woman he'd ever seen. Even Maura.

Maybe they were two of a kind. They both came from the servant class; they were both too clever by half for the social niche that fate had set them in. They both had guileless faces and kind, innocent eyes. But Maura had possessed a treacherous heart. How fortunate that Lily Troublefield's heart didn't interest him even remotely.

Her body did, though. Her body interested him quite a good deal. He fingered the soft gold threads at the end of the bell pull while he stared into the still-glowing coals across the way. A minute later he gave the rope a violent jerk, then four more after that, evenly spaced, each harder than the last. In his eyes there wasn't a particle of amusement.

Breathless, Lily skidded into the kitchen half a minute before the bell rang. She had time to greet the cook, the scullery maid, and one yawning footboy, the only ones up at this hour, when the bell in the wall over the door jangled and all heads turned. Number 4, the master's bedroom. Amazement registered on every upturned face. "I'll go," Lily said quickly, confident that no one would challenge her; there was no one else up yet who *could* go.

She hurried out into the hall. But at the foot of the stairs she pivoted and made a right turn into the open door of the estate agent's office. She hurried to the far end of Mr. Cobb's cramped but tidy room, away from the door and out of view of anyone who might pass in the hall. There she waited, counting off the minutes she estimated it would take to walk upstairs, listen to the master's order, and come back down. She smoothed her skirts with damp palms, wondering if Lowdy had missed her last night. The girl had made no mention of it just now when Lily had crept into their attic room for a clean apron—but she had just woken up, and coherent speech was beyond her so early in the morning.

When it seemed to Lily that enough time had passed, she returned to the kitchen. "Mr. Darkwell wants his breakfast immediately," she told the cook. "He's not feeling well. He asked for hot broth and dry toast and an egg. And a pitcher of beer."

Mrs. Belt peered at her in surprise, but didn't hesitate. "Dorcas, fetch an egg from the larder and be quick," she directed as she took down the grill to set over the hearth for toast.

The butler and a few sleepy servants drifted in, mumbling good morning. Lily kept an apprehensive eye on the progress of the master's tray, praying it would be ready before the housekeeper arrived. The topic of the day was Mr. Darkwell's "illness," and there was much

speculation on what time in the night he might have
come home.

"There, it's ready." Mrs. Belt laid a cloth over the tray
and gestured for Lily to take it.

"What's this? Where are you going with that?" Mrs.
Howe stood blocking the door, black-garbed and bulky,
impenetrable as a boulder. Behind her Lily saw Trayer,
his face a hostile, goading replica of his mother's.

"It's—it's the master's breakfast," she stammered.
"He rang early and told me to bring it up. He's not
feeling well."

"Told *you* to bring it?" Trayer shoved into the room on
his mother's heels and stood in front of Lily with his fists
on his hips. "That's Rose's job. I'll take it up myself if
she's not down yet."

Lily tightened her grip on the tray in near-panic. This
was exactly what she had feared! "Mr. Darkwell told me
to bring it," she said as calmly as she could.

"I'll take it," Trayer repeated.

"No. What I mean is, he said for *me* to bring it.
He—said he didn't want anyone else. And he said for
you not to come to him today. He—doesn't want you."

The kitchen went silent. She looked at no one except
Trayer, but she could feel the focused eyes of every
person in the room. Measuring her. Judging.

Trayer spoke in a low snarl. "You're lying."

She shook her head, and the tense stillness flowed
back.

Mrs. Howe finally broke it. "Go on, then," she said in a
quiet voice that frightened Lily more than if she had
shouted. "You don't want it to get cold, do you? Get
upstairs quick, then come back and help cook with the
baking."

Lily muttered, "Yes, ma'am," and escaped, head
down and face expressionless, careful not to look at
anyone. But she heard the soft, surly growl of gossip
start before she was halfway down the hall.

When she pushed Devon's door open, she found him

leaning against the high bureau, white as chalk, trying to shave.

"Judas!" She set the tray on the desk and rushed toward him. "What are you doing?" She took the razor from him and moved him toward the bed with a firm, insistent hand at his back. "I thought you had better sense," she clucked under her breath, "I truly did. Sit down before you faint. How do you feel? You're as pale as the sheet. What got into—"

"Lily." His voice was stern, but Devon imagined he didn't cut a very commanding figure when his hands were trembling, he wore nothing but his breeches, and three-quarters of his face was covered with drying soap. "I'll remind you that it's not your place to tell me what to do. Your job is to do exactly what I tell you to do. Is that clear?"

"Yes, that's perfectly clear. I beg your pardon, my lord, I forgot myself. What is it you would like me to do?"

It was impossible to tell whether her remorse was genuine. He studied her limpid gray-green eyes, serious mouth, and demurely folded hands, and decided it wasn't. For some reason that pleased him. "I'd like you to help me finish shaving," he conceded gravely. "I don't think I can manage it on my own."

Her pique dissipated. "Well, then. Sit down." She hurried to the bureau to retrieve his shaving things. "The soap's dried out," she murmured as she wet her hand in the basin and moistened the lather on his face by making little circles with her fingertips. She dipped the razor in the basin, shook it off, and began scraping the whiskers along his jaw, her other hand resting on his throat. "I'm sorry the water is cold; your valet probably heats it."

"Mm." He was thinking how pretty her mouth was. "Did Trayer give you any trouble?"

"Oh . . ." She shrugged.

"Did he?"

"Nothing to speak of. Do this." She pulled her top lip under her teeth. He copied her, and she began to shave under his nose.

When she finished, he said, "You've done this before, I see. For your young man?"

She busied herself scraping away at his left cheek. "Certainly not. When my father was living, sometimes he needed help."

"Why?"

He certainly was full of questions. She decided to tell him the truth. "Sometimes he drank too much. If he'd shaved himself the next morning he'd have cut his throat. There." She wet the face cloth and wiped away the last traces of soap. "That's done. Your breakfast is getting cold. Why don't you lie down—if it pleases you," she remembered to say, "and let me bring the tray to you. Do you think you can—"

"Never mind that. I want you to help me get dressed."

"But *why?*" His black scowl, hostile and supercilious at the same time, made her draw in her breath. "I beg your pardon again," she got out stiffly. But she couldn't let it lie. "Forgive me for speaking out of turn, but you have a serious injury. In my"—she wouldn't say *humble* —"in my opinion you need to rest in bed. You won't have a doctor, so the wound can't be stitched. If it should open again and start bleeding—"

"Damn it, I know all that." He watched her frown and press her lips together to hold back more advice. Sensible advice. He sighed. "Listen to me. It's very likely that I'll be receiving visitors sometime today. I need to get ready for them. For reasons that don't concern you, it's important that the nature of my—mishap not become known to them. Do you take my meaning?"

"I understand you don't want these 'visitors' to know that last night you were stabbed in the shoulder. I don't understand why."

"Nor do you need to. Now get me a clean shirt. Please," he added magnanimously.

"Tell me one thing. Is your brother safe?"

He went stiff. "That's none of your business."

Lily didn't move. She waited with the razor in one hand, the bowl of soapy water in the other, and returned his steely glare with steady, clear-eyed composure.

Devon shook his head in disgust. If he wanted his shirt, he'd have to tell her about Clay; the woman was like a hound after a fox. "Clay's fine. Not a mark on him. I was the lucky one."

Is it true that he captains his own ship and leads a gang of smugglers? she wanted to ask next. But the moment of candor was over, she was certain, and instead she said, "Where do you keep your shirts?"

She got him dressed in a clean shirt and stock and a velvet smoking jacket, once again ignoring the fact of, the very existence of, his breeches. But this time her luck didn't hold.

"Lily," he said patiently, perched on the edge of the bed and clinging again to the post, "this maidenly shyness is very charming, but also irritating under the circumstances. I can't wear these buckskins any longer. Apart from other considerations, they're in deplorable fashion with my velvet jacket. Even Trayer would be offended, a man not fluently conversant with the *bon ton*." He rested his temple against the post, exhausted by his speech, and privately surprised by his own levity. "Find me some breeches," he finished with his eyes closed. "We'll contrive a way to get them on without debauching your sensibilities."

In the end they managed it fairly easily, aided by the fact that his white cambric shirt hung down almost to mid-thigh, sparing Lily the sight of anything so overtly masculine as to distress her. His lighthearted mockery helped; she knew she was behaving like a ninny, and getting her skittish nerves out in the open between them somehow soothed her.

"I think you should lie down now," she told him as she knelt at his feet and put his stockings and shoes on for him. "If your 'visitors' come, you'll have plenty of warning and can be sitting up before they come in."

"I'll greet them downstairs."

"But that's absurd!" She saw his expression and ducked her head. "I meant to say, my lord, that you—"

"I told you to stop my-lording me."

"Yes, sir. I only meant to say that in my opinion that would not be wise."

"And what gives you the idea that your opinion matters to me in the slightest?"

Lily finished buckling his shoes and rose smoothly to her feet. "Nothing at all. Forgive me. I can't imagine what I was thinking."

She kept her eyes downcast, but her lips were stiff with anger. He watched her fingers clench at her sides twice, three times, before she was calm enough to lift her chin and look at him. He admired her self-control; her face was quiet, the green eyes level and composed. But behind their surface placidity he saw fires burning.

The curtsey she bobbed was flawless and utterly without connotation this time. If he didn't need her any longer, she murmured, she begged to be excused. But she gave herself away when she turned and went to the door without waiting for his permission.

"Lily."

"My lord?"

They engaged in a brief staring contest.

Lily backed down. "Sir?" she corrected tersely.

Another moment passed. Then Devon said, "Perhaps you're right. Perhaps I'll see them here. Sitting at my desk."

"Very good, sir." But what she longed to say was, *What gives you the idea that anything you do interests me in the slightest?* It would have given her great satisfaction, in spite of the fact that it wasn't true. "Can you manage breakfast on your own?" she asked impassively.

"Yes. Thank you."

His voice was civil now, almost kind. It was a truce, of sorts. "Then I'll leave you. Mrs. Howe will be looking for me. I'll come back, if you like. As soon as I can." He nodded. Their gazes held for another second, and then she went away.

It hadn't seemed to Lily that she'd been gone that long, but when she went into the servants' hall she discovered that breakfast was over and no one was about except Dorcas and another girl, clearing the table. Dorcas's usually pasty face was bright pink with excitement.

"Mrs. 'Owe d' say you're t' come to 'er room," she informed Lily as soon as she saw her.

"When, Dorcas? When does she want me to come?"

"Now, miss. She'm ever so mad!" Her lackluster eyes sparkled, but whether with fear or anticipation Lily couldn't tell.

She scanned the long table for anything that might have been left over from breakfast—a piece of biscuit, a saucer of cold tea—but it was bare; locusts couldn't have stripped it any cleaner. A wave of fatigue and depression washed over her. And now Mrs. Howe was angry, would doubtless punish her with some tedious chore because she was late, and there was no plausible excuse she could give her.

The housekeeper's suite was at the short end of the narrow, L-shaped corridor. Being summoned to it was reputedly a harrowing experience, something to be feared and dreaded. It had never happened to Lily, but it had happened to Norah Penglennan, a sixteen-year-old chambermaid who had been at Darkstone only a few months before Lily arrived. Below-stairs rumor had it that her crime was neglecting to change young Mr. Darkwell's sheets on wash day. The fact that she'd fainted twice that day—from some undiagnosed condition—evidently did not figure in her defense. What went on between the girl and Mrs. Howe was never learned; Norah returned from the encounter trembling and white-faced, but she would not speak of it. A few days later she ran away.

*I'm not afraid of Mrs. Howe,* Lily told herself as she walked down the corridor. She wasn't hurrying along, though, she noticed; an impartial witness might even say she was dragging her feet. She sniffed and squared her shoulders. I'm not afraid of her because I'm not someone like Norah Penglennan, a poor, uneducated girl who can be intimidated by threats and harsh words from a petty despot. I am Lily Trehearne. My mother was a lady and my father was a gentleman. Most of the time. He had to work for a living, and a few of his occupations might not have been perfectly respectable in the strictest sense of the word. But he was gently reared and tolerably well educated, and to Lily's knowledge he had never done anything dishonest.

Oh, what nonsense! Her father's respectability was hardly the issue right now. For that matter, neither was hers. She had to get through an unpleasant interview with a mean-spirited tyrant, that was all. But what if, after having impersonated a servant for more than two months, she'd begun to think like one, feel like one? Nonsense, she thought again. She mentally shook herself, drew her fist back, and gave Mrs. Howe's closed door three sharp, fearless raps.

"Come in."

She pushed it open and went in. The scent of fresh baking still lingered, no doubt from the scones Mrs. Belt had made this morning and which, of course, no other servant had tasted—with the possible exception of Trayer, Lily amended. The housekeeper was sitting at her desk, poring over what looked like a list of accounts. She didn't move, and Lily understood that ignoring her was to be the first arrow fired from Mrs. Howe's sheath. Lily folded her hands and assumed an attitude, probably exaggerated, of polite submission. The seconds ticked by and she began to feel almost amused; she'd expected a tactic more sophisticated, less childish from her adversary.

But something about the shape of Mrs. Howe's hands on the desk—blocky and crude, nerveless, a man's hands—made amusement seem inappropriate. Irrelevant. In spite of herself, Lily's unease deepened.

At length Mrs. Howe laid down her pen and looked up. She stared without speaking for so long that Lily thought she herself might burst out laughing, or blurt out some incoherent confession of nameless crimes—anything to put an end to this silent, nerve-wracking staring. It's a trick, she warned herself. Designed to bully and harass frightened little girls. Even so, it was hard to imagine those bright black bulldog eyes missing anything. Perhaps at this moment they were searching out the telltale places where Lily's gown was still damp, or worse, the faint stains of blood that still lingered underneath her apron. Somehow she kept her own gaze tranquil and didn't look away. But she wanted to. And Mrs. Howe, she knew, wanted her to.

The housekeeper got to her feet, the great cluster of keys at her waist rattling ostentatiously. For a heavy woman, she moved with an unsettling fluidity that struck Lily, in her present mood, as grotesque. "You missed breakfast," she observed, standing beside her desk, in a voice much too soft to be genuine.

"Yes, ma'am." Lily bowed her head penitently.

"But that's against the rules, isn't it?"

"Yes, ma'am."

"Why did it take so long to hand the master his tray, I wonder?"

"I can't say."

"Can't say? Is that because you don't know?"

Lily's mind went frighteningly blank. "I . . . went up to my room afterwards to . . . I had forgotten my . . . I changed my stockings."

"Changed your stockings? Why?"

"I—don't know."

"Was it stupidity? Was it because you're a stupid girl, Lily?"

"No, ma'am, I just—changed them." God, how she hated this! Anger coiled inside, tensing all her muscles.

"But I told you to come right back and help cook with the baking. Didn't I?" She still hadn't raised her voice.

"Yes, ma'am."

"Did you disobey me?"

"I—yes."

"Why?"

She gritted her teeth. "I don't know. I forgot."

Mrs. Howe came closer. They were exactly the same height, and now their faces were inches apart. To avoid her eyes, Lily fixed her gaze on Mrs. Howe's grim slit of a mouth. Her lips fit together like two halves of a muffin split with a razor. "Forgot?" she murmured. "Because you're stupid?"

Lily couldn't answer.

"Are you stupid, Lily?"

"No. No, ma'am."

"No? Then why didn't you do as you were told?"

"I . . . didn't think."

"Because you're stupid?"

Her throat was so tight she couldn't speak at all.

"Say it," Mrs. Howe urged, her voice a throaty purr. "Say it."

Lily's chest was burning. "Please," she whispered.

"Say it."

"I'm not. I'm not stupid." But a treacherous, icy-hot tear slid down her cheek, and it was worse than an admission. Lily bowed her head in defeat.

The housekeeper backed up soundlessly. On a table beside the desk were two metal buckets. She picked them up, her manner brusque now, her eyes no longer crafty, only cruel. "Stupidity is one of Satan's disguises. It must be punished, for wickedness hides under it, beneath the serpent's belly, waiting for the innocent and the undefiled. It must be punished." She came forward and gave Lily the buckets, one in each hand. They were small; each held no more than a gallon.

"We've run out of sand to scour the floors, Lily. I want you to fill both bins in the kitchen garden shed. To the top. Don't use any but these pails. Don't stop until the bins are full. If you do, I'll have to punish you again. Do you understand?"

"Yes, ma'am." Impotence had solidified into rage, defeat into hatred. She wanted to do harm to Mrs. Howe with her own hands.

"We'll cast the devil out together, Lily. Thank me for it." She came closer. "Thank me."

"Thank . . . you."

"Thank you—?"

Lily closed her eyes for a second. "Ma'am." Mrs. Howe smiled. In the pitch depths of her black eyes, Lily saw real wickedness. Shaking, she turned and got away.

The sun at high noon was a blinding lemon-yellow disc in the center of a colorless sky. It beat down on the dark rocks that emerged from the sea like prehistoric beasts. The tide was out, but the sand was wet and foam-covered all the way up to the sand hills and the shingle and the granite cliff's base.

Lily crouched down at the last of the stone cliff steps and filled her two small buckets with sand. Straightening, she stared across the glittering rollers at the sharp knife edge of the horizon. Perspiration had soaked through the back of her gown; her face was beaded with it. Here by the shore the salt wind blew feebly, but above, behind the house among the outbuildings, not a breath of air stirred.

She grabbed up handfuls of her apron on either side and used them for padding between the buckets' thin wires and the tender pads of her fingers, but nothing helped much anymore. Blisters had formed hours ago, and now the sores only stuck to the fibers of the cloth and made releasing the buckets at the end of her journey that much harder. Head down, shoulders hunched, she started the climb back up the cliff steps.

There were seventy-two steps. At the twenty-seventh there was a wooden landing. She paused there to catch her breath. The sudden cessation of movement made her dizzy, and she clung to the rough railing with one hand, eyes closed and heart pounding. Fainting would be too easy; she wouldn't give Mrs. Howe the satisfaction. But one bin in the kitchen garden shed was still empty, the other not quite half full. Elemental arithmetic told her she had about seven hours of sand-hauling left to do.

She wished she could cry. Now that she was alone and no one could see, it would be all right——she would give herself permission. But, curiously, the tears wouldn't come. She was holding them in, along with her fury and frustration. Or perhaps she was punishing herself for that moment of weakness, of shameful capitulation when she'd wept in front of Mrs. Howe. Sometimes she was able to think about Devon, and wondered what he was doing now, if he was all right, if his "visitors" had come yet. But most of the time she was in too much pain to think about anything. Mrs. Howe had found a vulnerable place inside her—pride or confidence, self-respect —and injured it. She was wounded. She hurt.

She picked her buckets up and started to climb again. The muscles between her shoulders were burning, and there was no way to ease the painful ache low in her spine. The sun blazed; her mouth felt as dry as the sand she was carrying. Twelve steps from the summit, she looked up. At first she didn't recognize the man standing on the top step, holding the railings on either side with both hands and blocking the way. Then, squinting against the bright sun, she brought him into focus. Trayer.

Of course. He'd come to gloat.

Even though her legs felt sheathed in lead, she stepped up her pace, straightened her shoulders, and stuck her chin out. She tried to make her face serene, but she knew it was damp and red, probably freckled—and then suddenly the idea of pretending for Trayer Howe's benefit repulsed her. Not a bone in her body cared what he thought of her. She trudged on until she was three steps below him, then stopped.

"Excuse me," she said clearly, wondering how long he would taunt her, how long before he would let her past.

His satisfied grin widened predictably. He didn't move. "Hot today," he observed conversationally. "Could be you need some help with those buckets." He raised his eyebrows but didn't take his hands off the wooden rails.

"No, thank you. Please let me pass."

Malice flashed in his black eyes, so like his mother's they made her shudder. "'No, thank you, please let me pass,'" he mimicked, rolling his hips in an exaggeratedly feminine way. Lily looked away in disgust. "Even fetching sand, you think you're the goddam Queen of England. You don't look it, though. Right now you look just like the slut you are."

"Get out of my way."

"Think you've landed in a soft spot, don't you? Did a spread for the master, and now everything's going to be easy." She tried to squeeze past him, but he shifted his bulk to the side, cutting her off. "It won't work, not for long anyway. But I'll tell you what would work."

"Trayer—"

"If you was to give *me* a bit o' snug for a bit o' stiff, now, that would ease things up for you considerably. What d'you say, Queen Lily?"

She was rigid with anger, too furious to speak. She shoved one shoulder at him with all her strength, but it was like pushing on a rock. All of a sudden he reached out with both hands and grabbed at her breasts. With a cry of outrage, Lily dropped her buckets and batted his hands away. "Bastard!" she swore, while his ugly laugh rang in her ears. Weak-kneed, she backed down a step and stared at him, holding onto the rail.

"Oh, now, ain't that a shame. Lost your buckets, did you?" He peered over the edge of the railing at the beach below, where her two empty buckets lay half buried in the sand, and shook his head in mock sympathy. "Now you'll have to start all over. Want me to help you, your highness?" He took a step toward her, holding out a paw of a hand and grinning at her.

Lily imagined him backing her all the way down, one step at a time, laughing all the while. She planted her feet. Gripping the rail with one hand, she made a fist of the other.

"Miss Lily."

Trayer whirled. Galen MacLeaf stood on the brow of the headland above them, legs spread, roguish blue eyes darting a challenge.

"I was told to fetch you. Lowdy says master d' want you right away."

Trayer turned back. She looked away to avoid his eyes, but as she brushed by him he murmured, "Next time, bitch," in her ear. A shiver tingled up the length of her spine to her scalp.

"Thank you, Galen," was all she could say to MacLeaf. But the gratitude in her eyes told him how timely his arrival had been.

"I'll pitch his fat arse into the sea if you d' want un, Lily," he said softly, touching her arm.

"It was nothing, truly. Best to leave it."

He grinned his cocky, gap-toothed grin. "That's as you please. But there's the offer, whenever ee d' need it."

Although she tried to smile, she couldn't quite manage it. She left him and set off toward the house, aware that behind her she'd left a friend and a dangerous enemy.

# Nine

Devon came out of the lightest of dozes when he heard the door open and saw Lily tiptoe in. "Where the devil have you been?" he wanted to know. His eyes narrowed. He pushed himself up on his elbows painfully and asked a different question, in a softer voice. "What the hell have you been doing?"

Ignoring him, Lily went to the bedside table, where half a pitcher of beer still rested on the tray. She poured most of it into a glass—his glass—and drank it down without stopping. "What is it you want?" she asked directly, dragging the back of her hand across her wet forehead.

With lightning-quick speed she would not have given him credit for, his hand snaked out and caught hold of her wrist. He tugged on her arm, and she stumbled against the side of the bed. Turning her hand over, he stared at the raw, blistered flesh of her palm. He looked up at her in amazement, then reached out for her other hand.

She whipped it behind her back. "It's the same," she said stolidly. "What is it you want with me?"

Dropping her hand, Devon slid back against his pillow. "I want you to sit down."

"Good," Lily breathed, and sank down on the chair beside the bed. Every muscle in her body was screaming with exhaustion. But it was so cool and dark here, so quiet. When a moment passed and he didn't speak, she let her eyelids close. She could almost fall asleep, right now. Later—a second? a minute?—she jerked herself awake in alarm. He was still staring at her. "How do you feel?" she asked guiltily. She thought he looked a little better, maybe not quite as pale.

"What do you do, Lily? What chores do they give you?"

The question startled both of them.

"I clean your house," she answered simply.

"Yes, but what do you do?"

She sighed and leaned her head against the back of the chair. "Polish the furniture. Scrub the floors and beat the rugs. Dust. Tidy. Help in the kitchen, the laundry, sometimes the dairy." Her eyes had slid closed again; she opened them to see if he was still listening. "Do what I'm told," she finished tiredly.

"Why do you do it?"

"Why?" She laughed without any amusement. "To live." She glanced across at him, into his serious face. The conversation had taken an odd, dangerous turn. She was afraid her own face might give something away, and slowly got to her feet. She tried to sound brisk. "Have you had your dinner yet?"

"I don't want anything."

She opened her mouth to argue with him when there was a light knock at the door. She had time to jump away from the bed and busy her hands with the plates and glasses on the tray before it opened.

It was Stringer, the butler. Lily thought he made a

point of not looking at her. "Gentlemen to see you, sir. From the Revenue, they say."

"Bring them up, Stringer, I'll speak to them here."

"Very good, sir."

As soon as the door closed, Lily went back to the bed. "Are you sure you should be doing this?" she asked anxiously, helping him to sit up, then to stand. They walked to his desk together, her arm around his waist, and he sat down heavily. Already his face was gray and perspiring. "You shouldn't be doing this," she muttered, aware that she might as well be talking to herself. "You look terrible." She ran the fingers of one hand through his hair to straighten it, mumbling, "Excuse me," and then peered at him critically. "Should I open the draperies? You look ill, but with them closed it looks like a sickroom. I'm not sure—"

"Yes, open them." With one hand he lifted his heavy ledger book from the top of the desk and opened it to the current date. "Fix me a pen, quickly."

She opened his ink bottle, then took the knife he handed her and sharpened one of the quills from a jar on the desktop. "It's lucky you're right-handed," she murmured distractedly, giving it to him. "Will you stand up when they come?"

"Certainly not. The Viscount Sandown doesn't trouble himself for trifling government pettifoggers."

The dry humor in his tone cheered her enormously. On an impulse, she reached down and pinched his cheeks. "For color," she explained when his blue eyes widened. Just for a second her fingers lingered on the hard flesh of his jaw. She jumped when another knock sounded. "Good luck!" She reached the door just as it opened.

Preceding Stringer, two men came through. Devon recognized one as Polcraven, the Customs Collector at Fowey; the other was a stranger. Devon folded his hands and leaned back in his chair. At the movement, a sharp, agonizing pull in his shoulder had him gritting his teeth and willing his face not to flinch. "Gentlemen," he got out with what he hoped was lazy disdain. "To what do I owe this unexpected pleasure?" Before either could answer, he said to Lily, who was still standing by the door, twisting her hands, "That's all, thank you." She curtsied and went out. But he noticed she left the door open.

"Your lordship," Charles Polcraven intoned with a low bow, endangering the security of his bagwig. "Forgive the intrusion, I beg you, we won't keep you two minutes. The simplest questions you can imagine, that's all we need to ask. And let me assure you it was not my idea to come here and disturb you in this unseemly way, without notice or—"

"No, it was mine."

Devon steepled his fingers and peered over them at the tall, ax-faced man in uniform standing beside Polcraven. "Indeed? And you are—?"

"Lieutenant Edward Von Rebhan of the Revenue Service, Commander of the cutter *Royal George*." He executed a precise military bow.

"Lieutenant." Devon let mild surprise flicker for a second in his eyes. "How may I help you?"

"You can tell us where you were last night," Von Rebhan answered boldly, while Polcraven bounced on his toes and made little sounds of distress and apology.

"Really? Why would I do that, I wonder?"

"Because the penalty for assaulting an officer of the Revenue is hanging."

"My lord!" cried Polcraven, flapping his fat hands in the air and beginning to dance in place. "I beg your pardon, I most humbly do, this is not at all what we mean to say to you!"

"No? What do you mean to say to me?"

The cold, quiet tone of his voice made Polcraven go pale and apparently lose the ability to speak.

Lieutenant Von Rebhan got a better grip on his cocked hat. "I apologize if I was too direct," he said stiffly. "Allow me to explain the circumstances of our visit, my lord."

"I look forward to it." Devon crossed his legs and tapped two impatient fingernails against his desk—a distraction for the hand he passed over his face, wiping away the sweat that had beaded under his nose. His head was clear enough, but the throbbing pain in his shoulder was unrelenting.

Von Rebhan cleared his throat. "Yesterday morning, my lord, on routine patrol out of Fowey, my cutter came upon a sloop lying in a hidden cove."

"A 'hidden cove?' " He let a suggestion of amusement shade his tone.

"Indeed, sir, a *hidden cove.* One of many along the river in that area where smugglers' vessels put in to off-load their contraband cargos. This particular sloop was unmanned at the time. We confiscated it immediately."

"I'm delighted to hear it. I'm sure your superiors will be pleased."

Von Rebhan's gray eyes hardened. "I doubt that, sir. Twelve hours later, as they waited for help from the Waterguard at Falmouth, the men who were holding the sloop were attacked."

"Attacked?"

"By more than a dozen ruffians, carrying pistols and swords and cutlasses. My men were routed, thrown over the side of the vessel, and left to drown."

Devon massaged his mouth to hide a smile; in fact, there had only been five "ruffians." "Left to drown?" he said quizzically. "But I thought the sloop was tied up in a 'hidden cove.' "

The lieutenant reddened slightly and began to stroke his mustache. "They *might* have drowned," he said doggedly; "two of them couldn't swim."

"Ah."

"At the time, my cutter was lying at the mouth of the Fowey, waiting for the Falmouth mariners. The *Spider* was seen to—"

"The what?"

Von Rebhan's shrewd eyes narrowed, measuring him. "The *Spider*," he enunciated, and this time it was *his* voice that held a hint of mockery.

"That would be the smuggling vessel?" Devon asked blandly.

"Precisely. The *Spider* was seen to draw close to the shore and discharge one passenger before heading out to sea. The *Royal George* gave chase."

Devon rubbed his hands together. "Lieutenant, I trust there's a point to this story eventually, but in the meantime I must say I'm enjoying it tremendously. It seems to get more exciting as it goes along."

Von Rebhan flushed again, and twisted at his mustache as if he wanted to screw it into his face. "The *Spider* carried twenty carriage guns and twenty swivels," he went on tightly. "And she had a carronade. She came in close and fired at us for over a quarter of an hour. In the end, my cutter suffered thirty shots in her sails, two dozen in her boat, and her mainmast and mizzen halyards were blown away."

"Did you lose any men?"

"No."

Devon masked his intense relief with a show of impatience. "Good, good. Is that the end of it, then?"

"Not quite. I thought you might be interested in what happened to the passenger the *Spider* discharged near Polruan, my lord."

"No, I'm not. But if it will speed things along, go ahead and tell me."

"Evidently this man had left a horse tied nearby. Under cover of darkness, he began to make his way west. Toward Trewyth."

Devon   smiled.   "Trewyth?   Toward   St.   Austell,

Mevagissey, and Portloe as well, then. Not to mention Truro, Redruth, Hayle, Penzance—"

"Thank you, sir, you're quite right. At any rate, just north of Dodman Point, he was overtaken by Riding Officers sent out from Falmouth to help with the confiscation of the *Spider*. Four of them."

At least he had that number right. "And did they capture the man?"

"They did not. He overpowered them."

Devon lifted his brows. "You astonish me, lieutenant. How could such a thing happen?"

"I wasn't there, my lord," Von Rebhan said through his teeth. "I can't explain it. All the officers were disarmed; two are still recovering from head wounds."

"Incredible. And this man got away unscathed?"

"By no means. One of the Riding Officers assured me he was wounded seriously, perhaps mortally."

"And yet you haven't found him?"

He hesitated for a fraction of a second, then said evenly, "No, my lord. Not yet."

"How unfortunate. Why have you told me this story?"

Now that the moment had come, the lieutenant seemed to lose his nerve. Polcraven screwed up his courage and spoke for him. "I've told Lieutenant Von Rebhan a dozen times his suspicions are groundless, your lordship, but he won't listen. He has it in his head that young Mr. Darkwell captains the *Spider*, and that you yourself were with the men who seized it from the Revenue Officers last night!"

Bleeding hypocrite, thought Devon; there was no doubt in his mind that Polcraven was one of the Customs men whom Clay regularly paid off in exchange for keeping his mouth shut and looking the other way. He barked out what he hoped was an incredulous laugh. "Is this true, lieutenant?"

"It's a possibility I've been instructed to look into," Von Rebhan said steadily.

"By whom?"

"By the Surveyor of Sloops in Exeter. Who, by the way, is under orders from the Home Secretary himself."

"Fascinating. And do I take it that you believe *I* am this man who was 'mortally wounded' a few hours ago by Riding Officers?" Von Rebhan was silent, his consternation obvious. "Well? Is that what you think, lieutenant?" Devon stood up abruptly and walked across the short space of floor to the spot where the two men were standing. Polcraven retreated; the lieutenant, to give him his due, held his ground. "Do I look like a mortally wounded man to you?" he asked softly. A momentary dizziness, nothing more. But he wished he'd gotten up more slowly.

"I'm only doing my duty, sir. It's not my intention to insult you. This entire matter could be cleared up in minutes if you would be good enough to tell us where you were last night."

"And I say that's none of your damn business."

"Several of the servants have told us you were not at home for supper last night, nor did you—"

"You've questioned my servants?" Devon roared. The thunder in his voice sent Polcraven scurrying backwards toward the door.

But Von Rebhan would not be intimidated. "Yes, sir," he admitted staunchly. "Neither you nor your brother was at home last evening."

"Are you telling me, lieutenant, that my ancestral home is nothing but an owlers' den, a hotbed of thieves and cutthroats, vice and violence?"

"I've no opinion on that score whatsoever, my lord; I'm merely making an inquiry. Would you be good enough to tell me where your brother was last night?"

Devon heaved a defeated-sounding sigh and moved back to sit on the edge of his desk, hoping he didn't look as if he were collapsing on it. "Very well, I'll tell you, to get rid of you. Clay is on his way to London, via Devonshire to visit his mother. Also via Epsom,

Petworth, and Newmarket, to throw away his money. I don't know when he'll arrive in Russell Square; I should think it would depend on which horses he chooses to back en route. Now, go away."

The lieutenant planted his feet. "Meaning no disrespect, would you mind telling me your own whereabouts as well?"

"Yes, I would mind. You try my patience, sir. You come to my home uninvited and question my servants. You have the effrontery to tell me that assaulting Revenue Officers is a capital crime, and the impudence to use the Home Secretary's name in a pathetic attempt to threaten me. I sit in the House of Lords, sir. The Home Secretary has been a guest in my home. I could make threats, too, but you strike me as a man of decent sense. I'm relying on you to see the light within the next few seconds, lieutenant, take Polcraven with you, and get the hell out of my house."

Von Rebhan's face was beet-red. "You won't answer?" Devon sent back a frigid stare. "Then you're correct, there's nothing more to say. But I must leave you with a word—and I assure you it's not intended as a threat: This matter is far from closed, and you will be hearing again either from me or my superiors in the very near future. Good day to you."

By God, Devon couldn't help but admire the bastard. He didn't envy him his thankless, underpaid job, and he'd wager that Edward Von Rebhan was one of the few honest Revenue men in the whole of Cornwall. "Good day," he echoed, and watched him leave. Polcraven scuttled out after him sideways, like a crab, trying to bow and escape at the same time.

Devon got up from his desk and went to the window, where he leaned against the sill and mopped his sweating face with his handkerchief. At least he hadn't fainted—he could take some comfort from that. But bloody hell! Von Rebhan was no fool and he wasn't bluffing: he would be back. And the next time he would not be put off by haughty words and trumped-up indignation. He, or someone in his stead, would politely insist on answers. Devon had to invent some in a very short time, and then he had to implement them. "Implementing" them, he knew, would mean bribing people to lie.

Damn Clay to hell! No doubt he'd find all this amusing when he came back and heard the details. Devon wanted to wring his neck. He wouldn't, of course; he'd be cajoled out of his ill humor by Clay's damnable boyish charm—as usual. But at twenty-three, his brother was closing in on the far side of boyishness. The only good thing about this idiotic *Spider* affair was that it was bound to wake Clay up to some of life's simple realities. In the meantime, Devon was being forced to use his wits to thwart an investigation he would otherwise have championed. He was on Von Rebhan's side, for God's sake—he'd voted for bills that would finance the requisition of more men just like him! This was intolerable; the more he thought of it, the angrier he got.

He dropped his forehead against the glass and stared out across the rocky headland at the mirror of the sea. Where was Lily? He felt like hell, and she ought to be here, taking care of him. Perhaps he hadn't made it clear what was expected of her. He would do so as soon as she—

A loud rap at the door made him jolt up straight and swipe at his face again with his handkerchief. "Come in!"

He relaxed when he saw that it was Lily—then tensed again when Von Rebhan and Polcraven walked in behind her. He was about to say something indignant when he noticed that they all wore identical expressions of embarrassment. Of the three, Lily's was by far the most embarrassed. Now what? He managed to fold his arms without wincing, and waited.

Von Rebhan glanced at Polcraven; Polcraven glanced back and resolutely closed his mouth. Von Rebhan cleared his throat and started to speak, then appeared to think better of it, went back to the door, and closed it.

"Well? What is it now?" Devon demanded when the taut silence resumed. Lily was twisting her fingers, pink-faced, looking as if she wanted to disappear under the carpet.

The lieutenant got hold of himself. "My lord, this girl has just told us a story, and I—I'm obliged to ask you to confirm it."

Devon's hands clenched inside his coat pockets; it seemed as if a bomb had exploded in his chest. But he thought his voice sounded miraculously casual. "Indeed? And what has she told you?"

Something in his tone made Lily jerk her head up. *Dear God, he thinks I've told them.* Without warning, her eyes filled with tears. She bent her head to hide them, and wondered at the dull pain that made her throat ache. How could he think it, even for a second? How could he?

Von Rebhan went back to twisting his mustache. "She tells us, sir, that she spent all of last night, beginning around ten o'clock, in your guest house on the grounds. With you." He cleared his throat violently. "She says you were together there until a little after dawn. And she says there are no, ah, wounds whatsoever on your . . . person." He looked at Devon directly, in defiance of the faint flush on his cheeks. "Is she telling the truth?"

Lily risked another upward glance. Now Devon's face was a mystery; it was impossible to tell what he was thinking. She felt her own face grow hotter and looked back down at her feet. For her the tension was all but unbearable. What was he thinking? How would he answer?

After an eternity he spoke, in a cold, quiet tone that chilled her. "Yes, she's telling the truth. But let me warn you, gentlemen: If I ever learn that this piece of information has reached the ears of anyone beyond the four walls of this room, I'll see to it that your jobs in the Customs Service are terminated and that you find no others in Cornwall for the rest of your lives. You may take that as a threat if you wish. I mean it as a promise. Do we understand each other?"

"Yes, certainly, my lord, absolutely, without question," babbled Polcraven. Devon shot him a look of contempt—for he had no doubt that the story would be all over Fowey by nightfall.

Von Rebhan's reaction was more complicated; Devon could almost hear the debate going on in the man's head as he tried to separate truth from fiction. But presently he appeared to come to a decision. "Given what you and the woman have told us, it seems there's no point now in pursuing the investigation. I know of no practical reason why the—subject that has just been discussed should become known to anyone beyond ourselves. As a gentleman—and I'm sure I speak for Mr. Polcraven as well in this regard—I'm obliged to respect your personal business, sir, and I can tell you that any reports I submit will be vague enough in this crucial regard to insure that your privacy is not breached."

"Right, right," muttered Polcraven.

"Then I can take it the matter is closed?"

After the slightest hesitation, Von Rebhan answered, "Yes, my lord. I doubt that we'll be troubling you again."

"Fine. Then I'll bid you good afternoon." Devon inclined his head in dismissal and watched them go, his relief barely hidden.

When Lily started to trail out after them, he called her name, quietly.

She stopped. "I've—I'll—come back, but Mrs. Howe has given me a task and I've already—"

"Come in and close the door."

She breathed a deep, silent sigh and did as she was told. With her back pressed against the closed door, she watched him across the width of the room and wondered who would speak first. He did.

"Why did you do it?"

Then the words came tumbling out. "I know I shouldn't have—I'm sorry if I've caused you more trouble, but I knew they didn't believe you and it was all I could think of to do. I know I've embarrassed you. I apologize. I don't believe they will tell anyone, though, not after what you said to them. So you needn't worry about anyone finding out, I don't think. Really, I don't think they'll speak of it, you made it so clear—"

"Lily, do you think I'm angry with you?"

She folded her hands together to keep from fidgeting. "I don't know. Yes, I think you might be. Are you?"

"No, of course not. You've saved my hide—why would I be angry?"

"Oh." She felt ridiculously glad. "But I've embarrassed you."

"Is that what you think?" Perhaps she really was that naïve. "I wanted Von Rebhan to think you had, to explain why I didn't tell him the same story you did right from the beginning. But we live in a wicked world, my dear; no one in my acquaintance, with the possible exception of my mother, will be scandalized when they hear that I've been trifling with one of my housemaids."

"Oh—I see. Yes, of course."

Belatedly he realized that that was not quite what he should have said. Her cheeks were a bright pink, as if he'd slapped her, and she was staring in a frozen way at something over his shoulder. By God, she was prickly! Apologizing seemed excessive, though; he wasn't sure what he'd done anyway. Instead he asked her a question. "What about you, Lily?"

She made herself look at him. "Me? What do you mean?"

"If your young man should learn of this, what will he think? Will he be angry?"

"I expect so," she said faintly. "Yes, he would be."

Devon scowled. The answer didn't please him. "Then I'm doubly grateful to you, for risking his displeasure for my sake. I'd like to repay you. Come here. Come."

She came, reluctantly. He was holding out his hand. She wanted to go away, to be alone. Instead, with deep unwillingness, she put her hand in his.

He held it lightly, wondering at how work-rough it was, the nails chipped and short, and rubbed a soft forefinger in circles around the injured palm. "Whatever Howe's got you doing," he said gruffly, "I want it to stop." Before she could say anything to that, he asked, "What sort of reward would you like?"

She looked up, startled. "I want no reward. I think you should lie down now."

"But where's the incentive? We've already established that you won't lie with me." As disheveled and weary-looking as she was, she was still beautiful. Her eyes were still extraordinary. And she had the softest mouth.

"You're feverish."

"It's true, I am. Burning hot." He wrapped his hand around the back of her neck and drew her close, but she squirmed away immediately. He let out an involuntary grunt of pain.

Hiding her concern with a stern look, Lily took hold of his arm and tried to lead him toward the bed. "Meaning no disrespect, that serves you right," she scolded. But halfway there he snaked a hand around her waist and pulled her close again. "I see you're not quite as sick as I thought," she observed, a little shakily, standing still this time so she wouldn't hurt him.

"Not true. I'm in desperate pain and there's only one remedy."

"I wonder what it could be. Come to bed now, you'll only—"

"Not until I find the cure. Ah, I found it. It's here." He

touched her mouth with his fingertips. "Right here."

"Devon, Mr. Darkw—"

"Shh, I'm taking the cure." He dropped a light kiss on her lips, wondering a bit at his own playfulness. That was all he intended, just to tease her a little, and to touch her. But she sighed, and the soft, surprised sound of it beguiled him. He had almost forgotten how sweet she was. The kiss deepened in the most natural way, and the pure pleasure of it was enchanting—for the time it lasted, he really felt cured. But then it was over, and reason returned, and they stepped away from each other self-consciously.

"You're strong enough to find the bed yourself, I see," said Lily, out of breath. She backed away toward the door. "I'll bring your supper up in a little while. Go to sleep."

"Wait, Lily, you can't leave yet."

"I am leaving."

"Dammit! Oh, hell." Now that he wasn't kissing her, he felt terrible. He hobbled over to the bed and sat down gingerly, holding his bad arm against his chest. "Where the devil are you off to?"

"I still have a job, you know." He just stared at her, waiting, and she finally explained, although she hated it. "Mrs. Howe has set me a task. I have to finish it."

"I don't want you doing this 'task.'"

"If I don't finish, she'll only give me another."

"What is it she's got you doing, Lily?"

She looked away, then back. "Something—what difference does it make? Something I've got to do." Why couldn't she tell him? It made no sense to keep this secret. But to tell would be to admit that she needed help, because she was beaten.

"Is it a punishment?" Her face fascinated him; fleeting, complex emotions paraded across it too swiftly for him to read. When she wouldn't speak, he had his answer. And now he could even guess what she was being punished for. "Did you sleep at all last night?"

She moved one shoulder. "As much as you, I suppose."

"No, I doubt that. Have you eaten anything?"

She didn't answer.

His eyes narrowed grimly. "Go to bed."

She laughed, but she wasn't amused. "I've told you—"

"And I've told you that you work for me, not my housekeeper. Since I don't need you right now, I'm ordering you to go to bed. Immediately."

She thought of it, going to bed. Of lying down in her dark, quiet room and going to sleep. Right now. She closed her eyes and shuddered.

"Go."

"But—"

"*Go.*"

"But—she—" How to explain it? "If you could—" No, she wouldn't ask that. She hid her clenched hands behind her apron, tense with indecision.

Devon reached up for the bell rope and yanked on it. "I'm sending for her," he said shortly. "I'll explain to her what I want. And what I want is for you to wait on me exclusively for the next few days."

"Oh, but she'll think—"

"I don't give a damn what she thinks."

*But I do.* But obviously that carried no weight with him. He thought he was being generous.

"Go to bed, Lily," he said again, kindly this time. "I don't want to see you again before dark."

"All right," she conceded after a long pause, "I'll go. But I'll come back in an hour or so—" she kept talking over his impatient snort—"to bring you something to eat. Yes, I *will*. Now go to bed yourself. Sir." For the briefest moment they both smiled.

Then she was gone. And Devon cursed himself for not thinking of telling her to go to sleep in *his* bed.

# *The Master*

# Ten

"Why is it that sick people are called patients, I wonder, when it's their nurses who must have all the patience?"

"Ha ha," said Devon, not smiling.

"Are you going to drink this or not?"

"Not. It smells like boiled dung."

"It's a special kind of chamomile infusion; it's supposed to be calming."

"I'm sure it calms down dung beetles."

Lily clucked her tongue and set the cup on the bedside table with a clatter, sloshing tea over the side. "You're impossible. This is good for you—Cabby Dartaway showed me how to make it."

"That explains it. Cabby Dartaway's a witch."

"A witch! What nonsense. She's also the one who taught me how to make the poultice you said eased the pain so much in your shoulder."

"That thing that smelled like a dead ferret?"

"No," she demurred, pressing down a smile, "that

was the comfrey roots. You're thinking of the wilted burdock leaves. You said they smelled like pond scum in late July."

"Worse."

"Yes, well, it's your own fault. If you'd had a doctor in the first place, I wouldn't have to play witch's apprentice. I think it's time you stopped complaining and said a prayer of thanks because you're still alive."

"Is that what you think?"

She put her hands on her hips. "Yes, it is."

It was almost impossible to intimidate her anymore. In fact, he'd given up trying. He found it infinitely more interesting to try to provoke her and then see how she would react. But her patience seemed limitless; she really was the perfect nurse. She could be stern, but more often she used a disarming gentleness to manage him. And, he had to admit, there had been times in the last four days when he'd needed managing.

"I'll leave you, then, so you can have a nap."

"I'm not sleepy."

"You would be if you'd drunk your tea."

"But since I didn't, you may as well stay."

"But I have to go downstairs and speak to Mrs. Belt about your supper."

"Ring for a servant and send a message."

"I—I'd rather not trouble anyone; I'd rather go myself."

"I'd rather you stayed."

Lily shook her head, torn between exasperation and amusement, knowing that these tests of will to which he constantly subjected her were designed to nettle her in hopes of provoking some unsuitable response. This one was especially irksome, but she doubted that he would understand why. He could have no idea—and certainly no interest in—how her reputation had degenerated below-stairs, where among the servants it was commonly believed that she was sleeping with him.

"Very well," she said equably, not rising to his bait,

"I'll ring for Dorcas and speak to her in the hall." She reached for the bell pull on the wall above his opposite shoulder. At the moment she did so, he put his big hands on her waist and gave her a squeeze. She glanced down and saw the wolfish gleam in his eyes. Once such a liberty would have shocked her; but now that it or something like it happened daily—*hourly*, lately, as his strength returned—it only stirred her to the mildest annoyance. And sometimes not even that. "Thank you, I don't really require assistance," she murmured as she tugged on the rope the appropriate number of times to summon the kitchen maid.

"Sure?"

She sent him a quelling frown. But a part of her was beginning to suspect that there was really very little she wouldn't do to kindle and sustain that rare flicker of good humor in his cool blue-green eyes. She removed his hands from her waist matter-of-factly and folded her arms. "Shall I read to you? We've only a few hours left of Mr. Fielding's book, I should think, before we finish it."

"You read very well for an uneducated housemaid, Lily."

"Thank you. I do think Mr. Allworthy's sister Bridget is going to save the day, don't you?" she rushed on, anxious not to dwell on that particular subject. "If anyone can convince him that Tom is good and Blifil is a bounder, it's she, don't you think? How is your shoulder now? Is it still aching? If you won't take the tea, I suppose I could make you a Cromwell."

"A what?"

"A toddy."

This was a huge concession, thought Devon; usually she was as stingy with the brandy as an old maid aunt. "What's a Cromwell?"

"Haven't you ever had a Cromwell? It's brandy, cider, and a little bit of sugar. That's as opposed to a Cromwell with his head on."

"What's that?"

"The same thing, only double the brandy."

He chuckled. "And are you fond of Cromwells?"

"Oh, I've never had one. I've never had anything but wine. 'Twas my father who enjoyed his Cromwells."

"Ah."

"Do you not care for Mr. Jones just now, then?"

"No, I don't think so. And I don't think I'd care for a Cromwell, either."

"Cards?"

"Aha—*now* I understand. You're trying to get me drunk so you can beat me at piquet."

Lily smirked. "Intending no disrespect, Mr. Darkwell, I don't have to get you foxed to beat you at cards."

"Is that so? Get them out, then. At the risk of losing the last candle wick in the house, I accept your clumsy challenge."

She reached for the deck of cards on the table and pulled her chair closer; he slid over, leaving a foot of clear white sheet for their playing area. "Oh, don't feel you have to play on my account; I'd as soon do some mending. What was the score when we left off?" she asked innocently.

"As if you didn't remember perfectly. Fifty-nine to seven this time, I believe. Playing to a hundred."

"I believe you're right." She shuffled, offered him the deck to cut, and started to deal. "You wouldn't care to raise the stakes, I don't suppose," she mentioned while the cards flew.

"To what?"

"Mmm, oh . . . what about spools of thread? Something I could actually use."

"I haven't got any."

"No, but you could get them by ringing the bell."

"Lily, I'll play for money if you like."

"That's very generous of you, but I'd hate to clean a viscount out of his fortune while he's sick; 'twould be embarrassing for both of us."

He laughed out loud at that. It was the first time Lily

had heard him laugh. She forgot what she was doing and just stared at him, smiling back in delight. The sound was rusty and unused, tentative, almost experimental. She liked it immensely. She made a secret vow then and there that she would try to induce it as often as she could.

Still grinning, Devon lay back against his pillows and contemplated the expert way she arranged her cards with her long, thin fingers, discarding and retrieving from the stock. What an elegant body she had— graceful, long-limbed, lithe. Looking at it distracted him, and partly accounted for why he lost most of the games they played. But only partly. The main reason he lost was because she was the best card player he'd ever met. Her sense of when to be cautious and when to be bold was uncanny and unerring. And her face confounded him utterly. Try as he might, he could never discover what she was thinking about the cards she held, no matter what game they were playing. Usually she maintained a pleasant, faintly bemused expression that revealed exactly nothing, but sometimes she might lift an eyebrow in seeming approval, or frown as if dismayed. But when he would raise the stakes or make a judicious retreat on the basis of these elusive visual clues, he nearly always lost. Thinking to outwit her, he switched to making wagers based on the *reverse* of what she seemed to be signaling—but with no better success.

"Who taught you to play cards?" he inquired irritably after she'd scored for point and triplet without once varying the bland, artless look on her face.

It wasn't the first time he'd asked the question. Lily had always hedged before, not knowing how much she should tell him about herself. Her inclination was to tell him everything, but experience had taught her the bitter wisdom of caution. And yet it had been so long since she'd spoken naturally and truthfully to another person. "My father," she answered. What harm could there be in telling him that?

"Was he a gambler?"

"Sometimes."

"What was he when he wasn't a gambler?"

"Mm . . . other things."

"What?"

She frowned down at her cards, running her fingers indecisively along the edges. "An inventor," she said finally. "He invented things."

"What did he invent?"

"Nothing you'd have heard of."

"He wasn't a successful inventor?"

She couldn't help smiling at the understatement. "You might say that."

"Tell me what he invented." Just then she took the last trick and announced the new score—eighty-seven to seventeen—in a voice so determinedly neutral and devoid of gloating that it set his teeth on edge.

Shuffling the cards for the next hand, taking her time, Lily thought to herself, Why not tell him? What harm could it do? She let him cut, then dealt again, twelve cards each. "Well, there was the self-sharpening knife. Then—"

"The what?"

"The self-sharpening knife."

"How did it work?"

She resisted the easiest answer—"It didn't"—and attempted to explain. "It was based on a theory of his that was more, um, metaphysical than physical, you might say. He thought if you placed a knife in a particular way relative to certain stones, it would eventually sharpen itself."

"Certain what?"

"Stones. *Particular* stones. With abnormal powers." She looked up to see him smiling. "It wasn't a great success, as I say. The portable folding furniture did better, but most people found it too heavy to lift. Especially the bed. I have *repique*, by the way—thirty-one."

Laughing, Devon threw down his cards. "I give up."

"My father also invented a version of two-handed whist; would you like me to teach it to you?"

"No. You've cleaned me out of candle wicks."

"I'd be willing to take your marker," she offered magnanimously. "Move over a little; we need more room for this game."

He obliged with a grunt. The pain in his shoulder was bearable now, but he was still stiff. He settled back and watched her shuffle the cards in her brisk, rather masculine way. "What else did he invent?"

"He invented the 'heatable clothes press.' It was supposed to iron clothes in a matter of seconds, all at once."

"Did it work?"

"Occasionally. But more often the garment inside would go up in flames. Then there was the 'automatic door-opener,' for the busy householder with no maid. It was very complicated, I remember, lots of ropes and pulleys and hooks in the walls. If you were upstairs and someone rang the bell, you could open the front door by pulling on the ropes. That one almost hanged the cat."

She continued to tell him stories about her father's inventions, sometimes exaggerating their outlandishness to try to make him laugh again. Once she succeeded so well that he groaned in agony, holding his shoulder, and ordered her to stop.

Soon after that the maid knocked, and Lily got up to speak to her in the hall.

"Tell her I want something to eat, Lily! Real food this time, not that damn broth you keep pouring down my throat."

She sent him a look of pained forbearance. "Don't peek at my hand while I'm gone," she warned, and went out.

He shook his head, still smiling. In the last four days she'd done everything for him—tended his wound, bathed and shaved him, fed him his meals. He didn't know if it was luck, her diligence, or Cabby Dartaway's noxious potions, but the gash in his shoulder was healing perfectly, without stitches, and for the last two days he hadn't even had any fever. Now that he was almost well, he found it impossible to imagine what he'd have done without her.

He thought of the visit his housekeeper had paid him four days ago, after Polcraven and Von Rebhan had gone away and he'd sent Lily off to bed. Before he could tell the woman what he wanted, she'd announced with heavy self-importance that *she* would be nursing him from now on, having heard from "the Irish girl" that he was a bit under the weather. He'd eyed her with distaste, thanked her, and told her her solicitude was unnecessary. "Lily's going to wait on me for a while, until I say otherwise. Tell Trayer. Don't give her any other chores in the meantime."

"But, my lord—"

"Why does she have only one dress? Get her something to wear, Mrs. Howe."

"Yes, my lord, but—"

"And tell Stringer to send up a bottle of brandy. Immediately. The Nantes that my brother recently, ah, acquired. That's all. Was there something else?"

She'd clasped her sturdy, mannish hands and fixed him with a black stare. "My lord, your will is always my solemn duty to obey, but my loyalty won't allow me to keep silent. I feel I must speak."

Bloody hell. "Speak, then."

"This girl—I'm suspicious of her. She does her work middling well, but she's not what she seems."

"No? How's that?"

"To begin with, in my opinion she's no more Irish than I am. And she's devious—you can't trust her. I haven't caught her at it yet, but it's my belief she's stealing from the larder. I don't think the character she gave is genuine, either. I think you might like to write to this 'Marchioness of Frome,' if there really is such a person, and find out if she ever worked for her.''

Devon's first impulse had been to dismiss the suggestion with a nod and a curt word. But after a moment's thought, he'd answered instead, "Perhaps I will. Yes, I think I will." Her look of smug satisfaction had annoyed him. "That's all, Mrs. Howe. Don't forget to send Stringer with the brandy."

He hadn't gotten around to writing the marchioness yet, but he would. In many ways he was as interested in learning the truth about Lily Troublefield as his housekeeper was. He didn't believe she was devious and he doubted that she stole food from the larder, but he was certain she was hiding something. He'd quizzed her repeatedly in the last few days, directly and circumspectly, trying to discover what sort of life she'd led before she'd appeared in Chard and asked Howe, in a phony Irish brogue, for a job as housemaid. But she always evaded him with vagueness. Where did she come from? Oh, she had no real home, she'd traveled around quite a lot with her father. When did he die? Not too long ago. And her mother? Many years ago. How had she come by her education? Oh, a little here, a little there, from a pupil-teacher her father had once hired when she was little, or an occasional book. How had she learned her ladylike manners? She'd pretended to be terribly flattered by that. She was a naturally good mimic, she told him, and simply tried to emulate the style and manners of her high-society employers. So the dowager marchioness hadn't given her her first job? Oh no, there had been others before her. Who? Where? Different people, all over. They were dead now, or traveling, or they'd moved.

He didn't believe a word of it.

She came back into the room then. Her new gray dimity frock was plain, but at least it was clean and unpatched. But he wanted to see her in something finer, silk or velvet, softest satin. Or better still, he thought slyly, in nothing at all.

His expression mystified her. "Were you looking at my hand?"

"Yes, and it's clear you're going to beat me again, so I forfeit the game. Lily, I'm as stiff as a plank; come and rub my back."

She made another clucking sound and put on her sternest expression while she gathered up the cards, muttering under her breath that she couldn't abide a cheater. But these were merely diversions to disguise the flutter of nerves his request had set off. Lately he required a back or shoulder rub every few hours, it seemed, and the intimacy of the chore troubled her. No, that wasn't quite it—what troubled her was the degree of pleasure she took in performing it for him. The last few days had been like an idyll for Lily, a lovely respite from the drudgery of housework and the loneliness of impersonation. It was a shock to realize how starved she'd grown for simple conversation, with someone she could almost be herself with. Devon, although far above her and by no means an equal, was at least closer in education and accomplishment and social adroitness than Lowdy. Lily was like her father—gregarious, a naturally sociable person—and the weeks of silence and isolation at Darkstone had oppressed her spirit. Being with Devon these last few days had revived it. He could be chilly and remote; he was often moody and melancholy. But beyond the wall of reserve that circled him, she sometimes caught glimpses of kindness, even warmth. That he trusted her was a source of deep satisfaction. In odd, tentative ways, it seemed to her they had almost become friends.

But there was an edge to their friendship, a physical —well, say it, a sexual—consciousness that was never absent, never not there no matter how mundane the conversation or ordinary the situation. Sometimes he teased her, and then it was a relief because the tension was, more or less, out in the open. But usually it lurked under the surface, coloring everything, imbuing the simplest contact with an electric awareness that was as disquieting to Lily as it was thrilling.

"Turn over, then," she said brusquely as she perched on the edge of the bed, back straight, face prim. "What—what are you doing?"

"Unbuttoning my nightshirt. Skin's itchy; give me a nice scratch too, will you?"

Ridiculous, she knew, to feel this agitated—she'd seen him all but naked a dozen times by now. She helped him ease his shirt over his wide shoulders, wondering at the variety of emotions aroused by just the sight of his hard, dark-furred chest. He pushed the pillows aside and carefully turned over on his stomach, crossing his hands under his cheek. She put her palms on his shoulder blades, and his groan of exaggerated ecstasy made her smile. "Silly, I haven't even started yet." She began at the base of his neck and worked downward very slowly, using her thumbs along each vertebra with just the amount of pressure he liked. As always, his strength amazed her. She loved the supple feel of his skin over ridges of muscle as hard and smooth as polished metal. His powerful body tapered to narrow hips, and sometimes it was an excruciating temptation to pull the covers down and satisfy her intense curiosity about what his bare buttocks looked like. Of course she did no such thing. But sometimes she was afraid she might, and it was the same sensation she'd experienced standing at the summit of the headland—that she might suddenly, for no reason at all, lose control and jump off. Today she conquered the temptation, as she always did, but her hands lingered rather longer than necessary on the intriguing strip of naked flesh below his waist and above his bunched-up nightshirt.

"Don't forget the scratch," he murmured, eyes closed, his hard mouth relaxed for once in a dreamy half-smile.

She used her nails in a light graze all over his back and shoulders, and again his hum of pure pleasure made her smile. It was no wonder he was strong, she mused, watching his hard muscles ripple and flex under her fingers. She'd known from the beginning that he was no idle country squire, but in recent days she'd discovered that he was as involved in the running of his estate as any workman he employed, and this period of enforced inactivity vexed and frustrated him. She'd also learned, from meetings she'd overheard in this room or in her capacity as message-carrier between him and Mr. Cobb, Francis Morgan, and others, that his authority was absolute, and yet his employees respected him for traits like fairness and consistency and farsightedness, not simply because he was "the master." Lowdy had told her he was a troubled, unhappy man, at odds with the world. If that was true, she knew now that he did not allow whatever devils plagued him to intrude on his working life. He controlled them. But occasionally she wondered at what cost.

Her musings reminded her. "I'm sorry, I forgot to tell you—Mr. Morgan would like to speak to you on a matter about the mine this afternoon. He sent a note, and wondered if four o'clock would suit you."

"Fine," he grunted, pushing himself onto his back. "I wasn't going anywhere."

She plumped his pillows and stacked them behind him, and he sat up. She reached for the nightshirt at his waist, to help him put it on again, but abruptly he took both of her hands and brought them to his chest. It was a maneuver that forced her to lean over him until their faces were quite near. She'd learned by now that she was invariably the loser in anything approaching a physical struggle with him, and that a facade of imperturbability was her only defense. But he was opening her hands and pressing her palms to his chest, and the dark, tickly hair under her fingers was a disconcerting surprise. So was the strong, steady thudding of his heart.

Her voice was anything but steady when she said, "I'd better go, then, and tell the footman to take your message. To Mr. Morgan. That you'll see him at four—" She had to stop when he put two fingers on her lips.

"You're beautiful, Lily. You're lovelier today than you were yesterday. Or the day before." He was besotted, and yet he could swear it was true. Healthy color glowed in her cheeks, and her extraordinary eyes seemed brighter, greener.

She knew she was blushing. "I'm eating better," she blurted idiotically, "and—and sleeping more since I've been keeping your hours."

"Then we must make sure you continue to keep my hours." He cupped his hand behind her neck to draw her closer. She smelled like no other woman he'd ever known: she smelled like soapsuds.

His mouth was beautiful, and he was going to kiss her. She wanted it so badly it frightened her. "I don't think you need me anymore," she got out huskily. "I don't think you're very sick."

"Wrong," he contradicted, shaking his head slowly. "I've never needed you more." He surrounded one of her open hands with his and dragged it down the hard length of his chest, his flat belly. She only realized his intention when he murmured, "Let me show you."

She jerked her hand away and jumped up. Her heart was racing and she felt out of breath, and relieved and disappointed at the same time. It was hard to know what to say to him. *How dare you?* had an insincere ring; after all, this was only what their intimate game of advance-and-retreat had been leading to for four days. And it was hard to stay angry when he was grinning up at her with that cocky, utterly unapologetic gleam in his eye. Odd—what she wanted to do most was laugh at him.

But she made her face stern and began to fumble with

plates and glasses at his bedside. Turning away, she got halfway to the door with the tray, intending to leave without speaking at all, when he stopped her.

"Where do you think you're going?"

She made a quarter-turn toward him. "Downstairs."

"All right. You have my permission to leave." He didn't miss the tightening of her lips or the subtly acrid glare she shot him. "But come back in half an hour. I want you to help me get dressed. Then I think I'd like to walk outside. You'll accompany me."

She made herself face him, concern momentarily overcoming her pique. "Are you sure you're strong enough for a walk?"

"Oh yes," he said, folding his hands over his stomach and smiling suggestively. "I'm strong enough now for lots of things."

A lame double entendre, thought Lily. Nevertheless, it made her blush—which, of course, was exactly what he'd intended. "Very good, sir," she said through her teeth. That only made his leer of a smile widen. She whirled around, dishes rattling. Something that sounded surprisingly like a chuckle followed her out the door.

"Is it really necessary for you to hold *on* so?" Lily muttered, making her voice cross.

"Why, certainly. I'm recuperating from a serious wound; I'm still desperately weak. If I fell, I could do myself a grievous injury."

She slanted him a disbelieving glare. He'd tucked her hand under his arm so that to an observer—and she imagined there were many, for as they strolled along the headland path they could be seen from any window at the back of the manor house—it might appear that she was supporting him. Since he was perfectly capable of maintaining this sedate, unhurried pace without assistance, she knew it was just one more of his tricks, an excuse to touch her. She ought to be annoyed. Annoyance was the farthest thing from her mind.

But she couldn't help wondering what he was thinking of. Not very long ago he'd been careful—insultingly so—not to be seen with her by anyone, even his staff. Now their roles seemed to have been reversed, for she was the one who worried about the appearance of impropriety that the intimacy of their new relationship created. Because she was not a Cornishwoman, she'd never really been accepted by the other servants, and nowadays she was more isolated from them than ever. No one insulted her to her face, but only because it was assumed that, as his mistress, she was under the master's protection—at least for the time being. Trayer's insolence took subtler forms, while his mother treated her with a silent, dangerous contempt. The maids twittered and gossiped when they thought she couldn't hear; the male servants watched her covertly and exchanged knowing looks. Only Lowdy, broad-minded and unshockable, seemed indifferent to her fall from grace, although she badgered her all the time to know what was going on. When Lily would answer, "Nothing —he's ill and I'm minding him, that's all," Lowdy would lift her eyebrows in a comically worldly-wise manner and say, "Mm-*hmm*," with heavy skepticism.

"Have you ever seen the running of the pilchards, Lily?" Devon asked, breaking in on her thoughts.

"No. What's that?"

"It's a wild sight. They come from the deep water west of the Scillies and run along the coast in huge shoals. Once when I was a child, there was a school of them that stretched all the way from Mevagissey to Land's End. That's over a hundred miles if you figure the windings of the coast. My father took me to see it."

She glanced up at him again, intrigued. This was the first time he'd spoken of his family to her, or of anything personal.

"The whole town comes out to watch from the cliffs. The water looks as if it's alive with a great seething army of fish, being chased by hordes of hake and cod and seagulls and people. A kind of mania comes over everybody. Fishermen on the shore and in boats all along the coast stretch drift nets, and the pilchards struggle to escape, and you can't hear yourself think for all the shouting and laughing."

"When does it happen?"

"It starts in July. You'll see it."

July was two weeks away. Yes, she supposed she would see it. She hoped she would. The thought staggered her.

"Did you grow up here, then?" she asked shyly, thinking that a few days ago she would not have dared to ask him that question.

"Part of the time, when I would come to visit my father. The rest of the time I lived in Devonshire with my mother."

She waited for him to go on, but he didn't, and she lacked the nerve to ask him why his parents hadn't lived together. But she wondered. "Do you have other brothers besides Mr. Darkwell?" she ventured after a minute.

"No, but I've a sister. She lives in Dorset. I don't see her often." At the top of the cliff steps, he stopped walking and looked down at her. The afternoon sun was behind her, back-lighting strands of her heavy, dark-red hair like a halo around the delicate oval of her face. Her eyes were a guileless gray-green, grave and intelligent, and she watched him with complete absorption, as if everything he said fascinated her. She was lovely, and he'd had enough of talk.

The new look in his eyes stirred Lily, made her cast about anxiously for something else to say. "Do you— expect your brother back soon?"

"Soon, yes. Let's go down to the water, Lily."

"But—are you sure? You ought not to tire yourself on your first day out." He only smiled, and courteously preceded her down the steep stairs. After a second's hesitation, she followed.

A pile of jagged stones jutted out from the base of the rock cliff, across the tawny shingle to the shore. The tide was out; sun dazzled the choppy surf, dancing on wavelets, casting black shadows on the dark sides of the huge, hulking boulders that seemed to doze in the sucking sand. *I will miss this*, Lily thought unexpectedly, breathing in the wild salt wind. The idea shocked her, for she had not been happy here. But it was true—she would miss this remote splendor, the beauty and loneliness of the sea and the unkempt, inhospitable land.

He led her along the shore a little way and stopped among a silent circle of sea rocks, dry now, a safe distance back from the foamy line where the waves broke. They stood with their backs to a rugged, waist-high boulder and stared out at the Channel. As their silence lengthened, Lily threw a furtive glance at Devon's hard-edged profile, but as usual it told her nothing. He was a strange man in many ways, and her intuition had warned her long ago that he would be capable of hurting her. Yet she missed him when he wasn't with her, and was unexplainably happy in his company.

She glanced away, blushing, when he turned his head and caught her watching him. "How do you feel?" she asked, to cover her nervousness.

"I hurt, Lily. I'm in terrible pain." The stark alarm in her eyes made him smile quickly, to reassure her. "I need the cure again, and you're the only one who can give it to me."

In her relief, she couldn't help laughing at him. He touched his knuckles to her cheek, silencing the saucy reply she had ready. Heat gathered inside, so swiftly it scared her. He stepped closer, and she felt solid rock against the backs of her legs. "You—I thought you wanted to get some exercise, Mr. Darkwell."

"I intend to, Miss Troublefield."

He bent to kiss her, and just for a second she stiffened—because the name he'd never called her before unlocked so many unsettling memories. But the gentleness of his kiss melted her, scattering thoughts of anything but this moment and the heavy sweetness of his lips on hers. His tenderness disarmed her completely. One of her hands crept to the side of his face; the other opened on his chest, caressing him shyly. Holding her breath, she let him nibble at her lips. He moved his head slowly from side to side, and his open mouth stroked hers with each skimming pass. Her arms went around him in the most natural embrace, and the kiss deepened while everything seemed to slip away from her, all the boundaries and restraints she was used to. "Oh, don't," she sighed when his hands slid up so softly to touch her breasts. But she didn't stop him—couldn't stop him.

He murmured, "No?" and through her dress began to trace slow circles around the soft swell of her bosom with his fingers. She ought to stop this, it was wrong, it couldn't lead to anything but disaster. But she was drugged, and deprived of every sense except the one that was monitoring the achingly gradual progress of his fingers toward the sensitive tips of her breasts. "Let me love you, Lily," he whispered. "Say yes. I have to make love to you."

She tried to shake her head, but he was kissing her again and it wasn't possible. She was poised on the edge of something indescribable, and each second was separate from the past or the future, each moment new. She did not know what she would do. So she held perfectly still, eyes closed, and let the delicious fondling go on; she even forgot to kiss him back. He left her lips to murmur his urgent message in her ear, punctuating it with the soft, persuasive caress of his tongue. She was melting, weakening; she longed to give in to him. It was the helplessness of her desire that alerted her to the danger, and the fear of losing herself that gave her the strength to stop him.

"No, I can't," she whispered as she wrenched his hands away and twisted out of his reach.

In disbelief, Devon watched her walk away, hugging herself, staring out across the glittering water. He shut his eyes, just for a second, and said through gritted teeth, "Are you trying to drive me crazy? Because if you are, it's working."

She turned back. "I'm sorry—I made a mistake!"

"No, I did."

"No, *I* did. I shouldn't have let that happen." Her voice was quaking. "I apologize if I misled you into thinking there could be something between us. There can't."

"Why not?"

"It's just—it's impossible. I can't do what you want me to do." *What I want to do.*

"Why?"

She shook her head, helpless, at a loss. "Please, don't make this so hard. I can't—see you anymore, like this. You don't really need me now anyway. I have to go back to my old work. Please!" she cried when he swore and started to interrupt. "You're a gentleman, you won't take advantage of my situation, I know you won't. Let me go, Devon—sir—" She curled her hands into fists and drew a shuddery breath. A major part of her dilemma was contained in those stumbling last words, for in truth she didn't know what he was to her, or what she should be to him.

Her explanation hadn't settled anything, she saw; he was still glaring at her with smoldering eyes. She had an idea. It had worked with him once—it might again. "It—it's because of my young man. He would not like it if I—if we—" Blister it! How could she convince him she had a lover if she couldn't bring herself to say the simplest words? "If I was unfaithful," she said finally, feeling like a child. She took a step back when he came toward her, because the fire in his eyes frightened her. But his voice was low and controlled.

"Tell me about your young man, Lily. What's his name?"

For a terrifying second, she couldn't think of a single man's name, not one. "John," she got out belatedly.

"John. Where does he live?"

"In Lyme."

"Is he your lover?"

"No—yes."

"No, yes? Are you engaged?"

"No, we—"

"How long since you've seen him?"

"Two months."

"Do you write to him?"

"Yes!"

"How does he make a living?"

"He's—" She went blank again. "I don't have to tell you—Why are you asking me this?"

"Because I don't believe in him," he all but snarled as he took her by the shoulders with his big hands. "I think you made him up. What I don't understand is why."

"He's a stonemason! He builds cathedrals and houses and—buildings. He's an apprentice—I mean a journeyman, he became a journeyman a few—"

Out of patience, he gave her a shake. "Why are you lying?" But then, all at once, he understood, and wondered how he could have been so stupid. He'd thought such naïveté had been safely consigned to his past. Gentling his hold, he smiled thinly. "I'm sorry, I should have made it clear from the beginning. I'm not asking you to give me something for nothing; I assure you I'd make it worth your trouble."

Mistaking his meaning, she blushed and gave a little half-hysterical laugh. "That—that's—I don't have any doubt of it!"

"Well, then?"

She turned her face away and didn't answer.

"What is it you want? Name an amount. How much, Lily? Or is it a place of your own you want? Just tell me."

Her eyes widened and she stared at him, dumbfounded. "Money? Are you asking me to take money?"

Either she didn't want money or she was an extraordinarily gifted actress. "No? What, then?"

She was too appalled to be angry. That would come later. "What do I want?" She couldn't put a name to the things she wanted because they were all secrets— freedom, vindication, respectability. Friendship, affection. And, yes, money. "Nothing! Nothing you could possibly give me. Let go of me, Mr. Darkwell, you've made a mistake."

"I don't think so."

"Let me go!"

"What game is this? I don't need coyness, Lily. I'll pay you well, if that's what it—"

"Damn you—I'm not playing any game."

"Like hell you're not. You're no shy virgin. What is it you want from me?"

"How do you know what I am? You don't know anything about me!"

"I know because I listen to your lies. You tell me this 'stonemason' is your lover. Is it true or not?"

"Yes, it's true!"

"Then I won't be your first."

He jerked her to him and she started to struggle. "Touch me and I'll be your last!" That only made him laugh. "Don't kiss me!" She craned her neck sideways to avoid his mouth. "Don't!" she cried when he pulled her closer and buried his face in the hair behind her ear. "Damn you, I don't want this!"

Devon shut his eyes tight. For a long moment he just held her, feeling the rapid hammering of her heart and the tremors that shuddered through her. He'd never touched a woman this way before, in anger, demanding what she didn't want to give. He felt disgust for himself even as he acknowledged that he was not going to let her go. He told himself that no one understood the kind of woman she was better than he. She was toying with him, raising the stakes as high as she dared before granting him what Clay would call the "last favor." But there was one way in which she was *not* like Maura, and it would be her downfall: she really was hot-blooded. Lily's desire for him had never been an act.

That was what he intended to use against her. In cold blood, he would seduce her. The callousness of the plan troubled him not at all. Besides, he'd make it good, so good she wouldn't even be sorry afterward. Then he would be free of her.

He kept his arms around her, but relaxed his urgent grip. "I'm sorry for what I said," he murmured against her hair. "Forgive me, Lily, I misjudged you. I would never hurt you."

"Let me go, Devon, you must."

"Say you forgive me. I was angry, and those words— they were not well said. If I hurt you, I'm sorry." She stayed rigid, fists tight against his chest. "But I wanted you so much. I still do. I can't stop thinking about you, Lily, you've taken over my mind."

Her heart was racing. She ought to hate this painless but unbreakable embrace, but she didn't. "Don't say these things to me. Nothing's changed. It's impossible."

"Why is it?" One hand began to stroke the slim length of her back, slowly, shoulder to waist and back again. "I would never hurt you," he told her again, and this time he almost meant it. "You liked it before, when we kissed. Let me kiss you again, just once. Let me, Lily." He brushed his lips along the dainty line of her jaw, breathing softly, seducing her with gentleness. "Your skin is so sweet." He knew the moment she started to tremble. Nuzzling her resolutely closed mouth, he coaxed a tiny opening and slipped his tongue between her lips, caressing the velvety undersides. She sighed, shuddered, and turned her face away.

But he could be endlessly patient. "Do you know you taste like flowers?" he whispered as he ran his tongue lightly across her fluttering lashes. "Kiss me, Lily. I'm dying for you."

She tried to call back her defiance, but it was skulking away like soldiers in retreat, outnumbered by a vastly better-armed enemy. She wasn't pushing him away anymore, she was clutching at his shirt with both hands, holding him. "This isn't fair," she pointed out, ready to weep. She kept her face averted, but every sense was concentrated on what he was doing with his tongue—and now his hands, softly skimming her sides with restless, pent-up need.

"I know. I can't help it," he said as he walked her slowly backwards to the rock they'd leaned against earlier. It was almost true, he thought; he could probably stop now, but in another minute it wouldn't be possible. He touched her soft cheek. With gentle, insistent pressure, he turned her head until she had to look at him. The beginnings of surrender had darkened her eyes, from gray-green to jade. That was just as well, he had time to think, because he was through asking. His mouth came down, hot and hard, and captured hers in a fierce kiss devoid of art or gentleness. She swayed and he caught her, held her fast, pulling her arms around his neck and making her embrace him.

"Your wound," she got out, the words muffled. "I don't want to hurt you!"

He raised his head long enough to laugh out loud. Immediately he returned to her lips, savaging them with his tongue and his teeth. In seconds, his groping fingers untied the ribbons of her dimity dress and pulled her bodice apart. She whimpered when she felt the warm air on her skin, and then his warmer hands as he eased

her breasts out of the constricting folds of her chemise.
He stopped kissing her to look at them. "Oh, Lily, how
beautiful," he murmured, tugging her hands away when
she tried to cover herself. "Let me kiss you. Here, yes."
He made her turn until her back was against the rock
again, and then he leaned over her until she half lay on
it, bent backwards at the waist.

"Devon, oh *God*—!"

"Shh, love, it's all right, it's all right." He crooned
comfort into the warmth of her throat and the hollow
between her breasts while his fingers stroked slow rings
around her nipples. She sucked in her breath; he felt her
clench and unclench a handful of his shirt at the
shoulder. "Lovely," he murmured, touching his tongue
to the tip of one tight peak, and she groaned, high and
loud, as if he were torturing her.

She ground her teeth and raked her hands through
the cool sleekness of his hair, meaning to pull his head
away; but somewhere between the intent and the act her
will deserted her, defected to the enemy, and instead
her traitorous fingers held him close, coaxing, urging
him shamelessly. He chanted passion-words she could
barely hear, some coarse and some honey-sweet, while
his lips tugged and sucked one breast and his rough
palm slid urgently over the other. The roaring in her
ears was too loud to be the sea, it must be the sound of
her own desire, frantic, pleading for release. He took
her mouth again, and she felt herself giving up the last of
her control. She was floating up to a high, new, frightening place, a whirling wall-less funnel where there was
nothing but sensation. In self-defense, she put her hands
on either side of his face, filled with a sudden compulsion to see him and understand what manner of man he
was. Words were useless, irrelevant. She searched his
eyes, hot with wanting, and traced the harsh lines at the
corners of his mouth, as if they could reveal to her
something true and vital.

But the last thing Devon wanted was to be understood. Holding her intent gaze, he used his knee to part her legs. He felt the panicked clenching of her thighs, watched her eyes widen with dread and excitement, and muffled the start of her ragged, uncertain protest with a ruthless kiss. Groping now, blind with need, he dragged up her skirts to bare a long, sleek thigh. Soft, oh God, she was soft. Her little gasps, quick and desperate and uncontrollable, made him burn for her. A sound, an impossible, unthinkable sound, tried to penetrate the wall of pure feeling that surrounded him like armor, like a second skin, but he would not let it in. Lily's soft, wet mouth tasted like sugar water. He buried his fingers in the springy web of hair at the top of her thighs and shut out the sound by making her moan.

But the sound came again, and this time Lily stiffened and tore her mouth away. Her frightened eyes searched his, begging him to tell her she hadn't heard what she knew she had—the sound of feet on the stone steps above them. The next thing she heard was Devon gritting out the foulest swear words she had ever heard.

In one swift, jarring motion, he pulled her upright and stepped back. "Don't," he warned hoarsely when she made an instinctive move to turn around, bare-breasted.

"My lord?"

She recognized Trayer Howe's voice, and a mad thought crossed her mind that the burning outrage in Devon's eyes might set Trayer on fire where he stood.

But Devon's eyes were nothing compared to the raw, barely controlled fury in his voice. *"What do you want?"*

"You, uh, you have visitors, my lord. Your mother and Lady Alice Fairfax. They're waiting for you in the house."

It seemed to Lily the sound of the sea increased then to a violent roar. She saw Devon's face darken and tense, the jaw muscles flex and relax in a dangerous, uneven rhythm. "I'll come," he said, but she wondered how Trayer could hear him over the deafening thunder of the tide. His eyes traveled upward slowly, and she knew Trayer was hurrying away; but she could hear nothing now except the sound of water.

When Devon reached for her, she stepped nimbly away, turning her head so he couldn't see her face. He let her go, let her walk down to the tide line, and gave her enough time to fasten her dress. Then he went to her.

"Lily." He put his hand on her shoulder. She flinched as if he'd stuck her with a pin, and he dropped his arm. To see her, he would have to walk into the surf in his shoes. That was what she was counting on, he knew.

He did it. She was so surprised, she backed up; that gave him a piece of dry land to stand on. He said her name again.

"Don't make me talk. Please, I can't talk to you."

"You know we haven't finished. Come to me tonight. Meet me here."

"Please go away. Please."

He'd never heard this note in her voice, this desperate sound of defeat. "Nothing's changed," he insisted. "Meet me later, after—"

"I will not meet you. Ever. Devon, for God's sake—!"

She was close to tears. He could make it a test, force her, keep at her until she agreed to what he wanted. He was good at that. She was blinking her eyes and swallowing repeatedly, but she wouldn't look away. And suddenly he couldn't stand the thought of making her cry. But he had to tell her, "It's not over, Lily. We're not through."

"You're mistaken."

He watched her for another minute. A gull screamed overhead; far out to sea, the sun cast horizontal bars of light and shadow on the glittery waves. Then, because it was the kindest thing, he left her alone.

Finally she could cry.

# Eleven

"We can only stay two nights—we're due in Penzance early on Friday for the Lynches' house party. After that we're with the Trelawneys at Mount's Bay for the whole month of July. I don't know why you're looking so surprised, Devon; I wrote you all of this in my last letter."

"I remember perfectly, Mother, and I'm not in the least surprised." He kissed Lady Elizabeth's cool pink cheek, smiling fondly into skeptical eyes the same blue-green as his, then turned to his other guest. "Alice, how good to see you. And how brave of you to agree to such a long sojourn in the country with my mother. But I always knew you had courage."

"Hah," was his mother's answer to that.

"Hello, Devon," Lady Alice Fairfax greeted him, shaking hands warmly. "How are you? It's been a long time."

"Yes, it has. Thank you for your last letter. I had not

gotten around to answering it yet because things have been rather hectic this summer—"

"Never mind, I never write to you expecting a reply. I do it to keep in touch."

"I'll do better in the future, I promise."

The ladies resumed their seats in the drawing room, then described a hot but uneventful journey from White Oaks, Lady Elizabeth's estate near Witheridge in Devonshire. They said no, they wouldn't take tea, because they'd just stopped for it in Lostwithiel not more than an hour ago and didn't want to spoil their dinner. "Although that's a useless precaution if Mrs. Belt is still your cook," Elizabeth noted acerbically. "She spoils it quite adequately by herself."

"She's not quite that bad, Mother."

"You say that because you don't care what you eat. I suppose that Howe woman is still your housekeeper?"

"I believe so. The last time I noticed."

"Odious woman. You ought to fire her."

"Why? She takes care of everything and leaves me alone. She's perfect."

Lady Elizabeth clucked her tongue and glanced around, patting down stray tendrils of brown and silver hair. "How gloomy this room is, Devon. Why don't you paint these apartments? The whole house is looking shabby these days, if you ask me. If you let it go, it'll only cost more when you finally get round to fixing things."

"How is Clay?" Alice interjected, flashing Devon a sympathetic smile. "Stringer said he's not at home."

"No, he's gone up to London, I believe," he answered smoothly. "Said it was too dull here. He'll be sorry to have missed you."

"We hear the oddest rumors about him, you know. It's hard to know what to believe."

"Believe them all," he returned with a laugh. Seeing his mother's face, he went on quickly, "He's all right, though, in perfect health and all that. I shouldn't be surprised if he decided to settle down one of these days. That should please you, Mother."

"It will please me when I see it. I don't know which of my sons is a bigger disappointment to me." Devon crossed his arms and sent her an amused smile, and after a few seconds she gave in and returned it. "You haven't asked about Catherine," she observed brusquely.

"Yes, I was going—"

"She's having another child."

"Good God. That's—"

"Seven, now. Yes, I know. I've never known such a woman for having babies. She didn't get it from me, and I hardly think she got it from your father. It must be some throwback to another generation. She says to tell you she's not writing another letter until you answer at least one of hers. Really, Dev, she's your only sister, you might at least try to stay in touch."

Before he could answer, a parlormaid appeared in the doorway. She bobbed a nervous curtsey, unused to such important guests, and announced her errand. "I'm sended t' tell your ladyships your rooms are ready, and t' take you up if you d' care t' rest afore your supper."

Lady Alice rose. She was a slight, small-boned young woman with pretty light-brown hair and hazel eyes. "I believe I'll go up. You two have a nice chat. I'll join you at dinner."

Elizabeth nodded approvingly; Devon stood up and walked Alice to the door.

The maid had one more message. "I'm t' say as well that Midge's been walked and watered and's having a nap in your room, m'lady," she said to Elizabeth.

"Good Lord, Mother, you didn't really bring that snub-nosed wheezing machine, did you?"

"Certainly; I go nowhere without my little dog. Thank you—what is your—?" But the maid had already disappeared, following Alice. "What's that girl's name? She's new, isn't she?"

"Is she? I haven't the slightest idea."

"Honestly, Devon, you ought to pay more attention to the running of your own house. Your servants could be robbing you blind and you'd never know it. Alice is looking well, isn't she?" she went on without a transition. "Some women bloom later in life, you know. I believe Alice is one of them."

"I'd say she has a few good years left. What is she, all of twenty-four?"

"Oh, if that. She's a handsome girl, isn't she?"

"Yes, Mother."

"She has such a lovely, calm temperament. Why, I feel as comfortable with her as I do with my own daughter. She'll come into quite a large fortune when the baron passes away, of course. There'll be men swarming all around then, I expect. Not that there aren't now, but she's such a modest, unassuming—"

"Mother."

"Yes, dear?"

"Alice is a bright, attractive, good-hearted woman, we're agreed on that, and someone ought to marry her. It's not, however, going to be me."

Lady Elizabeth raised innocent eyebrows. "Goodness, I never suggested that you should!"

"Oh, come now."

"Very well," she conceded easily, "I admit it's crossed my mind that the two of you do suit rather well. The Fairfaxes are old friends; you and Alice have known each other all your lives, there would be no surprises. It's not as if you aren't *fond* of each other. And Alice needs someone to take care of. It might not be an *exciting* match, but it would be a strong one, based on liking and trust and respect. And," she added deliberately, "I should think you've had enough excitement in that other sort of way to last a lifetime." As she'd half expected, Devon's face closed up at that. But she went on, leaning toward him, eyes intent. "My dear child, don't you *want* to be happy?"

"I don't think of it," he answered shortly. "You say you love Alice as a daughter, but obviously you haven't thought of her happiness. If she's so dear to you, how could you wish someone like me on her?"

"What nonsense. You could be a good husband to any woman if you'd—"

"You're wrong. And this is a pointless conversation." He turned his back on her and stood gazing out the open window across the shadow-dappled terrace. The sea was a quiet, insistent murmur far below. On the horizon he could see a trio of herring boats from Looe, bobbing on the water like peas on a glittering silver plate. To the east, a thin disk of a moon was creeping into the blue sky.

He turned back. "I'm sorry, Mother. Let's not quarrel." He crossed to the sofa and took a seat beside her. The late-afternoon sun strayed across her delicately lined face, illuminating more silver hairs than he remembered from the last time he'd seen her. "Tell me about yourself. How have you been?" He didn't really expect an honest answer; well or ill, Elizabeth's routine response to that question was invariably, *"Very* well, thank you," followed immediately by a diversionary question about the health of the inquirer. She was uncomfortable talking about herself, and believed that describing one's physical or emotional state to others, unless it was perfect, was vulgar.

So Devon was surprised when she said, after only a moment's hesitation, "I've been sad. I've tried to shake it off, but I can't." He reached for her hand, and she eked out a stiff little smile for his benefit. "It'll be four years in August, you know."

"Yes."

"I miss him very much."

"So do I."

"It's odd, isn't it? Our marriage was stormy, to say the least; sometimes I was only happy when we were apart—he here, I at White Oaks. But I would give so much to have him back now. I think I would even consent to live here, just to be with him. It's what he always wanted."

"I never thought I would hear you say that. You hate it here."

"Yes, it's ironic. But you're mistaken—I don't hate it; I just couldn't live here. Devonshire has always held me, in the same way Cornwall held him." She squeezed his hand. "You're like him in that way. We quarreled over naming you, you know."

Devon nodded; he knew this family story well.

"I said I'd live here the year round if he'd let me call my firstborn son Devon."

"But you didn't keep your promise."

"No." She sighed and looked away. "He was a difficult man, your father. You're so like him, much more than Clay. He was moody, like you, and intense. He loved and hated with equal passion, and he was as reckless as he was cautious. He could feel great sadness, but also tremendous joy. Like you, he loved Darkstone."

"Because of the sea."

"He said it saved him from going mad. I would laugh at that—thinking he was exaggerating, trying to get my attention." She bent her head. "I wasn't as good a wife as I should have been, Dev. I loved him very much, but I couldn't live with him. Or so I thought. Now . . ."

She looked up. To Devon's relief, her voice lost its melancholy heaviness and grew strong again. "Regrets are foolish, of course. If Edward were to walk in that door right now, we would be happy together for a few hours. After that, the hard words would start again." She put her head against the back of the high sofa. "Still, you know, one of the biggest regrets of my life is that I wasn't with him when he died. I should have been here, with you."

"But you didn't know he was dying."

"It doesn't matter. I should have been here. He was my husband."

They fell silent. Each knew the other too well to offer false comfort. Tragedies happened; facile explanations for somber reality no longer consoled them. Both had lost their heart's desire, and they had become experts in the elaborate art of compensation.

"Well," Elizabeth said at last, turning brisk. "I think I will go up and change now. We've both brought our maids, did you know? Quite an impressive entourage we make. I assume your Mrs. Howe will make arrangements for them—something else you needn't think about. Are you still keeping country hours, with dinner at five?"

"Five is late for us." Devon smiled, helping her up. She was not as spry on her feet as she'd once been, he noticed. "We'll be famished by then. But by God, we'll be fashionable." Elizabeth chuckled. "I'll walk up with you, Mother," he said, and took her gently by the arm.

"You don't really expect us to *dine* at that table, do you? With all the under-servants?"

Lily paused, clutching a handful of silverware, and looked up. It was Miss Turner, Lady Alice's personal maid, poised in the doorway in a crisp gown of puce silk. Miss Kinney—Lady Elizabeth's maid—loomed up behind her in the next second, and together they regarded Lily with identical expressions of tolerant amusement. "We're really in the country now, Mary," Miss Turner said to her companion. "This girl was actually going to seat us at the servants' table." They chortled together.

Lily straightened slowly. They were about her age, perhaps a year or two older. Before she'd come to Darkstone, she hadn't known about this powerful, zealously guarded line of demarcation between upper and lower domestics in a great household. The highest female rank was lady's maid, higher even than housekeeper, and a woman who attained that exalted post never let anyone under her forget it. Lily despised the whole business. She hated the petty nastiness of a system where a girl promoted from scullery to kitchen maid could finally be greeted by the parlormaid with "good morning." But at least she had learned that it wasn't only the rich who could be arrogant and condescending about rank; that was a *human* trait, unrelated to fortune. The truth was, rigid class distinctions brought out the worst in everybody.

She laid down the last fork and put on her politest smile. "Where do you think you might like to 'dine?'" she asked, giving the word the same artificial emphasis the regal Miss Turner had.

The maid's eyes narrowed in suspicion. "In Mrs. Howe's room, of course. But not on that gruel the cook calls fish stew, I trust."

"Oh, surely not," agreed Lily. "If you're 'dining' with our estimable housekeeper, I'm confident you'll enjoy better. For *country* fare, of course."

Miss Turner sniffed. She felt insulted, but she wasn't sure why. "Impudent girl. Where do you come from?"

"From Cornwall, of course. The land of pilchards and barbarians. Excuse me, I'll just go and lay two more places in Mrs. Howe's room." She sidled past the two ladies' maids, and felt their astonished eyes follow her out of sight.

When she returned they were still there, seated languidly at the same table they'd recently spurned— evidently finding it more gratifying to be important before an audience than only with each other. The butler's society was deemed worthy of their notice, so while pretending not to see the other servants who had come into the room, they told the taciturn Stringer all about the prodigious amounts of luggage their mistresses were traveling with. Miss Turner described the distress of Joshua, Lady Alice's Negro footman, when he learned he would not be accompanying his mistress on the trip. Joshua was the pride of the Fairfax domestic household with his sumptuous emerald green livery, silk stockings, and powdered hair, and Miss Turner vowed he smelled sweeter than her ladyship sometimes. "What a peacock he is, truly, and so devoted to my lady. She takes him everywhere, of course, and positively dotes on him. 'Twas Lady Elizabeth who said he mustn't come, for she would bring her little dog along, and she said there wasn't room for *two* mascots. When Joshua heard, he wept like a baby, and the tears made little black trails down his powdered cheeks."

Miss Turner surveyed her spellbound listeners with satisfaction. Tales of the high life were rare at Darkstone; the servants were drinking in her words like sponges. Encouraged, she went on to tell of a ball that Lady Alice's family had given in the spring, providing lavish details about the lengthy preparations, the gown her ladyship wore, the hair style Miss Turner herself had helped create, the food served and wines drunk, the orchestra that had played. Lily busied herself with finishing the table, barely listening. It was the sudden coy note in Miss Turner's voice that caught her attention, even before she understood the words.

"I've heard a rumor that there'll be another celebration at Fairfax House soon . . . or perhaps at Darkstone Manor. Maybe you've heard it too, Mr. Stringer." She had everyone's attention now. "It's said," she murmured, leaning close in a pretense of confidentiality, "that there's going to be a wedding between my mistress and your master before the year's out."

Lily stood quite still, palms pressed against the coarse homespun tablecloth until the odd numbness passed. It could only have lasted a few seconds, for in the next moment she became aware of a murmur of excitement greeting Miss Turner's news. A moment later she felt the speculative, surreptitious stares of some of the servants, gauging her reaction. She set the last plate down, straightened a crooked spoon, giving what she hoped was a credible imitation of indifference. Inside, she felt as if she had been punched. *Foolish, foolish girl*, she chided herself. The day had been full of harsh lessons, but this one was the hardest; it put all the others in perspective.

Lowdy appeared in the doorway, behind a kitchen maid carrying a tray. The smell of fish stew brought Lily to the brink of nausea. Suddenly it didn't matter what any of them thought of her, or what they might say behind her back. She went to Lowdy and spoke low and fast.

"Tell Mrs. Howe I'm sick, Lowdy. Tell her I can't eat anything. Say I'll come back down in an hour to help clean up." She went out without waiting for Lowdy's answer.

The headland path, treacherous on dark nights, was almost as bright as day tonight. Silver moonlight spilled over the sea in a glittering triangle whose tip pierced the horizon and whose sides widened toward shore until the light broke on the rocks below in a radiant spray. Lady Alice Fairfax's voice was cool and pleasant over the grumble of the waves, her conversation easy and undemanding. Still, Devon had to struggle to keep his mind on it. They had paused to stand directly above the spot where, a few hours ago, he'd come so close to seducing Lily Troublefield.

He made an effort to shut his mind to the bright, erotic memories, but they kept flooding through him, leaving him edgy and his concentration in fragments. Hardest of all was trying not to imagine a very different ending to their short-lived tête-à-tête. She'd been on the verge, the very edge of giving in, and it had only been his valet's execrable timing that had stopped her. In the midst of his frustration, the thought gave him a rush of pleasure.

"Devon? Are you listening to me at all?"

"Alice, forgive me, I—was thinking about the mine, some problems we've been having," he muttered arbitrarily. He took her hand and got them walking again.

They hadn't gone far when she stopped again and asked earnestly, "How are you, Dev? Are you getting along? Have you been happy at all?"

He flashed a sardonic smile. Twice he'd been asked that question today. "I don't think in those terms anymore, Allie."

"You haven't called me that in ten years," she said softly, touching his arm. "I miss you, Devon. I wish you would come to White Oaks more often, the way you used to. It would make your mother so happy. And—of course, my family would love to see you at Fairfax House."

"You sound like Clay, always trying to get me out of Cornwall."

"It's because we miss you."

"You miss me because you don't see much of me. If you did, my company would wear thin very quickly."

"That isn't true."

He glanced down at her, and was relieved when he could see nothing more than affection and concern in her pretty hazel eyes. But Alice was an old friend; he would not risk hurting her because he was too preoccupied to make things clear between them. "My mother has us all but married in her mind, you know," he said lightly.

"Yes, I'm aware of it."

"You've always been a good friend, Alice. I hope you always will be."

A minute passed; then she slipped her arm through his. He searched her cool profile for a hint of her mood. She was smiling, but there was a slightly fixed look about it. "Dear Dev," she said, patting his hand. "I hope you'll always be my friend, too."

"You can count on that."

They walked on a ways without speaking. "Tell me all about Clay," Alice urged suddenly. "The stories I hear are positively shocking. Is it true he's the captain of a pirate ship called *The Ravager*, and that he's rescuing French émigrés and ferrying them to the Netherlands?"

Devon threw back his head and laughed. "Now, that's one I hadn't heard." They walked on, their faces close together, holding hands.

Lily watched them out of sight from her bench on the moon-bright terrace. The sound of Devon's laughter rang in her ears for long minutes after they disappeared. How fortunate that Alice Fairfax had arrived in such a timely way, she mused, for the other woman had helped her to see her squalid encounter with the master this afternoon in the proper light. It seemed unrelievedly sordid now, and she flinched when she thought of the contempt he must feel for her. But it was a good lesson, and long overdue. She held it close, like a bouquet of thorns to her breast.

Although it was the stifling heat that had driven her out of her attic room, Lily shivered. A bitter-cold resolve congealed inside her. Very soon, penniless or not, she had to find a way to leave Darkstone.

# Twelve

"'Ere, Lily, take this."

"What is it?"

"What's it look like, an? Master's sheets?" Enid Gross let out a raucous cackle as she pushed a basket of clean linen into Lily's arms; her friend Ruth joined in appreciatively, arms thrust to the elbows in a great tub of soapy water. "Master's clean nightrail?" More laughter, both girls doubled up with it, while Lily stood frozen, waiting. "Naw, tes Cobb's," Enid explained when she could speak, "and you're t' take 'em with ee to 'is house and clean it, 'Owe d' say."

"I'm to clean Mr. Cobb's cottage? Now?"

"Ais."

"But she told me to help Dorcas with the churning when I finish here, and then to scrub down the back stairs!"

"Then ee d' best 'urry," Enid smirked. "She've stuck on this chore t' your list, it d' seem."

Lily whirled away before they could see her face,

ashamed to show them how close she was to tears.
Shutting her ears to their spiteful snickering, she
trudged up the washhouse steps and stood still in the
hard-packed yard. The afternoon sun was blinding.
Shielding her eyes, she took deep, steadying breaths,
and in a little while she had her emotions in check. But
fatigue was with her all the time these days, like a
lingering illness her body couldn't shake off. She went
about her chores in a daze, silent, obedient, and numb.

She took hold of the basket in both arms and set off
listlessly down the dusty path. The air was feathery with
the billowing seedpods of dandelions at the sides of the
path. Two red deer strolled across the drive not twenty
yards away, into the bright bracken that waved in the
breeze, but Lily didn't see them, nor did she hear the
restless cawing of rooks in the hazelnut trees overhead.
The habit of thinking about Devon Darkwell was always
with her too, because she couldn't summon the energy
needed to cast his memory from her mind.

Their ladyships had gone off on their holiday, and
after a day or two life at Darkstone had resumed its
quiet, orderly pace, the brief flurry of excitement fading
quickly. Lily's life had resumed its hard, tedious routine
as well, for the idyll was over, the servants' perception of
her as being under the master's "protection" a thing of
the past, and Mrs. Howe had lost no time in reinstating
her to under-housemaid status. It seemed now that
there was no job too arduous, no task too demeaning for
Lily, and she knew it was not her imagination. Mrs.
Howe was having her revenge.

Still, things could have been worse. Lily derived a
morsel of comfort from the thought that, if nothing else,
at least Mrs. Howe and the others were confused,
unable to decide exactly where she stood with Mr.
Darkwell—for twice in the last four days he'd sent a
servant to bid her to wait on him, and twice she had
ignored the summons.

She had done it with a feeling of impunity, confident that the Viscount Sandown would never stoop so low as to fetch her himself from her tiny attic room, or seek her out in the midst of some servile piece of drudgery. Her assumption had proven correct, for he had not come. But mixed with her relief was a sense of foreboding: one flouted the master's wishes at one's own peril, and Lily had a strong and instinctual fear of Devon's anger.

But something else frightened her more, and that was the abdication of her own will when she was with him. At their last meeting she had learned the harrowing lesson that he was stronger than she, and that his desire for her was much more potent than her ability to refuse him. As many times as she'd gone over the events of that unforgettable afternoon in her mind, it still seemed incredible, *impossible*, that she had been ready to give herself—there on the beach, in broad daylight!—to a man who cared nothing for her. She wasn't that kind of woman! Or so she had always thought. But then, she'd never been tested. Devon Darkwell was the only man who had ever touched her—she discounted the fumbling attentions of the landlord's son in the Portsmouth boardinghouse she'd lived in with her father two years ago. But in her heart she knew she was not a wanton woman; she was decent and principled, and the awful, indisputable fact was that it was only he, Devon, who could make her throw all her scruples away by smiling at her. Or murmuring sweet, intoxicating words in her ear. Or touching her.

She had to stay away from him. To save herself, she had to keep out of his way. It wouldn't be for long, just until she made a little money and thought of a place to go. In two weeks her debts would be paid and she would begin to earn her wage. Then, soon, she would be able to leave.

She'd gone forty feet past Mr. Cobb's cottage before she realized it. She turned back tiredly and moved

toward the flagstone walk curving to the small,
thatched-roof dwelling in the park, set back from the
gravel drive. With her arms full of the laundry basket,
she managed to unlatch the door with one hand and
kick it open the rest of the way. A peculiar odor assailed
her, sweet and sour at the same time, and there was
something familiar about it. But the cottage looked
empty; she could see no one in the shuttered dimness.
She found the table and put down her basket. The odor
was stronger now. She went to the window; the sash was
up but the shutters were closed. She unlatched them
and threw them open.

"Leave that!"

She jumped—almost screamed; spinning around,
she saw a man huddled on the floor by the hearth in the
rear wall, knees drawn up, back pressed against the cold
brick. Seconds later she recognized the land steward.
"Mr. Cobb, you gave me a fright! I thought you weren't
here, I—I've come to clean your house." She trailed off
in confusion and peered at him. He hadn't moved. His
arms were wrapped around his knees. His black hair
and beard looked wild, and behind them she couldn't
read his expression. She took a step closer. "Are you ill?
Do you need help?"

Even in the dimness, she thought his fierce black eyes
glittered. "Tes you that needs help," he told her in a
guttural rasp, completely unlike his usual voice. She
suppressed a start when he unwound from his peculiar
crouch and got to his feet. "Tes you did ought t' take
care, little miss. A Darkwell bain't a man for a young girl
to rely on."

Again she almost cried out when he lurched toward
her, but he stopped in the middle of the room, swaying.
All at once it dawned on her that he was drunk. In all the
weeks she'd been at Darkstone, she had never seen Mr.
Cobb behave with anything but dour and irreproachable
propriety. She understood now why the sour-sweet

smell was familiar: it reminded her of her father's room in the morning after one of his infrequent alcoholic binges.

Lily held out her hand. "Here, let me help you."

White teeth flashed against the blackness of his beard. "Do ee want to help? Want to take my hand?" He stuck out his left arm, the one that ended in a mutilated stump. With an ugly laugh, he shuffled toward her.

Lily blanched. Her eyes never left his face, but in her peripheral vision she saw clearly the scarred white butt that poked out of his coat sleeve. He stumbled closer, and now she could read a dare in his reckless eyes. Revulsion lay under a multitude of other emotions, but she held her ground and didn't drop her outstretched hand.

When his arm was only inches away, he jerked it back and shoved it into his coat pocket. His black brows lowered in fury. "Get out of here. Get out!" Immediately Lily turned and ran. He followed her to the door. Leaning on it, he hollered after her, "Get away, you'll regret it if you don't! Get away from here!" He kept shouting until she couldn't hear anymore. Flying along the path, lungs aching, she imagined him standing in his doorway and yelling, yelling, with no one to hear but the jackdaws and the circling gulls.

That night, long after the other servants had said their prayers and gone to bed, Lily remained in the kitchen, standing on a chair to scour the blackened bricks of the fireplace chimney with a hog-bristle brush. It was a punishment for using sand instead of ground oyster shells this morning to polish the pewter. Mrs. Howe said she'd scratched it, but Lily could see no damage. But that was nothing new, and she was growing used to being singled out for scoldings and punishments and the dreariest jobs, for no better reason than that the housekeeper detested her.

"You, get down from there."

She fumbled and almost dropped the brush. For all her bulk, Mrs. Howe had a way of sneaking up on people as silently as a reptile. Lily scrambled down from the chair and faced her, wondering, dear Lord, what now?

She was holding something in her hand. "Look what I found."

That tone—silky, satisfied—should have warned her. She went forward hesitatingly, trying to see. When she was four feet away, Mrs. Howe opened her strong, masculine hand. In it was a pile of silver coins. Lily looked up blankly. "What is it?"

Howe's laugh was only a harsh exhale. "So you're going to lie, too."

"Lie about what?"

She dropped the coins in her pocket and folded her arms across her shelf of a chest. "I wasn't gone out o' my room more than five minutes. You're light on your feet, I'll give you that."

"What are you talking about?"

"But you should've put 'em somewhere besides your own drawer. That's the first place I looked."

Lily gasped as understanding dawned. "You think I stole your money!"

"Housekeeping money. Come with me, now."

"I didn't! I swear I didn't—you *couldn't* have found it in my drawer." She moved back in haste when Mrs. Howe took a step toward her. "Listen to me, I tell you I didn't—no!" The hand that clamped down on her upper arm was as implacable as a metal vise. "Let me go!" The housekeeper gave her a savage jerk, and she suppressed a cry of pain. Worse than the pain was the indignity of being hustled out of the kitchen, down the corridor, and up the stairs to the first floor. With deepening dread, it dawned on her that Mrs. Howe was taking her to see Devon. Humiliation washed over her like scalding water. But when they arrived at the door to the library, his usual haunt between supper and bedtime, she saw that the room was dark and empty—and went weak with relief. She tried to squirm away, but Howe's bruising grip on her arm only hardened. She seemed to be considering her next move. Seconds later she set off down the hall again, alternately pushing and dragging Lily along beside her.

Lily hung back again at the bottom of the wide walnut staircase. "I did not steal your damned money—" she got out through clenched teeth before Howe struck her in the face with the flat of her hand.

"Wicked girl. Foul, blaspheming slut." She took her by the shoulders and shook her until Lily felt as if her neck would snap. Then she grabbed her arm again and marched her up the stairs.

Devon's bedchamber door stood open. This is a dream, thought Lily, a nightmare. Swiping at tears of fury and embarrassment, she watched Mrs. Howe's manner change from viciousness to stolid concern in the time it took her to rap out a polite knock on the doorpost.

Devon glanced up from the book he was reading by the light of a branch of candles. Peering into the gloom, he made out the broad black outline of his housekeeper. "Yes, what is it?" Then he saw who was with her. He put his book down and slowly closed it.

His first thought was that Lily was ill, because she looked pale and exhausted and Howe seemed to be supporting her. He hadn't seen her in five days. If she'd been ill, he had time to think, that explained why she hadn't come when he'd sent for her. Before he could rise, Howe spoke.

"My lord, I beg your pardon for disturbing you this time o' the night, but I didn't like to wait—I thought you'd want to know right away." She yanked on Lily's arm to pull her into the center of the room, closer to the light. "I caught this girl in a theft. Fourteen pounds o' the housekeeping money was in her drawer in the hall, wrapped in a handkerchief. I found her all but in the act of it."

"I didn't—"

"Quiet, until you're told to speak to the master," Mrs. Howe ordered, giving her a rough shake.

"But I—"

"Let her go," Devon said softly.

When Howe released her, Lily held her aching arm and took a step closer, trying to see him better. He was coatless, shirt sleeves rolled up; a bottle of rum, a carafe of water, and an empty glass stood at his elbow. "I didn't steal anything," she said directly, eyes intent. "I swear it. It's a mistake."

He leaned back, wrists draped over the leather chair arms. He said, "This is a serious charge, Mrs. Howe," but his cool blue eyes never left Lily's. "Be good enough to begin again. You say you caught her in a theft?"

"Very nearly, sir. I left her in the kitchen, cleaning the hearth, and went to my room. I was settling some o' the accounts, so the box I keep the housekeeping money in was out and open. Enid Gross came in to tell me Rose was down with the toothache and would I come and bring the clove oil so she could rest. Naturally I went straight up, not liking to see one o' my girls in pain if there's something I can do to help."

Lily turned to her and stared.

"I went to the kitchen to fetch the clove oil, and that's when Enid told this one what was up. That's how she knew I'd be gone. Enid came up with me, so no one was about below-stairs except Lily. I wasn't away more than five minutes, and when I got back the box was empty, except for a few shillings at the bottom.

"I went straight to the servants' hall and started looking in the drawers—each has got a drawer o' their own, you see, for sewing or pen and paper and what-not, personal items. Inside Lily's drawer was the money, the exact amount, wrapped in a handkerchief." She reached in her pocket for the coins and held them out, flat in her palm.

Devon didn't speak. He stared at Lily with unnerving intensity, stroking his lips with a thoughtful forefinger. When she couldn't bear the silence any longer, she straightened her shoulders and said quietly, "I didn't steal this money. I can't explain how it got in my drawer, but I did not put it there."

"She's lying. She wants to leave here, can't wait to get away. She's still in debt for clothes and coach fare, so she stole the money. If I hadn't caught her tonight, she'd've been gone tomorrow."

A different light came into his eyes. For the space of a heartbeat, Lily thought she saw anger. "So you want to leave here, do you, Lily?" he asked softly, gently.

She didn't know why, but something warned her the gentleness was deceptive, that under it lay a trap ready to spring. There was a long pause while she tried to decide whether to lie or not. In the end, she couldn't. "Yes. I do."

His face didn't change. "Leave us," he said to Howe, not looking away. "I'll take care of it now."

"Very good, my lord." A twitch of satisfaction pulled at one corner of the housekeeper's traplike mouth. She bowed obsequiously and walked out of the room. Soon they heard her thudding footfalls on the stairs.

Devon neither spoke nor moved. Lily stared hard at his closed, formal countenance, from which all traces of anger were gone now, but she could make nothing of it. Fearful again of the tense, expanding silence, she blurted out, "Do you believe her? Do you think I stole the money?"

"I have no idea. If you wanted to leave Darkstone, I suppose you'd need it."

She closed her eyes for a second, wondering why she wanted to cry.

"And you did say you wanted to leave, didn't you, Lily?" He pressed his fingers together under his chin and spoke with chilling matter-of-factness. "Perhaps I can help you."

Her mouth went dry. A dark place inside knew what he would say next.

"I know of a way you can make quite a lot of money. Very quickly. Very simply."

Everything went still, but she kept hearing the dreadful echo of his words as if he were saying them in her ear, again and again and again. When she couldn't stand it anymore, she whirled around and darted toward the door.

"Stop!" He brought his fist down on the desk top in time with the shouted order. Lily jumped, stopped, but didn't turn. Devon stood up. "Close the door," he told her, more quietly but with the same ferocity. She didn't move. "Do it." He saw her hand go out to the doorpost, as if she needed it for support, and he came toward her slowly. When he was five feet away, he saw that her shoulders were shaking. "Lily?"

Her throat had closed; she didn't think she could speak. But she had to tell him. "I did not—" Dry sobs racked her before she could finish. Her chest was burning, she couldn't catch her breath. She felt his hands on her shoulders, and then her tears came. "Steal—your—money," she got out in a series of hiccuping gasps, and hid her face in her hands.

"No, I know. Shh. It's all right." He put his arms around her and held tight, pressing her back against him, absorbing her convulsive shudders. "Shh, Lily, it's all right now." He tried to turn her around, but she resisted; she didn't want him to see her face. He bent his head to put his cheek next to hers. "Don't cry anymore." She said something, but her voice was so thick he couldn't make out the words. He put his lips on her throat, tasting her tears. "Look at me, Lily." Very gently, he turned her in his arms. Her face was ravaged and tragic; she still wouldn't look at him. But she spoke again, and although her voice sounded strangled, he understood her this time.

"Do you believe me?"

"Yes, of course. Of course I believe you." And at that moment he did—but in truth, it didn't matter to him one way or the other. He brushed his fingers across her slippery cheeks. "Don't cry anymore, love. How can I kiss you if you keep crying?" She couldn't smile back, but she let him dry her face with his handkerchief, and then she let him touch his lips to the corners of her mouth.

"I didn't, I didn't."

"I know. Hush, now." He kissed her with all the tenderness in him, a long, slow, soothing kiss that he broke abruptly when he felt the passion in him rising too fast.

She wiped at her cheeks with the backs of her hands. "Why would she say it?" she asked brokenly. And then, "Do you really believe me?"

"Yes, of course. You would never steal, you *could* never." To his amazement, she put her arms around his neck, sighing, "Oh, Dev," and offered him her mouth. He didn't hesitate. He kissed her hungrily, holding her still with his hand at the back of her head while he coaxed her lips apart and tasted her tear-salty mouth with his tongue. She made a soft, ambiguous sound deep in her throat and took half a step back. He followed. Eyes closed, he found the door with one hand and closed it. He felt her stiffen and try to say his name, but he was kissing her too deeply, the word was muffled. "This is an abomination," he muttered, dragging off her maid's cap. Fingers tangled in her hair, he pulled her head back and covered her mouth again, drinking in the wet, intoxicating taste of her. She began to shake uncontrollably. He pulled back to look at her. Her lips were wet and bruised-looking, her eyes cloudy, the lashes spiky from crying. Very slowly, very deliberately, he began to unfasten the front of her gown.

"Oh," said Lily—all she was capable of saying—for until now it had almost been possible to pretend that they were only kissing, that he was only comforting her. What he was doing now bared the flimsiness of the pretext. She brought her hands to his wrists and tugged —but so feebly it made him smile. And in that moment, that instant when his rapt, intent face softened and his eyes glowed with warmth, the fleeting wisp of a thought crossed her mind that she loved him. He had her dress open now, pushed back over her shoulders, and he was whispering sweet, extravagant praise against her lips. "Devon?" He bent to press moist kisses on her throat while he stroked her breasts. "Devon, I think we should talk."

He didn't bother to raise his head, but she heard the low rumble of his chuckle, warm on her skin. For a giddy moment she almost joined him. But then he covered one breast with his hot, open mouth, and she forgot what was amusing. Later, with great care, he drew her arms out of the sleeves of her gown, her shift. And when he hooked his fingers inside all the bunched-up cloth at her waist and yanked down, all she could do was hold on to his shoulders and try not to shake.

Immediately he took her in his arms and held her, just held her. His body was warm and real; when a little of her trepidation subsided, she wrapped her arms around him and pressed close, loving the hard feel of his chest, his solid thighs against hers. All at once he lifted her in his arms. She held on to his neck and buried her face there; all her turmoil returned and the realization struck that if she was ever going to make a choice, not just give in to the loveliest seduction she could imagine, the time was now.

She hadn't noticed that they were moving, so the bed

was a soft surprise when he laid her in the center and sank down beside her. She bent her knees, bringing her legs up. He ignored that, but when she crossed her wrists over her chest he said, "Ah, Lily, don't do that," and dragged her hands away. Unaccountably, she obeyed. He smiled. Her eyes went wide when he licked his thumbs, touched them to her nipples, and made soft, raspy circles around the hard little tips. Her head fell back against the pillow; she tried not to make a sound, but her breath was coming in quick pants and it wasn't possible. His mouth replaced one thumb, and his free hand drifted down to her stomach. She couldn't help it—the soft kneading of his palm there made her moan. Then he slipped his hand between her clenched thighs.

"Devon—wait—I think we should wait—" She saw his head move from side to side in the negative, in time to the remorseless flicking of his tongue across her nipple, while his fingers pressed her legs apart with gentle but unrelenting pressure. She grabbed at the collar of his shirt, whether to push him away or hold him she no longer knew. The oddest thought crossed her mind.

"But I still have my shoes on."

He looked up. While she watched, the scorching intensity of his stare faded and his mouth, wet from kissing her, twitched with amusement. He laughed. Astonished, she found herself smiling back. The sound of his laughter was so free and hearty that she felt as though some gentle balm was being poured over an old wound and she was healing. And she knew that they were going to make love, that there had never been a choice, or she had made it long ago.

"Why is that funny?" she asked. That only set him off again, and this time she laughed with him. They kissed with frantic abandon, while he ripped all the buttons off his shirt and stripped off his breeches. He took her

shoes off next, and then her thin, patched stockings. He
stared a moment, bemused, at one of her dingy garters,
monogrammed in black thread with her initials, L.T.
"You need some new clothes," he told her. Then he
stretched out beside her and took her in his arms.

Lily didn't know what was more exciting, her nakedness or his. "I've never done this before," she confided
in a whisper, touching a shy hand to his chest. She knew
he thought otherwise.

He didn't believe her, but it didn't matter; she could
have told him anything at that moment and he would
not have cared. He smoothed back strands of dark red
hair from her face and kissed her until she was breathing hard, and then he slipped his knee between hers.
Her eyes flew open and she tensed. "It's all right," he
murmured, "I won't hurt you."

A sliver of leftover reality flickered in a far corner of
her mind, like an old moon on the wane. "And afterward?"

His seeking fingers found her most sensitive place.
She gasped. "Afterward?" He caressed her intimately,
deeply, while his soft, tugging lips suckled at her
breasts, then he said hoarsely, "There's no afterward.
There's just now." He slid both hands under her buttocks and sank into her all at once.

She was tight. Hot. Indescribably soft. And so sleek
and wet he could have finished then, not waiting for her.
Instead he held still inside her, feeling the deep blend-
ing of their pulses. She'd turned her face away, into the
pillow. He put his lips to her ear and whispered, and
delicate shudders shook her, lodging him higher. Her
eyes were shut tight. "All right?" he breathed. She made
a soft sound, and he began to move in her.

Lily lay quietly, alive to every sensation. The pleasure
had faded at the moment he'd come into her, but faint
tendrils were returning ever so slowly, curling in her
loins and belly like a flower blossoming. She turned her

head on the pillow to find him watching her. Self-conscious, she touched his face, stroked her thumbs along the deep lines at the sides of his mouth. His thick, straight hair tickled her cheek; she raked her fingers through it, pulling him nearer. Their mouths joined in a rapacious kiss, and the curling sensation tightened and gathered deep inside. She found his rhythm, and then it seemed to Lily that the mystery was solved. Her body strained, muscles taut, laboring, but inside she felt weightless and airy. And she was rising, floating, flying, her pleasure acute and growing, all but unbearable, an excruciating promise that must be fulfilled now, now—

"Are you with me, love?" Devon asked in a ragged mutter, face buried in her hair.

"Yes, yes," she answered, although she didn't quite know what he meant.

He slid his hand between them, to caress her just above their intimate joining. Lily's head went back and her mouth opened on a long, soft cry. Mistaking her, he plunged deep and hard again and again, holding her in a fierce, possessive grip. His climax was silent and wrenching, a wild unraveling. He lost himself, forgot who he was, staggered by the intensity of the pleasure, and in the aftermath he felt weak and new. Free.

Frightened.

He withdrew abruptly and rolled away. But he took her hand and held it to his lips, not looking at her.

Lily threw her free arm across her forehead and stared up at the candlelight flickering on the ceiling. After a minute her breathing slowed and her pounding heart returned to normal. But her nerves still tingled, her body still felt stripped—*skinned*—vulnerable. What was this throbbing expectancy? Something had eluded her; that was all she knew. Still, she treasured the closeness, the unspeakable intimacy they'd shared. Had it meant as much to him? She stole a glance at his profile and saw that his eyes were closed. Impossible—

he couldn't be sleeping! All her senses were alert and
alive and she was desperate to talk to him, reestablish
the contact she could tell they were losing. He still held
her hand, but she was afraid he was falling asleep—
leaving her alone. "Dev?" she whispered. Saying his
name excited her. "That was good, wasn't it?"

A moment passed in silence. She was about to repeat
the question, unable to let it lie, when he answered,
without a smile and without looking at her, "Yes." And
that was all.

She felt a treacherous prickling of tears behind her
eyes. She lay still for many minutes, listening to his quiet
breathing. If he wasn't asleep, it was clear he didn't
want to talk. Her presence in his bed began to seem
more and more unnatural. She waited a little longer,
praying he would speak, or move, or do something.

"Well," she said at last. She sat up, her back to him. "I
have to go now."

Devon opened one eye and laughed, low in his throat,
while his hand shot out and grabbed hold of her wrist.
He gave a tug and she fell back to the mattress with a
little cry. Facing her, securing her in the crook of his
arm, he ran a lazy hand across her breasts, back and
forth, establishing a soft, abrasive friction. Lily shifted
restlessly. As he had before, he wet his fingers, then one
of her nipples with them, and afterward he blew on the
hard little peak. The icy, shivery sensation took her
breath away and made her stiffen. Pleased, he made a
circle around her navel with his forefinger, then dug
gently into the delicate whorl, tickling her, making her
back arch.

She turned her head to look at him. Their lips were
almost touching, but he didn't kiss her. He watched her
eyelids widen and then flutter closed when his slow
hand dipped lower. He used his leg to pull hers apart
and keep them open. He cupped her with his hand, and
curled a long forefinger inside her. She arched up again

and cried out, something loud and unintelligible. He sleeked his finger in and out, softly, ever so slowly, watching the play of emotions on her damp, flushed face. All at once she set her teeth and stopped breathing at the top of a deep inhale. He took his hand away.

The disbelief, the look of cheated indignation on her face almost made him laugh again. "Ah, Lily, you are so beautiful," he breathed against her lips, "and I want to be inside you when I make you come."

Her voice was thready, a little hoarse. "When you what?"

Spreading himself over her, he parted her legs wider and made her put them around his waist. "When I pleasure you," he explained, his voice not altogether steady either. He drove into her gently, embracing her, feeling the wild thud of her heart against his. Tenderness, new and unused and awkward, rippled through him. He drank in the achingly sweet taste of her mouth, and the wisp of a thought crossed his mind that he never kissed when he made love to women. Lily sighed against his lips, and her breath was warm and moist on his skin, gentle as a blessing. "Dev," she whispered, so amazed. The straining weight of his body on hers felt perfect. She pulled him closer. They kissed with fierce, greedy passion until the last second. Then they just held on to each other, stunned and humbled, while time stopped and they suffered together the tumultuous recoil of an identical explosion. Lily thought she was lost, that it would never end, and the minuscule piece of herself that was still intact knew a second of panic—no more. But the storm subsided, and time started again, and Devon kissed the tears on her cheeks with such tenderness that her heart cracked open and she loved him.

She started to tell him, but the words that came out were "Thank you." His face was beautiful. How she loved him! They turned on their sides together and held each other.

They might have slept. It astounded her that they could make love again, but they did, and again after that. Every time it happened her wonder grew. This was, quite simply, too good to be true. Mere humans could not experience pleasure this profound, this *often*. This was a kind of happiness she'd thought heaven promised, not lowly earth.

Alongside the awe, the need to tell him everything increased as the long night slipped past. Each time she began, he kissed her into silence, for Devon did not want to talk, or to think. He only wanted to hold her, because she was a woman and it had been a long time for him. She was skin and flesh, warmth and heat and wetness, and he did not want to think about how it felt on the inside—only on the outside. Because she was just a woman. Close to dawn, Lily fell deeply asleep in his arms, and dreamed of him.

She awoke to the sound of rain blowing in gusts against the half-closed windows. The room was pearl-gray and chilly, and she was naked except for a tangle of wrinkled sheet around her ankles. She shivered and sat up. The same sleepy, sweeping glance that told her Devon wasn't beside her soon spied him across the room, standing by the south, sea-facing window. Fully dressed in brown breeches, coat and waistcoat, white cravat. Watching her.

She smiled. "Dev," she murmured, wondering how long he had been standing there.

"It's almost daylight."

"Yes," she agreed, puzzled because his voice sounded odd. She wanted him to come to her and touch her.

"It's time, Lily."

"Time?"

"For you to go back to your room."

"Oh." She stared at him, not thinking of anything. But suddenly she felt ashamed because she was naked. She wrestled the twisted sheet up and covered herself while a deep flush rose to her face. "You want me to—" She stopped and swallowed. "You're sending me away?"

He raised his straight black brows and smiled slightly. "What did you expect?"

"Nothing. Nothing." In the flash of an instant she knew the worst, understood it all. She scrambled off the bed, dragging the sheet with her. She spotted her clothes in a puddle by the door, and spoke quickly. "If you will leave me for just a minute, I'll get dressed."

"Shy, Lily? What difference does it make now?"

"Very little. But I would be grateful to you all the same."

He shrugged casually and walked out.

As soon as the door closed, she collapsed on the edge of the bed. She felt strangled with tears; they were in her throat, her chest, everywhere but her eyes, which were quite dry. Stupid. Oh, stupid! The magnitude of her folly was awesome and unendurable. Oh God! But she mustn't think about it now—if she did, she was afraid she would drown. Later, when she was alone, there would be plenty of time to think. She staggered up and dragged her clothes on with jerky, graceless movements, fingers bloodless and clumsy. She put her cap on last, shoving all her hair under it, trying not to remember what he'd said when he'd taken it off. For a split second she caught a glimpse of herself in the wardrobe mirror, chalk-white and pitiful in her dry-eyed grief. She whirled away, but the remembered image finally brought a flush of anger. She opened the door with her shoulders squared, her head held high.

He was leaning against the opposite wall, hands in his pockets. He looked bored. And she knew he was not even going to bother to pretend, with sweet words or kisses or lying promises. The ashes in her heart fanned to life. In that moment, she hated him.

"We didn't speak of an amount beforehand," he

mentioned, reaching into his jacket pocket. "Will this be enough?"

He couldn't have said that; she didn't believe her ears—or her eyes when she saw the wad of folded bills between his fingers. Her body felt thin and brittle, ready to break. "Devon! You—" Then it hit her. "You think I stole your fourteen pounds." It was the only explanation she could think of. "But then—*how could you touch me?*"

"That part was easy." His smile didn't reach his cold turquoise eyes.

Lily recoiled. Two spots of color streaked her pale cheeks like slap marks. *"Bastard,"* came out in a dry hiss.

"Take the money, love. It's all you'll get from me."

"No, not all," she whispered, backing away. "There's shame as well. You've given me that." She spun away from the sight of his outstretched hand and ran.

# Thirteen

"Some hot." Lowdy planted her fists on her hips and blew upward at the hank of hair stuck to her sweating forehead. "Whyn't the ol' cow make us club rugs in springtime, 'stead o' nigh August? Meanness," she supplied, before Lily could answer. "Meanness pure an' clean. You d' know it, and so does all the world. She'm meaner'n a razor, I'd as lief nuzzle a snake as turn my back on 'er."

Lily made a sound of agreement, listening with half an ear. The heat was intense; they'd lost their hour of morning shade when the sun had climbed beyond the manor house's western chimneys, and now it beat down on them in dry waves, unrelieved by the lightest breeze. She sat back on her heels and wiped the perspiration from her face with the back of one hand, while a wave of dizziness made her cheeks pale. Her knees hurt and her arms ached from brushing dry tea leaves into a floral-patterned wool carpet spread out on the grass above the area steps. Nearby, Lowdy was resting from the task of beating a wire paddle against another rug strung up on a line.

"An' ee can think what you will, Miss Mullygrub Sad-Face, but there bain't hardly a person in the whole house who thinks ee stole 'er splatty ol' housekeeping money. Ask 'em if ee don't b'lieve me."

"No, I won't ask them," Lily said tiredly. "And you're wrong, Lowdy. They don't know me—they have no reason to think I wouldn't take the money."

"Ask 'em, is what I say. Stringer don't think ee did it, an' cook said—"

"It's best to leave it. It doesn't matter anyway."

Lowdy shook her head and said, "Phaw," in disgust.

The smell of hot wool and tea leaves was overpowering, taking Lily to the brink of nausea. She sat back dully and watched a drop of sweat splatter on the hand that lay limp in her lap. Lowdy chattered on, about Mrs. Howe, about Dorcas's elevation from scullery to kitchen maid, about Galen MacLeaf and the Methodist revival he'd invited her to attend. Lowdy's words were punctuated by violent, irregular blows of her paddle against the hanging rug. Lily closed her eyes—then snapped them open a second later to stare at Lowdy, breath suspended, limbs frozen with dread and hope and astonishment.

"I said, 'Maybe I can and maybe I can't, Mr. MacLeaf; I'll 'ave t' go an' look at my calendar, like, t' see if it's my 'alf-day.' " Lowdy chortled merrily and gave the carpet a dusty wallop. " 'Look at my calendar t' see if it's my 'alf-day,' " she repeated, giggling in gales, relishing the joke. A thought occurred to her. "Maybe you d' care t' join us, an? Ee could use an airing, Lily, no mistake. Tes next Sunday in Truro at the Coinage Hall."

Lily's voice sounded like a croak. "Who did you say the preacher was, Lowdy?"

"Reverend Soames, from Exeter. Twur on a bill in Trewyth, Galen d' say. 'Ave ee ever been to a Methody revival? No? Gawm, there'm naught like it. Onct—"

"Are you sure it was *Soames?*"

"Ais, Roger Soames. My chum Sara from orph'nage, her as lives in Launceton now, she seen 'im in Redruth last year and said it fair give 'er the shakes to 'ear 'im. Myself, I'm that fond o' preachin', for it puts me in the queerest mind. It's like God and the divil are flailin' over my soul, and I can't decide which of 'em to let have it. Well, Lily, do ee want to come wi' us, an?"

"What? No, Lowdy, I can't."

"Phaw." The younger girl grumbled for a minute, then threw her paddle on the ground. "By Jakes, I'm parched. I'm goin' for water, and I don't care what 'Owe said. I'll fetch you a cup." And off she sauntered, round hips swaying.

*He's alive!* Lily exulted, her mind awhirl. *I didn't kill him!* A great burden lifted; for the first time in weeks, she felt at peace with herself, at least on one score. Reverend Soames was alive—and *well*, if he was preaching next Sunday in Truro. But what did he think of her? Had he told the authorities that she'd assaulted him and stolen his money? Dear God, could she come out of hiding if he had not?

She had to find out. Not by meeting him in Truro, of course; that would be too dangerous. But now surely she could take the risk of writing to him. She would send a letter to his home in Exeter and ask him to write back in care of Mrs. Troublefield, her old neighbor in Lyme. To that kind lady she would send another letter, asking her to forward any mail for Lily to Darkstone— but on no account to reveal her whereabouts to anyone. She had wanted to keep Mrs. Troublefield out of her dangerous personal problems, but now it seemed she had no choice. And anyway, the possibility of arrest no longer terrified her as it once had. Darkstone Manor, she mused grimly, had become almost as much a prison to her as the Bodmin Gaol.

"Where's Lowdy?"

Lily was jolted up on her knees, startled by Mrs.

Howe's stealthy, unnaturally silent approach. "Lowdy? She's—she had to use the privy." The housekeeper had told them that they mustn't stop work, even for a drink, until dinnertime. *Oh dear God*—Lily's heart leapt painfully and she dragged her eyes back to Mrs. Howe's red, angry countenance, praying her own face hadn't given away what she'd seen over the woman's shoulder—Lowdy traipsing toward them, head down, a dripping dipper of water in one hand and a filched apple in the other.

Hopeless. Howe spun around, almost as if Lily had pointed behind her and shouted "There she is!" Lowdy stopped dead in her tracks. A nearly comical look of chagrin lumbered across her wide, friendly face. Then Lily's view of her was cut off by Howe's bulky back, moving with uncanny swiftness. She heard Howe's voice raised in interrogation, Lowdy's low in impudent answer—and then the crack of Howe's hand across the girl's flushed cheek. Lily stumbled to her feet and ran toward them, her own voice stuttering "Stop!" in a frightened, breathless gasp. Howe struck again, and this time Lowdy screamed. The tin cup clattered; the apple rolled sideways. Lily reached them just as Howe brought her hand back again. "No, don't!" Lily shrieked, and Howe whirled around, fist raised.

"I'm all right!" shouted Lowdy, holding her cheeks, blood streaming from her nose. "I'm all right, I'm all right, Lily didn't do nothing!"

Howe turned from one to the other, breathing hard, black eyes venomous. Lily thought the white streaks blazing back from her temples made her look mad— rabid. "You, Lowdy, go up to your room! For your disobedience you'll have no dinner nor supper, and tomorrow you'll spend the day watering the kitchen gardens—with that cup. Out o' my sight, now, unless it's a beating you want, too. Go on, I said!"

Lily stiffened in fearful anticipation, seeing rebellion in Lowdy's bloody, tear-streaked face. But a second later

Lowdy mumbled, "Yes, ma'am," eyes downcast to hide the welling of new tears, and scuttled toward the house at a graceless, uneven trot.

"Well? Go back to your work or you'll get the same and worse. What're you staring at?"

Lily didn't try to hide her disgust. Behind Howe's flat black eyes she could see nothing except malevolence, but for once Lily's anger was stronger than her fear. "Lowdy didn't deserve that, Mrs. Howe, and you know it," she accused, ignoring the quake in her voice. "You hit her because you wanted to—because you like frightening people if they're weaker than you. You're a bully and a tyrant—and a hypocrite." She planted her feet, braced for whatever would come, but with no regret for what she'd said. Watching Howe's huge right hand clench into a fist, she thought of one more thing to say. "I don't believe Mr. Darkwell knows how you treat the servants, and I—I intend to tell him what you did to Lowdy!"

To her amazement, the housekeeper's grim slit of a mouth loosened in a repulsive smile. "So," she said in a soft hiss. "You'd tell the master on me, would you? Good. Very good." She slid back a silent step. "Excellent," she sighed, and the sibilant syllables raised the hair on the back of Lily's neck. "Do that. Do it soon. Be sure to let me know what he says. And remember, Lily: 'God is not mocked; for whatsoever thou soweth, that shall you also reap.'" Her smile grew, revealing two white eyeteeth as sharp as fangs. A dreadful moment passed. Then she turned and walked away, black bulk sliding swiftly, feet slithering over the grass as silently as adders.

Lily shivered in the blazing sun. A prickle of fear, or premonition, fluttered across her shoulders, leaving a sheen of ice-cold perspiration. She shook herself, but the terrifying sense of helplessness, of having inadvertently been captured, would not go away. She gazed up at the blunt stone walls of Darkstone, the flat, implacable bulwark of tower and chimneys and black balustrade against the bright, cloudless sky. For the first time since the night she'd come here, the house looked sinister to her. Malign, not indifferent—not insensate stone and mortar bur a force, a consciousness within the thick granite walls that bore her a personal ill will.

Fancy, she scolded herself, turning her face away, blinking into the hot sky above the blinding sea. Childish imagining, and she could not afford to indulge in whimsy. In an impetuous moment she had issued a challenge. She regretted it now, deeply and profoundly, but that was too bad. Lowdy deserved better from her than craven acquiescence to the status quo. Speaking to Devon would be hellish, crushing, a far worse torment than anything Howe could devise. But she had no choice; she'd made a promise and now she had to keep it.

She knew where he was: in his library. She knew too that he was alone, working at his big table. The accuracy of her knowledge of his whereabouts at almost all times dismayed and appalled her, but in spite of her best efforts she could not rid herself of this uncanny and destructive *awareness*. He was nothing to her—she was less than nothing to him!—so why couldn't she forget him? She would. She would—as soon as she got away. Roger Soames was alive, and tonight she would write to him. Her captivity was ending—surely! Dry-mouthed, shoulders squared, Lily wiped her damp palms on her apron and moved with reluctant haste toward the house.

Devon raked his fingers through his hair, loosening his neat queue in the process. He tore the thin velvet ribbon away and threw it on his desk, out of patience with everything. It was the heat that made it impossible to concentrate on his tenant registry, he told himself, staring grimly at the same column of figures he'd been trying to add for four minutes. The whole exercise was pointless anyway—Cobb handled his rental accounts, and he could count on one hand the times he'd caught his steward in an error. Still, better to sit here by himself, shuffling numbers about on a ledger sheet, than go out and recommence swearing at his employees. For a man who prided himself on his self-control, this new inability to curb his temper was disconcerting. And all he had to do to exacerbate his anger was to remember two facts: that he'd only felt this way during one other period of his life, and that he'd vowed five years ago that he never would again.

He heard no sound over the restless murmur of the sea. Nevertheless, something made him fling his head up, tossing the curtain of straight brown hair back from his forehead. Lily was nothing but a dark outline against the blaze of the day, but he recognized her instantly, and felt a queer twist of pleasure. She was standing between the open French doors, poised in diffident silence. Forcing his hand to relax before he broke his quill pen in half, he said her name in a quiet, questioning voice. Tall, willow-slim, impossibly graceful, she took a hesitating step toward him.

She could barely see him in the sudden darkness. He was sitting at his cluttered library table, exactly as she'd known he would be. Despite the heat, he still wore his black coat, somber-looking against the white of his frilled shirt front. As her eyes grew accustomed to the dimness, she saw that his expression was patient and disinterested, a little stern. Although she'd never seen a judge, he made her think of one. Good. That was good, she told herself, for if she'd seen anything to hint that he remembered, if there had been the vaguest flicker of acknowledgment that once a thousand years ago they had been lovers, had sighed and touched and laughed together, naked in his bed—then she'd have lost her courage and run away without speaking to him. But then, why did his indifference make her heart ache so?

She cleared her throat and made herself take another

step closer. "I beg your pardon for disturbing you, but I have to tell you something important. It's about Mrs. Howe."

He didn't know what he'd expected her to say, but it wasn't that. He leaned back in his chair, conscious of a violent rush of disappointment, and stroked the feather of his pen with apparently idle fingers. "Mrs. Howe? What can you have to tell me about my housekeeper, I wonder?"

She heard condescension in his voice and pulled herself up straighter. "You couldn't know what she's like—you *couldn't*, or you would not keep her." She swallowed hard; that wasn't at all the way she'd meant to begin!

"Indeed? What's she done? From the look of you, Lily, I'd say she's made you jump in the well to retrieve the bucket." He stroked the quill across a tight smile, letting his gaze flick over her damp, disheveled gown and disreputable-looking apron. Her already pink cheeks flamed red with embarrassment, and she tossed a long tangle of escaped hair out of her face with the back of an angry hand.

"She's done nothing to me, it's Lowdy. She *struck* her!"

Devon scowled. "Why?" he snapped. "What did the girl do?"

"Nothing!"

"Nothing? Come, now. Nothing at all?"

"She stopped working in the hot sun to get a drink of water." She desperately wanted to leave it at that, but couldn't bring herself to lie. "And she st—she took an apple from the kitchen larder."

"She stole?"

"An apple!"

"I see. And what is it you expect from me now?"

She spread her hands, staring at him in gathering hopelessness. "Something!"

"What?" He shoved back in his chair impatiently and folded his arms over his chest. The impulse to explain himself to her annoyed him, turning his voice surly. "Mrs. Howe has been here for four years. She's a capable woman; I leave everything about the running of my house in her hands and I don't interfere. We leave each other al—"

"I can't believe this," Lily broke in, anger and incredulity making her forget her awkwardness. "She hit Lowdy, I tell you. She *hurt* her. And Lowdy's not the first. Do you condone that?"

"It depends," he answered coldly, his eyes a pale, arctic blue.

"On what? What could it possibly 'depend' on?"

"On whether you're telling me the truth."

She gasped her outrage. "Why would I lie? Listen to me, this is *important*—"

"Why would you lie? I can't say. But I don't believe my housekeeper would strike anyone for stealing an apple."

"She did, I tell you! And you won't do anything about it!"

"I'll do what's fair—I won't tolerate abuse in my house." He paled with anger when she laughed, a harsh, disbelieving sound that edged into derision at the end. "But if you *are* lying, we both know it wouldn't be for the first time."

Lily closed her mouth, frightened by the accuracy of his thrust.

He smiled unpleasantly. "You can't answer that, I see." A silent moment passed. "I'll speak to Howe," he conceded stiffly.

"No," she cried, rallying. "Speak to Lowdy. For God's sake! She'll tell you the tr—"

"Enough!" Her righteous ire goaded him again. "I told you, it's not my affair. I don't get involved with . . ."

She didn't cry, didn't look away, but an odd, opaque film gathered in front of her eyes, blinding her. The word hung between them, unspoken for as long as she could stand it. "With servants."

Devon stood. He said, "Lily," with no idea of what he would say next. But it didn't matter—she spun away and ran out through the French doors, disappearing into the dazzling brightness before he could speak another word.

He came out from behind the table, striking his knee against the sharp-edged corner. Cursing, he drew his booted foot back and kicked viciously at a heavy oak leg.

"That's telling it. Son of a bitch won't try *that* again."

Devon swung around. His hard face split slowly into a glad smile. "Clay, you miserable bastard. Thank God." They met in the middle of the room. Clay ignored the hand Devon held out and threw his arms around his brother in a jubilant bear hug, pounding him on the back. Devon grunted in pain; Clay jumped away.

"God, Dev, what is it? Are you hurt?"

"No, I'm fine."

"No, something's wrong."

"A scratch. It's nothing now." And he was doing exactly what he'd said he wouldn't—minimizing the consequences of one of Clay's idiotic follies in order to save his bloody feelings.

"What is it, your shoulder?"

"It's healed—only acts up when some fool attacks me." Might as well explain it. "One of the Falmouth Riding Officers got a bit too close with his bayonet. But I put his lights out," he couldn't help adding, modesty be damned. "I have a lot to tell you, you scurvy son of a bitch."

Clay's blue eyes twinkled. "Not as much as I have to tell you." He was bursting with secret news, but his mouth pulled sideways with impatience. "Trouble is, I *can't* tell you. You never want to know."

"Clay—dammit—you said you'd stop, you made a promise—"

"I *have* stopped. Except for Wiley Falk, my whole crew's disbanded, left the area. This isn't smuggling anyway. Not exactly. It's something really big. I won't say what it is—"

"Thanks for that."

"—but I will tell you that it's safe, it's finished, it's my last adventure, and if I weren't already a rich man, I would be now!" He laughed, partly at his exciting news, partly at the consternation on his brother's face.

Devon swore, long and foully. "Just tell me this: Did you sell that bleeding sloop?"

"Not yet." He held up a placating hand. "But I'm *going* to. Christ, I've only been back for two days."

"Two, eh? I won't even ask why you're just getting home."

"Let's just say I had something to take care of."

"Something you wanted as few witnesses to as possible?"

"Maybe." He laughed again, then slowly sobered. "Listen, Dev, I'm awfully sorry you got nicked. I'd never have asked for your help if I'd known it would end like that, I swear."

"I know it. Forget it."

"No, I can't. I wish it had been me instead of you, or at least that I'd been there with you when it happened."

"Best that you weren't; they might have recognized you. Anyway, it's over. They could stick me like a pincushion and I wouldn't care, as long as you're really through being a goddamn pirate."

"I am, I swear I am. I'm going to be so bloody dull you'll soon get sick of the sight of me."

"I doubt that." They smiled at each other. "So," he said, trying to sound casual, "think you might be staying around for a while, do you?"

"I might be. Might even go to work in your damn copper mine."

"Not *in* it, for God's sake, I never—"

*"For* it, then," Clay chuckled. "Manage it, or whatever the hell you want."

Devon couldn't stop shaking his head. "I must be hallucinating."

"I say maybe—we'll see how things go. Brandy?" Devon nodded, and Clay poured out two generous glasses from a decanter on the side table. "But I won't work for Francis, Dev. That's the only condition I'll make, but it's final."

Devon searched his face, looking for a clue to his brother's long-standing antipathy to his mine agent. "I've never understood why you dislike him so," he said slowly. "Is it something I should know about? Something about Francis that I ought to be on guard against?"

"If I knew the answer to that, I'd tell you. For myself, I don't trust him. But you went to school with him, you've known him longer—you *do* trust him. Since I can't prove my suspicions, I don't think it's right to blurt 'em out."

"Well, that's high-minded of you. All the same—"

"Just watch him, that's my advice. Keep an eye on him. And if I'm wrong, nothing's lost."

They heard footsteps in the hall; a second later Stringer appeared in the doorway to announce dinner.

Clay put an arm around Devon's shoulders—gently. "I missed you," he admitted ingenuously. Devon clubbed him on the back and nodded vigorously—his way of returning the sentiment. "Do you know what else I missed? Women. I haven't been with a girl since the day before I left. Not tonight—I'm too tired—but tomorrow night, let's go to the Hornet's Nest. Come on, Dev, I mean it, it'll do you good, you don't get out—"

"Yes, I'm saying yes. Fine. Let's do it."

Clay eyed him in amazement. "Well—great! We can have dinner at Rosreagan's first, maybe play cards afterward. Then spend the whole night at the Nest if we want to." He grinned in gleeful anticipation. "It'll be like old times!"

Devon's smile was drier, but his anticipation was almost as sharp. "You know, for a hare-wit, once in a while you have a good idea," he said approvingly, guiding Clay down the hall toward the dining room. "As it happens, a whore is exactly what I need."

# Fourteen

". . . beg you will believe me when I tell you how much I deeply regret the terrible events of our last meeting. I have prayed every day for your full recovery, and believe God's hand must surely be behind the miraculous news I have just received that you are well. Now my fondest wish is that you have found it in your heart to forgive me for the part I played—inadvertently and without malice, I swear—in that unfortunate mis- understanding, and that, with God's help, we can find a way to resolve our differences. I dare even to hope that, if you would allow Lewis and me a little time to know one another, the Lord's will and mine may draw closer together, and the union you once desired between us might one day come to pass. . . ."

Head down, Lily turned off the high road and walked through the gates of the twisting, sandy drive that led to Darkstone. *Liar,* she taunted herself, compulsively re- calling the words she'd written to her cousin. *Schemer. Canting hypocrite.* She sent a clod of earth flying with the toe of her shoe and fisted her hands in her apron pockets. It wasn't all a lie; she *had* prayed for him every day—at least that part was true. No matter; it was done, the letters were posted, and she would just have to learn to live with her perfidy. Desperate straits drove people to desperate acts, she consoled herself. Hearing the defensiveness in that, she gave a defiant mental shrug and kicked at another dirt clod. Nothing had changed, and she would do it again, write another letter full of half-truths and outright deceptions to Roger Soames without hesitation. There was no point in compounding one hypocrisy with another by pretending to regret it.

What she had done was to buy time, and it no longer concerned her that she was buying it with stolen currency. What mattered was getting out of Cornwall. If by some miracle her cousin still wanted her to marry his son, she was going to take advantage of his inexplicable obsession and pretend to consider it. In a little over nine months, she would come into her inheritance. Although it wasn't much, it would pay for the most precious commodity she could think of: independence. In the meantime, all she had to gamble on was her ability to stall. Almost certainly she wouldn't be able to stretch Soames's patience and credulity for the whole nine months. But for now, she needed sanctuary, and if getting it meant deceiving him and accepting his help and hospitality under false pretenses—so be it. She was at the end of her rope. And it wasn't as if she would be *stealing* from him, she told herself. If he took her in and gave her protection, she would pay him back someday—when she had money.

Enough. It was done. The likeliest outcome was that Soames would ignore her letter, so she might as well forget that she'd sent it, go on as if nothing had changed; that way she couldn't be disappointed. Even if he responded favorably, she probably wouldn't hear from him soon. If he traveled around the west of England preaching the gospel to his "flock," he might not receive her letter for weeks. All she could do in the meantime was wait, and try not to hope.

It was late; her errand had taken longer than she'd expected. She'd met Francis Morgan in the village, and he'd engaged her in conversation outside the chemist's shop for at least ten minutes. Afterward he'd walked with her part of the way back to Darkstone, delaying her further because his lazy pace was slower than her long-legged stride. At first she couldn't imagine why he had spoken to her. He'd never noticed her before, and today they'd talked of nothing of consequence. He was about thirty, tall, yellow-haired—under his wig—and elegant-looking. Despite his undeniable good looks, Lily had never quite been able to take him seriously, perhaps because his habitual style of dress, fashionable and flamboyant, was so out of keeping with his provincial surroundings. He looked more like a London dandy than the manager of a Cornish copper mine. He'd spoken to her pleasantly enough, but when he'd finally tipped his hat and turned back, Lily had felt relieved. Looking back on the incident, she realized it was because of a new look she'd caught in his eyes, an expression of curiosity and sly speculation—the cause of which was distressingly obvious. She was known to him by now—known to all of them, she didn't doubt—as a woman who was easy and available.

The birds were silent, the sea inaudible here. It was a peaceful time of day, but the profound stillness seemed more ominous than tranquil. A wisp of a breeze was warm, but she shivered and quickened her steps, wondering what time it was. She'd asked Lowdy to tell Mrs. Howe she was feeling poorly and didn't want any dinner, calculating that she could be back from posting her letters in Trewyth before time to start her afternoon chores. Now she was late, and the consequences could be anything.

Circling the house to the servants' entrance, she encountered no one, and counted it a blessing. Still, something abandoned-looking about the place made her uneasy. Her job this afternoon was to wash all the basement half-windows, inside and out. She filled a bucket from the well and carried it down the area steps to the basement, pausing to snatch a rag from the kitchen cupboard, and wondering where the cook was, or Enid or Rose. The house was unnaturally quiet. Surely dinner was over by now; where was everyone? With growing alarm, she hurried toward the servants' hall, her footsteps sounding shockingly loud in the uncarpeted corridor. In the doorway she stopped—so abruptly that water sloshed from her bucket and hit the floor with a slap.

Fourteen heads turned at her entrance, and at the foot of the long, cleared table Mrs. Howe slowly rose to her feet. Lily's heart turned over. She saw Trayer at his mother's right and noted his nasty, triumphant leer. But far worse was Lowdy's face, ghost-white and set with fear. Lily lowered her bucket to the floor, slowly, fingers numb. Straightening, conscious of a feeling of imminent catastrophe, she drew in a deep breath and waited.

"You're a bit late for dinner, aren't you?" Mrs. Howe began, mildly enough.

But Lily wasn't fooled. Her mind raced, searching for a way to leave Lowdy out of it. "Yes, ma'am, I'm sorry," she blurted out in a rush. "I told Lowdy I was sick, but—then I—went for a walk. On the path. I'm feeling much better now."

"Are you? I'm so glad. We're all relieved, aren't we?" The housekeeper glanced down the table at the others. Lily thought most of them looked extraordinarily uncomfortable. But a few smiled back at Mrs. Howe, as though sharing a joke, and one of the footmen licked his lips in anticipation. "If you went walking on the path," she resumed, moving forward on a silent glide, "you must've found it hard to post your letters."

"My—" Lily swallowed painfully; her heart began a rough, erratic pounding in her chest. "My letters?"

From the corner of her eye, she saw that Lowdy was looking down at the table and had started to cry.

"Your letters, yes. The ones you left your work in order to mail. After you persuaded Lowdy to lie for you."

"No, Lowdy didn't know, I lied to *her*—"

" 'Whoso diggeth a pit shall fall therein; he that rolleth a stone, it will return upon him.' "

"Please, Mrs. Howe, I swear, Lowdy didn't know—"

"First a thief, now a liar. But nobody here is surprised. 'The dog is turned to his own vomit again, and the sow that was washed, to her wallowing in the mire.' "

Lily shuddered. It was useless to argue. She waited stoically for her punishment.

Howe lifted a heavy arm and pointed toward the wide brick hearth across the room. "Go and kneel there, wicked girl. You'll stay on your knees all night on the cold stone, with no dinner and no supper. In the morning, you'll drink a cup of vinegar to scour your lying tongue. And then you'll—"

"You must be out of your mind. I'll do no such thing." Lily hadn't thought the deathlike silence in the hall could intensify, but it did. And suddenly she couldn't stop her tongue, in spite of the prickle of perspiration on her palms and the shiver of panic across her shoulder blades. "What I did was wrong, but I don't deserve this." She thrust a hand toward the stone hearth. "I'm sorry I lied. I needed to post some letters, and I knew you wouldn't let me. I'm all of twenty minutes late, and I'll make it up tonight after my other chores are done." She stood straighter and strove to conquer the tremor in her voice. "But I won't kneel all night on that hearth, and I certainly won't—" she heard a hysterical laugh bubbling up in her throat—"drink *vinegar* tomorrow to satisfy some vicious, barbaric—"

Intent on her argument, she didn't see the wide palm flying toward her until a half-instant before the impact.

She cried out, in surprise as much as pain, and clutched at her stinging jaw. Afterward, she would try to recall the thoughts that passed through her mind in the seconds that followed, but nothing would focus except stunning, red-hot rage. Obeying a reflex as involuntary as breathing, she brought her own hand back and smacked Mrs. Howe across the face as hard as she could.

It was as if a cannon had exploded in an empty field, so loud was the blow, so complete the stillness in the room in its aftermath. A mist of gray dots clouding Lily's vision gradually disappeared, and in the new clarity she saw Mrs. Howe's face change subtly from shock to exultation. Lily waited, filled with profound dread.

Howe's thickset body seemed to get bigger, swelling and expanding, darkening the room. "Go upstairs," she intoned softly, almost sweetly. "Wait for me in your room, with meekness and fortitude. For though your sins be as scarlet, they shall be as white as snow, and bathed in the blood o' the Lamb."

Lily stood still, fighting her fear, groping for courage somewhere in the waves of pure hate that were drenching her. She said one word—*"Monster"*—in a hissing whisper meant only for Howe's ears. Looking at no one, she turned and fled.

The moon beaming in the window was full, and so bright she could have read a book in her little room without a candle. But she had no book, no letter to write and no mending, nothing but her own thoughts to keep her company while she waited. She didn't think about Mrs. Howe's "punishment," although she did not doubt that, whatever it was, it would be exceedingly unpleasant. Instead she was tormented by images of the past and the future, and her normally resilient spirits were lifeless and heavy from an unfamiliar feeling of regret. Her father's death had been a tragedy, but she'd learned to accept it and carry on with her life in the dark, straitened aftermath. No one avoided catastrophes forever; when they occurred, one did one's best to live through them and come out whole and hopeful on the other side. But the things that had begun happening to her life two months ago did not seem natural to Lily. They were beyond the realm of her experience, at odds with her expectations. Roger Soames was at the heart of her troubles, but his obsessions were out of her control. Nothing she could have done, short of total capitulation, could have changed the outcome of their last encounter.

In the same way, Mrs. Howe's enmity was frightening and inexplicable, a powerful mystery; standing in its violent path, Lily felt completely helpless. Nothing made sense anymore; nothing was orderly. Actions had no relation to consequences. She'd lived her life with a barely conscious conviction that she had a hand in her own fate, but that consolation no longer existed. Complacency was gone. Survival, which had once been a given, was now a contingency.

Where Devon Darkwell fit into this new philosophy, she couldn't say. She would be glad to leave him, glad never to see him again. He had given her very little except pain and anguish, hurt and humiliation. And yet, incredibly, she didn't hate him. When she thought of him, before her mind had a chance to throw up its thick bulwark of defenses, sometimes a deep, exquisite joy assaulted her, made up as much of pain as pleasure, and so strong it could make her lightheaded. She would be *happy* to leave him, and yet his—companionship, if it wasn't too much of a joke to call it that, had been the only bright spot in all of the long, dreary weeks she'd been at Darkstone. Odder still, and most distressing of all, was the knowledge that she would never forget him: she would take his dark, provocative, frustrating memory to her grave.

She heard a step on the stair. It's Lowdy, she told herself, for it seemed as if hours had passed; surely it was almost bedtime. But no—now she heard a second set of footsteps, and a moment later she saw a flicker of light under the crack in the door. Lowdy would have no candle.

Stiff-limbed, heart pounding, she got up from the bed and stood in the center of the small room, her back to the window. She heard a rattling at the knob and watched the door swing open. Mrs. Howe stood four-square in a rectangle of yellow light; behind her, Trayer held a lantern. In the next second she made out what Mrs. Howe had in her hand. It was a leather strap.

"You won't beat me," Lily got out defiantly, backing up, skin tingling with dread. Trayer set the lantern down on the bureau.

"'The wrath of God cometh upon the children of disobedience. Whom the Lord loveth, he chasteneth.'" She moved closer, black eyes gleaming, her mean buttonhole of a mouth pinched with purpose. "It's time, Lily Troublefield. This is the day of salvation."

Lily kept shaking her head. "You won't do this. *You won't.*" She stared at them, and just for a second her absolute certainty stopped them. But then they started toward her again, and she felt the fine, icy prick of terror on her scalp. She backed away until one heel struck the wall behind her. She saw Trayer advancing on her right. He put a hand out to grab her and she feinted toward him, then dodged the other way. Horrifyingly agile, Mrs. Howe shifted her wide bulk to block the door, and in the next moment Lily felt Trayer's hands gripping her arms.

She kicked back at him, futilely. He spun her around, pulling her close against him in an obscene travesty of an embrace, arms tight around her waist. The first slash of the strap cut like a blunt knife. She howled in pain and fury, beating against Trayer's hard biceps. Mrs. Howe struck again and again, vicious lashes across her buttocks and thighs, and at last Lily gave up trying to twist away. Slumped against Trayer, choking on tears of rage and shame, she endured the ruthless flogging—

until the unmistakable evidence of her captor's arousal made her flinch back in horror. At that moment Howe paused to rest. Trayer pulled away to grin lewdly in Lily's face. Without a thought, she snapped her knee up into his groin.

The air left his lungs in a rush as he gave a hoarse shout of agony, staggered backwards, and fell writhing on the bed.

Lily whirled. Howe had dropped the strap. She was standing in front of the door, sweating, furious. "God's word is quick and powerful," she panted, "sharper than any sword—"

Lily uttered a blasphemous curse and ran at her.

It was like charging a stone wall. The wide, hard bosom gave no ground, and instead she found herself ensnared in Howe's powerful arms and held in a grip of pure steel. She screamed her fury into Howe's mad-eyed countenance and kicked at her shins. The housekeeper only grunted, then captured one of Lily's arms and slapped her across the face, again and again, using all her strength. Lily tried to shield herself with her free hand, but Howe was as strong as a man. Panic snaked through her. This was real, it was happening now, and it wasn't going to stop.

All at once she was spun around from behind. Red-faced and snarling, Trayer struck her with his fist. Her vision clouded; silver streaks flared behind her eyes.

"No, not her face!"

The next blows were to her breasts and abdomen. When he struck her in the diaphragm, Lily lost her breath and dropped to the floor on her knees.

Half-conscious, she tried to stand, but the muscles in her legs were impotent. She heard Howe say, "That's enough!" just before a booted foot smacked into her ribs. She gasped from an explosion of pain and struck the floor hard. The last blow was to the small of her back.

"Stop, I said!"

Lily waited, braced for another kick. It didn't come. Through a haze, she heard footsteps retreating. The slamming of the door. Nothing.

"My fault—oh God! Can you raise up? But she made me, said she'd beat me unless I told. Lily? Oh God, I'm scairt. Sit up now, you did ought to. I'll help—"

"Don't. Don't, Lowdy."

"Oh God! What should I do? Lily, what's wrong with you?"

Lowdy must have lit a candle; Lily could see tear streaks on her worried face in the flickering light. Lowdy was holding her hand. Lily tried to squeeze back, but the gray fog started to roll over her again. She whispered, "Get Devon," and then it smothered her.

There was dust in her nostrils, and the musty-sweet smell of raw wood. Lying on her side, cheek pressed to the floor, she watched a particle of lint flutter and float in time with her shallow breathing. A sound vibrated in her ear: a step on the stair. She closed her eyes and mouthed a prayer of thanks. "Dev," she croaked, waiting for him. Lantern light streaked through the shadows where she lay. She couldn't move; she could scarcely turn her head. She saw his shoes before he dropped to his knees beside her.

"Hullo, your highness. How're you feeling, Queen Lily? You don't look so high and mighty anymore." Trayer grabbed her shoulder and shoved her onto her back, ignoring her choked scream of pain. Her hands flailed uselessly while he unlaced her dress and tore her shift open, then massaged her bruised flesh with deliberate cruelty. "You don't even look pretty anymore. But you know what? I'm gonna overlook that." When he yanked her skirts up and lay on top of her, she felt the gray fog swirling closer, closer. Her body was limp; the

fist she tried to beat against his side was loose and
pitiful. Something was wrong with her throat; a moan of
despair made her eyes fill with helpless tears. She
turned her head away from Trayer's black and avid gaze.
But a sound made her look back—to see if he'd heard it
too. Their eyes locked as the sound became running
footsteps, loud and fast and furious. Trayer had time to
jump up and move two steps away before the master
burst through the open door.

"I was trying to help 'er—my mother did this!"

Devon's steps faltered; he moved toward Lily in slow
motion, seeing her in sharp, unconnected streaks of
perception. Blood, bruises, torn clothes, torn flesh—
the picture coalesced with slow, terrible precision. He
bellowed his outrage. Trayer was sliding past him; it felt
like mercy, like a deliverance, to turn away from the
dreadful sight of Lily and lunge at him.

He caught him in the hall. His valet's face was blank
with panic until Devon struck him in the mouth with his
fist. Blood spurted; Trayer squealed and backed up
toward the steps, bulky legs churning. The second blow
doubled him over; the next hauled him upright again.
He lost his balance and flew backwards, striking the
balustrade. It split under his weight, and his body
hurtled across four steep steps before slamming against
the wall, shoulder first. Devon heard a coarse groan,
then the thud of bones hitting wood, violent and irregular, receding, as Trayer disappeared into the black pit of
the stairwell.

Devon backed up blindly and stumbled into Lily's
room. She was trying to raise herself up on her elbow.
He caught her just as she collapsed. He laid her down
gently, trying to smile into her anguished face, but the
sight of the blue contusions on her chest and throat
froze his blood. His fingertips grazed the dark swelling
on the side of her jaw, and she winced even though his
touch had been feather-light. She raised one hand
feebly, defensively, and he saw that the knuckles were

bloody—from trying to cover herself?

"Sir?"

He spun and saw Lowdy cowering in the doorway. "Get MacLeaf," he bit out. "Tell him to ride to Trewyth and fetch Dr. Penroy. Go!"

Lowdy scampered away.

Lily held his sleeve, pulling on it weakly. Her mouth moved, but he couldn't hear the words. He put his ear to her lips, and she whispered, "Something's broken."

Beating back his fear, he slid an arm under her shoulders. "It's all right, you're safe now, you're going to be all right." But when he bent to lift her, she rasped out a terrible cry and her eyes slid back in her head. Sweat broke out all over him. *Lily.* She'd fainted; he couldn't rouse her. His arms were shaking as he gathered her up again and lifted her. He glanced around the room, taking unwilling note of its meagerness, the ugly, cast-off furniture. He could not put her down on that thin straw mattress. Grabbing up the lantern with the hand that supported her knees, he headed for the stairs. On the second floor, he turned at the first room he came to—one of the guest bedchambers, a few doors down from his own—and laid Lily on the bed.

She roused to half-consciousness as he undressed her. He saw the strap marks on her thighs when she tried to twist away because he was hurting her. Worse was a blackening blotch below her right breast; when he touched it she flinched away, white-faced. He covered her with the sheet when she started to shiver. With his handkerchief he wiped a trickle of blood from the side of her mouth. Her cheeks were flushed and puffy, as if she'd been slapped repeatedly.

Lowdy came, but hung back in the doorway until he called to her. "Why did they do this?" he demanded.

"Twur a punishment, sir. Lily runned t' the village t' post a letter and were late gettin' back."

Devon stared at her in revulsion and disbelief. His face went dark with fury, and Lowdy shrank back.

"Get her nightgown," he snarled.

"She ha'n't un, s-sir."

"What does she sleep in?"

"Sleeps in 'er shift."

He whirled away, then back. "Get hot water and clean cloths," he said through clenched teeth, and Lowdy ran off again.

He sat beside her and took her hands—then dropped them when she bared her teeth and arched away from him in agony. "God, Lily!" he muttered, afraid to touch her. When Lowdy returned, they bathed her together as best they could, but everything they did seemed to hurt her. He held brandy to her lips, but she couldn't swallow it. After that he pulled a chair close to the bed and sat down. Finding it impossible not to touch her, he rested his arm lightly alongside hers. She was awake, but she couldn't speak; instead she listened with huge, pain-glazed eyes while he told her over and over that everything would be all right.

Clay appeared in the doorway. "My God, Dev, is it true?" He came forward slowly, appalled, staring at the still figure on the bed.

Devon stood up. He was overcome with relief to see Clay—even though he smelled like a gin mill. "I didn't think you'd be back until morning." They'd gone whoring together in Truro, but Devon had come home early, sick of it.

"I heard you'd gone home, and I was afraid something had happened. Stringer just told me about Lily." He cursed softly, peering over Devon's shoulder. "Is she badly hurt?"

"Yes. Do something for me, Clay."

"Anything."

"Get Howe out of the house. If I do it myself, I'm afraid I'll kill her."

Clay regarded him in surprise, taking in his taut face and haggard, haunted eyes. "I'll take care of it," he said evenly.

"Thank you." Immediately Devon turned back to the bed and resumed his chair. Clay waited another moment, then went out.

Dr. Penroy arrived a quarter of an hour later. Devon would have preferred someone else, he'd never liked Penroy, but there wasn't time to send to Truro. The elderly physician made him leave the room, and he went with deep unwillingness. He paced in the hall outside the closed door, listening intently for the smallest sound, the lightest cry. But there was nothing. Presently he heard Clay's quick step on the stairs and turned toward him expectantly.

"She's gone," he answered before Devon could ask. "I told her if she was still in the district this time tomorrow, you'd have her bound over and tried for assault."

"I will anyway."

Clay watched him curiously. "You and this girl, you . . ."

"Yes?"

Something warned Clay away. "Nothing. What in the world did you do to Trayer?" he demanded, to change the subject.

"He fell down the stairs. I hope he broke his neck."

"Not quite, but he's in bad shape. I couldn't believe it, Dev—the son of a bitch *cursed* me. After what he did to Lily, he cursed *me*. And then he had the gall to make threats—said he'd pay us all back!" He shook his head wonderingly.

"I should've killed him."

The unemphatic ruthlessness pulled Clay up short, silencing what he was going to say next. A second later the door opened and Penroy stepped into the hall. Both men crowded around the stoop-shouldered, irritable-looking physician in black wig, round spectacles, and old-fashioned pantaloons.

"She's been badly beaten," he announced, and Devon went rigid with impatience. "I've bled her to ward off fever. A rib or two is broken, and there may be other

internal injuries as well. Her larynx is inflamed from a
blow; don't let her speak. A soft diet, rest and sleep.
Oh—she might have a fractured wrist too—left hand—
but I can't be certain yet. Try to keep her quiet. I've
given her an infusion of Peruvian bark as a specific
against fever, and I've left laudanum—but give that
sparingly. She'll heal in time, as long as nothing's hurt
too badly inside." He looked back and forth between
their shocked faces. "There's nothing more I can do
tonight; I'll come again tomorrow if you want."

Clay roused himself to escort the doctor downstairs.
Devon stood still, looking at nothing, listening to their
low-voiced consultation fade with their footsteps. His
skin felt tender, his muscles taut with apprehension.
Penroy's words distressed him physically, as if each
injury were his.

Lowdy appeared from the dark end of the hall near
the servants' stairs. She approached him tentatively,
wringing her hands. "Want me t' go in and sit wi' Lily,
sir?" she ventured shyly.

He stared at her for a long time before her words
made any sense. He saw that she looked ready to bolt,
and realized he was frightening her. "Is your name
Lowdy?"

"Ais." She dropped an awkward curtsey. When he
didn't speak again, she began to back away.

"Wait. Yes, stay with her. Watch carefully and—take
care of her. If anything happens, if she needs anything or
she gets worse . . ." He trailed off, and his blind, burning eyes looked straight through her. ". . . tell my brother," he finished harshly, and spun around. He almost
ran down the hall and took the steps of the elegant,
curving staircase two at a time. Lowdy heard the great
front door creak open and slam against the stone wall
with a crash. Trembling a little, she went into Lily's new
bedchamber and sat down beside her friend.

# Fifteen

The moonlight was too bright. He cursed the clarity of sea and shale, rocks and sky. Blackness was what he had escaped the house for, in some vain hope that it might swallow him up along with his thoughts. But he could see the lines on his own palms in the silver light reflected from thin clouds that swathed but never blinded the white eye of the moon. He quickened his pace, away from the house. If he couldn't clear his mind with darkness, perhaps he could with movement. He closed his ears to everything but the sound of his own breathing, veering away at the bottom of the cliff steps to the stony track that sloped up to the woods and the mere.

The inland lake's waters were still tonight, black and bottomless, and the sea was a distant restless surge. He decided he would have a swim; that would distract him. He started to strip off his coat—and stopped with it hanging from his forearms behind him, remembering.

There across the sand was the black rock he'd trapped
her against that night with Clay, weeks ago. She'd been
embarrassed because she was naked, and he hadn't
hesitated for a second to take advantage of her distress.
She'd been nothing to him then, nothing except a body,
wet and sleek and exciting. Because she was a servant, a
part of him had reasoned—unconsciously or not, it
didn't matter—that her body was his, and that he was
entitled to at least a one-time use of it. He'd even
mentioned, ostensibly as a joke, the *droit du seigneur*.
That he'd wanted her, wanted *any* woman, had seemed
such a miracle that he'd allowed the wanting to justify
anything it took to have her. Later, when she resisted,
he'd leapt to the conclusion that she wasn't free but she
could be bought. For as long as he lived, he would
remember the look on her face the day he'd tried to give
her money.

Too bright here. He shrugged his coat back on and
hurried away from the mere, his shoes clumsy in the
thick sand. He walked quickly back up the stone track,
drawn to the dark, anonymous silence of the park. Oak
and larch and hazelnut trees enveloped him here,
shrouding him from the moon. He slowed his steps,
feeling the pumping of his heart in his chest and his
throat, and inhaled deep breaths of the black night air.
Far off an owl called to its mate, or its prey. The smell of
moss and damp earth was stronger than the salt tang of
the sea wind. He lost the trail and plunged through an
invisible copse of bramble and vine until he came out
on the gravel drive. Too bright here too—but at least he
wouldn't break his neck. He set off for the highroad
gates, head down, mind blank, hands shoved in his
pockets.

As he leaned against a stone post, another memory
assaulted him, of the night he'd come home wounded
and his horse had thrown him—here, practically at his
feet. He resisted the recollection with all his strength,
but his body betrayed him. He could *feel* her arms

around him, the warm weight of her pressing him back against the post, the firm touch of her hands on his chest. Her wet hair had smelled as sweet and wild as the storm, and in the bright slashes of lightning her eyes had glowed dark and huge, and tense with worry for him. Later she'd stabled his horse and hidden his clothes, for no reason except that he'd asked her to. When the Revenue men came, she'd lied for him.

And the morning after she'd given herself to him, betraying in the process some private principle he'd paid no attention to and hadn't cared a damn about, he'd offered her twenty pounds.

He shoved away from the gate post and began to walk back up the drive, striding swiftly, staring straight ahead. But the door was open now and the memories were jostling through. It wasn't long before the worst one, the one he'd been trying to avoid at all costs, hit him like a blow to the back of the head. He saw Lily standing in his library, weary and disheveled, struggling against her nerves and her pride. "But she hit Lowdy. She *hurt* her. Do you condone that?"

He'd told her he would speak to his housekeeper—but he hadn't. In the excitement of Clay's return, he'd forgotten. And by that act, he'd given Mrs. Howe carte blanche to brutalize her.

Up ahead he saw a light, from Cobb's cottage. What time was it? He had no idea. He turned off the drive and plunged down the short walk to his steward's front door. Without a thought, he pounded on it.

Cobb opened up immediately. He was fully dressed, and behind him Devon could see nothing to indicate what he might have been doing—eating supper, reading, repairing something; the cottage was as neat and spare as Cobb's office in the house, and just as unrevealing. "Come in," he said after a half second's startled pause.

The sight of his steward's familiar black-bearded face calmed Devon slightly. He said, "Arthur," and ducked his head to clear the threshold. "I've come to ask you about Mrs. Howe. What do you know about her?"

"Eh? Know about 'er?"

He pulled himself together. "She has beaten—one of the maids. Do you know Lily Troublefield?"

"Ais, I know who she is. Beat 'er, you say? What for?"

"For nothing!" He realized he wanted to slam his fists against the stuccoed wall behind him. He grabbed hold of one lapel of his jacket and stroked it compulsively. "Howe and Trayer beat the girl for nothing, some trumped-up charge of disobedience. I'm informed that it may not have been for the first time—I mean there may have been others before her. What do you know of it?"

"Nothing."

"You must know something!"

"No, I don't," he insisted stolidly. "Howe d' run the house wi' no advice from me or anyone else. Tedn my business, and I don't interfere."

With a sick feeling, Devon heard the echo of his own ignorance and indifference in Cobb's words, and wasn't hypocrite enough to chastise him for it. "I've thrown her out, and Trayer too," he said—defensively. Cobb blinked at him owlishly. Devon could think of nothing else to say. "Good night. I'm sorry for troubling you."

"Good night," Cobb echoed, standing in the doorway and watching Devon walk away until the blackness blotted him out.

Devon spent the rest of the night drinking in his library. He started with rum, but drunkenness stubbornly eluded him. With dawn bluing in the east, he switched to brandy, and at last his brain started to release him. His body felt weighted down, inert; he couldn't remember ever being so tired. Morning came, and he stretched out on the long sofa in the library, unspeakably grateful because oblivion was finally imminent. He slept.

When he awoke, he was sweating and tense, the vapory remnants of some dreadful dream nagging at the edges of his mind. His hands shook as he poured out a full glass of brandy. He brought it to his lips, but his stomach rebelled. He set the glass down carefully and stared into space.

Clay found him that way. "You look awful," he observed frankly.

Devon cleared his throat to ask a question. "How is—" But then he changed it. "Where is Cobb?"

"Cobb? In his office, I suppose." Clay looked back into his brother's bleak, austere face for a long moment. "Lily's the same," he said lightly. "Penroy came early this morning. He thinks her wrist is only sprained. He—bled her again and painted her throat with spirits of sea salt. She's resting."

Devon turned his back on him.

"One of the maids, the one named Lowdy, sat up with her last night, and another one is with her now. Penroy said he'd come again tomorrow."

Devon said, "That's fine," and nodded once.

There was a pause.

"Dinner's ready. Are you going to eat?"

"No. I have to go out." He looked through the French doors and noticed for the first time that it was raining. A chill, clammy mist was blowing in from the sea. "I have to . . ." He couldn't think what he had to do. "I'm going out." And he walked out into the sodden afternoon, leaving Clay to stare after him.

He spent what was left of the day riding to the farms of his most distant tenants, on unimportant errands Cobb usually ran for him. It was after dark when he returned. He came into the house through the servants' entrance and headed straight for the kitchen. A maid—he had no idea what her name was—almost dropped the pot she was scouring when she saw him. Neither spoke. He went to the larder, located the remains of supper, and ate it standing up: cold soup, pigeon pie, and a currant tart, washed down with a cup of beer.

It had rained most of the afternoon; his clothes were sticking to his damp, chilly skin. He ought to change his shirt, shave, clean himself up. He paused at the bottom of the staircase, one hand on the walnut banister, peering up into the darkness. If he went upstairs, he wouldn't go to his room. He'd go to Lily's. And he wasn't allowed to do that, because his punishment wasn't over yet.

He went back to his library instead, and stripped off his shirt. He unfurled a soft plaid blanket that lay folded on the sofa and wrapped it around his shoulders. Brandy tasted good again, and went down easily. Sitting at his long table, he opened one of his account books and put on his steel spectacles. He sharpened a quill. Outside, the sea grumbled and hissed under the steady downpour. The clock on the mantelpiece struck nine. He put his head in his hands.

"Mr. Darkwell, sir? Your lordsh—my—Mr. Darkwell?"

He wasn't asleep; the shy murmur was so softly spoken it had taken a minute to snag his attention. He lifted his head from the cradle of his bent forearms and peered at the girl hovering in the doorway. "Yes, what is it?"

Lowdy came half a step nearer. "Tes Lily, sir. I'm that worried."

Devon came out of his chair. "What's wrong?"

"I telled young Mr. Darkwell, as ee said, but he didn't know naught t' do. He said t' speak t' you about 'er."

"What's the matter with her?"

The sight of him moving toward her, big and bare-chested, a blanket draped over his wide shoulders, made Lowdy quail. "She won't stop cryin'," she said in a rush, her back pressed to the doorpost. "She didn't cry

# Thrill to the most sensual, adventure-filled Historical Romances on the market today…

## FROM  LEISURE BOOKS

As a home subscriber to the Leisure Historical Romance Book Club, you'll enjoy the best in today's BRAND-NEW Historical Romance fiction. For over twenty-five years, Leisure Books has brought you the award-winning, high-quality authors you know and love to read. Each Leisure Historical Romance will sweep you away to a world of high adventure…and intimate romance. Discover for yourself all the passion and excitement millions of readers thrill to each and every month.

## SAVE AT LEAST *$5.00* EACH TIME YOU BUY!

Each month, the Leisure Historical Romance Book Club brings you four brand-new titles from Leisure Books, America's foremost publisher of Historical Romances. EACH PACKAGE WILL SAVE YOU AT LEAST $5.00 FROM THE BOOKSTORE PRICE! And you'll never miss a new title with our convenient home delivery service.

Here's how we do it. Each package will carry a 10-DAY EXAMINATION privilege. At the end of that time, if you decide to keep your books, simply pay the low invoice price of $16.96 ($17.75 US in Canada), no shipping or handling charges added*. HOME DELIVERY IS ALWAYS FREE*. With today's top Historical Romance novels selling for $5.99 and higher, our price SAVES YOU AT LEAST $5.00 with each shipment.

## AND YOUR FIRST FOUR-BOOK SHIPMENT IS TOTALLY FREE!*

*IT'S A BARGAIN YOU CAN'T BEAT! A Super $21.96 Value!*

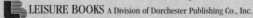

LEISURE BOOKS A Division of Dorchester Publishing Co., Inc.

# GET YOUR 4 FREE* BOOKS NOW— A $21.96 VALUE!

### Mail the Free* Book Certificate Today!

## 4 FREE* BOOKS 🐚 A $21.96 VALUE

## *Free * Books Certificate*

**YES!** I want to subscribe to the Leisure Historical Romance Book Club. Please send me my 4 FREE* BOOKS. Then each month I'll receive the four newest Leisure Historical Romance selections to Preview for 10 days. If I decide to keep them, I will pay the Special Member's Only discounted price of just $4.24 each, a total of $16.96 ($17.75 US in Canada). This is a SAVINGS OF AT LEAST $5.00 off the bookstore price. There are no shipping, handling, or other charges*. There is no minimum number of books I must buy and I may cancel the program at any time. In any case, the 4 FREE* BOOKS are mine to keep—A BIG $21.96 Value!

*In Canada, add $5.00 shipping and handling per order for first shipment. For all subsequent shipments to Canada, the cost of membership is $17.75 US, which includes $7.75 shipping and handling per month.[All payments must be made in US dollars]

*Name* _____

*Address* _____

*City* _____

*State* _____ *Country* _____ *Zip* _____

*Telephone* _____

*Signature* _____

If under 18, Parent or Guardian must sign. Terms, prices and conditions subject to change. Subscription subject to acceptance. Leisure Books reserves the right to reject any order or cancel any subscription.

(Tear Here and Mail Your FREE* Book Card Today!)

# Get Four Books Totally
# F R E E\* —
# A $21.96 Value!

(Tear Here and Mail Your FREE\* Book Card Today!)

PLEASE RUSH
MY FOUR FREE\*
BOOKS TO ME
RIGHT AWAY!

*Leisure Historical Romance Book Club*
P.O. Box 6613
Edison, NJ 08818-6613

AFFIX
STAMP
HERE

at all before, and now she can't leave off. I don't know what t' do for 'er, for surgeon said take care wi' the laud'num. I give it to 'er in little bits, but it don't help anyway. I'm that scairt, Mr. Dar—'' She broke off when Devon plunged past her and loped down the hall for the stairs, blanket billowing behind him.

Only one candle was burning beside the bed. In its feeble gleam he could hardly see her, huddled awkwardly on her side under a bulky weight of bedclothes. He didn't hear anything at first, but as he crept closer a faint sound came to him, part sob, part whimper. He froze for a second, appalled by the hopelessness in it, the quiet, unrelieved anguish. He stepped to the side of the bed. Her dark hair clouded the pillow; her face was absolutely without color. Her knuckles were pressed to her lips to stifle her ragged breathing. He put his hand on her shoulder, through the bedclothes. "Lily," he said indistinctly.

She opened her eyes. When she saw who it was, she wiped her cheeks with her hand and the cuff of her cotton nightrail and tried to sit up. Before he could help her, she collapsed back on her side. Sweat broke out on her forehead; she gritted her teeth and clutched at the damp pillow until the spasm passed, and then she lay still, panting.

A flare of panic scorched him. He dropped to his knees beside her. "What's wrong?" he murmured, touching her. "Where do you hurt, sweetheart?" She didn't answer. He pulled the covers back as gently as he could. Her left arm angled out from beneath her, the bandaged wrist limp on the mattress, palm up. "Is it your wrist?" She didn't speak. Her nightclothes were damp with perspiration, the pillowcase wet from her tears. He thought of the swollen black bruise under her right breast. "Is it your side?" A broken rib, Penroy had said. Or two. Tears slid out from under her tightly closed eyelids. "Is it your ribs, love?" he whispered, his breath fanning her face. "Show me, Lily. Tell me where it hurts."

Her wet lashes untangled and she opened her eyes again, but she didn't look at him. A moment passed, and then she let go of the pillow and slid her hand to her side. They both released their indrawn breath at the same time.

Devon stood up. There was a small bottle of brownish liquid on the night table, half-empty, as well as a cup of cold tea and an uneaten half-slice of buttered bread. "Have you had any of your medicine in the last two hours or so?" he asked, bending near. She mouthed the word "Yes." He straightened; his lips formed a grim line.

He crossed the room to the high bureau, on top of which rested a china basin full of water. He took the basin and the folded face cloth beside it back to the bed. She was curled up at the extreme edge of the mattress. Rather than move her so that he could sit, he kicked off his wet boots and got up on the bed behind her. She shuddered at first when he stroked the damp hair away from her cheek and bathed her face and her swollen throat with the cool cloth. Next he washed her hands and as much of her arms as he could reach under the full-sleeved gown, careful not to touch her injured wrist. Leaning over her, he unbuttoned the front of the gown and held the wet cloth to her chest, feeling the heat of her body penetrate the coolness in seconds. "Feel good?" he murmured. Her lips moved, he thought in assent. He rinsed the cloth in the basin on the pillow beside her and wrung it out. "Can you lie on your back? I'll help you."

With his assistance, and using her good arm for leverage, she started to turn. Halfway around, she drew her knees up and squeezed her eyes closed in silent agony. Devon blanched. "All right, all right," he whispered meaninglessly, holding her. Slowly, muscle by muscle, she relaxed, and after a minute she was able to finish the maneuver. Then she lay still, white and perspiring, on her back.

When his hands stopped shaking, he pulled the hot covers away and began to bathe her legs. He felt a surge of relief when she made a weak, one-handed effort to push her tangled nightgown down across her thighs, reasoning that she must not be mortally hurt if she could still care, in this dire hour, about her modesty. He spent a long time on her feet, first washing and then massaging them, sitting cross-legged at the bottom of the bed. As he worked, he thought a little of the glazed look began to fade from her grayish-green eyes—the only two spots of color in her face. Her head was elevated slightly on the pillow. She watched him sometimes with a grave expression, and other times she closed her eyes and seemed to be resting. After a while she began to shiver. He put the basin aside, tugged her gown down below her knees, and covered her with the sheet and a blanket.

He held the cup of cold tea to her lips. She tried to pull away, but he persisted. But when he saw what the effort to swallow cost her, he put the cup down and ran his hands through his hair.

"What should I do, Lily?" he said, struggling to hide his desperation. "I can't give you any more laudanum yet. What can I do to help you?" She only stared back, resigned, hopeless. Presently she grew restless; one hand went to her injured ribs and she twisted her head on the pillow, knees flexed. He didn't know what to do. She reached across for the side of the mattress and tugged. "On your side again?" he guessed. She nodded gratefully. It was another slow and painful process, but eventually they accomplished it. He knelt on the floor beside her, stroking her cheek, straightening the covers. "Try to sleep now," he told her. She closed her eyes obediently.

But she didn't sleep. There was no position in which she could be comfortable for long. He shifted and turned her when he could, and continued to bathe her limp, sweating body. The long night wore on, and pain and exhaustion ate away at what was left of her composure. Close to dawn, she gave up her silent suffering and went back to the frail, pitiful weeping he'd walked in on.

He could not bear it. He grabbed up the vial of laudanum, splashed some into the tea, and made her drink it, all of it. Then he went to the other side of the bed and got under the covers beside her. She tried to see him, peering around her shoulder, but her hair was in her eyes. He smoothed it back and settled himself on his side behind her. He kept his hands light and, as much as possible, impersonal, one tucked under her waist and the other resting on her hip. He started to talk.

He told her about the things they would do when she was well. Had she ever been to Penzance? No? They would go there first, then. The west winds were so warm that even in winter the fuchsias grew as big as trees. The gardens were lush with camellias and myrtle, tamarisk and hydrangeas, and the hedges were draped with Hottentot figs. Wild orchids grew on the moorlands, and rare clovers covered the cliff summits in a blaze of color. Had she seen Land's End? They would go there next. Desertlike and desolate, it looked like Life's End, looking out at the edge of the world. King Arthur had lived there, he told her, and maybe Tristan, too. He would show her the monoliths and stone circles and dolmens, and she'd understand why Cornishmen still believed in giants. After that they'd go to St. Austell and look at the great mounds of china clay, white as the Alps, strange moon-mountains shining in the sun. Would she like to go down in his copper mine? He'd take her if she liked. And he'd take her to Lizard Point and show her the serpentine rocks, deep green streaked with red and purple, the green as beautiful as her eyes.

He kept talking until his throat was dry and his voice was hoarse. While he talked he touched her, a light stroking across her shoulder and down her arm to the curve of her hip, and lightly back up again. At sunrise the rain stopped, suddenly, and in the dripping quiet he heard her deep, regular breathing. She was asleep.

He turned on his back carefully, quietly. Blood returning to his numbed left side made his body tingle. But he kept one hand pressed gently to the small of her back, fearful of losing contact. He closed his eyes. Beyond the exhaustion, a vast relief made him feel weak. She was going to recover. Gratitude flooded through him, humbled him. He hadn't thanked God for anything in years.

He did now.

The worst was over.

Once she was able to rest, Lily found she could bear the pain of her injuries, and soon the laudanum, still administered in small, careful doses, was sufficient to give her ease. On the third day she slept round the clock. Dr. Penroy congratulated himself for fending off a serious fever; still, to be on the safe side, he wanted to bleed her again. Devon forbade it, arguing that she was too weak already, she was as limp as a rag, and personally he didn't hold with bloodletting anyway. The doctor had drawn himself up, demanding to know who was the physician here. Devon replied that apparently it was young Dr. Marsh, from Truro, and he was sending for him in the morning. Penroy went away in a huff.

Appalled at his colleague's prescription, Dr. Marsh called for spirits of camphor to relieve Lily's raw throat, and almost overnight the inflammation decreased; soon she could swallow and even speak without too much discomfort. The worst was her ribs; that pain was lingering and acute, and endured long after her other aches and injuries faded. Nevertheless, after five days she could sit up; in a week she could walk around the room—slowly, and if someone helped her.

Usually it was Lowdy, or Rose if Lowdy wasn't available. Clay visited her almost every day, just for a few minutes. At first his solicitude astonished Lily. He didn't know her at all, and the social barriers between them—the real one and the one he believed was there—should have insured that his interest never went beyond the barest courtesy. But she soon came to believe that Clay was kind to her because he was a kind man, and perhaps also because he liked her. Her reserve melted, and she began to look forward to his visits because he always cheered her up. His high spirits were contagious, his good humor irresistible. The only disadvantage to his company was that sometimes he made her laugh—and that was excruciating.

Devon came every day too, morning and evening, with great faithfulness. But his company didn't cheer her. Much of the aftermath of the Howes' assault was a blur to her now, but the memory of his gentleness during the longest night of her life was crystal clear and indelible. So it was hard to reconcile this stiff, unsmiling, painfully polite visitor with the man whose patience and compassion had pulled her back at the last moment from the edge of despair. Now he was distant, stern-faced, uncomfortable, and he behaved as if he hardly knew her, or as if something in their mutual past deeply embarrassed him.

She could imagine what that might be easily enough. She began to dread his dutiful visits as much as she looked forward to his brother's. After inquiring about her health, he would run out of conversation, and she felt equally constrained. After that, instead of taking his leave, he would sit and stare off into neutral space, and wait until the silence between them was so awful she wanted to scream. Then he would mutter some courteous civility and go away.

One night he didn't come. He's late, she thought at half past eight, and wondered what he might be doing.

She told herself she was glad, that she hoped he wouldn't come. She plumped her pillows and went back to her book. At eight-forty-five she closed it, keeping her finger in her place. Was that a step in the hall? She heard the far-off, intermittent sound of waves charging and retreating, the unruly thud of a moth at the half-closed window. Nothing else. She stared at the long, smooth shadows in the corners of the room, the glimmering paleness of the ceiling. The scent of moonflowers drifted in from the garden below. The ticking of the ormolu clock on the mantel sounded petty and mean-spirited. She returned to her book, but the words looked random now, like ants parading across white sand. He wasn't coming.

At ten o'clock she heard footsteps. Her heart leapt; her hand fluttered to the high collar of her nightgown. The door opened, and Lowdy bustled in.

"Ee're red as a rose, all flushed-like," she observed, peering at her in the candlelight. "Are you sick?"

"No."

"Galen just got done askin', and I said, 'She'm doing brave, don't ee worry a speck about Lily,' and 'ere I find you all pink-faced and faint."

"I'm not faint. You startled me a little when you came in, that's all."

"Well, that's all right, then. Speakin' o' Galen, 'e give me this t' give to you."

Lily held out her hand and took the palm-sized object Lowdy offered her. "What is it?" From what she could see, it was two wooden cylinders one inside the other, with a handle protruding from the smaller one.

"Somethin' 'e whittled. Jerk that little top part."

Lily turned the handle, and the wooden cylinders emitted a loud, screeching chirp.

Lowdy laughed and clapped her hands. "Tes a bird-caller! Ain't it the cunningest thing? Do it again."

She did, and laughed too—then groaned and had to

hold her side. "Oh, Lowdy, I love it. Tell Galen I thank him, and I'll use it tomorrow to call the birds in right through that window. What a lovely present."

"'E likes you," Lowdy said simply. "If ee didn't 'ave a young man o' your own, I expect I might be jealous o' you, Lily Troublefield." Lily smiled, a little wanly, and Lowdy shrugged back at her. "'Ere now, drink this up, and then off you go t' sleep."

"But I don't want it, Lowdy; I don't need it anymore."

"This'm the last of it, and you're done. Come on, one last dose. Open up, Miss Button-lips. There, that weren't so terrible."

"Easy for you to say." She screwed up her face to keep from gagging at the bitter aftertaste of the hated laudanum. At least it was finished; she hoped never to have to swallow another mouthful of the vile stuff for as long as she lived.

"Guess what."

"What?"

"There'm a new housekeeper."

"No!"

"Mrs. *Carmichael*, if you please. Comes from Tedburn St. Mary, and talks regular English like you. Twur master's sister that found 'er and sent 'er, I heard. Came today, and didn't make us say prayers after supper. She'm youngerer'n 'Owe, and civil-like, not nasty. Galen d' think she's fine."

"Then she must be." Already her eyelids were getting heavy. A thought occurred to her. "I know you didn't get to hear your Methodist preacher that Sunday, Lowdy, because of—what happened to me, but did Galen go?"

"O' course not. 'E were that worried about you, and master sendin' 'im for surgeon and what-not, he didn't care t' go."

"Oh." Lily glanced down at her hands, twitching at the coverlet. "I might get a letter one day soon. Would you look for it, and bring it to me if it comes?"

"Ais, I will."

"Thank you."

Lowdy raised her black brows, waiting. But Lily said no more, and after a second the younger girl leaned down to put out the candle.

"Oh, don't blow it out."

"Ee'll be fast asleep in ten minutes."

"I know, but . . . leave it, please. I'd rather have it burning tonight."

"Have it, then. G'night, Lily."

"Good night. Thank you for taking care of me, Lowdy."

"Phaw," she exhaled, grinning, and scuffed out.

Lily sank back against the pillows and pulled the sheet up to her chin. The house was absolutely still, as if she were its only inhabitant. Drowsiness crept over her, and with it a thick, listless pall of depression. Howe's vicious beating and Trayer's attack had almost destroyed her; recovering from them had taken all her strength. But even at the lowest point, she'd never felt like this. She'd been in pain and distress, but always there had been something to fight for—even to hope for. At first it was Devon's sympathy, later his nerve-wracking formal appearances twice a day that had somehow made her forget how deep the rift was between them, and exactly what had caused it. And his company, odd and unsatisfying as it was, had planted a secret, unmentionable hope in her deepest heart. But tonight he hadn't come, and she knew he would never come again, and it mortified her to admit even to herself what that secret hope had been. Now there really was nothing to do except to wait until she was well, and then leave Darkstone Manor.

Something, the softest sound, made her open her eyes.

"I'm sorry if I woke you. Were you sleeping?"

"No. Almost, but—no." Except for the white of his ruffled shirtfront, he was almost invisible in the dark doorway. In the comparative brightness of candlelight, she felt vulnerable and exposed, and wondered how long he had been standing there. "Come in," she invited softly.

He moved into the room. "How are you feeling?"

"Much better, thank you," she answered in her rusty voice. They had said the same words to each other for the last ten nights, never varying the programme. She waited for her racing heart to slow, filled with a mixture of gladness and anger, the latter at herself because of the former. She saw that he wore a long, wine-colored waistcoat with his shirt and black breeches; he smelled faintly of leather and sweat, and she guessed he'd been riding.

"Lowdy said you seemed tired."

"You spoke to her?"

"Just now. Are you certain you're all right?"

"Quite certain." The inanity of this conversation rivaled all their previous ones, she was thinking when, all of a sudden, an ear-piercing squeak split the silence. "Oh!" She stifled a giggle. Devon's eyes widened. She'd forgotten all about Galen's birdcalling device. It still lay in her hands, and she'd turned the handle out of nervousness. "It's a present," she explained, holding it up in the light. "From Mr. MacLeaf. He made it himself. It—calls the birds."

"Very nice."

"Lowdy says you've hired a new housekeeper," she mentioned, determined to hold up her end of the conversation. A wave of drowsiness surged through her, then tapered off.

"Yes," he said, clearing his throat, coming closer than usual—actually standing at the side of the bed. "A Mrs. Carmichael. She seems . . . competent."

Lily thought of many things she could have said to that, some of them bitter. But she fingered her bird-caller and said nothing.

"But then, so did Mrs. Howe. I've learned that the

appearance of competence isn't the only quality one should look for when hiring a person to oversee one's household. And that . . . it doesn't excuse one from responsibility for the people in one's employ."

She looked at him closely for the first time. He looked extraordinarily uncomfortable, hands clasped behind his back, scowling ferociously, eyes fastened on something in the general direction of her knees. It dawned on her that he was trying to make an apology. The realization dazzled her. Devon Darkwell—*apologizing*. Stranger still was the strong impulse she felt to help him.

She said, "Would you like to sit down?" He looked behind him for the chair. "Here," she specified, smoothing the space between her hip and the edge of the bed. She felt his startled eyes on her, but kept her gaze on her hand lightly patting the mattress. He sat.

A minute passed, and she began to fear that another of their long, dreadful silences was coming. Half turned to her, he'd drawn one knee up on the bed; she could touch it if she wanted to just by reaching a hand out. She cast about for something to say, and seized on an observation about the unseasonably cool nights they'd been having. She was just about to utter it when he spoke.

"Mrs. Howe was stealing from me, Lily. I found out yesterday when I went over the household accounts. She'd been paying tradesmen a fraction of the figure she got out of me and pocketing the difference. One of her most profitable ploys was to charge me an inflated amount of money for food for the domestic staff, and then feed them the cheapest stuff she could buy. Swill, from what I've been told. The same with supplies— soap, linens, clothing, the simplest necessities. I gave her money for them, she kept it, and charged the servants for them a second time, behind my back."

Lily blinked up at him, aware of a powerful sense of relief. She had made an assumption that he knew all about the meager lot of his servants, that Howe's niggardly treatment of them was at his direction, or at least with his consent. To learn otherwise made her feel lighthearted—and strangely, like crying. She started to speak when she saw that his face had grown dark and grim.

"I'm sorry they're gone, Howe and her bastard son. If they were still here, I swear before God, I'd—" He halted, and clamped down on some powerful emotion. "What happened"—he took a deep breath—"what happened was my fault. If I could change—anything . . ." He stopped again.

Lily felt tears burn again at the back of her throat. She searched his eyes, so somber. The taut parentheses on either side of his mouth were white with tension; she wanted to soothe them with her fingertips. "It's all right," she whispered. "You didn't know."

"No. *I didn't know.* But that was my crime, not my excuse."

"But it's all right now."

Her understanding goaded him. "No, it's far from all right. You could have been killed. Or raped, or hurt so badly—"

"But I wasn't. And you—"

"But you could have been."

"Dev—" She stumbled over his name. She had no right to call him that now. They were both silent, hampered and uneasy, not looking at each other. But she couldn't stop her hand from going out to him, hesitantly. She laid her fingers on his wrist, ever so lightly. Just to touch him. To soothe him, and to take comfort for herself. She closed her eyes and felt another surge of blackness rushing toward her.

"Lily," he said, bowing his head. "I can't ask you to forgive me. I only want you to know that I'm sorry. I'm so sorry." He kept speaking, his voice low and intense; but in spite of her best efforts, her grip on the meaning of the words loosened and loosened until finally it seemed only fair to tell him.

"Devon, please stop talking before I fall asleep."

"What?"

She thought he sounded a little hurt. "Lowdy made me take the last of the laudanum just before you came. I can't keep my eyes open." It was literally true; she was speaking to him with them closed. "I don't understand why, but I know you want me to be hard on you, not to forgive you. But I really can't, it's not"—she yawned widely, barely getting her hand up in time to cover it—"not in my nature. What happened was dreadful," she went on sleepily, "but it's over now. I'm going to get well. Thank you for being sorry—" she tried to open her eyes when she heard his impatient snort, but she just couldn't manage it—"and thank you for telling me that you are. Now . . ." Now, what? She had no idea, and she was too tired to think about it. "Now I have to go to sleep." Her hand relaxed and fell open on his thigh.

He blinked down at it. He felt the beginning of a smile, his first in a long time. He enclosed her limp hand in both of his, examining the calloused palm, the long, slim fingers. He fought the impulse to laugh when she let out a delicate snore, just before pulling her hand out of his and settling gingerly onto her side.

"Good night, Lily," he said in a conversational tone. Nothing, not even a flicker of an eyelash. She was fast asleep. "Sweet Lily," he said in a whisper. He watched her a moment longer, beguiled. Unable to resist, he bent and pressed a light, lingering kiss on her cheekbone. Then he blew out her nub of a candle and left, closing the door quietly behind him.

# Sixteen

"Aren't you ready yet?"

Lily looked up, startled. "No, I'm—for what? Aren't I supposed to—"

"Meet Clay. I told him I'd come and get you."

"Oh."

Squinting, Devon moved farther into the room. Lily sat in a splash of sunlight before the open windows, dressed in her nightgown and cloth slippers and sewing on something mustard-colored and voluminous draped across her lap. Dusty sun bars touched color in her dark red hair and made the green specks in her eyes, usually subdued, look almost gaudy. But it was her smile that dazzled him. He returned it unguardedly, and for fully half a minute they were too absorbed in beaming at each other to speak.

Lily recalled herself with a becoming blush and finished pulling the needle through the narrow seam she was sewing. "I'm not quite ready. Your brother said two o'clock, and I'm about three minutes shy of finishing this."

"What is it?"

"A dressing gown. I haven't got one, so I'm altering this to fit me."

"Ah." He frowned down, observing the lengthening line of her delicate stitches. "How is it that you haven't got any clothes, Lily?"

Her fingers stilled. What was it she'd told Mrs. Howe? Something about being robbed at a hiring fair. "They were stolen, just before I came here." The words almost stuck in her throat. Lying to Devon repelled her now, but she shrank from telling him the truth. It wasn't time. Not yet. Working in haste, she finished her seam, looped a tidy knot, and snipped the thread with a pair of scissors. "There, it's finished. What do you think?" She held up the robe for his inspection, praying he would ask no more questions.

"Not your color," he said mildly. She smiled—a bit mysteriously, it seemed to Devon. "Why is that amusing?"

She grinned outright. "Whose color do you think it is?"

He looked at the robe, then back at her. The light dawned. "Mrs. Howe's?"

"Yes! Clay said it would be all right if I had her clothes—she left them *all*, Devon, a whole wardrobe full—and tried to make a few things from them for myself. This is my first attempt." She surveyed her handiwork critically; it wasn't too bad, she decided, although he was right about the color. She glanced at him expectantly. "Oh," she realized, seeing his face, "you don't like it."

"No, it's fine." He took the coarse cotton out of her hands and pretended to examine it. "You sew very well." What he was thinking was that he detested the thought of Lily working on Howe's—or anyone else's—ugly, cast-off garments in order to have something to wear. He was prepared to buy her all the clothes she wanted, and a great deal more. But first they had to come to an understanding. And it was too soon, she was still too ill, to broach the subject of the arrangement he had in mind.

"It's all right," she assured him, misunderstanding his expression. "I don't mind that they were hers, really I don't. In fact"—she smiled and looked away, a little embarrassed—"if you want to know the truth, I enjoy cutting them up. The *irony* of it pleases me. These are even her slippers. They're miles too big"—she stuck her feet out to show him—"but I can't help liking it that I'm wearing them. Do you think that's childish?"

He chuckled, then laughed. "No, I think it's delightfully human."

She blushed as if he'd paid her a rare compliment.

He reached for her hand. "Well, stand up, let's see how well you've done. If it falls off you, Howe will have had the last laugh after all." It astonished him that he—that they—could joke about his housekeeper in any way, any context. And it pleased him, because he knew it was a measure of the extent to which Lily had healed, in mind as well as body.

She stood, her borrowed nightrail billowing around her ankles. It was full, high-collared, and anything but sheer. Nevertheless, she felt self-conscious standing in front of him in it, he fully dressed. Silly; he'd seen her in significantly less. Still—

"Come on, put your arms in. There." She stood still while he settled the robe around her shoulders and joined all the frog fasteners down the front. The best he could say for it was that it fit. "It fits."

But Lily was thrilled. "Oh, it does, it really does. In fact, if I say so myself, it's perfect." She made a slow turn in front of him, ridiculously pleased with herself.

*You're perfect*, he thought as he took her hand and guided her out of the room at a sedate pace.

"Clay said today was an occasion, and not just because it's my first time outdoors. Do you know what he meant?"

"Ha! He's milking this for all it's worth, I see."

"What?"

"He's telling everyone today is his last day of 'freedom.' Tomorrow he starts work at the mine."

They stopped at the top of the staircase. Lily picked up her skirts, hoping she wouldn't trip in her roomy carpet slippers. But before she could step down, Devon put an arm around her shoulders and one behind her knees and lifted her off her feet. "Oh, no, I can walk, really, I'm perfectly—"

"Quiet. I'm not taking any chances with you," he said gruffly. True, but an even stronger motivation was the need to hold her. She'd lost a lot of weight, but the solid feel of her in his arms, the living, companionable substance of her filled something inside he hadn't realized was quite so empty.

As he carried her down the stairs and through the corridors of the cool, dim house, neither spoke, and a silent, breathless awareness replaced the lighthearted banter they were growing used to. At the doors to the wide, shady terrace, he stopped again. Lily breathed softly, hands clasped over his far shoulder, watching the steady pulse that throbbed in his neck. If he turned his head just a little, their lips would touch. The odor of roses was faint and teasing on the capricious breeze, the sea a subtle, gossipy whisper. Their expressive silence went on. She should ask why they were standing here, it occurred to her vaguely; but she knew why, and to ask would break the spell. More than anything she wanted to lay her head on his shoulder and press her lips to the side of his throat. Or tug on his earlobe with her teeth. The seconds wandered past, lazy and unnoticed, until Lily finally murmured, "I must be heavy."

He could have held her all day, all night. Forever. "Light as a feather," he answered. A banal analogy. "Or a lily," he amended whimsically, watching her soft, sensitive mouth. "A long, graceful lily, as white as your skin."

A drawn-out sigh was the only response she was capable of making. She wet her lips with the tip of her tongue and felt his chest begin to rise and fall against her bosom in a different rhythm. The longing to kiss him was like wine in a tall glass, rising to the brim, ready to overflow. She said, "Dev," in a husky whisper, and closed her eyes.

"Well, are you coming out or not?" called Clay from behind the lacy trellis of greenbrier and clematis they'd thought had concealed them. "What's keeping you? Is Lily all right?"

Devon made a noise in his throat that summed up perfectly all the frustration Lily was feeling at that moment, and stepped down from the shallow portico to the flagstone path.

"Finally. I was almost ready to come and get you." With a put-upon groan, Clay set down his lemonade, closed his newspaper, pulled his bare feet from the edge of the wrought iron table, and stood up.

"Yes, I can see you were eaten up with worry about us," Devon observed. He set Lily gently on her feet and pulled a chair out for her. Neither looked at the other, but they wore identical small, secret smiles.

"Lily, you look wonderful today," Clay said gallantly. "Pink and healthy and rosy-cheeked."

"Thank you." She could imagine exactly how rosy-cheeked she must look.

"But I can't say I think much of that dressing gown. No offense, it doesn't do you justice."

"So I've been told." She took a deep breath. "Oh, it feels lovely to be outside. What a *beautiful* day."

"Isn't it? My last, you know. From now on it's nothing but black, dripping pits for me, a candle in my hat, burrowing about in tunnels like a mole."

Devon rolled his eyes. "Clay will persist in this child-ish conceit that he's going to work *in* the mine," he explained for Lily's benefit. "He thinks it'll buy him sympathy."

"I see." She smiled across at Clay and asked, "Why are you going to work if you hate the idea of it so?"

"Because I can't stand Dev's nagging another day," he answered promptly. He held up his glass. "Let's drink to my last afternoon on the earth's surface," he proposed dramatically. Devon chuckled and poured a glass of lemonade for himself from the pitcher. He pushed something under a towel toward Lily, brows raised expectantly.

"Oh, no," she wailed when she saw what was under the cloth. "Oh, that's not fair." It was Dr. Marsh's "tonic," a yellow, viscous brew as foul as anything Cabby Dartaway ever dreamed of concocting, and she had to drink a glass of it every day. "You're just doing this to get back at me, Devon, and I don't think it's very nice of you."

He widened his eyes in pretended shock and covered his heart with his hand. "How could you think such a base, petty thing? I tell you, Lily, I'm deeply offended."

She giggled at his silliness; she'd never seen him so playful.

"That reminds me. I'm changing the toast." Clay's voice, serious for once, drew their attention from each other. "I've never thanked you, Lily, for taking care of Dev when he was hurt. It was my fault; I'm the one who got him into the whole stupid mess. It could have ended very badly. Mostly because of you, it didn't." He lifted his glass again. "To you, Lily. With my gratitude and friendship."

"Hear, hear," Devon seconded quietly.

The brothers drank while Lily stared down at her hands. She murmured something inaudible and turned her glass around and around in circles on the table.

"You still have to drink it," Devon reminded her, and they all laughed, a little self-consciously.

"Oh, very well." She squeezed her eyes shut and downed the noxious liquid in four swallows, shuddering afterwards and making exaggerated sounds of disgust.

"Good girl," Devon said warmly.

Her eyes watered, but she smiled back in pure pleasure, feeling again as if he'd given her the compliment of her life.

Clay looked back and forth between them, fascinated.

"So. Tomorrow you start a new job." A new life, she might have called it. She found it slightly odd, although understandable, that none of them ever alluded directly to what Clay's "job" had been immediately preceding his new one. It had affected all of them in one way or another, and yet a sort of cautious, well-bred tact prevented anyone from mentioning it. "Will you be Mr. Morgan's assistant, then?" It was an innocent question, so Clay's suddenly cool, hooded look confounded her. She wanted to bite her tongue.

"Yes."

The one-word answer was loaded with some meaning she couldn't fathom. She glanced at Devon in perplexity.

"Only at first," he put in smoothly. "Clay's going to find out if he likes doing an honest day's work. Then . . . some other arrangements will be made."

She felt as if she'd floundered into deep waters that were none of her business. For a tense moment she fiddled with her glass again. When no one spoke she said, "May I have some lemonade, please?" and Clay reached for the pitcher, grim relief evident in his face.

Devon said something incontestable, the conversation became general, and in no time they were all at ease again. Lily basked in a lovely, unwonted feeling of acceptance. The affection between Devon and his brother was obvious, and to be included in their companionable railery made her happier than she could remember being in a long time. She loved watching them laugh and joke with each other, sensing an understanding between them that went beyond brotherliness. She almost felt jealous of the easy smiles Clay could draw from Devon with such effortlessness, but her envy was nothing compared to the pleasure Devon's unusual high spirits gave her. She never considered that her own presence had anything to do with it, nor that Clay was as surprised and intrigued by his brother's uncharacteristic good humor as she was.

"Excuse me. Afternoon t' you."

Devon glanced up at his land steward, standing a respectful distance away, twisting the wide black brim of his hat in his hand. "Arthur," he greeted him, nodding. "Do you need me?"

"Ais, in a manner o' speaking."

Devon pushed back his chair and walked over to Cobb. The two men had a short conversation, then Devon turned back to the table. "I've got to go have a look at Robert Slopes's cottage. Cobb says his wife tried to burn it down last night."

He stared back impassively when Clay's first impulse was to laugh, and Lily had a swift insight into one of the differences between the two brothers. If Clay had been the firstborn, she wondered idly, would he have been the responsible one? Or was the distinction more fundamental, more a matter of nature than order of birth?

"Take care of Lily," Devon told his brother with a smile that didn't diminish the seriousness of the admonition. "Don't let her get too tired. I'll be back in a few hours."

When Devon turned his smile on her, she felt a queer twist in her chest. She watched him walk away, admiring his long-legged stride and the smooth, fluid movement of his wide shoulders, until he and Mr. Cobb were out of sight.

She felt Clay's intent gaze and turned to look at him, then away to hide a blush. She had let too much show in her face, she realized. What must he think of her—the girl who had once worn cap and apron and brought him his breakfast on a tray? Now she was his brother's coddled and protected . . . what? "Companion"? She had no idea. Clay's bewilderment over this odd turn of events must be extreme, although it could hardly be stronger than her own. She saw that he was still watching her, his expression frankly bemused, and blurted out the first thing that came into her mind.

"How did Mr. Cobb lose his hand?"

Clay looked startled, but answered readily enough. "It was a long time ago, when he was fourteen. Cobb's father was my father's steward. We grew up together at Darkstone, played together like brothers. When I was four, Dev and Cobb and I were playing where we weren't allowed to play—in an abandoned tin mine on the estate. It's been razed since then, but at the time there was a way to get into the main shaft if you were small enough and curious enough. We were."

"What happened?"

"I don't remember it very well, but somehow I got into a long, narrow crawl space above the shaft roof where the timbers were half rotted. And then for some reason I was afraid to come out. Dev crawled in to get me, and the strut collapsed. We were both trapped."

"How old was Devon?"

"Ten. So then Cobb climbed up and got his shoulders under the broken roof of the thing somehow, giving us enough space to slither out. And at the last second, everything came down on him. His arm was crushed. They had to take his hand off."

"How horrible," breathed Lily, imagining it. "You must have felt—terribly—" She stopped in confusion.

"Guilty? I suppose I should have, but I was so little. Devon's the one who really suffered."

Yes, thought Lily, he would have. Even at ten, he'd

have taken on his shoulders the burden of responsibility for Cobb's tragic accident.

"Dev was always the sober one," Clay said as if reading her mind. "Even when he was little he was serious and intense, like my father. He felt things more deeply than other people—or," he specified, laughing, "certainly more than I did. And sometimes that made him unhappy."

"I see." But she didn't, not really, and a natural reticence prevented her from asking questions.

"Do you know about Dev's wife?"

Lily started. Was her face that transparent? "No, I—that is, I've heard that she died."

"Yes, she's dead. Her name was Maura." He put his dusty bare feet on the chair Devon had vacated and folded his arms across his chest. He wore no coat or waistcoat, and he'd rolled his shirt sleeves up to the elbows. He looked completely relaxed, the picture of the indolent country squire at home, but there was tension in the set of his lips and a new seriousness in his fine blue eyes. "Devon fell in love with her when he was twenty-three. She was half Irish, half French. Black-haired, white-skinned. Very beautiful. She was my sister's oldest child's governess. Needless to say, it wasn't a suitable match."

"No," Lily said faintly. "No, I can see that."

"They had a clandestine affair. But Dev couldn't leave it at that. I don't know if it was his passion for her or his sense of honor, but he made up his mind to marry her. You can imagine the family's reaction."

"They must have been—shocked."

"Horrified. My father threatened to cut him off, everyone was universally against it—even after Dev found out she was pregnant and told them so. But he was set on it and nothing else would do. He told them he had to marry his own child's mother, and it didn't matter to him if she were a milkmaid."

He reached for his glass and swallowed a sip of

lemonade. Lily sat perfectly still, making pleats in the cloth belt of her dressing gown, waiting.

"So he married her. My father didn't cut him off—that had never been anything but a threat. He could have brought her here to live, or to my mother's house in Devonshire, but instead he bought a farm in Dorset with his own money and set out to learn farming. She was from Dorset. He thought it would please her." He grimaced and fell silent again, as if it hurt to recollect the rest of the story.

"Clay, you don't have to tell me."

He shook his head quickly. "I don't know what their life was like, because Devon won't talk about it. The baby was born—they named him Edward, after my father—and eight months later Maura took all the money she could find in the house and ran away with Dev's hired man. For some reason, God knows why, they took the child with them."

"My God."

"Dev went after them. He searched for weeks, and finally found his baby in Crewkerne. Dead from small-pox, in the cottage of an old woman Maura had given him to so that she and her lover could travel faster. A little later he found them as well, in a pauper's grave in Weymouth. They'd been waiting for a boat to take them to France when the disease killed them, too."

He stood up and went to stand at the top of the terrace steps, facing the deep blue of the Channel. Lily stayed where she was. She pressed her fingers to her lips and blinked back tears of sorrow. *Devon.* She wanted to see him so badly, to hold him. The terrible story filled her with grief for him and his infant son, and with a cold and murderous fury toward the woman named Maura. She'd thought of her from time to time, but only the bare fact of her; she'd never been substantial enough in Lily's mind to warrant more than an occasional twinge of unhappy curiosity. Now she saw her clearly, with her black hair and her white skin, her corrupt and treacherous heart. *Maura*. She even hated her name. She wanted to do violence to her.

When a little of her composure returned, she stood up and went to join Clay. She touched his arm; he pivoted to face her. She could imagine that the bleakness in his face mirrored the same emotion in hers. "Thank you for telling me."

"I'm not sure why I did," he admitted with a hint of his old smile behind his eyes. "Maybe because Dev seems almost happy these days."

She shook her head. "I'm afraid you're mistaken if you think that has anything to do with me. But I—care about him, and I'm grateful to you for telling me what happened. He . . . never would have."

They stood side by side, staring out at a restless high tide, thinking their separate thoughts. "He came back to Cornwall," Clay resumed after a minute, "and lived like a mad recluse for about a year. None of us could help him. He was literally untouchable. The only comfort he could find was in drunkenness. That was the worst time," he confided, turning to look at her. "We'd been so close before, but he couldn't even talk to me. I missed him," he said simply.

"Then my father died. It's ironic, but that's what made Dev start to heal. Finally he was able to come out of himself and look around at other people. His world was black, but he'd learned he could survive in it, so he was able to comfort us. Especially my mother, who was completely shattered. After that, he threw himself into the running of Darkstone. It wasn't for the money, of course—he could live like a king for the rest of his life without lifting a finger. But he needed the work, the routine, I guess, to give him back his equilibrium."

He faced her again, this time with a real smile. "He's still not the brother I grew up with, but he's a great deal better off than he was five years ago. And you can think what you like, Miss Troublefield, but part of it is because of you."

Simple words, spoken in a light tone. Clay could have no idea of their effect on Lily. She turned her face aside, fearful again that he would see too much. The thought of meaning something to Devon, the possibility that he might care for her — But it couldn't be. In her heart she knew better. Clay was being kind, or naïve. Devon's interest in her had always been quite narrow and specific. At least, having listened to Clay, she had a better understanding of *why*, what it was in him that would not allow him to see her, or perhaps any woman, as anything but a bed partner — and a temporary one at that. Someone to give money to in the morning — or perhaps, if she were very special, at the end of the month.

"You may believe whatever you like, too," she answered, striving to echo Clay's lightheartedness in her voice, "but what Devon feels for me is a very nice mixture of gratitude and guilt. Which is quite wonderful, and something a bright housemaid would be foolish not to exploit, don't you think? Why, if I play my cards right, I might even get him to buy me a new dressing gown. Then I won't have to listen to any more slanderous and unkind slurs on this one."

"You're no housemaid."

Her teasing smile froze; her heart stuttered. He couldn't know, he *couldn't*. "Would that that were true," she answered, hoping she sounded wistful.

"You're a lovely young lady who seems to have fallen on hard times. I doubt that Dev could do much better with a countess."

Too fast to hide, tears welled in her eyes and spilled down her cheeks. It was because she'd been ill that she was so emotional these days, she told herself. But Clay's sweetness undid her.

He laughed softly and brushed the tears away, then

took her hand and led her toward the house. "Enough excitement for you today, Miss Lily. You're to take to your bed for the rest of the afternoon."

"Oh, but—"

"No arguments. I want you hale and hearty on Saturday."

"Saturday?"

"Your first *real* outing. I'm selling the *Spider*, did Dev tell you? That's my ship. I'd like you to see her before I do—help me say good-bye to her and all that. She's lying in the Fowey, below Lostwithiel. What do you say?"

"Well, I—I don't know. Will Devon come?"

"Most certainly. He'd never trust me alone with you."

"You are very silly," she scolded him with a misty-eyed smile. "And, yes, I'd love to come."

# Seventeen

Lily awoke to the high, plaintive cry of stone curlews nearby, and for several blank seconds she couldn't remember where she was. A heavy footstep overhead confused her further. Then she heard the watery slap of waves and noticed the gentle rocking motion of the feather bed she was lying on, and memory filtered back. She was aboard the *Spider*, having a nap in the captain's cabin.

And quite a fine cabin it was. Not luxurious—too small and tidy for that—but wonderfully comfortable in a masculine, unadorned style that rather surprised her. The "young master," for all his kindness to her and his abundant charm, was not a man Lily had ever been able to take quite seriously. Now that she'd seen his ship, however, and listened to his energetic, informative—and exhausting—commentary on the sloop's innumerable seafaring attributes, she was ready to revise her opinion. Clayton Darkwell might be carefree, irresponsible, and immature, the classic younger son, but about ships and sailing he was plainly a bona fide, unmitigated expert.

He also had a fanatic's habit of assuming that everyone else shared his obsession. "I know what you're thinking," he'd told Lily thirty seconds after she'd stepped from the Darkwell carriage and beheld the *Spider*, tied up below in a picturesque river estuary. "For her size, she's grossly over-rigged. But that's what makes her so fast! Besides the gaff main, she carries double square topsails, roached and sheeted to that spread arm low down on the mast, and a big jib sail and a flying jib as well. That's why she needs those great running backstays, to take the driving strain. That's why she's clinker built, too, which is much stronger than carvel. Come on, let's go aboard."

Lily and Devon had exchanged blank, humorous glances before following him down the dusty, twisting path to the water's edge. Clay whistled, and across the way a head popped up above the sloop's gunwale. A man waved. Soon a small, single-masted boat Clay called a lugger was being rowed toward them by the man who had waved, and a few minutes later they were all on board the *Spider*.

The man was Wiley Falk, Clay's first mate, and he'd been overseeing "repairs" to the sloop for the past two weeks. When Lily asked innocently what kind of repairs, Clay only winked. Devon made a pained face and answered for him: "They had to do with the little matter of a false bottom and a thirty-foot bowsprit. It was thought that potential buyers might find such amenities a trifle odd. Not to mention illegal."

During the tour that ensued, Lily learned about the *Spider's* size (fifty-two feet long, twenty-two wide), top speed (nine and a half knots), tonnage (sixty, empty of contraband), and artillery (twenty eight-pound carriage guns, twenty swivels, and a carronade). She also got surprisingly tired in a short time. It was Devon who noticed it, almost before she did, and insisted that she lie down for a while in Clay's cabin.

She wondered how long she'd been sleeping. She felt wonderful. But what time was it? Through the single tiny porthole high in the wall—the bulkhead? the partition?—the sky was a soft, cloudless pink. She stretched—carefully; her ribs were still tender, and sudden movements could still cause searing pain—and sat up. What a comfortable bed, not at all what she'd have expected on such a trim, businesslike boat. The thought crossed her mind that in all likelihood the *Spider's* captain entertained ladies in his cabin, and in his bunk, from time to time. There was a soft knock at the door—the hatch? the companionway? Maybe it was just the "door." Her nap seemed to have scrambled all her new nautical terminology. "Come in!"

It was Devon. Although she still wore everything but her shoes, something made her pull the soft muslin sheet up to her shoulders and comb a self-conscious hand through her tousled hair. At the same time, a deep, stirring gladness welled up at the sight of him, and she sent him a sweet, welcoming smile. He was dressed casually today, in blue broadcloth coat and buckskin breeches, and she thought she had never seen him so handsome. He had to duck his head to clear the threshold, and once inside, the breadth of his powerful body made the cabin seem even smaller. He was holding a bulky, paper-wrapped package under one arm. "Hello," she said with a touch of shyness because of the way he was looking at her. "I just woke up."

"So I see. Did you sleep well?"

"Wonderfully well, thank you. What time is it?"

"Around six, I should think."

"Six! Heavens, you and Clay must have wanted to go home long before now. Why didn't you wake me?"

"There was no need; we've decided to stay."

"Stay?"

"Overnight, and leave in the morning. Clay's got a farewell supper planned for this evening—on deck. You don't mind, do you? We thought the ride back might tire you out again."

"Oh no, really, I'm—"

"And besides, he wants to stay. He says it's his last night on the *Spider* and he wants to have his friends with him."

"Oh." That Clay might consider her a friend moved her in an unexpected way. "Then I'd love to stay."

"Good." He came closer. "This is something for you, Lily. For tonight." He laid the package beside her on the bunk.

"What is it?"

"You'll see."

He looked mysterious, and quite pleased with himself. Lily fingered the string bow on top of the bundle and smiled up at him. He'd never given her a present before. "Thank you."

"You're welcome. There are candles here on the desk if you need more light." He went to the door. "Mr. Falk has managed somehow—we don't ask how—to supply us with a picnic. Everything's ready. Clay says to tell you to hurry up because he's starving."

Lily laughed. "I'll be with you in two minutes."

The mysterious look returned. "A little longer than that, maybe." Then he was through the door and gone.

"Did she like it?"

"I don't know, I left before she opened it."

Clay handed his brother a mug of rum and lemon juice and leaned back against the mainmast to watch the sunset. "To smuggled rum toddies and French silk," he toasted with a grin.

Devon eyed him narrowly. "To the *last* of smuggled rum and French silk. That's what you meant to say, I'm sure."

"Of course," Clay assured him, eyes twinkling. They drank.

It was low tide; oyster-catchers swooped down in a flash of black and white to feed in the mudbanks along the shore. Farther out a heron stalked, then stopped to brood, head buried in its feathers. Gazing inland toward the gently wooded slopes, Devon saw none of them. He was waiting for only one thing, the sight of Lily in a pale rose-colored gown made of the richest silk, low-cut and long-sleeved, with delicate Brussels lace on all the layers of the graceful full skirts. Would she wear her hair down? If she did, it would put the paltry red sunset to shame. He wished he could have given her shoes tonight too, fragile French slippers with little round heels. And jewelry. Jade and amethyst, sapphires and emeralds and aquamarine. She would look beautiful in diamonds too, at her throat and on her slender wrists. He saw her with gold loops in her ears and silver rings on her long, strong fingers. And pearls, wound into the softly curling strands of her beautiful hair.

He heard her footsteps on the ladder. He turned his back on Clay in the middle of a sentence and went forward to offer his hand. Her head and shoulders appeared above the companionway. His smile of anticipation wavered and disappeared; he stopped in his tracks halfway to her. She had on her plain gray dimity frock. He shoved his hands in his pockets and stared at her without speaking.

He was angry, she could tell from his eyes. But he was trying not to show it. Clay sidled around him; she took his outstretched hand gratefully and stepped up on the deck. She gave soft, meaningless responses to his too-animated chatter and sipped from the glass of Madeira wine he gave her, watching Devon all the while. After a few minutes the tension began to leave his shoulders and he made a few formal attempts to join in their conversation. Boldly, she moved closer to him. Clay was saying something about his ship. Devon looked at her directly for the first time, and she took the opportunity to send him a smile of apology, hoping he would understand. His flinty blue gaze softened while she watched, and her feather-light heart beat erratically. She resisted the urge to reach for his hand or brush her fingers across the hard line of his cheekbone. But over the rim of her glass, she sent him a fervent look that said *Thank you.*

The river was calm, the air soft. The sun threw a last, theatrical shaft of light on the water and disappeared behind a low bank of clouds. The sky turned from gilt to rust; an owl called from the pine trees across the glassy inlet. Clay lit a lantern. Then, with a flourish, he set out their supper of sausage pies and violet pudding on the upended flat bottom of a dinghy. They ate it sitting on line boxes.

The conversation was animated and eclectic. It began with Clay's provocative—and, Lily guessed from Devon's expression, rather shopworn—declaration that "free-trading," as he insisted on calling it, sprang from a fundamental human instinct to thwart the law, and that even an honest man felt a tingle of excitement when he succeeded. That led to a heated argument over the moral and economic implications of the smuggling trade. Clay claimed that as long as the damned government declared more than a thousand articles of imported merchandise dutiable, citizens would continue, without a qualm of conscience, to smuggle tea, salt, brandy, silk—even playing cards!—into the country at every opportunity. Devon argued just as passionately that smuggling was devastating the economy; the cure, he agreed, was to lower the tariffs on liquor and soap and all the rest. In the meantime, *responsible* men would do well to deal within the framework of the constitution—which, incidentally, provided them with more personal freedoms than any other government in the world—and work in *legal* ways to dismantle an archaic system of duties and excises and taxes.

At the gentlemen's feet was a half-anker of Marmande cognac whose origin no one was tactless enough to mention. The vehemence of Clay's convictions rose in direct proportion to his access to the cognac. The government Devon defended became the butt of his ridicule. He derided the popular wisdom that the poor ought to *save* more, that it was their own fault if they couldn't live within their means. Fat, gouty old men in Parliament had the hypocrisy to suggest that the problem was profligacy, not poverty. And they wanted to reform the poor through education—especially Sunday school, he noted with a sneer, so as not to interfere with their productivity on the other six days. Devon shot back that Clay was perfectly right, but that the way to change things was to give *jobs* to the poor—in copper mines, for example—not charitable handouts derived from the illegal profits of free-trading.

Lily listened, captivated. She'd never heard politics argued by men who were actually in a position to change things, to influence affairs of state. Her father had been a nominal Whig, but only because he'd distrusted Tories even more. She sat quietly, contributing little, and yet for some reason she didn't feel neglected. She had an idea that both men were aware of her, no matter how warm the discussion became. She also sensed that they were much closer to agreement than they pretended, and chose opposite sides of every issue mostly for the fun of arguing.

Her back ached a little. When the conversation shifted to the physical, moral, and mental shortcomings of the royal family, she murmured an excuse and got up to watch the moon and stars on the river from above the bowsprit. Across the water, beyond the sloping gorse cliffs along the shore, she heard a nightjar call, its cry a rhythmic rise and fall, faintly disturbing.

Nodding at something Clay was saying, Devon watched her. She stood at the edge of the flickering ring of yellow lantern light, gazing up at the star-strewn sky. Even in her shabby gray dress, she was beautiful. He had known that, of course, known it since the first moment he'd seen her. But he hadn't let her loveliness affect him in any way but physically; if anything, he'd held it against her. What had changed? He knew her now. Against his will—and hers too, he didn't doubt—he'd begun to understand her. Besides a beautiful face, he knew that she had a gentle and generous heart. She could no longer be neatly labeled as a woman who couldn't be trusted. Too many times she'd proven to him the opposite. If he continued to resist her, it would only be because of cowardice. Besides, it wasn't as if he meant to *marry* her. And regardless of the consequences of an affair between them, he could not lose everything. That only happened to a man once. Because it had already happened to him, he was safe. And she was irresistible.

"Well," said Clay rather loudly, "time I was on my way."

Lily turned around in surprise. "Where are you going?"

"I told Wiley we'd celebrate tonight."

"But—"

"In Lostwithiel. There's a kiddlywink there where my crew and I have spent many a happy hour."

"A what?"

"An owler's inn," Devon explained.

"Oh." At least she knew now that an owler was a smuggler. But Clay's leaving startled her. "Do you really have to go?"

He shot Devon a sly look. "Oh, indeed yes, it's been arranged for weeks. The captain and his mate, you know, enjoying their last night as carefree sailors together." He walked to the port side and threw his legs over in an agile leap, landing on the rope ladder. "Good night to you both. The evening's been a great pleasure, and I thank you for sharing it with me. See you in the morning." His head disappeared. A moment later they heard the creak of oarlocks and the splash of water, then silence.

He was deliberately leaving them alone; that fact was as clear to Lily as if he'd shouted it. And Devon knew it too. She leaned back against the gunwale, resting her forearms along the top, and watched him come slowly toward her.

He came so close she could see the turquoise in his eyes even in the pale moonlight. "Do you think he'll really be able to leave all this?" she asked in a stalling, not-quite-steady voice, with a gesture that included the *Spider*, the river, and the sky.

But Devon had no intention of talking about Clay. "I don't know. Why didn't you wear the dress, Lily?"

She searched his face for a hint of anger, but there was none now. "Why did you give it to me?" she countered softly.

"To make you smile."

She smiled now. "No other reason?"

He understood the question perfectly, and answered it with the truth. "I want to take care of you."

"Do you? Why? A few weeks ago you wanted to be done with me. You offered me money. You didn't want to see me again."

He wondered if the words hurt her as much as they hurt him. But she wasn't accusing him; her tone was gentle and sad, not bitter. Again he answered honestly. "I don't know what's changed."

But Lily thought she knew. She'd called his new feelings for her "a nice mixture of gratitude and guilt." Now she knew what had happened to him, and she was not so devastated by his distrust. But it still hurt. "Are you asking me to be your mistress?"

Her directness startled, then relieved him. "Yes."

"I refuse. I will never give you my body in return for money. Or pretty dresses, or a place to live." Trying not to tremble, she looked him in the eye. One hand stole to the sleeve of his coat, for courage. Her voice started out strong but ended in a whisper. "I will give it to you for nothing."

She hadn't planned to say it, hadn't even known she was thinking it. But she loved him. The knowledge made her ache, for with it came the certainty that he would hurt her. It didn't matter now. She had loved him for a long time, and she believed she always would.

He didn't move or speak. She brought his motionless hand to her lips and kissed his fingers. He was wrestling with disbelief, and Lily knew an instant of loathing for the woman who had made him this way. "Dev," she murmured. "My love. It's so simple." She put her arms around him and kissed his lips.

He embraced her automatically, but he was still incredulous. He drew back to see her, and the solemn sweetness glowing in her silvery eyes assured him it was true, all of it. The breeze caught a wisp of her hair and blew it across his cheek, a tantalizing caress. Desire rose in him, painful and pitiless, but he kissed her gently. Her lips, like damp silk, softened and opened for him; when he touched the tip of his tongue to hers, a wave of shivering seized her. "Are you cold, sweetheart?"

She smiled with her eyes closed. "No, no, I feel so . . ." Rather than search for the word, she hummed her satisfaction in a throaty purr, heartfelt, artlessly sensual.

His hand at her waist tightened. He traced the outline of her mouth with his forefinger, enchanted by her soft, fearless smile. Resting his forehead against hers, their noses touching, he murmured, "I want you so much, Lily. Everything hurts."

The shaking recommenced. She held his shoulders, pressing against him, feeling the leaping rhythm of her pulse—or maybe it was his. His hands, sliding up her hips and along her sides, pulled her arms up until she wound them around his neck. They kissed again. And inhaled sharply together, muscles tensing, mouths open, ravenous. "Let's go downstairs," she said in a tight whisper.

"Below," he corrected hoarsely. Holding hands, they walked toward the ladder.

It was pitch dark in Clay's cabin. "Stay here," Devon said, leaving her at the door. Lily heard a sharp thump and a pained exhalation; she expected a curse next, but instead a laugh came from out of the blackness. The sound of it warmed her to her bones. She heard the scratch of flint and steel; a moment later he lit a candle. He set it in the stationary holder on Clay's desk, lit another from it, and carried the second to the cabinet beside the bed.

Nerves quivered through her when he came to her. He took her hands clasped at her waist and kissed them, first the backs, then the palms. His thumb caressed the sensitive pad of each fingertip; the sensation was so startling that her breathing changed, began to come quickly.

"Did you like the gown?" he whispered, touching his tongue to the pulse point in her wrist.

She glanced past him and saw it lying on the bed where she'd left it, neatly rewrapped. "Oh, Dev, it's beautiful."

"It was part of Clay's last booty. I told him I wanted something for you, and he sent Mr. Falk to one of their hiding places for it. But do you know, I was wrong to think of it—"

"Oh, no—"

"—because you don't need it. It doesn't matter what you wear. In this dress or any other, you're the most beautiful woman I've ever known."

She wanted to weep. She brought her hands up to touch his face, thinking that he was the beautiful one. She ran the backs of her fingers under his chin, along his jaw, his strong throat. The desire in his flushed face made him look vulnerable, for once, and filled her with an unbearable tenderness. She felt him untying her hair in back, and in a moment it fell to her shoulders. Knowing that she would not stop him, that she would give him everything, made her feel weak and uncoordinated. They kissed again; she pressed her body against him, slipping her hands inside his coat to touch his back, his wide shoulders. He shifted the angle of his mouth and kissed her until her knees shook uncontrollably and she could feel her own seduction, the slow dissolution of her common sense.

"On the other hand," he murmured, then kissed her again.

She must have missed something; what had been on the first hand? She said, "Hmm?" and then opened her mouth so that he could go back to nibbling on her tongue.

Another lengthy silence. "On the other hand," he tried again. "You're more beautiful with no clothes on at all. Speaking from experience."

She sighed and pulled away. Smiling tensely, she held still while he unlaced her dress in front and eased it down over her shoulders. Her shift came next, and soon her breasts were bare. The sweep of his gaze was as efficient as a caress; she felt her nipples stiffen and pucker before he could touch her. Then he touched her. The electric thrill rushed downward and the trembling in her knees started over again. "You, too," she whispered, unbuttoning his shirt. "Speaking from experience."

In no time at all they were naked. Devon reached behind her to close the door. The working part of her brain was faintly amused, for the silence on board the *Spider* tonight, broken only by hushed sighs and soft whispers, testified to their absolute aloneness. But when he took her gently by the shoulders and shifted her so that her back was against the door, she realized that its true purpose wasn't privacy.

He swept his hands down her body and up again, caressing her belly, pausing to admire her breasts by lifting them and running his tongue across their silky white tops. The soft little sound she made was his reward. He bent lower to press his lips against the sensitive place under her right breast, where the skin was still lightly discolored. "It still hurts here, doesn't it, Lily?"

"Oh, no. Oh, hardly at all." The thought that they might not finish what they'd begun because of that made her go weak with anxiety.

"But a little," he insisted, straightening. "So we will have to take special care."

"Oh, yes," she agreed, dazed with relief, "let's take special care." She slid her hands from his waist to his bare buttocks, watching his eyes darken and smolder. The hot, hard throbbing against her abdomen told her they were both lost, and consequences no longer had any meaning.

"Open your legs, Lily," he chanted, pressing his mouth against her throat, her shoulder, and she obeyed. She gasped at the first skimming touch of his fingers. He pulled her head back by a handful of her hair and covered her open mouth with his. His deep caress made her groan pitifully. He started a slow, alternating rhythm of penetration with his fingers and his tongue. Very soon she was panting, unable to catch her breath. A fierce, uncontainable joy was filling her, rising higher and higher with incredible speed. She abandoned herself to it because she trusted him, and because she had no choice. Whispering his name once, she surrendered.

He couldn't get enough of her. Her wet, responsive mouth was delicious, and the strong, throbbing pulse in the hot depths of her beat in time with his intimate stroking. All at once—so quickly it amazed him—she pushed backward, drawing her face away. Her eyes fascinated him. They were glazed with passion, but even at the moment of her release they never left his. He kissed her again, hard, before she was finished, drawing her pleasure out for as long as he could. When it was over she gave a soft cry and dropped her head against his chest, shuddering.

For a long time they didn't move. Lily listened to the rhythmic pressure of his heartbeat against her cheek, eyes closed, feeling her impossible love welling up in her heart. *I love you*, she told him with everything but her tongue; a wispy vestige of self-preservation still prevented her from saying it. Sadness flickered in a far-off corner of her mind. But this was not a time for regrets. The man she loved was holding her, his steady pulse thudding in her ear. She tightened her arms around him and put her lips to his heart.

A little later she felt his hand, which she had almost forgotten, twitch to life. She stayed still and didn't move, didn't breathe. Unerringly, he found her secret place, and one of his clever fingers set up an unbearable, butterfly-light fluttering against it. She wanted to laugh at how easily he could arouse her. She said, *"Oh, Devon,"* in a voice full of wonder.

The pain of wanting her was more than he could bear. Her skin was magic; every place he touched was enchanted. "Lean back, Lily. Just your shoulders. Hold on to me." She did everything he said. Her bottom was soft, solid; it fit his hands perfectly. He pulled her hips closer and flexed his knees. Smooth and sleek, he glided into her until their bellies touched.

Not moving, breathing softly, they watched each other. A little later he took her hands and held them high on either side of her face while he moved into and out of her in the slow, deep rhythm they both wanted. Eyes closed, unaware, Lily whispered, "Please, please, please . . ."

He kissed her briefly, but he couldn't concentrate on it. "Put your arms around my neck, darling." She did, and then he lifted her, hands under her buttocks, still holding her against the door. "Wrap your legs around me." She did that too, and then he turned her around and walked toward his brother's heavy desk in the corner of the room. He kicked the ornate Italian chair—smuggled out of France, one of Clay's prize possessions—out from behind it. "Looks comfortable," he muttered, and sat down.

He didn't have to tell her to fold her legs back and straddle his lap: she figured that out for herself, almost instantly. But she loved his passionate instructions. Were all men so—talkative? she wondered. His volubility gave her courage. To hide her face she kissed him, then murmured against his lips, "I love the way you feel inside me. It's like everything is melting."

He dragged his mouth down her throat, her chest. "Lean back," he ordered in a guttural murmur; when she did, he took her breast into his mouth and suckled her with greed and thoroughness.

Gasping, she clutched at his shoulders. "I've never done this with anyone but you! Do you believe me?"

He answered, "Yes," immediately. Could it be true? He didn't care, didn't care.

He took her hips in a strong grip and moved her on him, over him, reveling in her helplessness, his absolute possession. But she streaked her hands through his hair and brought her mouth to his in the lightest, sweetest kiss, the bare brushing of lips, and her moist breath was perfume. His self-control teetered.

She pulled back, and they watched each other's eyes again, spellbound, gauging. He slid lower on his spine until she lay on top of him, her feet just touching the floor. She braced herself with her forearms against his chest and set the new rhythm herself. Nothing had ever felt like this, this wild mix of power and surrender, control and abandon. Finally it was need, raw and burning and urgent, that overpowered her. "Devon, I can't—I can't—!"

Hold back, she meant, but he thought she meant the opposite. He clapped his palms to her buttocks and thrust into her again and again, grunting, breath rasping, and suddenly her whole body convulsed. She shouted out something loud and incomprehensible, and he felt her helpless, uncontrollable quivering for a long, long moment before she softened and finally sank against him. He held her tightly—too tightly, he knew, but God! he couldn't help it—while he unleashed himself and plunged inside her over and over and over. He thought it would never end. When it did, they were both as limp as rags, and he was incapable of moving.

"Lily," he got out. Strands of her hair were stuck to his wet cheek. "Are you all right?" He moved one hand enough to touch her shoulder, but it was a tremendous effort. She was still trembling. "Are you all right? Did I hurt you?"

She tried to straighten up, to look him in the face, but she was much too weak. She moved her lips far enough away from his damp throat to make herself understood. "I don't know if I'm all right or not. Frankly, I don't care."

A deep, relieved laugh rumbled in his chest. He peered down through her hair at the lovely, erotic sight of her splayed thighs on either side of his, her saucy buttocks gleaming white above his bent knees. Shifting a little, he used his legs to push hers together. She understood immediately and squeezed her thighs around him. But the sensation was too much; he uttered a hoarse cry of combined agony and ecstasy and she stopped, laughing softly. They both sighed deeply, stroking each other, nuzzling. "We should get in bed," he said after a while.

"Yes, I suppose. I like this chair, though. I'll miss it."

"We'll come back to visit."

She looked up at that. "Will we?"

"Mm, soon. And often."

She shivered delicately.

"How are you, Lily? Seriously." He stroked the bruised skin over her ribs tenderly, watching her face.

She answered with the simple truth. "I've never felt so well in my life. I love what we do, Devon. You make me feel . . ."

"What?"

"I don't know the words. Lovely."

"You are lovely."

"Perfect."

"You are perfect."

She began to laugh again. "Delightful! Irresistible, beautiful—"

"You're all of them."

She kissed him exuberantly. She didn't believe any of it, but she felt intensely happy.

When they finally found the strength to move to the bed, they lay quiet in each other's arms, listening to the gentle lap of water close by. Time passed unnoticed, could have stopped for all they knew. Lily wanted to talk, to describe all the new things he could make her feel. She wanted to tell him who she was, and most of all she wanted to tell him that she loved him. But Devon's trust was fragile and brand new; if she spoke, it could disappear. She would not be able to bear that. Silence, even deception—they were a cheap price to pay for happiness like this. The future was out of her control; if nothing else in the last few months, at least she had learned that lesson. For now, for this night, she was content. What else mattered?

In the morning she awoke gradually, coming out of a dream she couldn't quite recapture; she only knew that it was beautiful. She moved her knee toward the center of the bed, then her hand, searching for him. She knew he was gone before she opened her eyes because the place where he'd lain was cold. The last of the dream fragmented. She sat up.

She saw him immediately. Facing the porthole, staring out. Tall and straight and stiff. Fully dressed.

Nausea rose in the back of her throat. The dreadful memory of their only other morning together made her heart hammer, her hands go clammy with perspiration. "Dev?" she whispered. He turned, and the sight of his face confirmed every fear. She couldn't utter another sound.

So, finally, she was awake. He fisted his hands in his coat pockets and leaned against the wall, resisting an urge to go closer. The sun streamed in a golden shaft across her bare shoulders, gilding them, lighting a fire in the wild tumble of her dark red hair. While he watched, she crossed her breasts with her wrists, and a dull rose stain crept into her pale cheeks. Her unspeakable loveliness caused him pain he couldn't endure. He looked away and said, "It's late. Get dressed." His voice came out too harsh. "Clay will be here soon," he added, softening it but still not looking at her.

Everything hurt. She tried not breathing, but her blood still pumped, still carried the deep, pitiless ache to every part of her. Her throat was swollen, but somehow she asked the question. "What has happened? To you?"

"Nothing, what do you mean? It's late—"

"No, don't."

He looked at her then. Past the glitter of her unshed tears he could see all her pain. He recoiled. Bitterness rushed through his veins like acid; contempt for his own cowardice brought a dark flush to his face. He had to turn away from her again.

"Was it too good, Devon? Did you feel too much?"

He couldn't answer. He could only wait, hoping that anger would come soon and rescue him.

What was the point of taunting him? He was what he was; she could never change him. She stared at the stiff, bleak line of his shoulders until she couldn't bear it. Then she dropped her head. How easy it would be to weep. But a second later, she discovered that her love was even stronger than her pride.

He heard the rustle of covers, the creak of the bed ropes. When he turned and saw her, her nakedness drove all the words he'd thought to say from his mind. "Oh, Lily," he murmured with a grim smile. "Not fair."

Ignoring that, ignoring all the voices in her head that were shouting, *You're a fool*, she went to him. She drew one of his clenched hands from his pocket and held it between both of hers. "Don't do this, Dev. I know why you're afraid, but I would never, ever hurt you. I swear it."

He swore foully.

She held tighter and told him. "I'm in love with you."

He heard, but he kept it out. "Then I feel sorry for you." Her nostrils thinned; she was holding herself very carefully. Heat rushed through him. "Don't say that," he told her, without the snarl this time. "I don't want to hear it."

She yanked at his hand. "Don't tell me not to love you! And don't you dare leave me again, Devon, I will not allow it."

He saw that every muscle was tense; even her skin looked tender, vulnerable. "My dear, I never meant to hurt you. But what you want is not inside me. If you like, we can—make an arrangement, an agreement we both—"

"Stop it, stop! I told you last night, I want no 'arrangement.'"

"Then—"

"We can make each other happy, Dev. For just a little while. Don't you feel it? Don't you know?" He put his hands on her face, cupping the sides, holding so tightly her bones hurt. But she didn't move, and she didn't drop her urgent gaze. "I love you. You're everything to me. You're in my heart, there won't ever be anyone else." She saw the anger and fright and shock in his eyes, and faced it down. "I would never deliberately hurt you. I'm me, *Lily*, I'm not like anyone but myself. And I love you so much."

"But I don't want your love."

"It doesn't matter what you want. It's free, I give it to you."

He wanted to push her away, her and her unwanted gift, but he couldn't make his hands let go of her. Something tore inside, and it felt like the tender, jagged edges of a wound that had never healed. "I don't want you," he whispered, shaking his head over and over. "I don't want you, Lily."

"Too bad." She shook her head right back. How confident she sounded! Whatever happened, she must not cry.

"You're a fool."

"Doubtless. I love you."

He cursed again—not her, but life in general—and then his brain shut down and he pulled her into a rough, angry embrace. "You'll regret this," he said into her tousled, sweet-smelling hair.

Oh, yes, she knew that. But she was so in love that she even appreciated the warning. She was standing stiffly, holding her breath, because the grip he had on her hurt her ribs. He noticed, and instantly lightened his hold. She felt his lips on her temple and sighed deeply. "I have to tell you about myself," she said, moving her hands up and down his back in slow, ardent strokes. "I have so much to tell you."

He swore again.

She went rigid, thinking he didn't want to know. Then she heard it: a thump, and the soft scrape of wood against wood. Clay was back. "Judas," she swore softly.

He pulled back to look at her. She was dry-eyed, but her face was full of emotion. How could he let her go? How could he not? Love and relief glowed in her serious gray-green eyes, and strength, and pain, and a dark, stoic knowledge. Whatever happened, and for as long as he lived, he would never forget the way she looked right now. He kissed her lips with a sweet, weary promise that said, *I will try.* God help him. For once he meant it.

The clatter of footsteps on the companionway ladder jolted them apart. Five fast knocks. Devon stepped between Lily and the door instinctively—and not a minute too soon. Before either could speak, the door opened and Clay loomed in the threshold. Lily watched him over Devon's shoulder in speechless disbelief.

"God damn it, Clay—!"

"Oops," he exclaimed, but he didn't leave. In fact, he grinned at them cheerfully, eyes alight with curiosity. He even stood on his toes a bit, trying to see over his brother's shoulder. "Too early, am I? It's almost ten, I was sure you'd be up."

"Would you get the hell out of here?"

Devon sounded more exasperated than angry, and it amazed Lily that she felt the same. She wasn't half as embarrassed as she knew she ought to be.

"I'm going, I'm going. I just wanted to tell you, Dev, that Trayer Howe's been seen in the neighborhood. He's limping around on a crutch, but he's been making some interesting threats against you. And Lily, and me. Which is pretty stupid since I didn't do anything," he added to himself. "Lily either, of course. Anyway, I thought you'd like to know. In case you wanted to arrest him or something. Shall I go on deck now and wait for you?"

"Good idea."

"Right you are. Morning, Lily. You're looking lovely. At least, what I can see of you is certainly—"

"Out!"

"Right. On my way." He winked broadly and pulled

the door closed. Devon turned to Lily, then spun back around when it shot open again. "Shall we have breakfast in the village? Wiley's a little under the weather this morning and wasn't able to supply us with—"

"Out! Damn it! Get out!"

"Testy in the morning, aren't we?" He chuckled and shut the door again, and presently they heard his ascending footsteps.

Devon turned back. "Idiot," he muttered, but he couldn't hide the twinkle in his eyes behind the scowl. "What's wrong?" She was as white as a sheet. "He didn't really see you, Lily, it's—"

"No, not that." She knew she was being foolish, but she couldn't help it. When his arms went around her, she clung to him.

"What, then?" She wouldn't answer. The warmth of her skin fired him, but he kept his touch comforting. "What is it? Tell me, love."

"I'm afraid."

"Of what?"

He would keep at her, she knew, until she admitted it. "Trayer."

"Oh, no." He encircled her with his arms, backed her against the wall and pressed gently against her, all to tell her she was safe. "He won't hurt you. I won't let him."

"Clay said you could arrest him?"

"Certainly. If he stays in the neighborhood, he'll be caught and I'll have him sent to prison."

"But not if—how can you?"

"It's easy, I'm the magistrate. The parish constable's already been notified to watch for him. If he comes anywhere near you, he'll be captured. I'll have him bound over for the Bodmin assizes. I swear to God, Lily, I'll see him hang."

First she went stiff, then limp and lifeless in his arms. "Lily?" Her shoulders shook; he thought she was crying. "Darling," he breathed, and drew away to see her. She wasn't crying, she was laughing. But there was an edge of something, an ironic weariness in the sound of her laughter that disturbed him.

"You're the magistrate?" she said weakly.

"For the district. So you're safe, love."

"Safe. Oh, Dev." She leaned back, and her smile was steeped in regret.

"Lily, what's the matter?"

"Nothing. Hold me." She drew him close, and his warmth eased her, helped her to forget. They kissed. Afterward, he forgot to ask her what it was she'd wanted to tell him about herself. He wouldn't think of it again for a long time.

# Eighteen

For Lily, the weeks that followed were a nerve-wracking combination of happiness and anxiety, euphoria and distress. The joy sprang from the fact that Devon was her lover, and the trepidation came from exactly the same source. Only at night were things clear and simple between them. Who she was to him, what he was to her—in each other's arms, it was all a matter of indifference. They were lovers, and for those hours their hearts and minds and bodies were in harmony.

But Lily was aware that he didn't know what to do with her, how to place her in his life. Like him, she had no idea what her new role was. She'd told him she wanted no "arrangement"—but what else was it when she ate his food and slept in his bed, in exchange for nothing more than her body?

When she'd been too ill to work, she could rationalize things into a prettier picture. But now there was nothing to prevent her from doing housework—nothing except

Devon's nearly violent refusal to allow it. So instead she busied herself with prodigious quantities of sewing and needlework, for him and his household and his numerous servants. But even that couldn't alleviate her deep, persistent uneasiness. She was in limbo, taking her meals in her room, rarely going out, engaged in her endless mending. On the rare occasions when she saw him during the day, she never knew how to greet him. He was invariably cordial, and yet ever so slightly reserved. His reticence hurt, and made her more determined than ever to keep out of his way . . . until night fell and he came to her again and made her his.

Once she thought of moving back into her attic room with Lowdy. His reaction was predictable: he forbade it, refused even to discuss it. But what game were they playing? Lily was not accustomed to self-delusion. The fact that he did not repeat his offer of hard cash in return for her favors did not alter the facts of the case. She knew what a "kept woman" was. She was not accustomed to hypocrisy, either. If things continued as they were, she would either have to leave Darkstone or accept the fact that although she'd once refused, with fine indignation, to be his mistress, a mistress was exactly what she had become.

What was the solution? Sometimes she imagined that everything would be all right if only she could tell him the truth about herself. She was shrewd enough to recognize that his reluctance to involve himself with her was *partly* because he believed she came from the servant class. Women in that category—*women like Maura*—were venal and heartless, an unconscious, unreasoning part of him still believed, and they used men as tools for pulling themselves out of one class and into the next. But would it really change anything if she were to tell him she was educated, genteel, poor but respectable—that once she'd employed servants herself? She suspected not. Devon's distrust went deeper, extended to women in general; the more intensely his emotions were engaged, the faster he ran from them.

Besides, she *couldn't* tell him. He was the magistrate! What an unamusing joke. There was every likelihood that she was still wanted for theft and assault, and she'd fallen in love with a man who, if he knew it, would be duty-bound to arrest her. She hadn't realized that God's sense of humor was quite so ironic.

So there was nothing to do but wait. Perhaps a letter would come soon from Cousin Soames, saying that all was forgiven. Or perhaps Devon would fall in love with her. Perhaps one or both of these things would happen before his distrust returned and destroyed the fragile bond they were sharing, or before her own sense of shame forced her to leave him.

One day in August, when the warm wind slammed a light but unremitting rain sideways against the house, she heard a clatter of hooves and the jangle of harness in the gravel drive below her window. Carriages were infrequent at Darkstone; occasionally Francis Morgan arrived in one, but hardly anyone else did. Because she'd been sitting for hours, Lily got up from her chair, laid aside her sewing, and went to the window to see who it was.

It wasn't Francis Morgan. This carriage bore the Darkwell arms on its lacquered black door, and yet she'd never seen it before. A footman in livery jumped from the boot, opened the door, and pulled down the step. A lady descended. She was tall, thin, past middle age; she was looking down, minding her step, but when she achieved the ground safely and turned back to wait for her companion, Lily saw her face. She'd never seen her before, and yet she knew without a doubt who she was. Devon's mother.

That meant the small, graceful, brown-haired lady stepping down after her was Alice Fairfax. Lady Alice, of Fairfax House. Where, Lily clearly remembered Lady

Alice's maid confiding, there might be a wedding "one day soon, between your master and my mistress."

The two women disappeared from view. Lily pressed her cheek to the window and let the damp chill of the glass seep inside her. Once before she'd felt jealousy. She observed its sure, razor-sharp return now helplessly, despising herself, unable to stop it. Alice Fairfax was not really beautiful; Lily could console herself with that. But she was regal as a queen, every inch a lady, and she would make Devon Darkwell a perfect wife.

Shuddering slightly, Lily left the window to sit on the edge of the bed. A little later she lay down and pulled the covers up, fully dressed. Misery, black and heavy, permeated her like a dank, filthy fog. Time passed. It had been a dark day, and her clock had run down; she had no idea what time it was when she heard footsteps in the corridor and feminine voices. Doors closed; silence drifted back. Lily sat up. Good God, were they staying? On this floor? A few doors down the hall?

She got up and began to pace. When it grew too dark to see, she lit candles. Every sound made her go tense, straining to interpret it. A girl brought her a cold supper on a tray, and it was only by an act of will that she refrained from pumping her for information. The night dragged on. Occasionally she heard laughter coming from downstairs. Her nerves stretched tighter. She bathed, put on her nightgown. Lying in bed in the dark, stiff-limbed and wide-eyed, she felt such contempt for herself that she wanted to disappear. Wretchedness made her body feel wooden, foreign, not even human. Much later, she heard steps again on the stairs, in the hall, and presently the murmur of quiet good nights. She waited. Breathless, motionless. Transfixed with anxiety.

He didn't come. For the first time since the night on the *Spider*, Devon didn't come to her.

The moon climbed halfway across her window,

paused, and sank back into the blackness. The silence was absolute: she couldn't even hear the sea. She rose—to pace her room again, she thought. But before she knew it she was in the hall, bare feet soundless on the cool floor, stealing toward Devon's room. Without knocking, she opened the door and slipped inside.

He'd heard nothing, but he knew she was there. He sat up. She was only a white blur against the door, pale and insubstantial as a ghost. They watched each other across the dark breadth of the room for endless minutes. The longer it went on, the surer he grew that something irretrievable was slipping through his fingers. But he could not speak. Did not know the words.

"Poor Dev," she said, and her voice sounded low and disembodied. "You don't know what to do with me, do you? How awkward this must be for you—your fiancée and your mistress under your roof at the same time. It must make you—" He spat out an oath and leapt from the bed, and the rest of the words stuck in her throat. Some part of her noted that he still had his clothes on, and she took a particle of comfort from it: at least he hadn't been fast asleep.

"What is it you want from me, Lily?" he demanded, looming over her.

The rawness in his voice made her wonder, incredulously, if he could be in as much pain as she. It gave her the courage to touch him, a light hand on his chest. "I want you to love me."

All the fight went out of him. He gathered her into his arms and buried his face in her hair. "I do. God help me. As much as I can."

She hated the qualification, and the reluctance, the agonized unwillingness of his tone, as if uttering the words had cut his throat. She whispered, "Will you marry me?" with no idea where the courage, or the insanity, came from to ask him such a question. She felt his body stiffen, and fought an immediate premonition of defeat. He drew away slowly. She was thankful for the darkness that hid her face. "Just say no. For God's sake, spare me your kindness."

"Listen to—"

"No!" She pushed at him violently. "You won't because I was your housemaid. That's part of it, isn't it? What would I have to be before you would marry me? How much money would it take?"

"Lily, for—"

"What if I were a seamstress? What if I made hats? No? It's a lady or nothing for you, isn't it?"

He reached for her shoulder and gave her a rough shake, as angry now as she.

"How many thousands of pounds a year, Dev? Twenty, thirty?"

"God damn it, Lily!"

"What if I were a governess?" She was shouting now. "You'd never marry me then, would you? Because even if you loved me, I'd be too much like your dead wife, your beloved *Maura*, the woman who made you this way! But I'm not like her, Devon, I'm me, I'm Lily, and I—"

He shoved her backwards. She hit the door hard with her shoulders. The noise was much worse than the pain, but his violence stunned both of them. He whirled and walked to the window, to put time and distance between them as much as to tell her, without words, that she was safe from him.

"You don't understand. It's not that I want to hurt you. Lily, if I could—" The latch clicked and he spun around. She was gone. His breath left his body, as if he'd been punched in the gut. The closing of her bedroom door sounded across the silence, soft and final. He waited interminable seconds, and then he heard it: the turning of the key in the lock.

"No more business this evening," Lady Elizabeth Darkwell decreed. "Alice and I are leaving early in the morning, and after that you two can talk about ticketings and the price of ore all you like. Until then you have to be sociable."

"Yes, Mother," mumbled Clay, flashing a dry smile at his brother.

"Yes, but what *is* a ticketing?" Lady Alice wondered. "Just tell me that, Dev, and then you can go back to being sociable. Or start, rather."

"It's an auction. Representatives of the copper companies bid on the parcels of ore that the mine agents come to sell. The man with the biggest parcel for sale acts as the chairman. This time our mine has the most ore, and—"

"And Dev thinks I'm too stupid to be the chairman."

"Clay, for—"

"Excuse me, too *inexperienced*."

Devon shook his head, exasperated. "Well, you've only been to one ticketing in your life, am I right? They're tricky, that's all I'm saying, and Francis has been attending them for years. The price of copper is down, it was sixty-one pounds a ton last month, and sometimes there are strategies that can be worked to keep it from plunging deeper. You and Francis—"

"Devon."

He halted sheepishly. "Right. Sorry, Mother. I'll ring for the tea." He did so, then applied himself to the task of being sociable. Clay's antipathy to Francis Morgan went deeper than petty jealousy, he knew, and he still didn't understand its source. Devon had known Francis for ten years; they'd been at Oxford together and had stayed in touch afterward when Devon had gone back to Cornwall, Francis to Lancashire. When Devon decided to reopen the mine and needed someone to manage it for him, he'd thought of Francis because he was talented and competent. He was also poor, and not succeeding very quickly with his tiny law practice in Manchester. It had seemed to be the perfect solution for both of them. And Francis had done well, justified

Devon's faith in him; lately there had even been vague, preliminary talk of a partnership in the mine. But now, with Clay in the picture, such plans no longer seemed appropriate.

Alice was speaking to him, showing him two serpentine rings she'd bought in Mullion. Where was Lily now? Devon wondered. She would be in her room, no doubt, probably hunched over some damnable piece of mending. He hadn't seen her since last night, but she'd rarely been out of his thoughts. "Poor Dev" she'd called him. Alice put one of the rings in his hand and pointed out the long red striations. They bent over the stone together, faces almost touching, and he caught a faint breath of her rose-scented perfume. Lily never wore perfume. But sometimes she smelled like flowers. Her hair was so many subtle shades of red, alive and luminous. Magical. He loved her mouth. The delicate, self-conscious shapes it made when she spoke fascinated him. She had a way of looking at him through her lashes when she smiled, lips curving up at the fragile corners, sweet, not coy, and completely charming. And when she cried, her nose got red and her gray-green eyes swam, and it always broke his heart. Had he made her cry last night? He'd listened, lying in his bed, afraid that he might hear her. But the sleepless night passed, and he'd heard nothing but the creaking of the house. *Lily*, he thought. *What am I going to do with you?* He felt a prickling sensation on the back of his neck. When he looked up, she was standing in front of him, handing Alice a cup of tea.

The ring dropped from his fingers and fell to the carpet with a soft thud. He was too stunned to move. Silent and graceful, Lily stooped to pick it up. For an instant she seemed to examine it in her hand. Then she offered it to him. His fingers went out automatically and she dropped the ring in his palm, careful not to touch him. Their eyes met. But her expression was shuttered; he couldn't read it.

"I say, are you taking tea, Devon?" his mother repeated.

"No," he got out.

"Clay?"

"Yes, please."

Devon watched, impotent anger blossoming slowly, as Lily took another cup and saucer from his mother and carried them across the drawing room to Clay. She wore her old gray dimity dress and tired apron, her hair tucked up into her dingy cap. Clay looked uncomfortable; he tried to catch her eye as she handed him his tea, but she curtsied prettily—mockingly, Devon thought—and turned away immediately. Alice was in the middle of some animated story; Devon barely heard Lily murmur to his mother, "Will there be anything else, m'lady?" Elizabeth said no, Lily made another shallow curtsey, and a second later she was gone from the room.

"Jimmy was flabbergasted and said to Justine—in front of *all* of us, Devon, even your mother—that he hoped never to hear such talk from his own wife ever again, and if he did he'd feel no remorse in beating her for it. As if he ever would. Jimmy *Lynch*, can you imagine? And her such a perfect lamb! Wasn't it droll?" she asked Elizabeth, chuckling in her easy, good-humored way.

"Very droll," murmured her ladyship. But she was distracted as she gazed back and forth between her sons, her eyes speculative. Clay was scowling down into his teacup; Devon had never taken his eyes from the door since the pretty, pale-cheeked parlormaid had glided through it. "Justine sends her regards to both of you, by the way," she mentioned. "You remember her, don't you, Dev? Clay, I *know* you do. A pretty girl, yellow hair; we all thought she'd marry Tom Wren, and then Jimmy—"

"Excuse me." Without looking at any of them, Devon strode toward the door.

"Dev? Is something wrong?"

He paused in the threshold. "No, Mother, I—" What? "I've remembered something I have to tell Cobb. I'll only be a moment." Three pairs of startled eyes watched him go.

She wasn't in the kitchen. The scullery maid looked terrified but swore she hadn't seen her. An instinct sent him sprinting down the L-shaped corridor, past the new housekeeper's room, and up the sagging stone steps to the empty courtyard at the side of the house. He spied her beside the garden shed, leaning against the wall, facing away from him. His boots were silent on the spongy ground; she didn't hear him until he was a dozen feet away. Even then she didn't turn. He reached her in four more strides. His fury had propelled him this far; he hung onto it as he made a grab for her shoulder and spun her around.

But her face defeated him. All the bitter words died on his lips when she threw up her hands—too late—to cover her tear-wet cheeks and swimming, anguished eyes. When she tried to turn away again, he held on. "A mistake," she sobbed, "I should never—" But she broke off because she was crying too hard, and put her face in her hands. What could he do but hold her?

She tried again. "I'm sorry, I don't know why I did it, I was angry, hurt, I thought if I—"

"Hush, it doesn't matter." It didn't anymore.

"She's so perfect—I've only made it worse—now that I've seen her—" She dissolved again into helpless weeping. Her fists were clenched against his shirtfront, to hold herself away from his comfort.

It took him a minute to realize she meant Alice. She'd spoken of her last night too. "Lily, Alice is not my fiancée. She never was."

"No," she choked, "but she will be."

"No, she—"

"Or someone like her. Someone; someday. It's true, you know it." She beat against his chest once and twisted out of his grasp. "I have to go away, Dev. I can't bear this."

He grabbed her back, acting on reflex, his hands no longer gentle. "No, you're not leaving. Don't make me angry, Lily, don't say stupid things."

He pulled her close, his hard arms circling her completely. She let him. This pain was excruciating, but to go away would be a hundred times worse. How could she give him up? Never to hold him again—how could she relinquish such terrible sweetness? Cowardly, maybe, but she couldn't leave him—not yet. It would be like cutting out her own heart.

She couldn't say "I love you" again; it hurt them both too much. He couldn't give her any hope. They clung to each other for a long time, not speaking, offering their bodies for comfort. Wondering what in the world they were going to do.

# Nineteen

Elizabeth and Alice were gone. Lily had heard them leave in the morning, but this time she hadn't gotten up to watch from the window. Afterward, she'd stayed in her room all day, brooding. Devon had not come.

It was a wild night. The southern wind blew in from the sea, buffeting the shore in violent gusts that tore at her hair and twisted her skirts around her legs. A good night for making decisions, Lily thought as she stood at the bottom of the winding cliff steps and watched the incoming tide inundate the last foot of dry sand at her feet. She was alone, solid rock behind her, nothing but the vast sea and sky in front. She already knew what she was going to do, but she wanted to think it out one last time. Impulsive behavior had only brought her trouble in the past; a few hard lessons had taught her she could no longer afford to indulge in it.

She was going to tell Devon who she was, and what she would and would not do, and then be prepared to take the consequences. The first two would be bad enough, but it was the last she wasn't sure she had the strength to face. For although he would be relieved to know she wasn't really a housemaid, she doubted that that knowledge would be enough to change his mind about marrying her. And she had made up her own mind that she would not be his mistress. "Mistress," as she had always known but lately had chosen to ignore, was only a euphemism for choosy whore.

What would she do, then? Where would she go? She'd thought she would have heard from Soames by now; it had been over a month since she'd written to him. If he would not take her in, she must find another place. A place where she could live cheaply while she waited out the nine months until her twenty-first birthday, when she would come into her tiny inheritance. Would Devon lend her money? she wondered. If he did, could she take it from him, even on the basis of a loan? Perhaps, but she would much rather make a clean break.

The wind blew a gust of salt spray into her face; she had to hang on to the rail with both hands to keep her balance. What a liar she was, she thought, despairing. If Devon offered her a living in return for her body, did she really think she could say no? However distasteful and humiliating it might be, did she truly believe she could decline and then leave him? She loved him enough to be his whore, and she would not care what the world thought.

She was weary of thinking. It was pointless to agonize over every eventuality before she'd even done anything. First she would tell him who she was and why she had run away from Lyme. Then she would worry about his answer. At least she was certain—certain enough to take the risk—that he wouldn't have her arrested. Magistrate or not, he'd once flouted the authorities himself to protect his brother; surely he of all people would understand that sometimes, when appearances were wrong and observing the law perpetrated a greater injustice than violating it, it was the better part of wisdom to ignore the law's absolute letter and act instead on principles of common sense. The worst that could happen was that he would send her away—in which case, except for the condition of her heart, she would be no worse off than the day she'd arrived.

She squared her shoulders. Her mind was made up. Devon wasn't home yet—he wasn't due back from a meeting of mine owners in Truro until late—but she intended to wait for him. In the library, perhaps, with Clay. Maybe Clay could cheer her up. Turning her back on the wind, she started the steep climb toward the house.

Devon threw open the tall casement window set between gilt-framed portraits of the first and second Viscounts Sandown. A blast of wind struck him full in the face. He shut his eyes and inhaled the cool, humid tang, hoping it would clear his head. The sea air had already wilted the stiff sheet of foolscap he still held in his hand. He read the short message again, folded the letter, and put it in his pocket. A moment later he resumed his pacing.

The gallery at Darkstone connected the second floor of the house with the west tower. It was a long, high hall, chestnut-paneled, with dark paintings of myriad illustrious Darkwells hanging between all the windows. The furniture was pushed back along the walls, leaving the carpeted center clear so that the master could pace up and down when the weather prevented him from pacing out-of-doors. That wasn't the case tonight, and yet here he was, back early from Truro, too lost in thought to bother finding his way outside again.

It was Lily, as usual, who occupied his mind. Preoccupied it. It seemed to him he'd thought of little else but Lily Troublefield since the day they'd met, but never more so than lately. He was aware that she wanted him to make a decision, come to some conclusion about his intentions. The problem was that what he wanted and what she wanted were worlds apart. He wanted to be with her, to enjoy her, to give her pleasure; she wanted promises of a lifetime and a commitment of emotions. But his emotions were all used up.

It didn't help that he understood perfectly why he couldn't bring himself to make a place for her in his life, his heart. Maura had been dead for five years, but he had forgotten nothing. He recalled with crystalline clarity the fierce heat in the beginning, his obsession with her, his compulsion to possess her. Just as clear was the memory of his bitter, withering disillusionment, the self-loathing and mortification when he'd discovered that the object of his most passionate and tender feelings was faithless and deceitful. She'd run off with his bailiff. They had stolen his money and his baby. They'd kept the money but thrown the baby away when it had become an inconvenience to them. Devon felt an ancient agony rising in him, like acid eating at his vitals, and shut his mind against the dreadful memory of finding Edward, his tiny son, dead in the old woman's cottage. Those memories led to black, bottomless despair, and he had traveled the road there much too often.

And none of it had anything to do with Lily. He repeated the words in his head, fervently. The top of his mind believed it, knew it must be true. Something underneath, though, something potent and unhealed, shifted restlessly, not sure. An image of Alice Fairfax came to his mind; he saw her quiet face and kind eyes. Alice was a lady to her bones. She would be faithful and trustworthy. She would be *safe*. Was that what he wanted? Was that what his life had come to?

A few months ago he'd have answered yes, without hesitation or regret. Then he'd met Lily, and all his staid, rigid, spiritless expectations about his life had caved in like rotten wood. He'd abused her, insulted and ignored her, done all in his power to keep her out of everything except his bed. But despite his best efforts, she had won. Against his will she'd renewed him, worn down the barriers he'd erected so skillfully, and given him a glimpse of a different future full of feeling and risk and joy. He'd tried to protect himself by insisting that all he felt for her was physical desire—and that had been novel enough, since for five years women had been nothing but unavoidable accessories to his joyless and infrequent acts of sexual release. To experience passion again had felt strange, dangerous. To feel more than passion had terrified him.

It still did. But he and Lily had to come to a resolution. He'd told her he loved her, but was it true? He thought about her constantly. Was that love? When he was with her, he was happy. Was that love? He had no idea.

He stopped pacing and leaned against the wall beside a formal portrait of his grandmother. His hand closed over the letter in his pocket. It was from the Marchioness of Frome. Her ladyship wished to inform him that she had never heard of Lily Troublefield, much less employed her in the capacity of housemaid. The problem of dishonesty among servants worsened every year; she feared to say it, but she suspected his lordship had been the victim of a deceit. She could only hope it had stopped at the hiring, and that Miss Troublefield had stolen nothing more from him than his trust.

The only surprising thing about the letter was how little it surprised him. From the beginning, he'd known that Lily wasn't what she claimed to be. It hadn't mattered to him one way or the other then; his interest in her had been circumscribed and quite particular: all he'd wanted to do was seduce her. Later, he simply forgot about it—forgot that she'd resorted to a phony

Irish brogue to get herself hired, that she was a thousand times too refined to be a maid, that she stringently avoided questions about her past and occasionally told him outright lies. Now he found it at least ironic that she demanded complete trust from him—"I'm me, I'm Lily, and I would never hurt you!"—while she'd evidently been a great deal less than candid with him about herself.

But all that was by the way. She was concealing something; he expected she would tell him about it when it suited her. Even now, he didn't particularly care what it was. The important thing was to decide what to do about her.

He resumed pacing. A sound—a shot?—brought him up short. He thought it had come from downstairs. It couldn't, of course, have been a shot. What, then? A shutter blowing against the house, probably; the wind was strong enough for it. But it had been sharper than that, more high-pitched. The house was quiet now except for the whining wind. He remembered that Clay had been in the library when he'd gotten back from Truro, going over copper ore weight figures for the ticketing tomorrow night. Devon descended the stairs unhurriedly, watching the candles flicker in sconces along the walls, buffeted by drafts of wind even here. A storm was coming up from the sea.

"Clay?" he called in the corridor, seeing lamplight glowing in the library door. He went inside. Clay wasn't there. But the doors to the terrace were open. One slammed against the wall now, and he knew with relief what the "shot" had been. Damn Clay, why hadn't he closed the doors? Papers from the desk had blown all over the room. In a corner of his mind, he wondered what Clay's strongbox was doing on the desktop. Clay usually kept it locked in the bottom drawer. He hurried to the French doors and pulled them shut.

He saw Clay when he turned back. Lying on the floor

behind the desk, face down. Blood in his hair, dark and dreadful, soaking his shirt.

Devon ran to him, knelt beside him, shouting, "Clay!" He touched him with desperate hands, then gently turned him over. A small black wound gaped in his hairline, above his right brow. His blue eyes were wide and glassy, staring up at nothing. He was dead.

Devon cried out an anguished, incoherent protest. He dropped his forehead on Clay's chest and squeezed his eyes shut, fingers tangling in his brother's shirt. "No," he said, over and over and over. He stopped when horror began to supplant his disbelief.

Then he felt it—something, a movement of Clay's chest. He jerked up, fingers tightening. "Clay!" he bellowed. He pressed his ear to his brother's heart, harder, harder, and finally he heard a weak, fluttery sound, so faint he was terrified he'd imagined it until it came again.

He jumped up and ran for the door, shouting for Stringer. When no one came, he rushed out, calling all the while, down the hall toward the servants' stairs. Stringer appeared in the archway, coatless, buttoning his waistcoat.

"Get a doctor! Send MacLeaf—Clay's been shot. A head wound, he's bleeding. Get Penroy from Trewyth, it's closer. Move!"

Stringer stood stock-still, blinking stupidly. Suddenly Cobb appeared behind him, and Devon sagged with relief.

"Clay's been shot. It's bad. Send MacLeaf for Penroy."

Without a word, Cobb turned and ran for the front door.

Devon told Stringer to bring blankets, then raced back to the library. Clay hadn't moved. He was dead-white, eyes open and unfocused. Devon sank down beside him, full of dread. He reached for Clay's limp wrist with terrible reluctance, and saw the pen in his hand. The paper under it. Two slanting, spidery words on the page said, "Lily shot," before snaking away to an ugly blot of black ink.

"Lily shot." His vision clouded. He blinked to clear it, but the words stayed the same. Black on white, clear and unambiguous and inexorable. "Lily shot."

He heard Stringer coming. He watched his own unsteady fingers surround the paper and pick it up like a handful of coins, crumpling it. Turning away from the hurrying butler, he slid the wrinkled wad into his pocket. For a moment he went blind and deaf. Then Stringer dropped blankets beside him, and the man's helplessness brought him back to himself.

They covered Clay up, tucking warm wool around him carefully. Devon reached again for Clay's wrist, and the thready hint of a pulse caused his own blood to beat again.

Cobb returned. Devon stayed where he was, touching Clay, watching his face. Clay's staring eyes were strange, disturbing. Devon closed them with his fingers, and a tremor of revulsion shuddered through him. Cobb said something; he didn't hear. Clay was absolutely still but Devon was trembling, as if from cold. He asked Stringer to light a fire. He could hear the other servants in the hall, huddling, whispering. Suddenly he got to his feet.

"Stay with him, don't leave him," he told Cobb hoarsely. Grabbing up a branch of candles, he went out.

He didn't expect to find her in her room but he went there anyway. And stopped in the middle of the floor as the wavering candlelight picked out the shine of a small tin trunk lying open on her bed. He went toward it slowly. A corner of a piece of paper showed under one of her garments. He pulled the cloth aside and stared down at four neat stacks of twenty-pound bank notes.

Lily saw Devon coming toward her as she toiled up the last of the twisting stone cliff steps. She felt the familiar jerky little dance in her chest, and smiled in anticipation. He was back early—how lovely. The seriousness of what she had to say to him and her uncertainty about his reaction to it were no match for the sudden wild delight that welled up inside at the mere sight of him. The wind shredding the clouds apart uncovered the moon for a few seconds; by its watery, glimmering light she saw his face. Her smile faltered.

"What's wrong?" she asked when he stopped in front of her. "What's happened?" Blackness lowered again; she couldn't read his expression. But something was terribly wrong. The tension in his body was visible, even in the murk. "Dev, what is it? Has someth—uh!" She cried out, more in astonishment than pain, when he caught her arm and yanked her to him, his other hand gripping her shoulder. She heard his voice like a low growl in her ear, saw his teeth bared in a feral grimace, sensed the effort he made to control his inexplicable fury.

"You weren't expecting me home so soon tonight, were you?"

"What? No, I—Devon? You're hurting my—" She broke off again when he gave her a violent, teeth-rattling shake and began to pull her toward the house. She trotted along behind him, wrenching at his fingers to loosen his numbing grip on her arm, but his hand was like a vise. "Stop it, why are you doing this? Don't, you're hurting me. Devon!" She fell, striking her knee on the terrace step. He didn't look back or break stride, only pulled harder so that she had to stumble to her feet and run, limping, to keep up.

"What is it?" she cried, weeping now. "What are you doing?" He made no answer, and she could see nothing in his face but rage.

He dragged her around the side of the house to the front door. Inside, he shoved her toward the main staircase, hauling her up when she tripped on the stairs.

She stumbled against the banister, and a piercing pain knifed between her ribs. She dropped to her knees, stunned, holding her breath. Without a pause, he cursed her, pulled her to her feet, and forced her to keep climbing.

When they reached the door to her room, he threw her inside. His face made her quail; his clenching hands terrified her. "I don't know what you think I've done!" she cried, holding her side. "Will you tell me?"

Her innocent pose infuriated him. Snarling, he leapt at her and grabbed her by the hair. "I'd have given you the money. Murdering bitch, you didn't have to shoot Clay for it."

Lily blanched. "Oh God, Dev. Clay?" she quavered. "Shoot Clay? Is he hurt badly?"

Devon's body was burning. He dropped his hands because he wanted to tear her hair out by the roots.

She felt the first wave of true panic. His violence was palpable, barely suppressed, and she sensed that it would take very little to push him over the edge. Speaking carefully, trying to sound calm, she said, "Devon, please listen to me. I didn't shoot Clay. There's been a mistake. Why would you think it?"

"Because of that."

She followed his wild eyes and saw the money. So much money. "But—*I* didn't—"

"What's your real name?"

"Trehearne," she answered immediately. "I'm Lily Trehearne, I come from Lyme Regis. My parents are dead, but my guardian wanted me to marry his son and I c-couldn't—" She started to stammer when he took a menacing step toward her. "It's true!" She fought hysteria, holding her hands up as a shield. "I ran away because he said I stole his money, and he was hurt, I was afraid he might die—" She heard what she was saying, and despaired. "Oh God! Mrs. Howe was in Chard and I spoke to her—Devon, *listen* to me! I was going to explain it to you tonight!'' She couldn't stop crying. It all sounded so outlandish, like a clumsy lie even in her own ears. "I don't know what this money is! I would never hurt Clay. Please, I was going to tell you everything, and then go away if you didn't want me."

"Shut up." Seizing her, he shoved her body against the wall behind her. She hit her head and uttered a cry of pain. He had to get out; he was so close to hitting her.

"Please, please, please, you have to believe me." She was babbling now. It amazed her that under the thick, coiling fear lay profound pity. Was Clay dead? Despite Devon's ferocity she wanted to comfort him, soothe the anguish she could see in his eyes behind the fury. "I'm begging you, don't do this," she whispered. "Let me help you. On my honor, Dev, I couldn't hurt Clay. Listen to—"

He cut her off by grabbing a handful of the front of her dress and bringing her face close to his. His lips drew back from his teeth in a bestial snarl. "If Clay lives, I'll see you hang. If he dies, I swear before God I'll kill you myself." With a vicious shove, he let her go. He yanked the key out, closed the door, and locked her in.

"I'm afraid I can't offer you much hope." Dr. Penroy pulled the gore-spattered piece of toweling out of the waist of his immaculate black breeches and used it to wipe the blood from his hands. "I've removed the bullet and stopped the bleeding, but his chances of surviving are very slim, very slim indeed. Even if by some miracle he should recover, he'll never be the same. The ball passed through part of his brain." Lord Sandown didn't answer; the doctor wondered for a moment if he'd heard. "I'm very sorry. There's nothing more I can do, at least for now. I'll come again in the morning to see how he is."

The doctor wiped his forehead with his sleeve and wondered how his lordship would take it if he asked for a brandy. "I'd advise you to leave him where he is now, on the sofa, and not attempt to move him. Keep him warm. You won't be able to get any food into him, but you could try liquids." Darkwell's utter stillness began to unnerve him. "You can call in Marsh if you want, I've no objection," he said, trying not to bluster. "But I daresay he'll tell you exactly the same thing. I'm sorry," he repeated. A minute passed. He straightened his wig with snuff-stained fingers, then went a step closer to the motionless figure standing in the shadows outside the library door. "I say, are you all right? Do you hear what I'm saying?"

"Yes," came a low response. "Get out."

Penroy drew himself up. He opened his mouth to speak, say something self-righteous and offended, and snapped it shut when he saw naked rage behind eyes that seemed to sizzle and spark in the dimness. "You're upset," he muttered, "naturally so. I'll leave now, and come again tomorrow. Good night." He went back into the library and picked up his surgeon's case. He slanted a glance at the still figure stretched out under a blanket on the sofa, shook his head in a slight, hopeless gesture, and went out of the room through the terrace doors.

Devon waited until he heard the doors close, then went into the library. Standing beside the sofa, he listened for the sound of Clay's breathing. All he could hear was the sighing of the wind. He went closer. Penroy had put a bandage around his head. In flashes, a memory of the bleeding black gash assaulted Devon, and he dropped to his knees. He could feel his strength draining away, all the props that had kept him upright starting to split underneath him. He took Clay's hand and held it. Tears he hadn't shed since the day he'd cradled his son's cold, lifeless body streaked down his face in a hot cascade.

*Don't die.* He clutched Clay's hand harder, as if he could hold him back. But death was like a yawning

mouth, gaping closer. Aghast, he felt its slow nearing.
*Don't go.* Terror of abandonment swamped him, made
him tremble. Why had she shot him, why? The pitiless
injustice of it ignited a barbarous emotion; he felt as if
he'd been set on fire. A sudden pressure on his shoulder
steadied him. He looked up and saw Cobb standing over
him, his black-bearded face grim. Devon put his lips to
Clay's pale fingers for a moment, then stumbled to his
feet.

Cobb had a glass of cognac pressed between his chest
and his handless wrist. He retrieved it with his right
hand and held it out. "'E mayn't die," he muttered
harshly. "Surgeon said he d'have a chance."

"Yes, a chance." Devon held the glass to his lips, then
lowered it without drinking.

"He'm a strong lad."

"Yes."

Cobb took a long breath and looked away from the
sofa. "I can take a message to your mother, if you d'
want. Leave now, be to Witheridge by—"

"No. Thank you. Not yet, I don't think. We'll wait until
tomorrow; we may . . . know something more then."

Cobb nodded heavily. "You did ought t' rest some.
Mrs. Carmichael can sit up wi' him awhile. Says she
knows some about doctorin' and such." Devon made no
answer. "Is there anything you want me t' do?"

Devon stared at him for a full minute. Now was the
time to send Cobb to Truro to fetch the constable. They
would hold Lily in a cell until the magistrate—Devon—
ordered her bound over for the assizes. She'd stay in the
Bodmin gaol for the two months before her trial, and
they would convict her—there was no question of her
guilt. Then they'd hang her. She would die.

It was what he wanted. It was all he wanted. Cobb
shifted, waiting. Devon thought of the noose tightening
around Lily's throat, her eyes dilating with horror. He
remembered the night he'd found her in her room,

beaten and broken, and how he'd wanted to take all her pain into himself, because she was precious to him. He remembered Clay's kindness to her. The money in her tin trunk. Clay's blank, staring eyes. The message in Clay's hand.

"Sir?"

He drank the brandy down in three bitter swallows. "No, there's nothing. Tell Mrs. Carmichael to stay with Clay." He thrust the glass into Cobb's hand, unaware of the nearly rabid look that had come into his face. He'd made a decision, or the beginnings of one. He would not have her arrested, could not, for reasons he didn't understand. But she had a hold on him—not love, not anymore—and the hold was strong, and he was going to make her pay for it. If Clay died, he might kill her; he didn't know. If he lived, she might wish that he had.

He walked out, leaving Cobb staring, and moved steadily toward the stairs.

He turned the key in the lock of her door slowly, imagining her fear, smiling. He pushed the door open just as slowly and swept the room with a glance. Empty. Impossible—she must be hiding. The thought pleased him, made his vicious smile widen. He stepped inside. He hoped she was cowering under the bed because it would be such a pleasure to drag her out, hearing her whimper and plead for mercy. He would show her as much mercy as she'd shown Clay.

But she wasn't under the bed. Behind the curtains, then—shaking with dread, praying he wouldn't—he saw the broken glass on the floor, under the sash, and went toward it numbly. She'd shut the casement and broken it out, made a larger opening. No! She couldn't have jumped, it would kill her! Clutching the frame, unaware of pain as the jagged edges cut into his palms, he leaned from the window and gaped down at the dark shrubbery fourteen feet below.

Nothing.

He whirled, growling like an animal, beating down the sick relief. He was halfway to the door when he noticed the tin trunk on the bed—with the money on top, exactly as he'd left it. Or was it? Was some missing? *But why hadn't she taken it all?*

He ran from the room, down the stairs, out the door. As he rounded the house for the stables, he saw Cobb hurrying toward him.

"I don't know what it can mean, but I thought you did ought t' know," he started before Devon reached him, breathing hard.

"What?"

"The girl called Lily has runned away on a horse. Stableman give it to 'er."

Shouting a wild, incoherent curse, Devon shoved Cobb out of the way and made a dash for the stables.

MacLeaf was coming out of the tack room holding a broken bridle. He halted when he saw the master coming toward him with blood in his eyes. His face turned as red as his hair, and the harness slipped from his fingers. He took a sideways step toward the corridor between the stalls that led to the rear door, but it was as far as he got. Leaping across the straw-strewn floor, Devon seized him in a violent grip and hurled him against a stall door. The mare inside screamed, striking the rails with her side.

"Where is she?"

"I don't know!"

Devon struck him in the mouth. He fell sideways, but sprang up immediately and darted for the door. Devon tripped him and he went sprawling. Small and fast, he was on his feet again and had taken two steps toward freedom when Devon grabbed his shirt and hauled him back. "Where is she?"

"She ran! She was scairt! Said ee'd kill 'er!"

"Where?"

"I don't know!"

He used the back of his hand to smash across MacLeaf's face; the force of the blow sent him flying across the floor. Before he could get up, Devon caught him and hit him again. MacLeaf's back slammed against the door to his own small room, and he fell inside. Devon followed. Straddling him, he wrapped his hands around his neck.

MacLeaf pummeled Devon's chest and belly with panicky fists, but Devon didn't feel the blows. As if he himself were being strangled, his blood pounded in his throat and his ears, his eyes, blinding him, blotting out everything but fury. Someone was shouting at him, but the words were a meaningless howl. He felt the tearing of his hair from his scalp, then a blow to the side of his face. He gave a roar and tightened his grip. Something sharp struck the back of his head and he pitched forward, enraged, flailing against darkness and nausea. He hauled himself upright and found MacLeaf's throat with scrabbling fingers, just as a heavy, stunning weight hurtled against him, knocking him to his side.

It was Cobb who lay on top of him, holding his arms; Devon cursed him, then broke off his words to struggle in earnest when he saw MacLeaf—choking, tears streaming down his face—jackknife to his feet and stagger to the door. Devon made a last desperate attempt to shake Cobb off, and got a hard knee in the abdomen for his trouble. He lost his breath and doubled up.

When he felt he could stand, he stumbled up, and immediately lurched against the wall. Nausea returned; he touched his fingers to the back of his head and felt the sticky wetness of blood. Nearby on the floor lay a pitchfork.

Cobb had collapsed on the cot, limp arms hanging between his knees. "I'm sorry," he got out, panting. "You'd've killed him. I had to stop it." His hair was wild, his face above his fierce black beard a mottled red.

Devon said nothing.

"I'll ride for Truro now, fetch constable."

"Why?"

Cobb looked up. "That girl—she must've shot Clay. She runned away, she—"

"Leave it. Say nothing of this, Cobb, to anyone."

Cobb stood up, tall and lanky, anger and bewilderment darkening his harsh features. His good hand clenched into a fist. "But she must be found!"

"I'll find her."

"And punished!"

A ghastly smile split Devon's white, haggard face. "Don't worry," he said, and the clipped savagery in his voice gave his words the cadence of a blood oath. "I'll punish her."

# Twenty

"Ah, Lily, there you are. Feeling better now?"

"Yes, Cousin, much, thank you. I was just dizzy for a few minutes, that's all. From all the excitement, I expect."

"Of course. You look lovely," Roger Soames added with a false, square-toothed smile.

Now *he* was lying; she looked dreadful and she knew it, had said as much to the wan reflection in her bedroom mirror not five minutes ago. But for reasons she was apparently never going to understand, her cousin was as anxious as she to ignore what was obvious and pretend that nothing was amiss. She wondered what Lewis made of it all, but had reconciled herself to ignorance on that score forever: her betrothed was a man of few words—at least to her—and what he thought of her or of his father's unaccountable eagerness for them to marry were mysteries she would never uncover.

"Have you met Mr. and Mrs. Blayney?" Soames asked, introducing her to a middle-aged, richly dressed couple whose formal smiles could not quite hide their avid curiosity. *What an odd gathering*, Lily thought for the second or third time, smiling back at the Blayneys with all the friendliness she could muster. The guests at this "informal" wedding-eve entertainment in Cousin Soames's new home were a strange assortment to Lily's mind, a highly curious mix of the fashionable and unfashionable, the secular and the devout. Mr. Blayney, it developed, was a banker. But Mr. McComas, whom she'd met just before a wave of illness had forced her to murmur an excuse and retreat to her room, was a preacher, a disciple of Mr. Wesley, like Soames, and there were others here like him.

Soames's house hadn't been what she'd expected when she'd arrived here three weeks ago. It seemed too large and sumptuous for the dwelling of a humble man of the cloth, an itinerant preacher of repentance and damnation. It was new, made of brick, L-shaped and two-storied, with a fine rear courtyard in the angle of the L planted with flowers and shrubbery and fruit trees. It was here that the pre-wedding festivities were going on—thank God; she couldn't have endured the stuffiness of an indoor party tonight—and where there was to be even more frivolity after the wedding ceremony tomorrow morning.

Soames himself was even more of an enigma. He was a man of God, a minister with a sizable "flock" of souls he was hell-bent on saving. And yet she couldn't believe in him. For all his outward rectitude, his worldliness showed through, at least to Lily. In fact, the longer she knew him, the more convinced she became that his strongest spiritual asset was his voice—a truly compelling instrument he used to good effect. Even in ordinary speech she was struck by the range and beauty of it and the variety of emotions it could evoke. She could imagine sinners falling to their knees in a rush to repent when that voice exhorted them, or the already-redeemed weeping with joy when it described the ineffable peace and happiness waiting for them in God's heaven.

She spied Lewis across the way; they nodded to each other decorously. Her fiancé conformed much better than his father to her image of the stern and humorless clergyman. Speaking to Lewis, she sometimes had the wild notion that he was watching hellfire flickering just over her shoulder. With a small sinking feeling, she saw that he was coming to speak to her now.

"Lily," he intoned, bowing slightly.

"Lewis. Are you having a nice time?"

His heavy brows went up, as though he found the question faintly unsuitable, or at least irrelevant. "Are you?"

"Oh, yes."

"I'm glad. But you must be hungry. Come, my mother has put the food out."

Lily excused herself from Cousin Soames and the Blayneys and went with Lewis toward the long wooden tables across the way, where Mrs. Soames and the servants had indeed laid out a feast. There were hot pasties, cold tongue and partridge, cakes and jellies, syllabubs and fruit, punch and wines. Lily could hardly bring herself to look at it, much less eat any of it. But Lewis prepared her a plate, and to please him she pushed the food around on it with her fork, even touched some to her lips. It was kind of him to take care of her this way, she thought with a twinge of guilt, since he himself had been fasting for the last two days in preparation for their marriage. With weak and weary chagrin, she contemplated this man she didn't love and hardly knew, whom she would marry in the morning. He was truly devout, about which she had mixed feelings. At least he wasn't a hypocrite like his father, but what kind of wife would she make for Lewis, and what sort of life could they have together?

Last night he had confided to her his dream, his "vision" as he'd called it, that God wanted him to go to Wales and preach His gospel to the poor coal miners. Lily's first reaction had been a kind of subdued horror over the bleak prospect. But her dread had faded, and now any feeble unwillingness she might feel was buried under indifference and inertia. If Lewis had told her that God wanted him to hunt whales in the North Sea, she would have followed passively and tried her best to be a good whaler's wife. She simply didn't care. She'd stopped caring the night Devon had shoved her against a wall and told her that she'd shot his brother.

She'd stolen a horse and enough money to pay for coach fare back to Lyme Regis. During every minute of the nightmarish journey, she'd expected him to ride up and stop her—and then kill her, or beat her, or at least arrest her. In Lyme, Mrs. Troublefield had taken her in. She'd already forwarded a letter to Lily in Cornwall, she told her. From Exeter? Yes—so Lily knew it must be from Soames. She'd written to him immediately, saying she'd missed his letter, would he please write again? She told him she regretted what had happened and thanked God he was all right. If he could find it in his heart to forgive her, and if by some miracle Lewis still had any affection for her at all, she would be honored to become his wife.

Soames had written back by return mail. All was forgiven; come at once. He'd even enclosed money for her to hire a post chaise.

Three weeks had passed since then. The banns had been published, the wedding would take place tomorrow. Soames's haste had appalled her at first, until she'd considered how perfectly it accorded with her own secret needs. *Need*, rather; she only had one now: to give the child she was carrying a father.

"Are you feeling better, dear?"

"Thank you, yes, Mrs. Soames, I'm perfectly all right now." Soames's wife, Ruth, was a silent, pathetic wom-

an, small and self-effacing, who spoke in shy bursts of
speech and then turned away or looked down to hide
some inexplicable embarrassment. Lily had hardly gotten a hundred words out of her since she'd arrived. She
was completely cowed by her husband, who ignored her
except to give her gruff orders. But she'd been kind to
Lily in her bashful way, and for that she would always be
grateful. Lily began to tell Mrs. Soames what a lovely
party it was and how delicious the food tasted, when
Soames and a man she hadn't noticed before bore down
on them.

"Lily, Lewis, will you come inside for a moment?"
Soames asked, smiling jovially. It wasn't an invitation
they could refuse, since he had a hand on their shoulders and was propelling them toward the house as he
spoke. "This is Mr. Witt," he added belatedly, indicating
the gentleman with him. "He has some papers for you to
sign—you know how lawyers are. The merest formality,
and then you can go back to our guests."

"What sort of papers, Father?" asked Lewis once they
were in Soames's study, a large, dark-paneled chamber
lined with shelves of new-smelling books and decorated
—rather incongruously for a clergyman, Lily thought—
with hunting prints.

"Just a formality," Soames repeated; "the signing
over of the dowry."

"Dowry?" Lily almost laughed. "But I have nothing."

"Not *quite* nothing." He smiled blandly. "It's hardly
worth the trouble, I know, but Mr. Witt advises us to
keep everything neat and tidy."

Lily glanced at the thin, gray-wigged, dry stick of a
man who was unfurling a document and laying it out on
Soames's desk. She'd always thought a husband acquired everything a woman owned on the day they
exchanged wedding vows. Mr. Witt must be quite a
stickler. She took the pen from his hand and scrawled
her name. Lewis signed underneath.

Soames proposed a toast.

"To the happy couple," he offered, handing everyone except Lewis a small glass of port; to his abstemious son he gave a glass of barley water. "May God grant you a long and blessed life together, and may your children spring up around you like olive branches."

Lily paled, but got the wine down without choking.

It was time to rejoin the party. When Lewis stood aside to let her pass through the archway that led to the courtyard, though, she hung back. She was tired all the time these days, and exhaustion hit her now with the force of a blow—no doubt because of the wine. Continuing to play this grotesque charade of bridal happiness was suddenly more than she could bear.

"Lewis," she murmured, touching his sleeve, "would you mind terribly if I went up early? It's a wonderful party, and it was so kind of your parents to think of it, but—I'm a bit tired. All the excitement has taken a toll on me, I guess, and I want to be fresh for tomorrow."

"Of course," he answered without hesitation or regret, and began to walk with her back through the house. At the foot of the staircase he paused, and surprised her by taking her wrist when she murmured "Good night" and started to turn away. "Lily," he said portentously.

"Yes?"

"A woman's highest duty to her husband is obedience."

She nodded slowly and began to try to frame some suitable reply.

"I've been watching you tonight," he went on, not waiting for a response. "Your speech and manners are too free; they invite misunderstanding. In the future, you'll have to curb your behavior around individuals of the opposite sex."

Her mouth dropped open. "But—I never intended anything improper, Lewis, I promise—"

"I don't doubt it; but I speak of the result, not the

intent. My father has been vouchsafed a vision from God that you and I are to marry. The match may seem unsuitable, even strange to us, but that does not signify. A higher Power has decreed it, and our duty is to accept His will with humility and gratitude." He tightened his grip on her arm and leveled her with a stern, gray-eyed stare. "You will be my wife, Lily. With discipline and patient instruction, you will become everything the Lord intends you to be."

It almost sounded like a threat. Lily squared her shoulders, suppressing an inner shudder. At least the mystery was solved: Lewis liked her no better than she liked him. She sent him a brave, determined smile. "I will try hard to be a good wife," she promised truthfully. "I will help you with the work you've chosen in every way I can. One day I hope you'll be proud of me."

His stern expression softened slightly. "I hope so too," he said, and bent to drop a dry kiss—his first ever—on her forehead. "Sleep well. I'll send the maid up to you."

"Good night, Lewis."

He walked away, tall and straight and bulky. She watched him go, wondering what he would do if he knew about the baby. A quick tingle of perspiration dampened her palms. It didn't bear thinking about. Hanging onto the banister, she dragged herself up the stairs and turned down the long corridor that led to her room.

It was small but comfortable, and all the furnishings were brand new. Without lighting a candle, she crossed immediately to the doors that led out onto a tiny balcony—the room's finest amenity, in her opinion. It was on the other side of the house from the courtyard, thank heaven, so the festivities going on there now were only a vague hum. Soames had built his house on the outskirts of the old cathedral city, away from most of the bustle. A bright September moon was rising above the

plane trees across the road, and somewhere among
them an owl hooted. Tonight, as it had every night since
she'd run away from Darkstone, Lily's unconscious
mind registered, just for a second, that something was
missing. Then, again as always, she realized what it was:
the sound of the sea. She missed it as an infant might
miss the sound of its mother's heartbeat.

She drew a shaky breath. There were many things she
missed, and much she had to regret. But she was getting
through these dreadful days by living in the moment,
suppressing thoughts of the past and looking no further
into the grim future than tomorrow. It had gotten her to
this day, this time, so it must be working; she had better
not tamper with success. The owl called again, the
sound hollow and haunted. Lily put her head in her
hands and wept.

Behind her she heard a light knock and then the
opening of the door. She dried her cheeks with her
hands and the sleeve of her dress, then turned around to
see the maid standing beside the bed, waiting to help
her.

She undressed in silence, too weary for chatter,
although she was aware that the maid, whose name was
Abbey, must think it odd that she had so little conversation on the night before her wedding. They bade each
other quiet good nights, and then Lily sat down at the
dressing table to brush out her hair. Again the mirror
was not her friend. The pale strangeness of her own face
almost frightened her; it revealed too much of her
desperate unhappiness. But she must not cry anymore;
it was weak and foolish, and it brought no relief anyway.
But she was weighted down with the twin burdens of
regret and guilt, with nothing to comfort her but the
certainty that at least she had not lied to Lewis about
one thing: she *would* make him a good wife. Wherever
he took her, and for the rest of her life, even if it killed
her, she intended to be everything he wanted her to be.

Personal happiness was ludicrously irrelevant now. What was happening was God's punishment, because she had given in to sin with a man who had never loved her. As long as no harm came to the baby, she could count herself blessed that her punishment was no worse.

She dropped her tired arms and bowed her head, staring at the hairbrush lying limp in her hands. The emptiness rose up again without warning; she closed her eyes, weary of tears. But she was so lonely. It was fatigue, she told herself, fatigue and stress that made it so hard not to think of Devon. Not of that last night— that was unbearable, unspeakable—but of other times they'd shared. For some reason she thought of the night beside the lake, Pirate's Mere, when he'd walked up behind her, he and his brother, and she had been wet and trembling and embarrassed. It had been an awful moment—and yet she'd never been able to remember it without a secret thrill of excitement. But why would she think of such a thing now? She couldn't help it; she clearly recalled the low, provocative sound of his voice in her ear, and even more clearly the way his warm fingers had pulled her dripping hair aside and lightly touched the bare skin of her back. A deep longing welled up inside, so strong it hurt her, made her throat ache.

Her breath caught. A touch—so light—at the back of her neck made her throw her head up, wild-eyed. A big hand whipped around and muffled her scream of fright.

They stared at each other in the mirror while her chest heaved and she tried to catch her breath. He took his hand away slowly, but the other stayed tangled in her hair, holding her still. *She's changed*, he thought, though he couldn't define how. He'd thought it before, observing from the trees outside as she'd moved among the people at her party, and again from her balcony when he'd watched her undress. She was as beautiful as always, more so, but there was a new fragility, a tentativeness, as well as an odd, heavy quality. Sadness? His fingers tightened in her hair; he remembered that he didn't give a damn what she felt, now or ever.

"Did all that Wesleyan merrymaking tire you out, love?" He watched her swallow, following the line of her throat into the neckline of her modest robe. He reached down and began to unbutton it, casually, down to her waist. She allowed it, seemed frozen in her seat, eyes wide and lips parted, still too shocked to speak. "What, no greeting for me, Lily?" His eyes locked on the rapid rise and fall of her breasts. "Haven't you missed me? I've missed you." He pushed the robe over her shoulders, listening to the flutter of her breathing. She didn't move. "What a relief to see that you weren't injured in the fall from your window, sweetheart. I've been so worried about you." He gave a little tug on the ribbon holding the front of her nightdress together, and her beautiful eyes darkened. At last she reacted.

She jumped up and tried to twist away, but he still had her hair. He pulled her into an embrace, intimate but unkind, and her eyes turned luminous with sudden tears. Detached, careful, he wiped them away with his fingers, noticing the bruised-looking crescents under her eyes. "Such a tragic face," he murmured, touching her cheeks, her lips, frowning intently.

"Why have you come?" It amazed her that she could speak any words at all, much less coherent ones.

"Why? To see you, of course. And to wish you well on the eve of your marriage. The wisdom of your choice eludes me, I confess, but I long ago gave up trying to understand women."

"Let go of me." Instead his arms tightened cruelly. But only for a moment; then, to her surprise, he released her. She backed away immediately, seeking distance, trying desperately to read his face. He was surveying the room, taking in its small ordinariness with a contemptuous glance. Shocked, she watched him walk to the bed and sit down at the foot, crossing his booted legs and smiling across at her coldly. She dreaded to ask, but she could not wait any longer. "Clay," she faltered, hardly above a murmur; "how is he?"

His smile stayed in place, but now it was patently unnatural. "He's recovered," he said tonelessly.

Lily's chin dropped to her chest; she closed her eyes and thanked God.

"But he's lost his memory. He can't remember who shot him."

She jerked her head up. "I didn't." Still his odd, wooden smile didn't change. "I've been thinking about it," she went on, unable to stop. "I think it must have been Trayer. Do you remember? He said he would pay you back."

"Trayer. Yes. That must have been who it was."

But he didn't believe it—she could see it in his eyes, hear it in his voice. "How did you find me?" she asked hopelessly.

"Simple. I opened the letter your estimable guardian had forwarded to you at Darkstone."

"But—"

"Then I went to Lyme Regis, where dear Mrs.—Troublefield, wasn't it? a vaguely familiar name to me—was persuaded to say where you'd gone."

She shivered; the thought of his persistence chilled her. "Please . . ." She lifted a beseeching hand, then let it fall to her side, conscious of the futility of asking him for anything. Instead she said, "What are you going to do?"

"Me? I'm not going to do anything." His eyes shone with a hard, peculiar gleam that terrified her. "But you are."

"What do you mean?"

"I only want one thing from you now, Lily. It's really

all I've ever wanted." He stood up, and Lily wrapped her arms around herself and stood straighter. He went toward her slowly, daring her with his eyes not to move. By the time he reached her she had gone pale with dread and the effort of control. He reached one hand out to her shoulder and caressed her under the robe, softly, almost absentmindedly. "I want to sleep with you." Her eyelids flickered, but otherwise she didn't react. "Just for tonight," he explained, running an idle finger under her chin, stroking her jaw. "One last time for us, hmm? For old times' sake."

She got out, "No," in an aghast whisper.

"No?" he repeated, pressing her lips now with his forefinger but otherwise not touching her. "Oh—but I forgot to tell you what I will do if you refuse. I'll have you arrested." He watched color come into her cheeks, then recede as she went even whiter. Her lovely gray-green eyes widened; for a moment he was lost.

"Dev . . ."

The sighed word recalled him to his purpose. "You know I can do it. They'll put you in prison, love. You'll stay there until November for the assizes, and then they'll try you. Clay can't remember, but his note will be enough."

"His—"

"They'll hang you," he said flatly, tired of sparring.

She took a step back. His cold, remote expression made her feel frozen inside. "I see." She pulled her robe closer and bowed her head, absorbing his terms and the hateful things he'd said. She thought of the baby. "But if I give myself to you tonight . . ."

"I'll let you go."

She looked up. He stared back, and she saw the utter ruthlessness in his face. Her decision wasn't automatic, and there was enough fight left in her to hope he knew it. But after a moment she answered, again in a whisper, "All right, Dev. You win." Before she could think too long about it, she shrugged out of her dressing gown and let it fall to the floor. His face went even harder. Taking that for a dare, she crossed her arms and seized two handfuls of nightgown at the hips, pulled it up, and whisked it over her head. She held the balled cloth in her arms across her middle just for a second, and then flung it on the floor. Her voice came out high and thin. "Where do you want me? In the bed?"

Devon dragged his eyes back to her face. *She thinks this is a game,* he thought, *that I'll relent because I'm bluffing.* "Yes, the bed," he answered softly, then repeated the last two words when seconds passed and she didn't move. Fascinated, he watched her smooth diaphragm contract with every panicked inhalation. Finally she turned and walked stiffly to the bed. She hesitated, both hands on the mattress, fingers spread. Her hair hung down her back like a dark flame; her skin was white enough to blind. She bent a little, and the movement of muscle in her thighs and buttocks made him stop breathing. With a natural grace that he remembered with shocking and painful clarity, she climbed onto the bed, then sat in the middle in a slightly awkward posture of waiting. "Lie down," he said hoarsely. Her thin nostrils flared, but she obeyed. "Yes, on your back. For now."

He moved closer. "Now open your arms and legs, Lily, as if you would welcome me." She turned her face away, toward the wall. A moment later she spread her arms out on either side. He waited. "Lily?" He saw that her ribs were shuddering faintly, then uncontrollably, and in the flicker of candlelight he made out the silver rush of tears on the side of her face he could still see.

The hollowness inside him shifted, changed, as if her tears were the ones he'd kept himself from shedding for so long and now his emptiness was beginning to fill. He walked toward the bed, stripping off coat and waistcoat as he went, dragging his shirt out of his breeches. He sat beside her, facing her, one knee drawn up in the hollow of her waist, and put his hand on the soft, silky skin of her thigh. She jumped. He lowered his head and kissed her just above the knee, once. She sighed and covered her eyes with one hand. He said her name, and as he did so he parted her legs with his hands, slowly but strongly, allowing no resistance. He watched her abdomen tense and harden. With his palm he caressed her between her legs; using the back of his middle finger he opened her, stroking side to side.

Lily took a quick gulp of air and faced him, one arm still spread wide. He saw her tongue touch the roof of her mouth as she started to say his name. To stop her, he put his fingers inside her. Her eyes squeezed shut; her head went back against the pillow. "Don't," she said brokenly. "Dev, for the love of God—"

"Don't talk, Lily." He watched her eyes, and the slow, slick movements of his hand. She drew one knee up; after long minutes her breathing changed and her back arched subtly. Her struggle to resist was fierce and obvious. He waited, resisting the invitation of her soft breasts until her hands curled into fists and every muscle went rigid. Then he bent to taste her, taking one stiff nipple into his mouth. She clutched at him while he suckled her and stroked her with thorough, remorseless skill. She didn't move or make a sound, but all at once he felt her strong, rhythmic contractions through his fingers and the palm of his hand.

The pulsing tapered away to soft, intermittent ripples. He straightened slowly. He wanted to see her face, but she kept it turned from him. Her breasts were flushed pink, wet from his kisses. He stared down at the still-intimate cupping of his hand, caressing her with a soft, insistent thumb. She jerked, and he stroked her again, but more gently. She moved her hand to cover his, stilling it, and looked at him.

She saw that his face was intent, aroused, but beyond

that she couldn't read his expression. Sorrow and uncertainty kept her motionless. It was not tenderness that had motivated the thing he had just done. But it was hardly cruelty, either. Something in between, she guessed, despairing. He had wanted her to feel defeated. She said his name, needing to connect with him in some way besides sex. His face didn't change and he made no answer. "Dev," she repeated, whispering. "Can you believe that I love you?"

Something flickered behind his eyes. She stared intently, straining to understand. Abruptly he got to his feet. She tensed, expecting anything. He began to pull off his boots, then his shirt and breeches.

She sat straight up, her face the color of ashes. "Don't. Don't do this. This is wrong, please don't." The sight of his naked body, powerfully aroused, filled her with primitive, unreasoning panic. Before she could move, he took her by the shoulders and pushed her down, sliding his big body over hers. She felt his knees forcing hers apart. "Please! Oh please, we have to talk, you—"

"I didn't come here to talk."

With a stab of anguish, she felt his maleness enter her quickly, sleekly. To her surprise he held still then, deep inside her. A truce. She tried to touch his face—if only she could reach him!—but he took her wrists away and pressed them back against the pillow. "Dev—"

"Don't say anything."

He began to move, seducing her with the slowness of his long, sensual stroking. The quickness of her response shamed her; for a few minutes she tried to dissemble, but it was useless. Tears filled her eyes. He stopped the wet tracks with his tongue, but when she moved her mouth to kiss him, he turned his face aside. His movements quickened and his eyes burned with purpose. She knew what he wanted. She said, "I can't."

"You can." He embraced her, releasing her wrists, and at last she was allowed to touch him—his heated skin, the cool sleekness of his hair. Now it was his body that was trembling as she slid her hands over his buttocks and the rigid muscles of his back. She was dying to kiss him. She trailed her fingers under the hard bone of his clenched jaw; watching his eyes, she drew his head down and traced the strong outline of his lips with her tongue. He sucked in his breath; his shuddering intensified. But he was waiting, wanting her to let go of her control before his own snapped. It was a matter of power. Realizing it, Lily almost smiled, for this was a game she could win.

She shifted subtly and pulled her knees up, lodging him higher, tighter. Legs locked around his waist, she began to rock him with the same slow, canny, devastating artistry he had taught her. His face was buried in her hair, but she thought she could hear him grinding his teeth. Patient and passionate, she gave herself to him, daring him to reject the gift this time. She knew the instant his resistance began to disintegrate. He raised his head; just for an instant, behind the desire, she caught a glimpse of haggard suffering in his eyes. Her heart contracted. Cradling his dear face, she touched her lips to his in a soft, gentle kiss. He shuddered, not moving, and then suddenly his open mouth slanted over hers and he returned her kiss with all the wild tenderness she had been afraid to hope for. He only lifted his head to grit out a low, hoarse shout when his climax came. It surged through him with a rough, tumultuous violence that she accepted gladly. She held him tightly, needing to shelter him until the storm passed. Afterward, he lay limp in her arms, sprawled across her, his breath rasping. But she could not tell from the heaviness of his body whether what he felt now was satisfaction or defeat.

And she couldn't ask. Words were their enemy, had always been, but never, she sensed, more so than now. She stroked his damp skin, treasuring the rare peace, if that was what it was. Her love was as strong as ever. But he would not believe her if she told him of it, and she would do anything to keep on holding him. She pressed her breasts and her belly against him softly, secretly, because the need to tell him about the baby was overpowering her. Not being allowed to speak those words made her cry.

He felt her tears on his cheek and pushed up on his elbows to see her. He had never been able to stand it when she cried. In weary wonder, Devon heard himself say, "Don't. It's all right, Lily, don't cry."

He slid away and lay on his side beside her. Lily dried her face on the sheet, determined to stop this weak weeping. But her emotions were closer to the surface than she knew, because in the next minute she found herself saying, "I love you, Dev. I do, I swear it."

A moment passed. Devon lifted his hand to her shoulder and patted it stiffly. "And I love you." She drew in her breath, turning to look at him. His downcast eyes eluded her. "But you must marry Lewis," he said in a sad, resigned voice. "I wish you happiness with him. He's probably not a bad sort. His father's rich, and that will help. But you already know that."

What was left of Lily's heart broke into pieces. "Will you remember me?" she whispered, eyes closed.

"Oh, yes. And you'll remember me."

Something in his voice made her heart stop. His fingers began to trail across her breasts in lazy, random patterns. A little later he covered her mouth with his, putting an end to speaking, arousing her in spite of a heavy listlessness that had begun to spread through her body. Turning her, he took her from behind this time, bringing her to her pleasure with slow, unrelenting patience. Heartsick, she fell into an exhausted sleep. Sometime in the night his skimming hands woke her. The candles had guttered; the room was dark and chilly. She suffered his strange, tormented loving in silence, too weary to speak now, or even to weep. The next time she awoke, she was alone.

# Twenty-One

"For 'The wife hath not power of her own body but the husband, and the unbelieving wife is sanctified by the husband. Else were your children unclean, but now they are holy.'"

Lily closed her eyes and tried to attend more to the fine, theatrical rhythm of Soames's marvelous voice than to St. Paul's uncompromising message. Kindly, soaring, avuncular, celebratory, the voice filled every inch of the enormous, high-ceilinged drawing room, empty of furniture this morning to accommodate the eighty wedding guests crammed between its ornate, frescoed walls. At least their faces were a blur to her, white, featureless blotches with staring eyes. She was thankful for the gossamer veil covering her head, for if the guests could see her face clearly underneath, it might alarm them.

It had alarmed Soames's wife a few minutes ago when she'd come to Lily's room to tell her it was time. "My

dear, you're ill!" Then, "Oh, heavens—Roger won't
want to put off the ceremony," she'd fretted, twisting
her hands. Lily had to summon all her strength to
reassure the good woman that she was not ill, only
excited, and of course the wedding must go forward.
But she felt another lurch of nausea now and pressed
the prayerbook Lewis had given her more tightly to her
stomach. She ought to have forced herself to eat something for breakfast after all, she thought distractedly.
What if she fainted?

"'Therefore as the church is subject unto Christ, so
let the wives be to their own husbands in everything,'"
Soames rumbled on, big square teeth bared for the
dramatic "e" sounds. Lily's knees had begun to tremble;
she imagined for a few seconds how very easy it would
be to slide to the floor, right here, right now. What on
earth was she doing, marrying Lewis Soames? Surely
this was a perversion, a sin, a willful crime against
nature. Her very soul was in rebellion against it, and the
battle inside was draining away the last of her physical
resources. She still felt empty and violated from Devon's harrowed, desperate lovemaking, and yet the
thought of giving herself to her lawfully wedded husband seemed infinitely stranger, a truly unnatural act.

"'For this cause shall a man leave his father and
mother, and cleave to his wife, and they twain shall be
one flesh.'"

She had no choice. "Unnatural act" or not, what she
was doing was a practical necessity, nothing more or
less. Her other two options were the poorhouse and
prostitution. Rather than marry Lewis, she might have
picked one of those—except for the baby. The solution
was not to think about it. Submit; let it happen. And
don't faint. Gratefully she felt the solidity of Lewis's
shoulder against hers. But it surprised her too, for she
hadn't realized she was leaning against him. Soames
had stopped reading and was addressing his "dear

friends," telling them why they were gathered here together.

It's not the end of the world; it's a wedding. To a good man, a respectable man. Just then he took her hand—his father must have told him to; she hadn't heard—and she looked down at Lewis's huge, blocky fingers, hers invisible inside them. She tried to imagine him touching her with passion, and everything in her shriveled and shrank. It was a sin, but she thought of Devon's hands, touching her. Even last night, in his anger and pain, there had been moments of undeniable tenderness between them—never mind that they had been against his will, half buried under some inscrutable torment. But he didn't love her; he had as good as given her to Lewis, without regrets: "I wish you happiness with him," he'd said. His heart was a mystery she would never unlock, because she would never see him again.

Marriage was an indissoluble union, Soames was saying, sanctified by the word of God and prayer. It was a sacrament proclaimed by Christ according to Mark, indivisible once undertaken save for the cause of fornication. Fancy, Lily knew, but it seemed to her that Cousin Roger's piercing gray eyes could see through her concealing veil straight to her wicked heart. *Submit,* she ordered herself. Don't think, just do it. Do it for the baby. Her hand in Lewis's was drenched with perspiration, but she was shivering as if with a chill. She heard a whirring in her ears, and despaired: dear God, she was going to faint after all.

But it wasn't whirring, she realized a second later, it was whispering; and now it was murmuring. People were *talking.* Impossible; was she losing her mind? Were they? What had Soames just said that could have provoked it? "In the absence of any impediment" was the last thing she could remember. She glanced up at Lewis, but he seemed equally bewildered. Soames stopped talking and peered, scowling, between her and Lewis's shoulders. They turned around together, still holding hands. The crowd behind them was parting in the middle, falling back to make way for a newcomer.

In the instant before she saw him, Lily knew it was Devon. Her first response was sheer, wild delight. Behind the veil, her face was transformed; she had to hold back a laugh of pure joy. He was here! He was going to save her! He was dressed formally, all in black; he even wore a wig. Had he been here all the time, pretending to be a wedding guest? Knowing it would be unseemly just now to flash him a huge, rapturous smile, she kept her veil in place. She saw him glance down at her and Lewis's clasped hands, and gave a tug to break the contact. But Lewis held on.

"I know of an impediment to this marriage," Devon announced in an idle, conversational tone that nevertheless carried to every ear in the long room.

But Lily saw through his seeming casualness; she could read the hot intensity in his eyes, and she felt its answering flame in her own heart. *Oh, my love,* she called to him silently; the jumping of a muscle in his hard jaw made her imagine he'd heard.

"At least, I should find it a bit of an impediment if I were standing in the happy groom's shoes at this moment."

"Who are you?" demanded Soames. "What do you want here?"

"I'm Devon Darkwell, Viscount Sandown, and I know a reason why young Lewis here might not wish to bind himself forever in holy wedlock to this woman. Are you interested in hearing it?"

The room had gone deathly quiet. Even Soames, for once, seemed incapable of speech. Finally it was Lewis who answered. "Speak your piece quickly, sir, and then leave us. You are not known here."

"Not entirely true, my friend. I'm known by one of you. Known rather well, in fact." His voice was still matter-of-fact; it was the slight sneer on his lips when he uttered the last words that sounded the alarm in Lily's brain. "But you asked me to be quick. I'm happy to oblige, for I've no more stomach for prolonging this unsavory business than you. Think you, sir, that you are marrying a virgin?"

A gasp went up. Lewis's fierce grip on her hand tightened painfully, and she was relieved; it took her mind off the agony inside as every hope died and each foolish dream crumbled. Devon had not come to rescue her, he'd come to ruin her. She had a swift vision of everything that would happen, like lightning illuminating a catastrophe, and then it all went black again.

"How dare you?" blustered Soames, his eloquent voice rising with indignation. "By what right do you come among us with your foul innuendos?"

"Let him speak, Father," Lewis said softly, and the murmurs of curiosity and outrage tapered off again to silence.

Devon cocked an amused eyebrow. "Thank you," he said with a mock bow. "I'll be brief. Assuming that, like most men, you don't care to find yourself encumbered with used goods on your wedding night, I think it might interest you to know that your betrothed is not precisely what she seems. Not even remotely, in fact. My acquaintance with the lady is short, a matter of months, so I can't speak of the past. But I can tell you that until four weeks ago she was my mistress."

Soames was beside himself. "Sir!" he thundered, raising one heavy arm and pointing behind Devon to the door. "Leave my house at once before I have you thrown out. By God, sir, I'll—"

"Have you proof of this?" interrupted Lewis.

"Alas, no. I can, however, prove one of the lady's more recent transgressions. Very recent, in point of fact; indeed, I'm speaking of last night."

A chorus of shocked exclamations erupted from the

guests. When she needed it the most, Lewis suddenly dropped Lily's hand; she wobbled, and felt Soames's strong, sustaining grip on her shoulder. Comfort from an unexpected source, she mused—and surely a temporary one. She folded her arms around herself and concentrated on not swooning. It would be too cheap a solution.

"I'm sorry to have to tell you this," Devon went on with the same ghastly confidentiality, "but better to find out now than later, eh? The fact is, I lay with your bride last night in your own bed. Well, not in *your* bed precisely, but you take my meaning. I had her three or four times, I forget which, and then left at dawn by way of that convenient little balcony." He smiled, and said as an aside, "If you decide to marry her anyway, I suggest you begin your new life together in a room without balconies, for your own peace of mind."

"Liar!" roared Soames.

"Not at all. Shall I describe the room to you? Small, the minimum of furniture; a rose-colored carpet of a vaguely floral design. White walls, plain ceiling. Truthfully, it's the bed I remember best—an oak tester with a carved headboard. Cotton coverlet of purple and rose and light blue, I think. You still don't believe me? Wait, I'd forgotten." He reached into his waistcoat pocket and pulled from it something white. "Voila! The lady's garter—I divested her of it myself. As you can see, it has her initials."

All alone now, thought Lily, feeling Soames's lifeless hand slide from her shoulder. It was almost a relief, because nothing worse could happen. This was the bottom.

Lewis was speaking to her. "Is this true, Lily, any of it? Do you know this man? Is he—"

"Of course it's not true," Soames interrupted, rallying, moving to stand between them. "The man's a liar, and very likely an impostor. Lily is family, my cousin's child. I'm a minister of the Lord—I've been blessed with the gift of seeing into men's souls, and I tell you this woman's heart is pure. Do you think I would countenance the wedding of my son to a common jade?" There was a gathering murmur of uncertain agreement. With his next words, Soames's persuasive voice rang with conviction. "Your lies don't convince us, sir. Leave my house at once. The wedding will go forward, on the strength of the word of this chaste girl. Lily," he boomed, eyeing her confidently. "We only wait for the truth from your lips. Tell us, do you know this man?"

"Yes, I know him." In another mood, she might have found Soames's expression comical, so obvious was his desire to rephrase the question. Summoning the last of her strength, she turned away from him and faced Lewis, drawing her veil away with an unsteady hand and looking directly into his shocked eyes. "What he says is true. I have been his lover. I ask your pardon, Lewis, I never meant to hurt you. I wanted to make you a good wife—" She broke off when Lewis snarled and shoved her away, hands trembling with suppressed violence, and turned his back on her.

His father confronted him immediately; their low, urgent conversation was drowned out in the rising din of shock and amazement of the scandalized wedding guests. Lily felt their rapt gazes on her as acutely as if she were naked, but she looked at none of them. It was Devon's glance that held her. Even when Lewis broke away from Soames's desperate counsel and announced in a strident voice that the wedding was off, she couldn't look away—no matter that the cruel triumph in Devon's face desolated her.

She became aware that the room was emptying. She felt a light touch on her arm and turned to see Ruth Soames standing at her side. The confusion in her shy brown eyes made Lily reach for her hand. *"I'm so sorry,"* she whispered. Ruth shook her head in slow bewilderment and started to speak. But Lily would never know what she intended to say, because Lewis pushed his way between the two women at that moment, and Ruth, as intimidated by her son as she was by her husband, turned away and wandered out of the room.

Knowing it was hopeless to try to make peace with Lewis, Lily simply waited. When she'd put on her pretty green wedding gown this morning, she'd been conscious of the irony that the day was glorious, the sun shimmering down from a sky of pure azure. Now, without surprise, she saw through the long drawing-room windows that a raucous wind had sprung up, blackening the sky and hurling dead leaves against the house. A much more fitting conclusion to the debacle of her wedding.

Lewis curled and uncurled his fingers into fists. With his back to Devon he hissed at her, "Lily Trehearne, you've dishonored my home and brought shame on my family. Leave this house; you're dead to us now. But know that God's wrath follows you and His justice is swift and terrible. Out, whore! Filthy, fornicating slut—"

She didn't truly believe he would strike her, even though his hands were clenched and raised; still, she felt relief when Devon seized him by the collar and pulled him backward, cutting off the tirade. "What, no words of denunciation for me? Not very evenhanded of you, Lewis, old man. A girl has to have a partner to be a filthy, fornicating slut—or hasn't your father explained that to you yet?"

"Villain! Spawn of the devil! Get out of my house, both of you! Here—what are you doing? Get back. Stop it, I said—"

Devon was marching Lewis backward toward the door, nudging him with a flat hand on his chest each time he stopped. "Go away, Lewis," he told him quietly.

"I'll leave in two minutes. But you'll appreciate that I need to have a word with Lily first."

"No, you—"

"Two minutes." He gave him a last firm shove and shut the door in his face.

Lily looked at the only seating accommodation, a loveseat set under the windows for some infirm wedding guest. But it was on the other side of the room, miles away; she would never reach it before her legs gave way. A long wainscoted wall was behind her; she stepped back until she felt its reassuring solidity against her shoulders. Devon sauntered over unhurriedly, hands in his pockets. The look of casual victory in his face and bearing was a mask, she knew, for there was nothing casual about him. He stopped in front of her and braced an arm against the wall beside her. She felt the subtle menace radiating from his body, but she was not afraid of him now.

"Too bad about the wedding," he murmured, smiling with false sympathy. "But I was wrong about Lewis— he's a canting arse. In my opinion you're well rid of him. What will you do now, do you think?" She didn't speak. "I expect you'll land on your feet one way or another. Your kind always does."

Numbness, not pride, kept her from weeping. It was hurtful to look at him, but she had to know the answer. She swallowed down the viscous lump in the back of her throat and got the word out: "Why?"

Slowly his face changed. Malicious whimsy faded to stark hatred, and under it, grief. "Clay," he said hollowly. "He isn't better, Lily. I think he must be dead by now. I stayed with him for a month, but he never woke up. The doctors gave him no chance." He pulled something from his pocket and handed it to her. "And you killed him."

She opened the worn, folded piece of paper. Her legs buckled; she steadied herself by locking her knees and

leaning all her weight against the wall. Her arms fell to
her sides and she closed her eyes as the hissing in her
ears became a roar. *Lily shot.* All the blood drained from
her face; she looked like a standing corpse. But it
passed; the spell passed and she didn't faint—another
mercy denied her. When she could move, she folded her
arms around her middle, protecting her womb. She wet
her lips with her tongue. "Why didn't you just kill me?"
she whispered. She saw him lean forward and realized
he hadn't heard. The words hurt her throat, but she said
them again.

"I wanted to. Want to. But this is better."

Because she couldn't look at him any longer, she
didn't know he was leaving until she heard his slow
footfalls on the carpet. A second later the door opened
with a soft click, and after that she knew she was alone.
Quietly, gradually, she slid to the floor.

She hooked her arms around her knees and rocked
herself, fighting nausea brought on by the sweet, relent-
less smell of carnations. The house was uncannily quiet.
With her cheek resting on her knee, she could hear the
blood pounding in her ears, feel it swishing through her
wrists. Inside her was another heart, tiny, beating fast
and birdlike; within her was another being, vulnerable,
helpless, innocent. It was her responsibility, the only
one now, to keep her baby safe. For that reason, Lily put
aside thoughts of self-destruction. And for that reason,
after only a few more minutes of quiet, empty-headed
numbness, she climbed to her feet and carefully made
her way from the room.

The house was silent enough to be empty, but she
knew it was not. She stood at the foot of the stairs,
gazing up at the dark hallway. Last night, on this spot,
Lewis had told her she was too forward with men. A
giddy laugh rose in her throat; she had to put her fingers
over her mouth to smother it. Was she expected just to
go now, with no more words? She said, "Good-bye,"

into the echoing emptiness, amazed at how clear and strong her voice sounded, and walked across the hall to the front door.

The wind blew a gust of grit and cinders in her face when she stepped over the threshold. Immediately her gaze fell on a rumpled bundle of cloth at the bottom of the shallow steps. She went closer and saw that it was her old dress, the one she'd worn when she arrived here three weeks ago. She bent and picked it up, and felt her old shoes, hard and lumpy, wrapped inside. Holding the bundle against her breast, she stared up at the flat facade of the house; the black window squares blinked back blind and empty, but she was not deceived: she felt the bright avidity of watchful eyes like sharp, bared teeth. Expressionless, she turned away and began to trudge up the lane, her high-heeled wedding shoes clumsy on the packed dirt, just as the first thudding drops of rain began to fall. Unknowingly, she was setting out toward Dartmoor.

# Twenty-Two

There is something inimical about the moor. It does not look habitable, it does not look like the earth. The bogs and bracken and seeping moss lie in a brown, monotonous expanse broken only by stark outcrops of granite called tors. Vipers live in the treeless moorland scrub, but few birds. The stillness is brooding and sullen, the prospect unfriendly even on the brightest days. But usually the moor is shrouded in mist, and then one has an urge to turn back, to get out into more wholesome air. Sometimes, in the middle of Dartmoor, a horse will stand still and sweat with fear.

On a cold September afternoon, when a clammy mist trailed white fingers over the dreary downland, an old woman drove a donkey cart along a trackless path of her own choosing. Her name was Meraud. Beside her on the hard seat sat a huge black dog. "Down now," said the old woman, and the dog jumped to the ground. The cart carried an extra burden today, and the aged donkey had to strain even on the shallow hills. The dog trotted alongside on the stony wasteland; when they were once again on level terrain, he leapt gracefully back to his seat.

Meraud buttoned the top button of her frock coat. It was a man's coat, green with age. "Getting cold," she said, huddling into it, "and that gel haven't so much as a shawl. Still sleeping, is she?" The dog, Gabriel, shifted his heavy ears at the question. "What were she doing in Bovey Tracy, I wonder. No place for a gel in a silk dress, that's sure. Damn rascally monkeys—ran when they saw you, didn't they, Gabe? Hoo hoo." It wasn't so much a laugh as a verbal representation of one, as one might say, "bang," to stand for a pistol shot. "Don't have to go back there for ages, maybe spring if we're lucky. Got everything, we did. You fancy the chicken, don't you?" She shrugged a shoulder toward the small wire cage on the floor of the cart behind her. "Admit it, you sod. But you leave 'er be, there's a good boy. You can have the eggs, for all I care; it's the other I'm wanting. Down again," she said as the cart started up another rise, and Gabriel jumped down. A little farther on, Meraud began to sing.

The mist thickened and thinned uneasily. In the intervals when it lifted, low-hanging bags of cloud jostled each other, so close to the seepy earth that it seemed an upraised arm could touch them. Lily gazed up at them blankly, imagining they were restless sheep, undecided what to do next. She shifted uncomfortably on a burlap bag full of sharp things; to her right was another large, heavy bag full of something foul-smelling. The voice that had awakened her came again, a high, light quaver on the heavy air: "How sweet my Savior is to me, His arms a refuge dear." Lily turned her head and stared through a wire mesh into the bright, unblinking beads of a chicken's eyes. After a moment she levered herself up on one elbow and glanced behind her. The black rump of an enormous dog filled her vision, two feet from her face. She hadn't noticed the chicken when she'd half crawled, half fallen into the cart, but she remembered the dog. His intimidating presence had saved her from a trickle of jeering urchins in the muddy lane of some no-name village she'd wandered through—how long ago? Undersized, barefoot, and scabby, they'd only insulted her at first, but then their beastly courage had grown and they'd begun to hurl rocks and clods of dirt at her. The black dog had trotted to her side, lifting his heavy flews back from sharp and astonishingly white teeth. Her tormentors had flown away like rumpled birds from a cat.

The thin soprano singing came to a quiet close. Lily heard a movement behind her, and then the voice said, "So, you're awake. What's your name?"

Lily twisted around, squinting in the dimness at the bony profile of a woman in a dark coat whose gnarled hands held the leads to the elderly donkey pulling the cart. "Lily Trehearne." The old woman nodded. After a few silent minutes, Lily ventured, "Where are we going?"

"Gabriel and I are going home." She turned her head slightly. "I'm called Meraud," she offered. "Have you got any people, Lily Trehearne?"

"No."

"Friends?"

"No."

"What'll you do, then?"

She shook her head. When she realized the woman wasn't looking at her any longer, she said, "I don't know. I can't think."

"If the parish constable catches you, he'll clap you in the workhouse. You got to have a place, you can't wander."

Lily lowered her chin to her chest.

"Can you work?"

"Yes, I can work."

"I need a helper. Couldn't pay anything, but you'd have food and a roof."

Lily took a breath. She said, "I'm pregnant." There was a long, long silence. She sank back down on her shoulders and closed her eyes, thinking of nothing.

"You could stay anyway. I live on the moor. You can help me with my work as long as you're able."

Lily gazed up at the gray swirl of the sky through tears of thankfulness.

A long time later, the donkey cart lurched to a stop. Lily got down stiffly. The moonless night was pitch-black. "Have a care," the old lady warned her when Lily, feeling lightheaded, walked straight into some bulky, looming shape in the murk, a tree or a stone of some sort, she supposed. She made out others like it all around her. Meraud took her by the arm and led her through the maze of dark forms to the door of a small cottage. Inside, it seemed colder, damper, and darker than outside. "Can you light a peat fire, Lily?"

"Yes."

"Here be the hearth at your feet, and there's the firebox. I'll come along in soon."

"But I should help you with your bags of—things."

"We'll let 'em set till morning."

"The donkey, then—"

"Have done, gel, you're already dead on your feet. Make up the fire and then hie you to bed." She ghosted away through the black door before Lily could say thank you.

She'd never laid a peat fire before, had only said she could to please her new benefactor. As her eyes grew used to the dimness, she made out the neat stacks of turf beside the stone hearth. She could see no kindling except the tinder in the tinderbox. Did you just—light it? She stacked the grate with four of the heavy squares, which resembled enormous bars of soap, and after much striking and scraping, succeeded in setting a spark to the linen tinder in the box underneath. Lo! The peat caught like magic, and in no time at all she had a merry fire burning. The smell was strong, though, and quickly pervasive; it reminded her of smoking bacon.

"Hie you to bed," Meraud had said. The bed must be this rush mat on the earth floor. Oh, but she would be taking *her* bed, then, or half of it anyway; was there nowhere else to sleep? She glanced around the small room—and drew in her breath in a gasp of astonishment. The wall! The one in the back, it was—*shining*, sparkling, glittering, sending back reflections of gold and crimson firelight from a thousand tiny prisms, specks of brightness on every surface of the wall from floor to ceiling. After a full minute of motionless wonder, Lily crept forward until she stood within touching distance of the colorful, blinking panel. Glass, it was, and mirrors. And metal. Small, oddly shaped pieces glued into the plaster, or whatever the wall was made of, to form a fantastic multicolored surface of blinking light.

She whirled at a noise in the door. Meraud came in, carrying the chicken in its coop and a sack over her shoulder. She kept her gaze down and didn't look up until she'd finished setting things down and storing her supplies on a shelf built into the bottom of a rough table, in what Lily took to be the kitchen area. For the first time, she saw the old woman in relative brightness. She might have been fifty or seventy, tall and angular, loose-jointed, slow-moving. Her face was deeply lined, dark as leather. Her yellow-white hair was cut short and covered her head like a metal cap. She had a witch's nose, sharp-boned, pointed on the end, and a small, thin-lipped mouth that revealed a number of missing teeth when she smiled. But her brown eyes were gentle as a madonna's. She glanced up now, and Lily was surprised to read shy anxiety in her expression. With a start, she realized Meraud was waiting for her to say something about the cottage, or more precisely, the wall.

She flung out an arm helplessly. "It's—*fabulous!*" Meraud's gap-toothed grin transformed her homely old face. In it Lily imagined she saw a sweet, forgiving nature that would understand and absolve every human folly and frailty. For no reason she could think of, tears sprang to her eyes. "I'm tired," she muttered, embarrassed, swiping at her cheeks.

"How long since you ate?"

She thought. "The night before last."

"Set down, lamb. Get dry and clean—there's water in this pitcher—and get under the covers. I'll make tea."

Lily did what she was told, glad to strip out of her damp silk dress and her new underclothes, her sodden shoes and stockings. She washed beside the fire, dried herself with a piece of cotton toweling, and crawled naked between the blankets on the rustling rush mat that Meraud had dragged close to the hearth. She heard scratching outside and watched as the old woman went to the door to let Gabriel in. He gave Lily an impassive stare before going to the fireplace, walking twice around a tight circle, and flopping down with a satisfied moan.

Presently Meraud handed her two mugs of tea and a plate of warm oatcakes, and lowered herself stiffly beside her on the mat. Lily scooted over, giving her the side nearest the flames. "You can't sleep bare after tonight, you'll freeze. Can you sew?" While she spoke, she drew her black dress over her head and folded it in a neat square for a pillow. Under it she had on a wool jerkin and pantaloons.

"Yes, I can sew."

"Good. You can make yourself a nightshift out o' some fustian I got in Bovey."

Lily ducked her head. "You're so kind to me."

Meraud slurped noisily at her tea.

"Do you live all alone?"

"Nay, there's Gabe, and Pater."

"Pater?"

"The donkey. And now there's that chicken. What should we call 'er?"

Lily couldn't think.

"And o' course I've my work." She reached out to hand Gabriel an oatcake; he chewed on it pensively, watching Lily.

"Have you lived here for a long time?" She felt a yawn rising, and swallowed it down with an effort.

"Middling long." On the floor at the head of their bed lay a small box heavily encrusted with stones and seashells; from it Meraud removed a short clay pipe and a leather pouch. She still had her gloves on, from which the fingers had been cut off. Watching her fill the pipe, Lily noticed that her bony hands shook slightly. Next she held out a long straw to the turf fire, ignited it, and lit her pipe from it, and presently the smell of tobacco mingled with the rich essence of peat.

Lily put her cheek on her folded hands. She had one more question, but she hesitated to ask it, fearful of offending Meraud. "Are . . . have you . . . do you ever get lonely?"

The old woman turned her head to look at her. Her face was in deep shadow, and Lily could see only two pinpricks of reflected light where her eyes were. But even in the darkness, she thought Meraud looked sad. "Lonely," she repeated in her high, sweet voice. "But how could I be," she asked gently, "when I'm never alone?" She reached out and stroked Lily's cheek, her rough fingers light and caressing. "Go to sleep, lamb."

Lily closed her eyes. She drifted off to sleep listening to Meraud's soft, raspy soprano, singing, "He walketh with me by a field of green, and He holdeth my trembling hand."

She was alone when she awoke. Thoughts of Devon crowded her mind—she must have been dreaming of him; but the images had fragmented past memory, and

for that she was glad. She sat up and was startled anew
by the gaudy spectacle of the cottage's far wall. She saw
a vague but gay reflection of her naked self at the
bottom, lit from the remnants of watery sunshine
streaming in through the half-open door, and the incongruous sight almost made her smile. She pulled her
clothes on quickly and stepped outside.

And stopped dead. Less than eight feet away stood a
giant. Every muscle in her body tensed, poised for flight;
she opened her mouth to scream. An instant later she
saw that it wasn't real—or not animate, rather, for it
was remarkably real. Not human, exactly, nor precisely
animal. Really, it was more like a partly human vegetable. She went nearer, and realized with a profound start
that this green vegetable-man was by no means alone,
that there were others—*dozens* of others—standing
around in the yard with him. Some were like the
vegetable-man, although in different postures, but there
were also owls and turtles, big-breasted women, cats
and rabbits and fish, giant balls, weird totems, monoliths, and countless other fantastical shapes and forms
whose identities could be known only to the one who
had made them. Meraud?

Studying the vegetable giant—which was eight feet
tall; Meraud must have had to stand on a table, or maybe
the donkey cart, to fashion his head—Lily saw that he
was made out of earth, predominantly, and that he was
still growing, as it were. Sprigs of greenery and tussocks
of reedy grass grew out of him in random unlikely
places, accounting for his inimitable look of edibility.
He had no face, and yet undeniably he had an expression. But Lily couldn't put it into words, and she
suspected that her perception of it would change with
her mood. For now, he struck her as whimsical, but at
another time she thought he might frighten her.

She heard violent coughing somewhere off to her
right. Following the sound, weaving through mermaids

and stars and wide-winged birds, she came upon Meraud wiping her lips with a handkerchief. She blinked moisture from her eyes and sent Lily the same shy, sidelong glance she had last night while she'd waited for her opinion of the spectacular glass-flecked wall.

This time Lily chose her words with care. "I didn't know what you meant before when you spoke of your 'work.' Now I understand. You're an *artist*." She watched a flush deepen the leathery old cheeks to the color of burgundy; her gap-toothed smile came and went, and her gentle eyes shone bright with pleasure. Lily smiled back, knowing she had said exactly the right thing.

"You slept for a good long time," Meraud noted, as if to change the subject. "How're you feeling?"

Lily looked up at the sky; from the position of the sun, she judged it was mid-morning. "I can't ever remember sleeping this late," she said wonderingly.

"Go and get us a cup o' tea, why don't you. There's barley crusts still lying in the ashes in a pan; fetch that, too. I like to eat outside when it's fair."

"All right." But she hung back. "What are your . . . sculptures made of?" she asked. The one Meraud was working on now, which was shaped vaguely like a horse, had a substructure of twisted wire, she saw, causing her to wonder if the new chicken still had its cage. There was a tub of something thick and brownish at Meraud's feet, and she was dabbing careful handfuls of it onto the wire shape. "It looks like mud and clay and straw. And feathers," she saw on closer inspection.

Meraud smiled again, pleased. "That's just what it be," she confirmed. "Oh, and a bit o' chicken shit. Wonderfully binding."

Lily's jaw dropped. She retrieved it when Meraud glanced up at her quizzically from a crouch beside her new horse. "I'll get the tea," Lily muttered, red-faced, and hastened away. Halfway to the cottage, she started to giggle.

Lily's primary job, she learned after they had eaten their breakfast and rested for a while on a blanket in the chilly sunlight, was to mix and haul Meraud's heavy tubs of ingredients for her statuary. The old woman wasn't strong enough to do it herself nowadays, she admitted, at least not in the vast quantities she needed. She was a prolific worker; if the weather was clear, she could complete a medium-sized sculpture in three or four days. She hated it when it rained—which, on the moor, it did more often than not—and had begun her mirror-wall out of desperation during a particularly long wet spell last winter. She spent the rest of the afternoon explaining proportions and mixing times to Lily, who learned that the process was far more complicated than merely stirring up a batch of mud.

Her other duties were domestic—keeping the cottage neat and clean, cooking their small meals, washing and mending their meager supply of clothing. The object was to free Meraud from the mundane so that she could spend as much time as possible on her "work," her true calling, about which she was completely and intensely serious.

The arrangement was agreeable to Lily, who welcomed the quiet routine their days subtly slipped into. More than anything she craved peace, for herself and for the baby. The only way she could find and maintain it was to extinguish thoughts of Devon. She went at the task with a vengeance, and found that it was not, after all, hard to do. Avoidance of pain was an instinct, as natural as yanking her hand out of a fire. Once, she had been distraught because Devon thought she'd stolen money from him. His belief that she would hurt Clay was much, much worse, and it had finally killed something in her—the core of her innocence, the wellspring of her hope and her optimism. How canny his punishment was; how clever of him to understand that having her arrested, even killing her himself, would almost have been a kindness. But to force her to live out her life alone, always remembering what he had done and how he hated her—that was the ultimate retribution.

The two women spoke little to each other during the day. If her chores were over and the day was fair, Lily would sit outside and watch the older woman's slow, rapt artistry. Gabriel would sit beside her, large and serious and steady. "Gabe don't take to everyone," Meraud said once approvingly, and Lily had felt absurdly flattered. She loved his powerful body, beautifully muscled, and his long, graceful tail—which he kept pointed straight back at a neutral, dignified angle, neither happy nor sad. She found his state of mind hard to decipher. Sometimes his huge brow would furrow as if in ferocious thought; at other times his long tongue lolled out of his mouth and he appeared to be a very foolish, leering sort of dog. He had a way of looking her in the eye, odd for a dog, until *she* looked away. Occasionally he would stare beyond her so intently that she would glance over her shoulder, expecting to see something unique. The fact that she couldn't see it never completely convinced her it wasn't there.

At night in the cottage, with no other light but the fire, Meraud sat in the only chair, a rough, handmade affair of splintery wood; Lily would crouch at her feet on the floor, a piece of burlap folded twice the only thing between her and the bare earth. It was November now, damp and already cold. One night Lily was bent over her wedding gown, letting the seams out of the waist for the second time. Her pregnancy was progressing—as near as she could reckon, she was in her fourth month—and yet she wasn't gaining weight the way she imagined she was supposed to. She worried sometimes that she wasn't eating enough. Meraud would touch no meat— "'Twould be like butchering a friend!"—and so their diet consisted of oatcakes and potatoes, apples, barley gruel, and an occasional egg if the chicken—whom they'd named Unreliable—was in the mood to give them one.

"I haven't always lived here," Meraud said suddenly, ending one of their lengthy, comfortable silences. "I had a husband once, and a son. They're gone now."

Lily sat quietly. They had a rule, unspoken but as inviolable as dogma: they never asked each other questions.

"After they went, everything turned, everything . . . shifted around. Where I lived, people said I got queer. Maybe I did. But they turned even more peculiar, to my mind—passing me on my right side, trying not to catch my eye. Foolishness such as that."

"They thought you were a witch!"

"Aye, they did. Light me a pipe, Lily."

"But it makes you cough." Meraud sent her a mild look. Lily sighed and reached for the pipe, tamping down tobacco in the bowl the way Meraud had shown her, lighting it, and taking a few puffs herself to get it started.

"A witch have got the means to ill-wish you."

"I don't believe that," Lily scoffed.

"Don't believe it?" She blew out a cloud of smoke, amazed. "Well, it's true! A witch can put a spell on you, make your cow sicken or your garden wither. Or you might fall ill for a long time."

"Is that what they thought you did?"

"Aye, it come to that in the end."

Lily laid her sewing aside and looked up. The firelight cast long, harsh shadows across the old woman's angular features, giving her for once a grim, almost sinister appearance. "What happened?" Lily asked softly.

She puffed stolidly, thin lips moving in and out. Finally she said, "Once you're ill-wished, there's just one cure: to draw blood from the witch that cursed you."

Lily went cold. Meraud said no more, but her silence only fueled the horror. A lurid image glittered and gleamed in Lily's mind, sickening her. To comfort herself and her friend, she put her arms around Meraud's skinny calves and rested her head on her knee. The old lady stiffened in surprise, just for a moment. Then she put one bony, quivering hand on Lily's hair and stroked it. Lily's eyes closed; she mentioned on a sigh, "My mother died when I was ten." Gabriel growled in his sleep. A block of peat split in half, sending up a fierce shower of sparks.

"This man you love—" Meraud said suddenly, quietly.

Lily pulled away. "I don't love him." She had never spoken of Devon, not one word—and yet somehow Meraud's knowledge didn't surprise her.

"This man you love," she reiterated patiently, "he might hurt you again. But you've got power you don't know about yet, and you can destroy him."

"What do you mean?"

"Be wise, lamb. Spite's not a good cause for doing one single thing in this life. It hurts you more than it hurts your enemy."

"I don't know what you mean."

Minutes passed.

"Did you see the moon?" Meraud asked abruptly.

"Yes, I saw it."

"A red cloud ran right across it, red as blood. Tomorrow we'll have to leave a gift."

"A gift?"

"At the well."

That's all she would say. A little later, they undressed and got into bed.

Meraud's gift was a doll, a figure of a woman she'd carved out of wood. She told Lily a goddess lived in the well—a dank pool of water behind two columns of piled stones, splotchy with moss and lichen and wind-browned ivy. Lily hoped the goddess appreciated the rough offering, because she knew how many nights Meraud's arthritic old hands had spent fashioning it. They walked back across the tussocky turf of the moor slowly, stopping to rest sometimes when Meraud's breath gave out. Gabriel ran ahead, snuffling at fox spoor and rabbit holes. In spite of her frailty, Meraud had a graceful, loose-jointed gait that Lily loved to watch; she swung a long leg out in a high kick for each step, slow and stately, completely unique.

As they walked, she spoke of other gods and the sacred places where they lived. Sprites and faeries and the spirits of the dead were everywhere, she said, in rocks and earth hollows, trees and hilltops, under stones. Lily listened in astonishment, for she had thought Meraud was a Christian. They paused beside a tall stone pillar on a slight rise of ground in the middle of nowhere. Lichen-covered, it bore no inscription, its top eaten away by the centuries. Lily gazed at it brood-ingly, impressed against her will by the silent, phallic power of it. "And does a god live here?" she asked, only half in jest.

"Aye, to be sure, a strong one. And another over there." She pointed to a blasted tree beyond the rise, barkless and gnarled and twisted as if in pain.

That night and on succeeding nights, Meraud ex-plained the spirit world. Creatures existed everywhere, cannily hidden in the simplest things—water, earthen barrows, rocks. They were as real to Meraud as their stolid hiding places were to Lily. Most of them were friendly or at least neutral, but some were actively hostile—and a few were evil. Placating them was a complex, worrisome, all-involving life's work, with sub-tleties and obscure nuances Lily didn't try to under-stand. But without thinking about it, she half believed in them when Meraud described them. In Lily's passive state of mind, Meraud's explanations of reality seemed as reasonable as any other.

As time went by, the moorings of Lily's rational, "civilized" mind loosened further, and gradually the grays, browns, and drab greens of the dismal moor began to play on her imagination. There *was* life in the twisted branches of some blighted half-tree the winter winds hadn't ravaged to death yet, or in the still, heavy stones set in a mute circle on the hill three hundred paces north of Meraud's cottage. Even the clouds had life, though it was a heavy, loutish, brutal kind of life as they lumbered across a leaden sky in the bitter-cold, silver-gray brightness of a moorland noon. Animation was everywhere once she began to look for it. For Meraud this transubstantial vitality was natural, unremarkable. For Lily it contained a subtle, brooding horror.

One night as they lay on the rush mat watching the dying firelight dance on the flickering glass wall, Meraud told Lily how she wanted to be buried. "'Neath the stone circle on the rise, with the magic stones from the well over me at head and foot. Do you remember 'em, the two at the top o' the columns? You'll need the cart to fetch 'em."

Lily lay still, stiff and cold with sudden dread. "Please don't talk like this," she whispered. "It frightens me."

Meraud reached for her hand under the covers. "Why, lamb?" she whispered back. "Don't be scared. Dying's naught but the center of a long, long life."

December came, bringing bitter cold. Meraud's cough worsened; she could only work outside for part of the day, and then only when the feeble sun shone. She was laboring on a special sculpture these days, more detailed than the others; it was inexplicably important to her, and there was a different kind of urgency in her that disturbed Lily. One afternoon she worked late, with feverish haste in a freezing wind, long after the light had

faded from the sullen sky. Lily called to her repeatedly
—Meraud would not let her near this sculpture, for it
was to be a surprise—until at last the old woman flung
her muddy gloves on the ground and shuffled toward
the cottage.

Lily met her in the yard. "I'll go and get the basin,"
she muttered, and started to walk past her.

"Nay, leave that, let it freeze. It's done. It's all finished
now. Help me inside, Lily, I'm worn to a nub."

Alarmed, Lily put her arm around her thin waist and
walked with her toward the door. That night, the old
woman's coughing brought up blood, and in the morning she could not get out of bed.

# Twenty-three

The wind blew for three weeks. Snow flew in flurries before the gale; drifts lay against the cottage, though the windswept ground was bare. Icicles hung from the roof over the door, and the water in the pail outside froze. Livid clouds writhed in a low sky, from which hail began to fall one dark afternoon, blowing sideways. The tallow candle smoked and started to gutter. Lily trimmed it again and listened to the wind roar like a beast, shaking the rafters and blowing thatch-dust around the cottage like chaff in a wheatfield. She pulled Meraud's ancient gray shawl around her shoulders more closely and knelt down again beside the rush mat.

"Thirsty?" she murmured. The old woman's eyes were closed; if she was truly sleeping, Lily didn't want to wake her.

But she shook her head, smiling dreamily, and opened her eyes a crack. "Wind's picking up."

"Are you cold?"

"I'm always cold." Lily stirred; Meraud reached for her wrist and held her still. "Don't," she said with surprising firmness. "It's too low. I told you."

"Then I'll get more," Lily smiled fiercely, gently removing her clutching hand. She got up and went to the fire, poked at the smoldering turf, and added two more blocks of peat from the dwindling stack beside the grate. They caught immediately and she closed her eyes to savor the sudden lovely heat on her cold cheeks and the chilled tip of her nose. After a few seconds she moved aside so the warmth could reach Meraud. She was already asleep. Lily sat down in the chair and listened to the mad howl of the wind.

"Lily? Lily?"

She awakened with a jolt. She'd fallen asleep in an awkward posture, and her neck hurt. "How do you feel?"

"You've got to go and get Pater, child."

"Yes, all right. Do you mean—bring him in? The house?"

"Aye, you'll have to. He'll die out in this wind."

"I'll fetch him, then. Don't worry. Do you need anything?"

Meraud shook her head and fell back into a restless doze.

Gabriel got up from his mat beside the hearth and stalked to the door, stiff-legged. "You're coming too, are you?" Lily took Meraud's coat down from the hook in the wall and wrapped her shawl around her head. She dragged away the heavy sack of barley meal that kept the door from blowing open, said, "Come on, then," to the dog, dipped her head, and stepped out into the gale.

A blast of frigid wind struck full-force, slapping sharp snow in her face. She hunched over, grimacing, clutching her clothes, and followed Gabriel through the maze of rimy sculptures—lonely ghosts in the barren twilight, snow-whitened, still and beseeching. Weaving among them, she fancied they felt the cold as much as

she, as much as Pater, but they had no voices, no way to
complain or ask for comfort. She stopped, as she always
did, when she came to Meraud's last statue, the one
she'd finished on that last day. Snow covered one side,
limning the soft curves palely and gentling the shape of
the mother—Lily—and her arm-cradled baby. Would
she have seen anything of herself in the crude shape if
she hadn't known it was meant to represent her?
Probably not. And yet there was something—a quality
of stoicism, perhaps?—that she thought she recognized,
or at least sympathized with. No matter; the sculpture
moved her to tears each time she looked at it, bitter tears
full of fear and loss. She reached out and touched
frozen fingers to the hard shoulder of the woman,
herself, and then to the tiny head of the baby. Gabriel
barked, startling her. She turned away, hugging herself,
and followed him toward Pater's lean-to behind the
cottage.

At first she had a wild idea that somehow, sometime,
Meraud had made another statue, one meant to look
like Pater. She crept closer with awful reluctance as the
truth dawned on her. The donkey stood on his four legs,
long neck bent and head to the ground, as if to nibble at
the snow with his velvet lips. Hoarfrost on his shaggy
hide made a sparkling fleece. His long, elegant eyelashes, ice-encrusted, were downcast; he looked sleepy
and peaceful. But no steamy breath blew from his big,
soft nostrils; his scrawny ribs were still. He had frozen to
death.

In the cottage, Meraud still slept. Lily stirred the fire,
then went to kneel beside her. The old woman's face
was gaunt and nearly fleshless, the bones like sharp
sticks under the flaccid skin. But it was the corpselike
pallor that frightened Lily the most. She took Meraud's
hand and rubbed the bony fingers to warm them. The
old woman opened her eyes and stared at her, just for a
moment, as if she'd never seen her before. Lily felt the
cutting edge of panic in a swift and terrifying premoni-

tion of her absolute aloneness. "Pater's dead," she blurted out. The words shocked her: she'd intended to lie. "I'm sorry," she whispered, and started to cry. "It's all my fault."

Meraud didn't cry. "You think everything's your fault," she chided gently. "Don't you know Pater's all right now?" She patted Lily's wrist and then put her skinny, long-fingered hand on Lily's stomach. "I wish I could've seen him."

"Who?"

"This baby." She moved her hand from side to side softly. "This sweet child." She sent her an unusually clear-eyed look. "This child's a gift. He makes a circle. A *circle*, Lily."

Lily shook her head in confusion. "Will he live, Meraud? Will he be all right?" Another shock: she'd never asked anything about the future, even though a superstitious part of her was positive that Meraud could foresee it. She regretted the question instantly, for the wrong answer would surely kill her.

But Meraud only said, "That's up to you, lamb," and closed her eyes tiredly. Her hand dropped away and she slept again.

The long night wore on. To Lily's distress, Meraud had stopped taking solid food two days ago and would only swallow spoonfuls of potato and barley gruel when Lily insisted. Lily wanted to kill Unreliable and make a nutritious broth, but she knew well enough what Meraud would say to that. So she was helpless. There was no doctor, not even a neighbor to go to. "Don't you know any—potions, any concoctions?" she'd wondered desperately, almost angrily, yesterday morning. Meraud had laughed at her. "So you think I'm a witch, too," she'd accused. "Nay, Lily, I know naught o' concoctions and magical potions. Leave me be, child, I don't need anything."

The wind blew and battered at the cottage all night.

Lily began to think of the wind as an enemy, something mindful of her that meant ill will toward her and those under her protection. She spoke soothingly to Gabriel when an especially violent blast shook the house and jolted him out of his sleep, but it was herself she was trying to console. The cold was bitter and could not be kept out. When the last of the peat beside the hearth was gone, she put on Meraud's old coat and went outside to get more. Meraud stored it next to the house under a slanting, makeshift roof that kept rain and moisture from soaking the absorbent turf. For the first time, Lily took full, panicky note of how low the pile had grown. Meraud had cautioned her to burn it slowly, but she hadn't obeyed—*couldn't* obey, because the cold was killing and brutal and she refused to let her friend suffer from that as well as everything else. Swallowing a dark fear, she filled the fire basket with as many of the heavy blocks as she could carry and hurried back inside.

Toward morning, the wind dropped. Because her body ached, Lily had abandoned the hard chair and stretched out next to Meraud on the floor. The novel silence woke her. She lay quietly for a moment, pondering what had changed. Suddenly she sat upright, aghast, and hovered over the silent, utterly still figure under the blankets beside her. As she watched, fists pressed to her teeth to drive back a moan of despair, Meraud abruptly drew in a deep, choking breath and released it. Lily's whole body went limp; her shoulders shook and tears of relief poured down her cheeks onto Meraud's clasped hands. She wanted to sob and sob for hours, forever. Instead she got up and rebuilt the fire.

Despite the new calm, the cold grew worse. She spent the day massaging Meraud's arms and legs and feet and hands, trying to warm them. Once, turning her, she noticed that the underside of her body was slightly darker in color, as if her blood were settling. What did it mean? She didn't know.

When she wasn't sleeping, Meraud drowsed peacefully in a dreamy half-world, murmuring of long-ago memories and reminiscences. Lily thanked God that she was not in pain. Sometimes she was perfectly clear-headed—precious times to Lily, who was fighting her terror of abandonment as hard as she was fighting her grief.

"Lamb," Meraud said in the afternoon, stilling the hand that was bathing her face with a damp cloth, "you can't stay here after I'm gone. Take Gabriel with you and go."

Lily felt as if an ice-cold hand was sliding down her back, caressing her bare skin. "Don't leave me," she whispered.

"I'll never leave you." She smiled, so sweetly that Lily's heart clenched. "Forgive the one who hurt you so badly." Lily leaned closer, certain she'd misheard. "Soften your heart and be patient. Wait for him to see who you are."

"What do you mean? I don't know what you mean. I'll never see him—"

"Be gentle, Lily, even though he's a fool. What good is being right if you're alone? Let go o' your pride, child, and you'll be happy."

Gabriel got up from his corner by the hearth, stretched, and padded over to them. Sitting on his haunches, he blinked down at his mistress, who wrapped her hand around one of his powerful forelegs and smiled at him.

"You'll watch out for 'er, won't you, Gabe?" Gabriel yawned. "Stay with him, Lily, or you'll get lost. Hear me? You'll get lost."

"I won't get lost."

"Good-bye, I won't be able to talk to you again. But I'll always be with you."

"Meraud. *Meraud.*"

She'd fallen asleep.

That night, dozing in her chair, Lily came fully awake all at once. Instantly her eyes found Meraud's in the smoky dimness; she was leaning toward her on one elbow, her arm stretched out. Lily scrambled up. Falling on her knees beside the old woman, she took her hand. The icy fingers were tense in hers, communicating a vital message. Neither spoke. Lily's swollen heart was bursting, but she didn't cry. The shining tenderness in her friend's gentle eyes dimmed as she watched, so slowly, and she was retreating, moving back and away. Lily squeezed her hand tighter, tighter, desperate to hold her. But a milky film blinded the old eyes, and the thin, transparent barrier was impenetrable. Meraud slipped away.

"I'm sorry, I'm sorry." Lily pressed her palms to the moist earth and wept. "I couldn't lift the magic stones. I tried but I couldn't, I was afraid for the baby. Oh, Meraud, I'm so sorry." Sobs shook her, the first she'd allowed herself since she'd been alone. It had taken all day yesterday to dig this shallow trough of a grave inside the stone circle; she'd sat up with her friend last night, and buried her this morning, dressed in her good dress and wrapped in blankets. At first Lily had been afraid that, because of the baby, she couldn't bury her in the stone circle at all. But then she'd discovered how pitifully light the old woman was, and in the end she had managed it with heartbreaking ease. But the special stones were too heavy; Pater was dead, and Lily couldn't lift them. The fact that she didn't understand Meraud's wish to have them was irrelevant: she'd made a promise and she had failed.

She sat back on her heels, wiping her cheeks with the back of a dirty hand. What prayer should she say? None she knew seemed quite right. So she sang one of Meraud's hymns—weeping, then almost laughing, poignantly aware that her voice was easily an octave

lower than her friend's. In the middle of the song,
Gabriel came and leaned against her. She put her arm
around his shoulders, thankful for his sturdy company.
When she finished the hymn, they sat together a little
longer. "Good-bye, I love you," Lily whispered. The
cold, which had relented in the last two days, had
returned on a sleety wind, and it was growing dark. She
climbed to her feet slowly. "Good-bye," she said again.
She hated to go, to leave Meraud here all alone. But she
was freezing. She took a step back, another, then turned
and walked blind-eyed down the hill.

The cold worsened in the coming days and the grim
moorland seemed to take on a new reality, one that did
not wish Lily well. She stayed close to the cottage,
occasionally conscious of her own oddness but not
alarmed by it. Nothing was the same. What had been
real was gone, and what was left had a sinister reality
which she knew, in a deep, fatalistic sense, she could
not escape. Perhaps Devon's true punishment was to
drive her mad. The idea appalled even as it intrigued
her. Sometimes, behind the wall of numbness she'd
erected between herself and memories of him, she
could feel the fiery heat of a blinding, spitting fury. But
numbness was better.

She stopped sleeping at night, but kept the fire up,
fearful that otherwise she really might go mad. Sometimes she could sleep in the day, in a slant of sunlight if
the sky was clear, huddled in a tight ball on the rush mat
if it was not. Her thoughts were wild and dangerous;
they frightened her. She wondered how Meraud had
found peace and friendliness in the same heavy, earthen
objects that seemed to her to warn of anguish and
disaster. She felt as if she were under the spell of
something unwelcome and unkind. She could no longer
control her mind, and it had become a struggle to see
the mundane in everyday objects—furze, peat, wood,
stone. Everything had a second self and it was hiding,

whispering—malevolent. Gabriel became her last link to normalcy. He followed her, stayed with her, watched her—and sometimes she fancied it was Meraud who looked at her out of his dark, placid eyes.

But his quiet presence was not enough to calm her. As near as she could tell, it was the middle of January now. If that was true, she was about six months pregnant. She had enough food to last until spring, but not enough fuel. Meraud had told her to leave, but she was afraid. Then one day, after waking from a dream that left her panting and terrified, she went outside and saw wickedness and danger in the sculptures around the cottage. Meraud's beautiful sculptures. That night she made up her mind to go.

The next day she packed all the food she could carry and put on all the clothes she could wear. "Come on, Gabriel," she called when he hung back in the doorway. "Come!" The dog didn't move. She went back and squatted in front of him. "We have to go now," she said softly, patting the knobby bone on top of his huge head. "It's all right, we're not really leaving her. She'll still be with us. Come on, boy." She straightened and walked away, but when she looked back he was still there. "Gabriel, come!" She started walking backwards. "You come!" she called, trying to sound angry. She set her bag of food down and clapped her hands. He just stared at her, looking patient and wise.

She put her hands on her hips and spoke to him firmly and at length. When he still wouldn't move, she heard herself threatening him. "I'm going to beat you if you don't come this instant!" she shouted, then wondered if that sounded as absurd to him as it did to her. She gave a groan of frustration and walked back to him.

"Please come, Gabe," she pleaded, bending over to look in his eyes. "We have to go or we'll freeze. I need you. Won't you come?" She moved back a little. "Please," she coaxed, holding out her hands. He turned his head to his right, and she imagined for a second that he looked disgusted. A plaintive moment passed, and then he raised his sunken hindquarters, shook his head, ears flapping noisily, and trotted after her.

An hour later she was lost. She had come here from Bovey Tracy, which was east, but beyond that she knew nothing of the way. There was no track, no path, and the day was dreary, the watery sun obscure behind a gaunt line of clouds. How had Meraud found the way? And there was no one to ask, no living creature anywhere. She veered suddenly at the sight of a badger, dead in a patch of stitchwort she'd almost walked on. Her pack was heavy, she'd brought too much; her back ached already. Gabriel walked behind her, not leading the way at all. When she would turn around to look at him, he would stop dead and stare back, hopefully, as if to see if she'd come to her senses yet.

After another hour it started to rain. The sun was completely hidden now and she could not tell east from west. Mist flowed in the gullies, white as a stream of milk, rising and thickening as she walked. The ground became soggy and treacherous; her unease turned to fear. She realized she was walking uphill, but she couldn't tell toward what. All at once a rocky outcrop appeared, whiter than the white mist, jutting up from the rough moorland scrub like a skull. The rock had a crack, large enough to squeeze into and take refuge from the wind.

But not from the rain, and in minutes she was drenched. The fog closed in. Waiting for it to clear was frustrating, maddening, and finally unbearable. She stepped out into the white world and began a slow, careful descent.

"Which way, Gabriel?" she asked hopelessly when her footsteps leveled off. The mist had lifted a little. In front of her the moor looked greener, slightly smoother. She hefted her pack and set off in that direction.

A mistake. The squishy turf ought to have warned her, but she knew nothing of bogs. One second she walked on solid ground, the next she stood thigh-deep in frigid water, her feet encased in mud that wouldn't release her. She shouted out, clutching her bag to her chest. Behind her, Gabriel barked excitedly. The bog stretched out as far as she could see, pea-green, steaming like a pudding. The longer she stood still, the deeper she sank. She got out at last by leaning backwards and pulling her legs out slowly, one at a time, straining against the oozing suction that wanted to hold her.

She found a stick and used it to prod and poke at the ground, but deception was everywhere and the mist was her cleverest enemy. Unable to see, she went into the bog again and again, a dozen times, until she was weeping with despair and helpless terror. She found a patch of firm ground and sat down, perhaps to die, for the marsh was all around her now. The secret was never to descend, when the mist lifted enough to see, toward the smooth, safe-looking pasture lying low, for that was where treachery lay. But the mist rose and fell purely to trick her, over and over, and she knew it would win in the end. She put her head on her knees and sobbed.

A damp snuffling on her neck warmed, then chilled her. She lifted her head. Gabriel sat beside her, watching her with his impassive, infernal patient look. "Why aren't you helping me?" Lily whimpered. "Meraud said you wouldn't let me get `lost. Oh, Gabe." She put her hand on his thick neck and bent her face to his, needing another creature to weep with. But he jerked away and backed up a step. She stared resentfully into his unfathomable eyes. "What? Will you lead me to safety? I don't believe you." He waited, tail out straight, face tolerant-looking. She muttered an obscenity, an actual obscenity, and got to her feet. "Lead on, then, you . . ." She trailed off, ashamed.

Gabriel led her out of the bog. She didn't believe it

until she'd walked for more than a mile on nothing deadlier than squelchy moss. But where were they going? The fog had lifted all at once, as if the whole planet had risen above the clouds. But now hailstones hissed in the bracken and the biting wind chilled to the bone. They passed a pool, slate-gray in the flying sleet, ominous and drear. She saw the bones of a dead lamb, and ringlets of wool scattered around it by the crows; farther on a sheep's skull leered at her from the peat. Gabriel trotted ahead, head down and purposeful, occasionally stopping to wait for her. Rubble from the granite tors around them made the going rough. She stumbled for the third time, landing heavily on hands and knees, and this time she didn't get up.

Gabriel ambled back to wait. She blew on her scratched and bleeding palms and hugged her stomach, rocking herself. Her clothes were wet through; she was freezing. "Where are we going?" Her voice sounded pitiful even to her. Gabriel gazed off into space. She still had her bag of food, though most of it was ruined from bog water. "Are you hungry?" She opened the bag and spread the contents out, offering them. Gabriel looked down, then away. "I'm not either," she admitted on a sigh. Nearby a stunted tree, dripping melancholy, looked grotesque against the winter sky. Afternoon darkness was setting in. Stiff-legged, she rose to her feet. Leaving her pack of food where it lay, she followed Gabriel into the deepening dusk.

Later, she would never know how much later, she saw something in the distance that might be a cottage. Her legs felt like lead and her body ached from exhaustion, but she quickened her pace. A little farther on she slowed, and finally stopped. And started to laugh. The demented sound of it scared her, but she couldn't stop. Gabriel looked back and grinned at her. They were standing in front of Meraud's cottage.

It was while she was lighting a fire in the hearth that

the idea came to her. Shivering uncontrollably, she knelt for a moment, frozen fingers almost touching the flames, steam starting to rise from her sodden skirts, and considered her choices. It seemed to Lily that they had narrowed to two: die now, or die later. Because she was a coward, she chose the first.

She had thought the peat was running low; the task of bringing it all in, load after load, changed her perspective slightly. But at last it was done: the enormous pile hulked on the fireplace hearth, dark and pungent and ready. Her plan was to burn every bit of it in one last, long, bone-warming fire, and when it was all gone, tomorrow or perhaps the next day, just to close her eyes and let everything go.

She pulled Meraud's chair closer to the flames and stirred them higher with her stick. She boiled a cup of tea. Gabriel plopped down beside her with a loud groan and put his head on his paws. She scratched his ears absently; with her other hand she rubbed her stomach. "I'm sorry, baby," she said out loud. "I thought we could be safe. At least we'll all be together and Meraud won't be alone. It's not your fault, Gabriel, it's mine. I forgive you for bringing me back. I should've known you'd do it and not gone with you. It's all right. It doesn't matter anyway." But it did, because she had wanted her baby to live. She put her head back and let the tears fall down her face, blurring the fire.

She woke up from a sound sleep because she was perspiring. No wonder, she thought; I have on so many clothes. She took some off, then added more peat to the fire. She heated up a pot of barley gruel and ate it standing up. When she was full, she set the pan on the floor for Gabriel. She made another cup of tea and sat back down.

At midnight she woke up again, flushed from the heat. She went to the door and opened it. Wind rushed in, cool and fresh; it felt wonderful. The stars shimmered in

a black, moonless sky. Gabriel trotted past her, panting.
Meraud's sculptures looked like immobile ghosts in the
dark. She shut the door reluctantly and went to rebuild
the fire, adding as much turf as the grate could hold.
The pile of peat was burning faster than she'd expected
—nearly half gone already. Good. With luck, she would
use it all up by morning. Tired of the chair, she lay down
on the rush mat, as far from the blazing hearth as she
could get, and watched the play of firelight on the wall
of mirrors across the way until her eyes glazed.

She dreamt she was burning. The flames were famished; they devoured her body in seconds, stripping
away layers of flesh while she grew smaller, smaller,
until there was nothing left of her except her baby. He
was a tiny, naked thing, sitting up in the thin air where
her belly had been, impervious to the fire. He had
Devon's face. And she was gone, she had ceased to be.
How odd, then, that she could hear Meraud's voice so
clearly. *Wake up, Lily*, it said in her ear, quavery and
insistent. *Wake up*. She opened her eyes.

The cottage was on fire. The mantel was gone; the
stone chimney was invisible behind a wall of flame.
While she watched, fire leapt in a hissing yellow arc to
the diminished stack of peat on the hearth. It caught
instantly. In the time it took her to scramble to her
knees, it turned into a roaring, funneling inferno. There
was no more air; with the last breath in her lungs, Lily
screamed. But no—the dazzling glass wall was a *mirror*
of the conflagration, not the fire itself, and she was not
surrounded. She got to her feet and staggered toward
the door. Fiery chunks of thatch rained down, scorching
her hair, her clothes. She found the door. But with her
hand on the hot rope handle, she dropped to her knees.
The earth floor felt warm on her forehead; she gasped a
chestful of smoky air and thought of burning to death. A
natural cremation. Why not? But Gabriel was barking
outside, and she couldn't breathe. She yanked on the

handle and crawled into the cold, sweet night on her hands and knees.

Air rushing through the open door stoked the flames higher, transforming the cottage into a furnace. The heat drove her back. Gabriel planted his feet and howled at the spitting, raging blaze. The noise deafened her. She put her hands to her ears and screamed back, at one with the chaos and the primitive synergy of fire and air and stone and earth. She could hear nothing but the bestial roaring of the flames, but she turned around, facing the blackness and the cold. Something prickled the hairs on the back of her neck. She saw a shape moving toward her in the murk. Death, she assumed. She braced herself, protecting her womb. She shrieked in mindless panic when she saw that it was not death but a man. Blood thundered in her brain, blinding her. She was fainting, the tide of blood rising too fast, too high. The figure closed in. Devon—it was Devon. She pitched forward and he caught her in his arms.

# The Gift

# Twenty-four

She was dressed in rags, layers and layers of them, all reeking of peat. He laid her on the ground a safe distance from the fiery cottage while he shot a wary glance at the stiff-legged monster standing motionless six feet away. He said something low and calming, but the dog only stalked closer, eerily alert. "It's all right, I'm a friend. I'm Lily's friend."

A lie, he thought. A cowardly, contemptible lie. Nevertheless, the sound of her name had an instantaneous effect: the dog sat back on its haunches and grinned at him.

Lily's face, ruddy in the livid glow of the fire, was thinner, he saw, the edges sharper. Was she ill? He thought she'd only fainted, but now her stillness frightened him. He began to loosen her tattered clothes, still warm from the fire. And then he froze. Not breathing, hand hovering, he stared down at the soft mound of her belly under the last layer of rust-colored homespun. His mind collided with the possibility, staggered backward, confronted it again. He touched her. His fingers were stiff with tension; at first he felt nothing, no sensation at all. Then, slowly, his rigid hand relaxed. The truth seeped into him as gently as his stroking palm rubbed across her abdomen.

He closed his eyes and felt a fullness in his heart rising, expanding, so poignant and powerful he wanted to weep. "Lily," he said, and she awoke. Her eyes were cloudy, her face uncomprehending. He whispered, "I've found you. Lily, I had stopped hoping."

Something gathered behind her eyes. He waited for recognition—prayed for welcome; the possibility of redemption lit all the black corners of his soul. Then she opened her arms, and they embraced.

Her hair was wild, a mad-looking halo against the flames that still curled and hissed behind her. He buried his face in it and held her tighter, trembling. The salt on his lips was the taste of his own tears. "Darling," he murmured, rocking her. "Thank God, thank God." He wanted to see her face, but he couldn't let go yet. "I looked for you everywhere. Everywhere. If I hadn't seen the fire, I would never have found you. Lily, thank God."

Finally he pulled away. "I went to Soames's house first," he told her, the words tumbling out. "He wouldn't speak to me. But his wife caught up to me as I was leaving, and she said she'd seen you walk west, away from the town." He remembered the way she'd scuttled up to him in the street like a crab, hanging onto his sleeve and hissing in a frightened whisper—*"They threw her clothes in the street!"*—and he shuddered, as he had then, unable to speak of it.

"I searched for weeks but I couldn't find you, Lily. Then, a few days ago—I can't remember how many—a little boy in Bovey Tracy told me he'd seen a lady with red hair. Last fall, he said. She went away with the witch who lives on the moor, whose dog is really a demon."

Lily didn't speak, and he couldn't read her expression in the dimness. "Are you all right, darling? Are you well? The child—"

She pushed his hand away when he stretched it out toward her, and got to her feet with clumsy haste. He scrambled up, helping her. "Careful, love, you're not—"

"Is Clay dead?"

Her voice startled him; he'd never heard that thin, emotionless tone. "No, no," he said hurriedly, "he's all right. He's still weak, not himself, but the doctors say he's going to get well." She looked away, toward the fire. He searched her sharp profile uneasily. She seemed so strange. "Who lived here with you, Lily? Were you alone?" He glanced at the outlandish maze of frozen statues all around them, glimmering weirdly by the light of the fire. Her dog stood beside her like a sentinel, watchful and impassive, waiting. Sparks floated in lazy spirals, flickering out before they touched the icy ground. "Lily, are you all right?" He took a step toward her; she moved back in tandem.

"I'm cold," she whispered, hugging herself.

Immediately he shrugged out of his heavy black cloak and draped it over her shoulders. "We'll go home tomorrow," he murmured, his cheek touching hers. She shuddered—from the cold, he thought.

The fire had dwindled. Within six feet of the cottage, the intense heat had thawed the ground in an ashen square. He led her to a clean place on the warm earth and helped her to sit down. He wanted to touch her again, but she was holding herself so stiffly he decided not to. "Talk to me, Lily. What's happened to you? Tell me how you've lived all these months. Have you been here all alone?" She didn't answer. *"Lily."* She lay down on her side, facing away from him, curled into a tight ball, hands clutching each other under her chin.

She was tired—she might even be sick; of course she

needed to rest. They would talk tomorrow. He leaned over her, trying to see her face. Shadows played on her pale cheeks and the sharp but still gentle line of her jaw. Minutes passed. Was she asleep? He shivered and sank down beside her, pulling her rounded back against his chest, seeking her warmth. His hand fell naturally across her swollen belly and he thought of the child. His child. He could not make out exactly what he was feeling beyond anxiety—for her, for the baby. But there was joy too, fragile, buried deep, a night creature frightened of the light. Out of habit, he distrusted it. But Lily was going to have his baby, and all at once he felt as if he were overflowing, as if he couldn't contain himself. *If this could really happen, if he could have Lily and the child . . .*

He could think of nothing to give in return, no equivalent in his sterile existence to match such precious gifts. But Lily had absolved him of so much already. He was afraid to want anything, afraid to hope, but he couldn't help himself. The last thing he'd have accused himself of was optimism, and yet he found that he was discounting all the dreadful possibilities that might lie ahead for them and was rejoicing instead in the miracle of this moment. For months his life had been a kind of oblivion, a nightmare storm of feeling so chaotic that there had been nothing outside it, nothing beyond himself. The nightmare was over now because he could protect her. She was here—*here*, in his arms. Her sweet profile softened the drab harshness of the moor. Her narrow shoulders grazed his chest in rhythm with her quiet breathing, and her smoky hair tickled his face. And tomorrow they were going home together.

He fell asleep. When he awoke, Lily was kneeling beside him, watching him. The dawn sky hovered low and menacing, a hostile shade of gray. He reached a hand out to touch her hip, but she leaned away.

"Will you do something for me?"

He sat up. "Yes. How do you feel, Lily?"

"I want you to move some stones." She got to her feet and backed away from him. "You'll need your horse."

He rubbed his eyes and the stubble on his cheeks. Then he got up and followed her.

"There," she said, pointing.

He hefted the second heavy stone from the donkey cart and carried it to the rock-piled tomb in the center of a circle of smaller stones. He dropped it in the spot she was indicating, straightened, and slapped the dust from his hands. Immediately she turned and walked off toward the blackened patch of earth that still smoldered and smoked in the distance. He set his teeth and followed.

Whose grave was it? What was special about these unwieldy granite boulders he'd had to haul from a fetid well half a mile away? Who had fashioned this mad array of birds and men and mermaids around the ruined cottage? Lily wouldn't answer, and he'd finally given up asking.

She was waiting for him at the bottom of the hill. His black cloak hung to her ankles, making him think of a small, pregnant bat. He suppressed a start of eerie recognition when he noticed the statue she was standing next to. It was of a mother and child; the woman had Lily's height and shape—former shape—and there was something in the posture and the calm, featureless face that made him certain she was the model for it. Staring at the cradled infant in the woman's arms, he felt disconcerted, almost disoriented.

"Why did you look for me? Why did you come here?" she asked abruptly in a voice devoid of expression.

"Why?" He had waited so long to tell her. "Because I love you."

She gave a short, violent exclamation, pivoted, and clapped her hands to her ears.

He was appalled. For a minute he couldn't move. Then he stepped around her so that she had to look at him. She lowered her hands slowly, the thin wrists shaking; her eyes looked blind, or as if they were looking inward instead of out. He tried to speak calmly. "Listen to me, Lily. I know now that you never hurt Clay, never could have. I—"

"How do you know?"

"I just know."

"How?"

His eyes sidled away. "I've come to my senses."

"You're lying."

How could she know? "No, it's the truth."

"Clay remembered something."

"No," he said honestly, "I swear it, he can't remember anything. I tell you I've come to my senses."

"Liar."

He flinched. "Will it help to tell you I'm sorry for what I did? I haven't said it before because I knew it couldn't—"

"Will you give me some money?"

"What?" She repeated the question—although he'd heard it perfectly the first time—in the same eerie, uninflected tone. "Why?" he asked gently.

"So that I can go away. So that I can live."

A chill traveled up his spine, spread across his scalp. "Lily—darling—" He saw a shadow of revulsion darken her sharp-boned features, and the rest of the words stuck in his throat.

"Will you?" she prompted.

"No," he said hoarsely.

"I didn't think so." She backed up when he stretched his hand toward her. "Don't touch me. I have no choice but to go with you—if I don't I'll die."

"Lily—"

"In three months I'll come into an inheritance from my father. I'll leave you then, and I'll take the child with me. It's not yours, it's someone else's."

He believed her, and his body went ice-cold with panic. But a split second later he realized she was lying.

Of course she was lying. "Whose is it?" he asked, humoring her.

"I'll never tell you."

He tried to smile. "You have to come with me, love, you have—"

"No choice. Yes, I know. But not for long—I'll leave as soon as I can. My child deserves better than you. If you try to take him, I'll kill you." Finally her voice broke; he saw that her whole body was shaking. He made a movement that made her take another step back. She wrapped her arms around herself, shivering uncontrollably. "Your baby died, but you won't have mine. You couldn't keep your wife, and you won't keep me. I despise you."

He turned around, white-faced, incapable of looking at her any longer. It was as if he'd been flayed, as if his skin had been stripped from his body. What lunacy had made him think forgiveness was at hand? He went to retrieve his horse, limbs moving mechanically. In the east, the sun was a watery orb behind the surly sky. When he returned, Lily allowed him to put her up on his big stallion. Her body was limp, she looked exhausted; but her eyes burned with enmity.

He knew it would be faster to ride behind her on the horse, but he couldn't bring himself to touch her again. So he took the horse's reins and led him through the frosty warren of sculptures, silent wraiths, their icy stillness as damning as a curse. The dog—Gabriel, she'd called him—trotted ahead, leading the way. A few snowflakes drifted on the chill wind, graying the brown tussocks of sedge and peat and the gaunt curves of some ancient earth barrow. He shivered, conscious of the dark moor's patient hostility, its low, snarling threat. He thought of his optimistic hopes of the night before. They struck him as pitiful, the crazed delusions of a madman.

"Will she come and dine with us?" Clay asked as Devon trudged up the terrace steps toward the manor house from Cobb's cottage where Lily had ensconced herself. Clay was wrapped in a blanket and slumped in a chair outside the open library doors.

"No."

"Why not?"

Clay's expression of sympathy set Devon's teeth on edge. "She didn't trouble to give a reason. What are you still doing out here? The sun set half an hour ago. If you catch cold, don't expect me to feel sorry for you." His voice was clipped, but his hands were gentle as he helped his brother to his feet and guided him into the library. As soon as Clay was seated on the sofa, Devon moved to the cabinet between the windows and took out a bottle of whiskey. He poured a drink and turned back, ready for Clay's disapproval—as predictable these days as the calendar.

"Does that r-r-really help?" Clay asked in his halting way, gesturing toward the glass.

"It helps." He peered down at the amber liquid, inhaling the harsh fumes, and took a swallow. A reflexive shudder shook him and his eyes watered. No, it didn't help. But he was used to it and there was nothing else.

"Look what Mac—MacLeaf gave me, Dev."

"What is it?"

"A horse. He carved it himself. It's Tamar, see? Galen says since I can't ride him, at least I can loo—look at him."

Devon managed a smile. MacLeaf had been back for a month now. He'd found work in a tin mine near Liskeard after Devon had driven him away from Darkstone. Apologizing to him had been painful and awkward, but he'd done it, and MacLeaf was glad to be working around horses again.

Clay was leaning back on the sofa with his eyes closed. Devon frowned. "How do you feel? Are you ill?"

"No, I'm fine. A little tire—tired."

"You stayed outside too long. Come on, I'll take you up."

Clay waved Devon away. "How far along is Lily's, um . . . Lily's"—the word finally came to him—"pregnancy?"

Devon set his glass down carefully. "I don't know. She won't tell me." And nothing closed her away from him faster than a reference—subtle, direct, oblique, aggressive, it didn't matter—to the child she was carrying. To save himself, he'd finally stopped, weeks ago, asking her any questions about it at all. But she was too thin; he worried about her incessantly.

"It's hard for you," Clay said softly. "But in a way, you know . . ." He trailed off, not at a loss for words this time, Devon knew, but in an effort to spare his feelings.

"It's what I deserve?" he supplied caustically. Clay smiled gently and lifted a shoulder. "Thank you for that insight. But you'll appreciate that it's occurred to me once or twice before now, and I'm sick to death of it."

"Right. But I still don't under . . . stand how you could've thought, even for a . . . sec . . . second, that Lily would sh-shoot me, it's—"

"Damn it!" Devon cursed with quiet ferocity. "There was a *note*, Clay, it was under your *hand*. Her trunk was full of money. I thought you were dying—I didn't think, I acted. Oh, hell." He closed his eyes and leaned back against the window. Those were excuses, not reasons, and he'd tormented himself with the magnitude of his stupidity a hundred times.

"Mother's coming—did I tell you?"

He finished his drink and looked up. "Yes."

"Oh—sorry. What day was it again?"

"Friday."

"That's right. Alice is c-c-coming . . . too, isn't she?"

"Yes."

"That's good."

Clay's smile provoked him to smile back. "Yes, that's

good. Then someone else will have the nuisance of taking care of you."

Clay grinned lopsidedly. "I'd much r-r-rather Alice nursed me than you. She's prettier and she doesn't growl at . . . me." His expression sobered slowly. "Dev?"

"Here."

"Do you want me . . . to talk to Lily? Try to, I mean?"

He laughed, but he wasn't amused. "What would you say?"

"I don't know. Maybe it would c-c-c . . ."

"Come to you?"

"Come to me. Something brilliant, something el— eloquent."

"I appreciate that. But I don't think so."

"Well, it can't hurt, can it? Just to try."

Perhaps not, but Devon thought it would be like forcing medicine down a dead man's throat; it wouldn't hurt, but it wouldn't help, either.

"I'll talk to her," Clay decided, rubbing his hands together.

# Twenty-Five

"How can ee stand that heat, Lily? Here it is April, an' you huddled up t' them coals like some witch over 'er kettle." Lowdy unfurled a clean sheet over the mattress and began to tuck it in around the edges. "Galen d' say they'm takin' more wood here than to all o' Darkstone since ee've come t' live in Mr. Cobb's cottage. Ee did ought t' get out more, is what. Ought t' be out walkin', not settin'. In the day, too, 'stead o' at night so nobody can look at you." She threw a sidelong glance at Lily, who made no answer and didn't look up from her sewing. "Gettin' peculiar, is what," she muttered under her breath as she spread the wool coverlet over the sheet and fluffed up the pillow. "Passin' peculiar. An' too skinny by half."

Gabriel got up stiffly from his place beside Lily's chair, stretched, and stalked across the small room to the door.

"Even the dog's burnin' up," Lowdy grumbled. She went to the door and knelt in front of Gabriel. "Oo, ee are such a love," she purred, kissing him on his fore-head. Gabriel blinked politely and looked away. "But 'e've only got eyes for 'is mistress, 'aven't 'e? Bless 'is heart, what a nebby boy." She stood and opened the door, and Gabriel escaped.

"Well, what's left t' do? Dust, sweep." She wandered closer to the fireplace. "What're ee makin' for the tiddler this time? Oh, a wee little cap, ain't it cunning? Pick me liver, this cheeil've got more clothes'n the queen an' she ain't even borned yet."

Lily cleared her throat and said, "He."

Encouraged, Lowdy retorted, "No, Mrs. Carmichael says tes a gel, an' she'm got the way o' such things."

"No, it's a boy," Lily said, and went back to her sewing.

Lowdy put her hands on her hips. "Is that all ee've got t' say, an? For the rest o' the whole blinkin' day? Fie, Lily, ee're wastin' away! Stay in this cottage o' Cobb's all day an' all night, eat by yourself, don't talk to anybody but me—an' not even that 'alf the time. Do ee know they're sayin' you're puttin' on airs an' 'ave got above yourself?"

"Who says?" she asked incuriously.

"Rose. Said it to Enid. I boxed 'er ears, so she won't be sayin' it again." She waited for a reaction, but there was none. She folded her arms. A sly look slowly replaced the exasperation in her plain round face. "Oh, well-a-fine, ee d' have t' live like ee must, I s'pose." She found the feather duster on the mantel and started to wave it around the furniture, humming. "Master slept in late today," she mentioned casually. Watching Lily out of the corner of one eye, she saw her stiffen, her busy fingers go still over her needlework. "Bain't surprisin', him stayin' up 'alf the night drinkin'. All by 'imself in 'is room, Stringer d' say. Used t' drink wi' young master, but 'e'm not allowed spirits these days, o' course, bein' still mucked up from 'is wound."

She stole another glance; Lily was staring intently at

the smoldering coals, and her face made Lowdy set the
duster down and go to her. "'Ere, now! All's well, Lily,
naught's amiss but what ee couldn't cure wi' a walk in
the sun. My blessed parliament, ee did ought t' get out o'
this place some. Tedn right, livin' like a moolly ol'
'ermit—"

Lily shrugged away from Lowdy's patting hand and
shot to her feet. "All right!" she cried, flinging her
sewing onto the chair. "I'll go. I can't *wait* to go for a
walk! Then I won't have to listen to your infernal
nagging tongue!" She crossed the room in four strides,
snatched up her straw hat, yanked the door open, and
slammed it behind her.

"Come on, Gabriel, we're going for a damn walk," she
called to the dog, who was chasing a butterfly among
the glassy-eyed forget-me-nots along the walk. The tiny
garden in front of the cottage was bright with sea-pinks
and lavender, she noticed, and wondered when they'd
started to bloom. Cowslips nodded along the sides of the
gravel drive, and the air was fragrant with heather and
clover and willow herb. Violets fought with primroses
for room between clumps of bracken and billowing
fern. A bosomy robin called from the green-tipped
branch of a willow, harsh-voiced over the twittering of
invisible larks.

Gradually Lily's angry pace slowed. She turned into
the path that led to the lake—no one would be there,
she was sure—just as a randy jackrabbit spotted her,
turned a somersault, and bowled away. Big hairy cater-
pillars climbed in the gorse bushes along the path. A
couple of red squirrels contended vigorously for the
affections of a third, round and round in the top of a
hazelnut tree.

Beside the lake, sunlight streamed across the soft
sand, turning it crocus-yellow. Lily plowed through it
toward her customary flat rock not far from the blinding
blue water. "Don't you dare bring me another dead fish
today, do you hear?" Gabriel gave no sign one way or the

other as he ambled away, disappearing among the black
boulders along the shore.

She took off her shoes and shook sand out. The sun
was warm on her toes. After a moment she stood up and
took off her stockings. Then it was impossible not to
walk down to the water and dip her feet in—and jump
back in shock, for spring might have come to Cornwall,
but Pirate's Mere was still icy cold.

She resumed her seat, brushing wet sand from the
soles of her feet, and thought about Lowdy. She hoped
she hadn't hurt her feelings. But lord, she could be so
aggravating! But only because she cared, Lily knew—
which only compounded her guilt feelings. Lowdy dis-
approved of the way she lived; she thought it "peculiar."
No doubt it was, but Lily had crafted her jejune,
lusterless days this way on purpose. She'd been a guest
at Darkstone for two months, albeit a reclusive, seldom-
seen one, living in Mr. Cobb's old house and keeping to
herself. Unless absolutely necessary, she talked to no
one but Gabriel and the baby. She reminded herself of
Meraud, and joked to Gabriel sometimes that it seemed
to be his lot in life to live in isolated cottages with
strange, lonely women.

She closed her eyes and leaned back on her hands,
chin pointed skyward, drawing in deep breaths of the
fresh-smelling air. The sun felt wonderful; it seemed to
penetrate to her bones—something the coal fire she
kept burning day and night never managed to do.
Perhaps Lowdy was right, perhaps she ought to get out
more. And not just at night when she wouldn't meet
anyone. When she wouldn't meet Devon.

That strategy had failed her last night. She'd been
walking on the headland a little before midnight when
she'd suddenly come upon his tall, broad figure after
one of the sharp turns in the path. The night was dark;
he'd had his back to her, gazing out over the water.
Three days ago, for the first time in weeks, he'd knocked
on her door. Would she take supper with him and Clay

tonight? he'd inquired. She'd refused, and sent him away with harsh words. Last night she felt awkward seeing him again so soon. She had prepared to make a quiet retreat—when he turned around and saw her. Neither spoke for long seconds, and then they both spoke at once. "I beg your pardon, I didn't see you"— "'Tis a dark night to be out alone—" They broke off simultaneously and resumed peering at each other through the next tense silence. "Well," said Lily, preparing to leave.

"Will you walk with me?" he'd asked hurriedly.

"Why?"

He'd stood straighter, stiffer, and his voice took on the sardonic edge he used with her nowadays and which she hated. "Because it's spring, it's a warm night, and we're going in the same direction."

"Good reasons, all," she had said after a taut pause. "Nevertheless, I decline. Good night to you."

He'd swept her a low, facetious bow. "Good night to *you*," he countered, and all at once she caught the strong and unmistakable odor of alcohol on his breath.

"Be careful walking home," she'd told him sharply. "You're not yourself."

"No? Who am I?" She made a sound of disgust and started to turn, but he reached for her wrist to hold her. "Would you give a damn if I fell over the bloody cliff?"

With great self-control, she had not tried to wrench her arm free. Ignoring the half-serious tone that lurked behind his fatuous question, she hesitated, as if thinking it over. Then she had said, "No," very distinctly. His hand had loosened. She'd picked up her skirts and walked away fast.

Gabriel returned, mercifully empty-mouthed. He put his heavy head in her lap and let her scratch his ears. Charlie kicked—she had named the baby Charlie, after her father—and she rubbed her stomach absently with the other hand. Sighing, she acknowledged the foolish part of herself that mourned because she had done something last night to hurt Devon. She comforted herself with the certainty that all she had hurt, all she *could* have hurt, was his pride; nevertheless, being deliberately unkind to someone, even him, was nothing she could take pleasure in.

Harder to acknowledge was the covert excitement she felt at seeing him—twice now in four days. She never missed an opportunity to tell him to leave her alone; and yet when he did, she could hardly bear it. Even on the moor after Meraud's death, she hadn't suffered this intense loneliness, this alienation that was so deep it felt like dying. Seeing Devon made her feel alive again, if only with bitterness.

But her resolve hadn't changed; she still felt nothing but contempt for him, would still leave him as soon as she could. How base of him to use Clay as an excuse to see her! The worst part of her self-imposed exile— nearly the worst—was that it kept her away from Clay. She heard news of the slow progress of his recovery from Lowdy and Mrs. Carmichael, the new housekeeper, but it shamed her that she herself had not gone to see him.

She made an effort to relax, to clear her mind. Distressing thoughts came too often; they upset her— they must upset the baby. She lay back against the sun-warm rock, one hand hanging over the edge to touch Gabriel's nose. But tears welled in her eyes unexpectedly before she could defend herself, and she felt her desperate sadness returning. "I'm sorry, Charlie," she whispered, not quite sure what she was sorry for, or why she felt so guilty and repentant. The rules she had made for this temporary time, this waiting period, weren't working anymore; her defenses had started to crumble, and she was helpless to stop it. It had something to do with the unfolding of spring, and the increasing impossibility of living alone. Isolation was a slow torture for her, completely unnatural, but she'd thought it was the price she must pay for safety and tranquility. More than anything she craved peace, but her strategies for achieving it were failing her.

She swiped at her cheeks. "What do you think of this day, Gabe?" she sniffed, determined to cease her "mooling." "Lowdy was right, we ought to get out more. Isn't the sky beautiful? That cloud looks like a man—see it? Smoking a pipe, with his hat slouched over one eye."

"Talkin' to the dog again, by Jakes."

Lily sat up jerkily. "Lowdy, for the love of—Don't sneak up on me like that!"

"Weren't sneakin' up, were trampin' loud as you please. I can tramp back, too, if ee don't want your note."

"What note?"

"This note. Footboy bringed it just now. 'E's waitin' for a 'response.'"

Lily accepted the slip of paper warily, assuming it was from Devon. It wasn't—it was from Clay. He wanted to see her. Would she join him for tea at four o'clock?

"Well? What's your 'response?'"

Lily refolded the note carefully. "Yes," she said, before she could think about it too long. "Tell the boy yes, I'll come."

"You'll come, eh? Well-a-fine, I'll tell 'im so. Well now, edn that grand? You'll come."

"I *said* I'll come. You can go now, Lowdy, go and tell the boy."

"I'm goin', I'm goin'. One weasly invitation from young master an' she'm all at onct a great lady an' giver o' orders," Lowdy said wonderingly. But her eyes twinkled and she sent Lily a glad grin before she whirled and slogged off through the sand.

"I've come to see Mr. Darkwell—Clay—Mr. Clayton Darkwell." How awkward she felt, speaking to Stringer as if she were a guest, a proper lady come to call. The staid, bland-eyed butler had always made her nervous, and never more so than now. "He asked me to come," she blurted out, defensive.

"Yes, miss. Come this way."

She followed him through the hall, surprised when he turned neither right nor left at the bottom of the great staircase but continued straight up without stopping. She had assumed Clay would see her in one of the drawing rooms downstairs. This was better—she hoped; she would be much less likely to meet Devon upstairs than down at this time of the day. The house was quiet. Time might have stopped, for everything looked exactly as it had a year ago when she'd first come here. She remembered polishing these stair balusters and dusting this wainscot, straightening the picture frames in the hall. It seemed like a lifetime ago.

Stringer arrived at Clay's door and knocked; a low voice bade them enter. The butler opened the door, stood back to let her pass, and closed it behind her.

"Lily!" Clay pushed himself up against the pillows stacked high at the head of his big canopied bed. He threw a paper and a quill pen aside, staining the coverlet with black ink in the process, and grinned a huge greeting. "Come in, come in!"

She'd been half-afraid he would reproach her. His gladness made her smile, and something hard seemed to dissolve inside her. "Clay, it's so good to see you." It felt natural to go to him and give him a soft hug. "But aren't you well? I had heard you were up and about now. I wouldn't have come if—"

"I had a c-couple of, um . . . bad days," he said carefully. "Sat outside too long on Sunday, Dev says. Now I'm fine. M-M-Marsh, Dr. Marsh, said I can get up tomorrow. Sit down! There's a chair, or you can sit . . . here beside me."

She chose the chair and pulled it close to the bed. She

hadn't known what to expect, and at first Clay's appearance shocked her. He was rake-thin and nearly as pale as his pillows. The bones in his face jutted out sharply, whitening the skin even more. His fine blue eyes looked huge; his Adam's apple bobbed prominently in his gaunt throat when he spoke. He looked like an invalid adolescent. But her distress faded while they spoke, for his voice and gestures and expression were still unmistakably the old Clay's; within minutes she felt comfortable with him, and remembered perfectly why she liked him and how much she'd once treasured his friendship.

"You look beautiful, Lily. No, truly. You've been here . . ." He frowned, trying to reckon it. "How long?"

She looked down, embarrassed. "Almost two months."

"Yes, two months, and I've only see-seen you once. From a distance. You waved to me and then you rrr . . ."

"Ran away." She colored. "I know. I'm sorry, I—"

"Oh, that's all right," he said hastily, "don't worry about it. Sorry to have to mee—meet you here, though. Must bring back memories." She looked quizzical. "Of the day we met," he explained, eyes dancing.

Lily laughed, and the unfamiliar sound amazed her. "Yes, that was a very *instructive* morning for me. Quite unforgettable." She began to relax, and commiserated with Clay while he told her of his excruciatingly slow recovery. "What's this?" she asked when he paused, fingering the paper he'd tossed aside when she entered. It looked like a drawing.

"It's a ship."

"May I see it? Oh, Clay, this is wonderful." It was only lines to her, with numbers printed on the sides—dimensions, she assumed; but it was done with such sure-handed skill that she was impressed. "It's really beautiful."

"Thanks. It's a sloop."

"Is it?"

"I was thinking of s-s-sending it to the Revenue Service. It's an—improvement over their cutters because the bow—bowsprit's longer and it retracts. And there's more room for canvas because I've extended the width amidships without increasing the size of the hull. See?"

She hmm'ed noncommittally. "Do you find it . . . a little ironic?" she had to ask.

"Me designing ships for the Customs? Bloody ironic. But it—it seems to be the only thing I can manage right now. And I like it, Lily, I really like it."

"Yes, I can see that."

"It's the only thing I'm really good at, even though my poor brain's not—much up to snuff yet."

They heard a knock at the door. Clay called, "Come in," and Francis Morgan came into the room.

"Good afternoon to you," he greeted them, smiling. If Lily's presence in Clay's bedroom surprised him, he was careful not to show it. Fashionable as always, he wore a pale blue coat over a silver waistcoat and bottle-green breeches; his immaculate yellow hair was lightly powdered.

"Hullo, Francis," Clay called genially. "How are you? Pull up a chai—chair, join us."

"No, no, I just popped up to say hello; been talking to Devon downstairs. How are you today, Clay?"

"Oh, tip-top. And you?"

"Couldn't be better. How do you do, Miss—Lily?"

Of course, she thought, he wouldn't know what to call her—or why she was here again, what her status could possibly be. And what must he think of her pregnancy? Her cheeks burned but she managed a smile, trying to ease his awkwardness. "I'm well, thank you, Mr. Morgan."

Clay and Francis exchanged a few more pleasantries. Then Francis said, "Well, I'm off, just dropped in for a second, as I say. Take care of yourself, Clay."

"You too, Francis. See you."

The door closed behind him.

Clay lay back against his pillows. "Dev tells me I can't stand Francis," he confided in a low tone.

Lily nodded. "That's what I recall."

"But I can't remember why. Seem—seems like a right enough fellow. He's been decent to me since the accident."

"Do you mean to say you're *friends* now?"

"Well—yes, I suppose. Odd, isn't it?"

"Very odd."

"Alice and my mother are coming. In a few days, I think. Oh—sorry, did I tell you that already? Alice has been wonder . . . wonderful, Lily. She was here when I woke up."

"From the accident?"

"Coma, yes. And she stayed until her fam-family made her go back. Her sister was sick; she was needed."

"She must be a good nurse."

"The best."

It was time to go; she didn't want to tire him. "I'm so glad to see you again, Clay."

"I'm glad to see you, too."

"I don't know how much you can remember, but you were kind to me before, and I thought of you as my friend."

"I remember."

"I haven't tried to see you, and I'm sorry if you think I've been distant or unfriendly or—uncaring since I've come back. But I haven't been able to be with people, you see. I haven't been able to talk."

"You've had a deuced bad time." He reached for her hand clumsily.

"Lowdy said you have headaches sometimes. I'm so sorry about what happened to you. I didn't want you to think that I don't care about you."

"No, I didn't think that."

She smiled, relieved because, as bad a time as he'd had, his charming self-assurance had not diminished a whit. She glanced down at their clasped hands. "I suppose Devon told you what he thought, at first. That . . . I had shot you."

His eyes filled with sympathy. "Yes. That must have been hard."

She acknowledged it in silence. "How long was it before you could remember?"

"Remember?"

"That it wasn't I."

He looked puzzled. "Well, you know, I *don't* remember."

"What do you mean?"

"A lot of time is missing, even before the shooting. *Months* are gone. The last thing I can really recall was a few days before, I think: I can clearly remember having breakfast with Dev. After that, it's hazy. But it's coming back to me in bits . . . um, bits . . ." He gestured impatiently.

"Bits and pieces."

"Yes, bits and pieces, all the time now. Fast."

Lily released her hand when she realized she was squeezing Clay's too hard. "You—you're saying you don't remember who tried to kill you? You don't know for sure it wasn't me?"

He laughed. "That's two different questions; no fair trying to confuse me." His smile faded when he saw her expression. "I don't know who tried to kill me," he said slowly, "and I know it wasn't you."

"Then—you didn't tell Devon it was someone else?"

"No, of course not. Lily, I have no idea who shot me."

She sat back weakly.

"Why? What did he say?"

"That's—nothing, I mean—that's what he said." But she hadn't believed him—she'd been so sure he was lying!

"Listen, don't tell anyone my mem-memory's coming back, will you?"

"No. But—why?"

"Well, Dev says I'm only . . . only safe as long as the person who shot me thinks . . . um, thinks I can't remember anything. So we've been keep—keeping it a secret. Did Dev tell you about Wiley Falk?"

"Who?"

"He was my first mate. You met him that day on the *Spider*."

"Yes, I remember."

"He's dead."

"Oh, Clay. I'm so sorry."

He ducked his head. "They found him shot to . . . shot to death in his house. Head wound."

Lily went white. "What does it mean?"

"We don't know. If only I could remember!" A look of panic swept across his thin face—gone in a second. "Marsh says I might n-*never* remember. Dev says to forget about it, just to think about *before* the shooting, try to remember who my m-m-middleman was."

"Middleman?"

"Someone sold the, um, stuff, the contraband for me and gave my share of the profits away."

"Gave it away?"

"To the poor," he smirked. "I was a philanthropist." His grin widened. "Don't look like that, Lily; you look just like Dev. He says I wasn't a—a philanthropist, I was an idiot."

She shook her head at him. "For once I agree with him."

"He says I told him when I got back from—from France that I'd come upon something 'big.' I told him if I weren't already a rich man, I would be now."

"And you can't remember what it is?"

"Or wh—*where* it is. Wiley was the only one left who knew."

"The rest of your crew—?"

"Gone. Scattered."

"And now Mr. Falk is dead," Lily said slowly. Clay rubbed his forehead, eyes shut tight. She stood up abruptly. "You're tired, I've stayed too long."

He reached for her hand again. "Will you come back?"

"Yes, of course."

"Good. Because I never—I forgot to talk about what I wanted to talk to you about."

"What is it?"

"It might take a while. It's about Dev."

"Oh." She slid her hand out of his grasp quickly.

"Lily, listen—"

"No, Clay, please don't. Don't spoil it, we've had such a nice visit."

"But—"

"*Don't.*"

He studied her intently. After a moment he cleared his throat and said carefully, "Lily, I'm sorry for everything that hap—happened. I apologize for my brother, all the hurt, all the pain he caused you. If there's anything I can do, amends I can make—"

She leaned over and gave him a quick hug to stop him. "You've nothing to apologize for," she whispered. "I'll come to see you again soon. Good-bye, Clay." She kissed his cheek and fled.

# Twenty-Six

Halfway down the staircase she saw Devon waiting for her. She halted and her heart stuttered; she grabbed at the banister, off balance. He was standing under the chandelier—repaired now—that he'd shot down with a pistol the night they'd met. Did he even remember that night? She would never forget it. She started down the steps again, slow and wary, conscious of her fear of him. It had intensified because of what Clay had said—that Devon had come to believe in her innocence on his own, without his brother's word for it. Something had softened deep in her heart, she could feel it. It terrified her.

She stopped again, three steps from the bottom, unable to go closer. He was dressed formally in a buff-colored coat with velvet lapels, brown breeches, a silk shirt. His handsome face was somber, but showed no aftereffects of his night of debauchery—if Lowdy's story could be believed. Out of habit, she spoke coldly. "Was there something you wanted, Devon? You seem to have a lot of time on your hands lately."

Devon's mouth quirked, easing some of the tension in his face. She looked beautiful to him in the red Chinese smock she'd bought from a gypsy for nine pence—Lowdy made an excellent spy for him these days—and holding her black straw hat in both hands. But she was pale, as always, and she didn't weigh enough. He guessed she was in the seventh or eighth month of her pregnancy, but she looked too small.

"Yes, there was something," he said with the faintly mocking formality he'd taken to using with her as a mechanism for self-preservation. "Will you come into the library with me? I have something for you."

Predictably, she stiffened. "What is it?"

His smile felt slightly battered. "Nothing fearsome, I promise. It's a letter."

"A letter? Is it bad news?"

"Not at all. I expect you'll find it very good news. Come with me, Lily, I won't bite you."

She lifted her lip in disdain, but gave in after a moment and preceded him down the hall to the library.

The dusk was deepening; Devon lit the lamp on his library table, then a branch of candles on the mantel. Lily waited, hands folded across her copious stomach, pretending she wasn't watching him. She loved to look at him, she realized glumly; the simple sight of him pleased her. But she wasn't in love with him, thank God, and these stirrings were only a residual sensibility, the twitch of an amputated limb, not real. She was safe from him now. And she had learned that it was childishly easy to affect him: she simply withheld everything, all her thoughts and feelings, and spoke to him as little as possible. She didn't ask herself why the results were not particularly gratifying, or why hurting him had never given her the satisfaction she'd once thought it would.

"This came for you today."

She took an envelope from his outstretched hand. There was an odd look in his blue-green eyes that she couldn't decipher. "It's been opened," she noticed.

"It was addressed to me. But it concerns you."

She moved around him, took up the lamp, and carried it to a small table between the terrace doors. With her back to him, she weighed the thick envelope in her hand. Feeling a strange reluctance, she pulled out the contents—folded papers, a letter wrapped around a thick, official-looking document. She tensed when the title of the document caught her eye—*Last Will and Testament*. Scanning the pages, she saw her father's signature at the bottom of the last one, Charles Michael Trehearne, in his familiar heavy, flamboyant script. Her heart gave a little leap. She opened the letter.

It was from someone named Matthew Bogrow, of the law firm of Bogrow, Griffin, Krowitz & Rice. Mr. Bogrow had ascertained from his colleague Mr. Witt, attorney to Rev. Roger Soames, that Lord Sandown might be in possession of knowledge of the whereabouts of Miss Lily Trehearne. Lily had to read that sentence again to absorb it. The name Witt sounded familiar—then she remembered: Mr. Witt was the man she'd met that night at Cousin Soames's house. He'd given her something to sign, she recalled, a paper that turned over all her possessions to Lewis in the event of their marriage.

She read the letter over—it wasn't long—then read it again. She whirled around, holding it to her chest, and laughed out loud.

Devon's heart missed a beat or two. He couldn't remember the last time he'd heard Lily laugh. Her face, radiant and unguarded, rendered him speechless. He came toward her out of the shadows, smiling—and stopped when she turned away abruptly, breaking contact, breaking the mood. He took a deep breath, steadying himself. A moment of unwary happiness between them had been too much to hope for.

"I'm glad for you, Lily," he said somberly.

She wasn't sure she believed him. "Thank you. It's—a surprise."

"Yes."

"My cousin told me he wanted Lewis and me to marry because it was God's will; he'd seen it in a 'vision,' he said. It seems God's will got a lot clearer to him after he became the executor of my father's estate." She shook her head slowly, wonderingly, confounded by the magnitude of Soames's hypocrisy.

Devon felt little surprise. He found it telling that Lily's reaction to her cousin's barefaced humbuggery was bewilderment, while his was cynical acceptance.

"Well. I had better go now."

"May I walk with you? It's almost dark."

She hesitated. "No, thank you, it's not necessary. Gabriel is here, he'll go with me."

Devon put his hands behind his back. "Thank you for coming to see Clay."

Lily looked down. "I should have done it sooner," she admitted.

"Will you come back?"

"Yes, I've told him I will." She paused again, uncomfortable. "Clay told me he can't remember who shot him." She lifted her chin and said steadily, "I apologize for not believing you when you told me that." He gestured, making light of it. "But I couldn't believe you had absolved me without any evidence—I thought surely he must have told you something. I beg your pardon for misjudging you."

The pale skin of Devon's cheeks went bronze; he wanted to squirm under her grave, ingenuous regard. He could hardly look at her. But he couldn't tell her the truth, and he couldn't stop himself from taking advantage of this rare softness.

He moved toward her and reached for her hand. It lay rigid in his, but he hardly noticed. Then he couldn't think what to say. "I'm sorry," came most naturally. He meant for everything. He'd tried to show her his remorse through his actions, but now the time seemed right for words. "Do you think you can forgive me,

Lily?" Hope surged in him; for the first time she was not hiding her feelings, and her indecision was as plain as a printed sign.

But at last she drew her hand out of his and took a step back. "I'm sorry too, Dev. I don't think so." Bleak sorrow in her eyes mirrored the same in his. She swallowed painfully. "What you're asking is not in me to give anymore. I don't want to hurt you, not now. But it's too late."

He saw her eyes fill with tears. She turned away, fumbling at the knob of the terrace door, and hurried out. Her dog sent him a sober, accusing look before he trotted after her.

Lowdy hadn't waited for her. Sometimes they had supper together in the cottage while Lowdy told her about Galen MacLeaf, how he'd looked and what he'd done or said that day. They were engaged—they were to marry in June. But tonight Lowdy had deserted Lily, leaving a sausage pie and a jar of cider on the table for her supper.

She lit a candle and took off her hat, hung it on the hook by the door. The room was absolutely silent. A panic of loneliness swept through her all at once. It passed, but afterward she felt edgy and unsettled. She wasn't hungry, but she cut a piece of pie and carried it to the bed, sat down, and kicked off her shoes. After a bite or two, she gave the rest of the pie to Gabriel.

Despair had a too-familiar feel. The irrevocability of what she had said to Devon weighed like sharp stones on her chest, crushing the life out of her. *God*, how could she bear this? But she was sick of tears. Desperate to cheer herself, she took out her letter and opened it again. She thought nothing anymore of talking out loud to Gabriel and the baby. "Listen to this, you won't believe it," she told them. Gabriel lifted his ears and watched her with every evidence of interest.

"'Inasmuch as Mr. Trehearne applied for and was

granted exclusive rights to make and sell the device known as Trehearne's Saccharometer,' "—just saying the words made her smile—" 'such rights secured by letters patent under Patent No. 1049, enrolled 29 January 1790; and inasmuch as the Solicitor General has determined that Mr. Trehearne's alcohol proof-measuring device is substantially and intrinsically different from and superior in accuracy to similar devices in use preceding its invention—' so on and so on—this is the good part—'all stipends, fees, and royalties earned from said patent now entail to his heirs and assigns'—that's me—'according to the terms of his Will.' Listen to *this*. 'As of current date, first payment of such royalties, to be compounded henceforward on 1 June per annum, amounts to the sum of four thousand, seven hundred fifty-four pounds, eight shillings!' "

She shook her head in amazement. "A Saccharometer! Oh, Papa," she exclaimed, then laughed softly. "It measures 'specific gravity,' whatever that is. Charlie, your grandfather invented something that—what was it?" She went back to the letter. " 'Proof spirit at 60° contains 49.24% absolute alcohol by weight; the degrees over or under proof ascertained by Trehearne's Saccharometer are percentages by volume of a standard spirit, which is the proof spirit.' Well, anyway, it measures how strong the whiskey is!"

Still smiling, she folded the letter and her father's will and returned them to the envelope. She lay back on the bed and stared up at the shadowy ceiling. Ever so slowly her smile faded, and with it her elation. Nothing had changed, not really. She would leave Darkstone wealthy instead of poor, but she would still leave. She didn't even know where she would go. Lyme, probably, at least at first, because she had one friend there. The irritatingly banal thought surfaced that money, which she had needed for so long, couldn't buy the one thing she really wanted.

She flung herself onto her side. "You're all I really

want," she corrected herself, rubbing a soft hand over her stomach. "You, Charlie, you're the one and only thing. And that's the truth." It had to be, for Charlie was all she could have.

"Oh, baby," she whispered, feeling the damned, useless tears start again. "We'll take care of each other and we'll be all right. We'll live in a big house. We'll make friends and we won't be lonely." She closed her eyes and listened to the sad, far-off rumble of the surf. "Maybe we'll live in a house by the sea," she murmured tiredly, and slipped into a dream.

She opened her eyes to the sound of knocking, and saw that the candle had begun to gutter. It wasn't terribly late; Lowdy must have come back.

But it wasn't Lowdy—it was Devon.

"May I come in?"

"Why?"

His face was shadowed, invisible; it was the sound of his voice when he said, "Please," that compelled her to open the door wide and step back.

He stood in the dim center of the room, hands at his sides. She had never let him into the cottage before. "It looks different. Cobb wouldn't know the place."

She followed his gaze. It looked the same to her. She'd brought in flowers, moved the furniture a little, nothing more. To fill the new silence, she said, "I see Mr. Cobb occasionally on the grounds. He never speaks, never acknowledges me. I can imagine what he must think of me. I shouldn't have taken his house."

"But that's what you wanted. Anyway, I've told you, Cobb doesn't care where he lives; he's content in the room next to his office."

More silence. Lily went to the table and trimmed the flickering candle. When she turned back, Devon hadn't moved. "It's late," she murmured. "What do you want with me, Dev?"

Instead of answering, he moved toward her. She

stepped back automatically, but he pulled the only chair out from the table and sat down. The light fluttered on his handsome face; she fancied she saw pain in his eyes. She opened her mouth to tell him to go.

"I was twenty-three when I met my wife," he said, watching her, his forearms on the table.

Lily backed up until she felt the closed door against her shoulders. "If you tell me this, it won't matter," she said tightly. "It won't make any difference."

"I was visiting my sister in Somerset," he went on as if she hadn't spoken. "Maura was the oldest child's governess. She was half-French, half-Irish. Long black hair, black as midnight, and black eyes. She came from Dorset; her father was a tenant farmer. She got her education from the local parson, some kind soul who saw a spark of intelligence in her and helped her to find a way out. She never looked back."

"I tell you I don't want to hear this."

"She was eighteen when I met her and— unbeknownst to me, of course—sexually experienced far beyond her years. It was her beauty that attracted me at first, but later it was the restlessness in her and the—energy, a kind of impatience that I'd already recognized in myself. She was pale and fragile, Lily, a tiny thing, incandescent, *burning* inside with needs and wants I thought I understood. I thought we were alike."

He unclenched his hands and put them on his knees. "So I married her. When it was over, my naïveté stunned me. I'd bought a farm in Dorset, thinking she'd like living close to home. But the very quality that had drawn me to her was restlessness—how could I have been stupid enough to think she would enjoy a life that was just like the one she'd tried so hard to escape?

"In moments not quite so full of self-disgust, I understood that part of it was her fault. She agreed to every suggestion I made, seemed pleased and flattered by every 'condescension,' as she called it. Not once did she give me a hint that anything was amiss. Until the night she left me a note on the kitchen table and took herself off with my bailiff and all the money she could find in the house. 'I can't live this life, I'm leaving you,' she wrote. She didn't bother to sign her name.''

Lily pressed her fists to her chin, hating what he could make her feel. But helpless tears slid down her cheeks, and there was nothing she could do about it.

"I never think about her now. I found the letters I'd written to her—needless to say, she didn't take them with her. Reading them again was the only way I could call back what it was I'd felt for her. I wanted to understand the passion, the—insanity. But they're only words. There's no feeling at all anymore. Nothing.''

He stared into space. A moment later he put his elbows on his thighs and buried his face in his hands. Drawn against her will, Lily moved toward him soundlessly. She knew as surely as if he'd spoken where his thoughts had led.

"But I never stop thinking about Edward," he said in a muffled voice. "She took him. Oh, Christ. He was eight months old. He could smile and laugh. When I held him he never cried." She crept closer and put her hands on his shoulders, standing behind him. "Sometimes his little body seems so real to me, Lily, I can almost feel him. He had black hair, soft as flax. And he was fat. And very . . . happy. I think he was happy." His shoulders hunched; he took a breath and sat up abruptly, the back of his head pressed against her bosom. "But sometimes I can't get out of my mind how he looked, his—corpse. Two days dead and still unburied. He looked so small. His skin was blue—his beautiful face—" He couldn't finish. A sob rose in his chest and shook his whole body. Lily embraced him and held tight, unable to console, helpless in the face of his despair. Their tears mingled and fell on her crossed arms. She murmured to him, her cheek pressed to his temple. He took a shuddering breath and drew his handkerchief from his pocket.

She stepped back. She was shaking because of what

she had to tell him, what she had to tell herself—that her heart had closed up. It contained one person now, the child in her womb, and could admit no one else.

"Devon." He turned to look at her. She was relieved to see that he had himself in control again. "I'm sorry for your pain. It hurts me—so much. More than I can bear. But this child"—she stopped and swallowed, and now she could only whisper—"this child is mine, and you can't have it."

He stared at her without speaking for so long that finally she couldn't stand it. It felt as if she'd thrust a knife into his heart, then into hers. Not knowing what he would do, she went to him again and put her arms around him. His body felt heavy, limp. She put her face in his hair and kissed him—a silent, secret kiss.

Then her arms fell away. She moved back, across the shadowy room toward the bed, and sat down on its edge. "I'm so tired. Please go now, I have to go to sleep."

He didn't move. Minutes passed, and she thought she heard him say, "Ah, Lily. You are my joy and my dark penance." He stood and came to her, pulled her gently up from the bed by her hands. The light was dim here; they could hardly see each other. He touched his fingertips to the dark smudges of fatigue under her eyes. "Let me help you," he said, stroking the back of her neck with his warm hand. "Let me do this for you."

His touch was soft—and she needed it so much. And he needed it, too. She closed her eyes. She would allow herself just a moment's pleasure, because it had been so long. So long.

Gradually she realized he was unfastening her gown in back. She turned around, away from him, but he slid one arm beneath her breasts to hold her. "Let me, Lily." Something in the touch of his hands reassured her; she stood quietly, her head bowed.

He eased the dress off her shoulders and let it slip to the floor. "Where's your nightgown?" She pointed to the foot of the bed. He started to unfasten her chemise.

"Don't. No, don't."

"Why not?"

"Because—I don't want you to see me."

He moved his hands down to cover her swollen stomach. "But you're beautiful."

"I'm not." She remembered to add, "And I don't need you to say that I am."

"No," he agreed. "But you are anyway. You're the most beautiful woman I've ever known. You always will be. Do you think that because your belly's big I don't want you?"

"I don't know—I don't care, I mean—"

"I remember everything about your body." He went back to unbuttoning her shift in front, his arms reaching around her, fingers light and gentle. "I remember how soft your skin is, how sweet it smells. How warm in my hands. I remember your hair, tickling my face, smelling of soapsuds. The bones of your face under my fingers, your eyelashes touching my cheek, my lips. Your mouth. God, Lily, I remember your mouth."

"Devon—"

"The taste of you, Lily, the sweet, sweet taste. Touching you was so good. Your breasts are soft and perfect and they filled my hands just right."

"Please—"

He had her naked now, but didn't turn her to face him. He spread his hands over her stomach again and took a deep, unsteady breath. Lily leaned back against him and allowed it, her heart full and aching. "I want you. There's no one else but you. Lily, I'm dying for you."

She felt his breath fan her neck, her shoulder. The thought of loving him, making love with him now, made her tremble. He moved his hands up to hold her full breasts, and the trembling became a palsied shaking she couldn't control.

"You're cold." He let her go, slowly. His voice sounded strange. He snagged her nightgown from the bed and gave it to her. She pulled it on jerkily, then faced him to sit on the edge of the bed and take off her stockings. She did it without coyness, and the intimate chore—the raising of the hem of her gown past her knees, the quick, efficient peeling of the cotton hose over her long calves—moved him as nothing else had; his whole body tensed with desire so desperate it frightened him.

She finished and lay down, covering herself. The blanket flowed in seductive shadows across the soft mounds of her belly and her breasts. "Let me kiss you," he said hoarsely.

Her voice was scarcely any lighter. "You mustn't."

He sat beside her and put his hands on either side of the pillow. "Don't you want me to?"

The question confounded her. The answer to it was so obvious she thought he must be taunting her. "It won't mean anything," she said shakily.

"It won't mean anything?"

She felt inexplicably ashamed.

"It will mean something to me," he said. He leaned over and pressed his lips to hers.

She was lost immediately in the warmth and the urgency and the sweetness. She made a sound of longing and defeat, and reached for his wrists. His mouth stayed gentle and undemanding; it was impossible to say who started the provocative caress of tongues or the deep, hot kisses and the hard, trembling, purposeful clutch of hands. Hunger, stronger than anything they'd known before, caught them off guard. Her blood sang a warm, surprised song, remembering everything they'd shared. He held her as tightly as he dared, and the firm, generous curve of her belly against him renewed something that had been dead, that he'd long ago given up any hope of resurrecting. At length, in a panic, Lily pushed back at his shoulders. She was panting, her face full of dismay and wonder.

"That meant something," he said when he could

speak. How close they had come. His body was still in rebellion. "Good night, my heart," he whispered. One last kiss. Their lips touched.

It started again instantly, all the helpless wanting, as if reason had never made its brief, unwanted interruption.

"I don't want you to seduce me!" Lily cried, but clutching at him with strong fingers.

"I'm not, Lily, I'm loving you."

"Don't say it—"

"I love you. I love you."

She wept, and let him unfasten the gown she'd put on minutes ago. "Tell me why you changed your mind," she begged, her mouth pressed to his throat. "About me, and Clay. What made you want me again?"

"Let's not talk."

"No, tell me now. Please, Dev, it's time."

He shut his eyes tight, feeling his blood cool. "I told you, I came to my senses." He touched her bare breasts with the tips of his fingers, and her breath hissed through her teeth.

But she wouldn't let it go. "But why? Tell me why. What were you thinking?"

"I was thinking of you, Lily, of the way you are. I remembered how sweet you are, how gentle." He'd thought it would be hard to lie to her, but it was the easiest thing in the world—because it wasn't a lie at all. "You could never have hurt Clay. I don't understand now how I could have believed it, even for a second. I'll never stop being sorry. You gave me everything, even though you knew I couldn't give you anything back. I was afraid I'd killed all that sweetness in you. Love me again, Lily, let me back in. I need you."

She wiped the last of her tears away and took him in her arms. His hair smelled of the sea. Their hearts beat together, and his body was like the other half of hers. She pressed soft kisses to his mouth, his closed eyes, whispering comfort against his skin.

What a rich blessing. He began to stroke his hand

across the solid swell of her belly. How long had he wanted to touch her like this? He felt himself healing, flourishing, and so close to her and to his child—all one. Their baby had been conceived in love, although he hadn't known it at the time. He knew it now. "I love you, Lily."

But she said, "Don't, Dev, just hold me, it's enough."

He wanted to keep saying it, but it made her sad. And she was right, this was enough—for now.

"I don't want to be naked," she whispered a little later when he started to push her nightgown down past her hips.

"Why? Oh, Lily, let me see you. I want to be close to you."

"All right." She couldn't deny him anything. "But you too—now."

"Yes." He smiled and sat up to strip off coat and shirt, boots and breeches. He tossed the covers aside and sank back down beside her. She was lovely, he murmured to her, desirable, delicious, he wanted her at this moment more than he ever had before.

"But I'm so fat," she insisted, but smiling, almost believing him.

"No, you're perfect." He kissed her with all his pent-up need and tenderness until they were panting, mouths starved and slippery, hands grasping. His fingers made a comb through the soft hair between her thighs. She parted her legs in invitation and he accepted, enthralling her with his slow, deep caress.

She shuddered, arched higher. "Dev, I don't know— *how*—"

"I know a way." Facing her, he pulled one of her long, sleek legs over his hips. "Like this."

"I can touch you this way," she marveled, demonstrating.

He groaned. "Yes, I know."

They kissed, side by side, exchanging sweet, hot

caresses, until they forgot to kiss. He squeezed her hand tighter around himself, rock-hard and throbbing, and ground out, "You do it. Slow, love, take it slowly, only as much as you—ah, Christ." She had taken him deep inside, all at once. They held still to savor it. "Lily, this—this is—"

"Yes," she whispered, in perfect agreement.

"No, but this—" Words were useless. He was connected again with his deepest feelings. He'd been solitary and alien, and now he'd come home. He, Lily, the child—they were together inside her kind and generous body. A storm of emotion shook him. He felt redeemed, and this intimacy was all but unbearable. He could have wept, but his sexual arousal was too intense.

His reaching hands were splayed across her breasts, hers on his stomach and his bent knee beneath her. Their bodies made a lovely, ungainly X. Lily let her excitement rise and blossom slowly, selfishly, taking his patience for granted because he had never been anything but patient before. It was as if she'd already been satisfied, and it was enough now to take delight in the miracle of this union, this amazing completion.

Almost enough. She could feel his passion building through the long, steady rhythm of his body's caress, and it fired her. Heat coursed through her, singeing her where his fingers stroked and pressed. The heat intensified. She'd known desire before, but not quite like this. She was aching. But she was big with child—how could her body respond to him this way? She had no answer; she only wanted. And loved.

And he was swelling, bursting, he couldn't bear the wait. This was need, not seduction, rough and uncontrollable, and he'd been on the edge of it for much too long. He rose up to take her near breast in his mouth while his fingers pinched and chafed at the other. Lily's head fell back, chin to ceiling, and she began the soft, rising moan, a sound he had never forgotten, that told him her climax was near. He thought of all the times he'd teased her, taunted her with his control and her helplessness, his mastery of her. Now he was master of nothing. He spoke low in her ear, love-words and soft, broken-off obscenities that were barely understandable between the hungry, devouring kisses he pressed to her throat, neck, shoulder. He could feel himself beginning to fall, beginning to overflow. "Hurry," he urged, trying to sound calm. She looked at him, and her eyes, before she closed them, were soft and opaque with her deep woman's knowledge. She smiled, and then her mouth opened on a long, silent cry.

He waited for her, surprising himself, but held fast in the grip of fascination while Lily surrendered, shuddering against him, gasping out her pleasure. His own followed instantly, a deep, endless release. When it was over, nothing was the same as it had been. Before he fell into sleep, still entwined with her in a lovers' tangle of sweat-damp arms and legs, he felt his baby move inside her body. Joy, an exquisite shimmering sensation, took his breath away. He kissed Lily's mouth, and closed his eyes in peace.

# Twenty-Seven

"Lily!"

She stopped, trapped. It was Clay who had called—she hadn't made her escape quickly enough. If she weren't so fat he wouldn't have seen her, she thought irritably. She turned and gave a reluctant wave and a nod. Perhaps it would still be possible just to walk away—but no. Now Devon was striding toward her along the cliff path, his face full of purpose.

"Come and meet Alice and my mother," he invited, smiling. "Last chance—Alice has decided to stay, but Mother leaves tomorrow."

"This isn't necessary," Lily said in a low voice.

He arched a brow. "Are you afraid?"

She started to deny it, but she saw the warm sympathy in his eyes and it provoked her to tell the truth. "Terrified." So far she had successfully avoided their ladyships, who had been at Darkstone for nearly a week, and until now Devon had respected her reticence.

"I won't let them eat you," he promised softly. He reached for her hands, his body blocking her from the view of the others. The look in his eyes melted her; everything blurred.

She thought of how patient he'd been these last days, letting her set the pace of their reconciliation. His wounds went as deep as hers, but hers were fresher—they didn't heal as quickly. And so they hadn't spoken of the future or given each other promises. At times like this, though, when his heart shone in his eyes, and when he stood close and she remembered everything about his body underneath the rough tan broadcloth and the soft white muslin—then she had no resistance at all, and her only defense was that he didn't know it.

"Come," he urged her gently, "you'll like them. And they'll love you." He took her arm. It seemed childish to hang back now; she let him lead her toward the trio waiting for them on the cliff path.

"Mother, Alice, this is Lily Trehearne."

Lily curtsied, murmuring, feeling extraordinarily uncomfortable. She'd made a mistake, she realized immediately. This was without a doubt the most awkward moment of her life; the more she thought of it, the more absurd it seemed. What could Clay and Devon be thinking of, wanting her to meet these women? Were all men this stupid? After the introductions, it didn't surprise her that no one knew what to say. Clay was holding Alice's arm in a comfortable way, she noticed. Lady Elizabeth was holding something too, a tiny ball of fur—a dog, Lily surmised—while making no effort at small talk. Instead she regarded Lily with such sharp-eyed interest that she wanted to squirm. Never had she felt so clumsy and tongue-tied. Or so pregnant.

"Lovely day," Clay mentioned presently, for the tenseness of the silence had finally registered even on him. Lady Alice agreed, and expanded on the theme for a few halting sentences.

"I was just on my way home," Lily remarked desperately. "Good day—I'm happy to have met you." She curtsied again, sent a private glance of misery at Devon, and made her escape.

In the cottage she paced, reliving the dreadful scene, chiding herself for going out at all today when she'd *known* that Alice and Elizabeth were here and there was even a small chance that she would meet them. Gabriel watched her from the open door, massive black head rotating with each of her hectic circuits. With a scrabbling of toenails he suddenly turned around; she peered past him to see what had caught his attention. Coming up the walk, skirts swaying, silk parasol swinging, strode Lady Elizabeth Darkwell.

She squinted in the doorway, finally making Lily out in the dimness. "May I come in?"

"Of course. How do you do? How good of you to . . ." She trailed off, aware that this was not likely to be a social call. Elizabeth was glancing about the rough room, cool blue-green eyes missing nothing. "Won't you sit down? The fire's still lit, I can make a cup of tea in no time if you—"

"Please don't bother." She sat at the wooden table in the room's only chair. Lily recalled the high stool by the bed; rather than stand over her ladyship, she went and got it, perched on it nervously, and folded her hands.

"I recognize you," Elizabeth opened. "I believe you once served tea in my son's drawing room." Lily stiffened. So the interview was going to be as unpleasant as her worst imaginings had warned. But unexpectedly Elizabeth smiled, and her rather haughty features relaxed. "You didn't do it very well, I noticed. It's lucky for all of us that your career as parlormaid was short-lived. Clay has told me all about you, Miss Trehearne."

"Sometimes Clay has a loose tongue," Lily said faintly.

"Yes, he does. Which is fortunate, considering that Devon never tells me anything." The two women regarded each other gravely.

"Whatever must you think of me," Lily murmured.

Lady Elizabeth spread her hands. "Quite honestly, I don't know what to think of you. You're more intelligent than I thought you would be; I can tell that from your face. No less beautiful—but Devon likes beautiful women."

There was an uncomfortable pause. "Did you come to tell me something in particular?" Lily inquired finally.

"Yes, I did. But I imagine you can guess what it is."

She didn't look away. "I imagine I can."

Her ladyship leaned forward earnestly. "My dear child, I wouldn't dream of hurting you, but surely you can see that a marriage between you and my son is impossible."

Lily's expression didn't change, but her heart beat faster. "Has Devon said something?" she asked evenly. "To make you think that such a thought has crossed his mind?"

"No," she admitted, "he hasn't. But as I told you, I'm not often in Devon's confidence. But there's a child involved; he may be contemplating marriage for the sake of the baby."

Lily flushed, and didn't answer.

"I've come to ask you to leave here, Miss Trehearne, before the baby's born. Before Devon sees it and decides he wants it. I'll give you as much money as you want."

Lily stood up abruptly, although she wasn't angry or even particularly surprised—this was only what she'd been expecting, after all. Then why did she feel so hurt?

Elizabeth rose, too. "I beg your pardon if I've offended you," she said quickly, measuring Lily with her astute, penetrating eyes. "Forgive me for speaking so frankly, but you must know that if my son married you he would become a laughingstock. He's only just begun to live down the scandal of his first marriage. You can guess what was said—a viscount marrying a governess, a woman who proved to be little more than a whore.

Now, if he were to marry a pregnant girl who was once his housemaid—"

"Please," Lily interrupted, face flaming, "I understand you perfectly. Devon has never offered marriage, and we have no understanding. I truly believe your fears are groundless."

"But if he did ask you?" Elizabeth pressed.

Lily honestly couldn't answer. She made a helpless gesture with her hands.

"Do you love him?" The older woman's face softened.

"Please," she said again, "there are things between Devon and me that I can't explain to you."

"I know what some of them are, I think. Clay has told me."

Lily almost smiled. Clay again. "I wonder if he's told you about my inheritance."

"Inheritance?"

"In a month I'll come into quite a lot of money—by my standards, at least; by Dev's, or yours, it probably won't seem like much. Nevertheless, I'll be able to support myself and my baby. Devon knows this."

"So you intend to go away?"

Again she couldn't answer.

Elizabeth folded her arms. "I like you, Lily Trehearne," she said candidly. "I admit that surprises me. I like a woman with pride. And good sense, too—it must have been hard to forgive Devon for the things he did."

Did she know everything, then? Lily could only nod, and murmur, "Yes, it . . . hasn't been easy."

"For myself, I don't think I could have forgiven him," Elizabeth confessed. "If it weren't for what the doctor told him, after all, he might still think the worst of you. I'm afraid I could not forget such a thing—or offer affection to a man who had shown so little faith in me. But I'm not much like you, Lily, I don't think. I'm harder, and more selfish. But do you know, if my

husband were alive today—" She broke off. "Well.
That's neither here nor there, is it? I'm—are you all
right, child?"

Lily was holding onto the back of the chair with both
hands. "I'm not sure I know what you mean," she said
carefully. "What did the doctor tell Devon?"

"You don't know?"

She shook her head. Lady Elizabeth paused uncertainly. "I would be grateful if you would explain it to
me."

"I'm sorry, please believe me, I thought you knew;
otherwise I wouldn't have spoken."

Lily waited.

"Clay's doctor, Dr. Marsh." She stopped again.

"Yes, I know him."

"It was he who told Devon that Clay could not
possibly have written anything in a note in the moments
after he was shot. The wound to his head was
devastating—he would have been incapable of it. The
injury was so severe, so traumatic that, as you know,
he's only beginning to recover the simplest faculties.
So—obviously someone else wrote the note, trying to
implicate you."

She went to Lily and touched her arm. "I'm so sorry; I
can see I've upset you."

"Would you please excuse me?" Lily whispered.

"I'm sorry," Elizabeth repeated helplessly. She
waited a few more seconds, then took pity and left
without another word.

Her ladyship's worried gaze was on the ground; she
was startled when her older son accosted her in the
middle of the gravel drive.

"Mother?"

"Oh, Dev—I'm afraid I've done something . . . rather
unfortunate."

Devon was familiar with his mother's habit of ironic
understatement. He prepared for bad news.

"That girl, Lily—"

"You spoke to her?"

"I did; I thought it best."

"What did you say to her?"

"I told her I thought the two of you ought not to marry."

He relaxed, even smiled with affectionate tolerance. "That was ever so slightly presumptuous of you, don't you think? I trust Lily took your advice in the way it deserved to be taken—politely but very sparingly."

Elizabeth looked more uncomfortable than ever. "Are you telling me you *would* marry her?"

"If she'll have me," he answered immediately.

Elizabeth put a hand to her forehead; she looked shaken.

"I love her, Mother," Devon said quietly. "And she's carrying my child."

"Maura carried your child." She put her hand on his arm when she saw his expression. "Forgive me for that! I hardly know her at all, and yet I can see this girl is nothing like Maura."

"No, she's nothing like her. But it took me a very long time to understand that. You must let me make my own happiness," he said more gently. "I can imagine what you told Lily."

"No, I don't think—"

"But I care less than ever what the world thinks of me. Lily's everything to me. All I want is to live with her and our children, here at Darkstone, for the rest of my life."

Elizabeth's smile was troubled and happy at the same time. "Then that's what I want for you, too. But I'm afraid I've done something stupid. But—I didn't know she didn't know, you see, and it just came out—"

"Mother, what are you talking about?"

"I thought she knew what Dr. Marsh told you about Clay—that he couldn't have written the note that blamed her because his poor brain was so badly injured that he wasn't able even to move, much less perform thought processes as complicated as . . ." She trailed off, chagrined anew by the look on Devon's face. "I've done it, haven't I? You hadn't told her. I'm sorry, I just assumed that you had."

"It doesn't matter," he said grimly; "in fact it's for the best. I'm glad you told her, glad it's out." He rubbed his face with both hands. "But you've set me a formidable task, Mother."

"Yes, she . . . seemed quite upset."

He could imagine. He looked over his mother's shoulder at Lily's cottage; a thin trail of smoke rose from the stone-and-mortar chimney in the thatched roof.

"I like that girl, Dev. I hope she comes around, because you could do much worse."

"I *have* done worse," he reminded her dryly. Then he gave her a quick kiss and walked off toward Lily's house.

There was no answer when he knocked. A bad sign. He started to turn the knob and walk in uninvited, but then he didn't. "Lily," he called out, "it's Devon. May I come in?" Nothing. "Lily!"

Another pause, and then he heard her voice, faint, almost querulous, calling, "Dev, is that you?"

"Lily, let me in."

"Well, come in, it's not locked."

He squared his shoulders and opened the door, expecting anything—except the sight of Lily sitting in front of the fireplace, calmly sewing embroidery on a child's blanket. All his breath came out in a slow exhale. "Hello," he said experimentally.

"Hello." She looked up for a second, then back at her sewing.

"'Tis a warm day for a fire."

"Is it? I was a little chilly."

He plucked a sprig of heather from the jar on the table and twirled it between his fingers, watching her. "How are you today, love? Feeling all right?"

"Oh yes, perfectly. Well, maybe a little tired." She smiled at him briefly. "Dev?"

"Mmm?" He crushed the heather blossom and held it under his nose.

"I was wondering if you might lend me some money." When he didn't answer, she went on, "Not much, just a little, and I'd pay you back when my inheritance comes."

He laid the flower on the edge of the table with great care. "What do you need money for, sweet?"

"Oh, you know—things. For the baby, for me, just—things."

Her voice was a parody of casualness. She was the worst liar he had ever known. He felt embarrassed for her.

"Lily," he said quietly, "I've just spoken to my mother."

Her hands went still. A long moment passed before she looked at him, and then her face was a stiff white mask. "Will you give me the money?"

"No."

She stood up so quickly her chair toppled over backwards and struck the floor with a crash. She threw her sewing after it and faced him, fists up and clenched, teeth bared. "Bastard!" She came toward him fast, hissing, "Lying son of a bitch!"

Shock kept him motionless; he'd never heard her swear before. When he realized she meant to sweep past him and escape through the door, he put an arm out to stop her. She shouted another oath and hit him— actually hit him—a hard blow to the side of his chest, her hands clasped to make a club.

"Bastard!" she cried again—her storehouse of curses was limited. "You bloody bastard, get out of my way!"

"Listen to me, I was going to tell you about Marsh—"

"Liar!"

"No, I was going to tell you, but the time wasn't—"

She ran at him, a spitting, sputtering, pregnant battering ram, and pushed him out of the way. "Lily!" He caught her arm and held it fast. Thank God her dog was nowhere in sight; he had time to think before she yanked out of his grip.

"Your mother will give me money!" she hurled at him. "She tried to before, but I wouldn't take it. Now I will!"

"She won't give you any money—I won't let her."

Her rage flared higher; she was weeping with pent-up fury and could hardly speak. The urge to escape receded, overcome by the need to fight. "I should have known you were lying, it's what you've always done! All you've ever wanted from me is sex. You lied so that you could seduce me again. Now you think you'll have this child, but you won't."

"Lily, please—"

"'I'll never stop being sorry,'" she mimicked, lips curling nastily in disgust. "You bastard! 'Love me again, I *need* you.' You're a—"

"For God's sake," he cried, "do you doubt it? Do you truly doubt it?"

"You don't know how to tell the truth! But this is the end, it's over."

Somehow he kept his hands at his sides. "Lily, have mercy. There was a note, words on it—I thought Clay wrote it."

"You should've known!"

"Yes. Yes, I admit it, I should have known."

"It's over, Devon. This is—not—forgivable."

"But you love me."

"I'll stop. I have stopped."

"Marry me."

She laughed. "Never. And thank God you can't force me. I'm leaving you, I'll forget you as soon as I can. I'll find someone else, a man who loves me and loves my baby—"

"You'd take the child from me?"

"Yes! Without hesitation! I would go now if I could."

Now Devon swore, with a viciousness that made her back away from him. "I don't agree to this," he said through his teeth, "I don't give you up."

"It doesn't matter—I don't expect anything from you that would help me. But I'm leaving you, and you'll *never* have this child, never even see it!"

"I will not allow this. I won't let you go. The child is *ours*, Lily, you can't take it from me." She shook her head, green eyes as angry as hornets. "I'll keep it!" he burst out, enraged. "I'll take it from you, I've got the power! It doesn't matter how much money you've come into, I've got more. I'm a viscount, I'm in Parliament, I'm the bleeding *magistrate*—"

"I knew it!" she crowed in sick triumph. "You don't want me, you only want a child to replace the one you lost! But I swear before God, Dev, you won't have it!"

She was crying hard, arms folded across her stomach in a desperate gesture of protection, panting with the violence of her emotion. Rationality returned to him in an icy rush. "Calm yourself," he warned; "you'll hurt yourself if you don't take care."

"Then get out. Get out! I don't want to look at you."

He couldn't stand any more. He felt battered, physically ill. "I'll send Lowdy," he muttered, backing out the door. When his feet hit the gravel, he turned around and ran.

The gray afternoon was windy and warm. The Channel waves looked like long glass rugs spiraling toward shore, pausing for a breath in midair before smashing on the shale in a million watery slivers.

Clay held Lily's hand as they stared out across the restless rollers. "Dev and I used to play here when we were boys," he told her.

"I know. He brought me here once." *And kissed me. For the first time. What a child I was then.* "He called it the drowning cove." She gazed past Clay toward the cliff's edge, and beyond it to the huge boulder below, almost completely exposed now in the low tide. The drowning rock.

"We used to play pirate in the caves under this cliff. One of the differences between Dev—Dev and me is that I grew up to *be* one."

"You were never a pirate," Lily scoffed, defending him. "You were a free-trader. A much nobler calling." She put a surreptitious hand to the small of her back and pressed, trying to relieve the ache there. "Shall we sit down again?" she suggested after a moment when the pain would not diminish.

They walked back to their blanket and the scattered remains of their picnic. Lily sank down gratefully; Gabriel flopped beside her and put his heavy head in what little space of lap she had left.

"I like this dog. There's something about him. He never leave—leaves you, does he?"

"Never." She shifted slightly, searching for a comfortable position. The low ache had started last night, and it seemed to be getting worse instead of better. Clay was watching her; she sent him a false smile.

"Are you mad at me, Lily?"

"No! Why would I be?"

"Because I wouldn't give you any money."

She mumbled something and hid her face by kissing the top of Gabriel's head.

Clay spoke earnestly. "We're friends, Lily, I'd do anything for you, I truly would. But Dev's my brother, I owe him my loyalty, too. And anyway, if you went away now, what good would it do? It would only—"

"It's all right," she broke in, "I understand, and I don't mind, honestly. I'm sorry now that I asked you—it wasn't fair. Let's forget it, Clay, let's pretend it never happened."

"But what will you do?"

She looked at him directly. "Wait."

He shook his head, dismayed. "Lily, this is crazy. I would never have thought you could be so stubborn."

She laughed, unamused. "Let's leave it," she warned again, coolly. "You really don't know anything about it."

"Ac-actually, I know all about it."

She shifted, uncomfortable again; Gabriel heaved a long-suffering sigh and squirmed away. "Oh, probably," she said irritably. "Let's leave it, anyway."

"All right." A minute passed. "Dev's miserable." Lily made a move to get up; Clay's hand shot out to hold her. "All right, I'm sorry! I'll stop." She settled back, face shuttered, and stared out at the waves, luminous gray cylinders winding tighter and tighter.

But he couldn't leave it after all. Lily's mouth tightened but she didn't move this time when he whispered —as though if he spoke softly enough she wouldn't run away—"Dev's an honorable man, Lily. You must know that. He made a stu-stupid mistake, a terrible mistake, and he's suffered for it. When will it be enough? When will you be sat-satis—Oh, Christ, I'm sorry." He reached out to brush away the tear that spattered on her hand in her lap. She seized his hand and held it tight. He squeezed back, and fell silent at last.

So, Devon was miserable. The news gave her no satisfaction; if anything, it only heightened her own misery. If he had mourned as she had in the last four days, then Clay was right—Devon had suffered indeed. Her anger, which had felt so righteous and pure at first, had abandoned her quickly, leaving her with nothing but distress. Finally it was the fear that she might be hurting the baby that had made her give up her solitary grieving and her weak, ceaseless weeping. When Clay had appeared at her door this afternoon, picnic basket in hand, pale and shaky but determined to make her come with him, she'd surprised them both by saying yes.

She wiped her eyes with her handkerchief one last time and sent him a watery smile. "Talk to me," she urged. "Tell me something about you. Anything, Clay, just talk to me."

He grinned, abashed but willing. "All right. Well, let's see. I posted my drawings to the Customs Office yesterday. Remember I was desi-designing a sloop?" She nodded. "I probably won't hear anything for weeks, maybe m-months."

"Oh, I know they'll like it."

"They ought to," he asserted, disdaining false modesty. "It's damn—*damned* good, as good as any tub they ever fl-floated." He found a scrap of cold partridge in the bottom of the hamper and began to nibble on it. "What else shall I tell you? Oh—I'm remembering things, Lily. More all the time."

She sat up. "Clay, that's wonderful. Anything . . . about that night?"

"Bits and pieces. I remember it was windy, ready to storm."

"It was," she confirmed, excited. "Anything else?"

"I remember being in the library, but I can't remember what I was doing." He scowled and rubbed his forehead gingerly.

"Don't worry, it will come."

"Yeah."

She touched his sleeve, seeing the confusion that bordered on fear in his fine blue eyes. It always broke her heart. "Everything's going to be all right, Clay. It just takes time." He nodded, not looking at her. "I don't know how I let you talk me into coming out on this picnic," she said to distract him. "It's most improper. My 'confinement' is a very loose state of affairs around here."

"That's what Dev's always liked about Darkstone, I think. There's no 'society' around here to disapprove of what he does."

Lily didn't answer.

"When, uh, what day do you, um . . ."

"Have the baby? Oh, today, probably." She waited for

his expression of shock, then laughed at it. "I'm not sure, silly, not exactly. Soon, though."

"I guess you'll be relieved when it's over."

"Yes. I have many . . . different feelings about it. You can probably guess what most of them are."

"I'd be afraid too," he admitted.

He'd misunderstood her ambivalence, she saw. It wasn't the pain of childbirth that troubled her—or not only that. It was afterward, when she would have to go away.

"I'd like to have children someday," Clay said suddenly.

"You will. I'm sure you will."

"Lily . . . do you like Alice?"

She raised her brows. "I don't really know her, Clay, I only met her once." Something more seemed called for. "She certainly seems to be an agreeable person."

"Oh, she is, she really is. I've known her forever. We grew up together, our families were friends. I wish you knew her better, I know you'd like her." He saw that she was staring at him in fascination. He blushed, then grinned, looking away. "I, um"—he brushed crumbs around on the blanket—"I, you know, like her."

Lily nodded encouragingly.

"Not the way I used to—as friends. It's changed since she came here and started taking care of me. I don't know what I'd have done without her, Lily. She's been so kind to me." He paused. "Actually," he confided shyly, "after I'm back on my feet, really all right again, I was thinking I might ask her if she'd like to get married."

"Oh, Clay." Lily's face was wreathed in smiles. "I'm so glad."

"Do you think she'd have me? She's a bit older, you know. Only a year or so, but still—"

"I think she'd be a perfect fool if she let a fine catch like you slip through her fingers."

He leaned over and gave her an impulsive kiss on the

cheek. Lily laughed at him. She lay down on her side to ease the pain in her back—it felt now as if someone were kneeling on her spine, trying to break it—and half listened to Clay extolling the perfections of the lovely, the inestimable, the incomparable Alice Fairfax, until her eyelids drooped. She was so tired. Clouds had begun to obscure the sun, but it was still warm and the whisper of the sea was restful.

When she woke up, the sky was black. The wind blew in warm, violent gusts and the sea had turned into a random swarm of foaming whitecaps. Clay awoke a few seconds later, and for a little while they watched the approaching storm in silence, hypnotized by the rude, inhuman energy of it. "How wild it looks," Lily murmured, and the wind whipped the words from her lips and away. She smiled and pointed at Gabriel; his ears were blowing straight out from his head. Finally they got to their knees and started to gather together the remains of their picnic.

"Hullo."

They turned in unison, startled to see Cobb striding toward them along the headland path from the east, away from the manor house. He stopped beside their blanket, courteously sweeping off his wide-brimmed hat. Until now he had seemed to make a point of keeping out of her way; this was the first time Lily had met him directly, close up, since her return to Darkstone nearly three months ago. Even now he didn't look at her; he spoke to Clay, exchanging pleasantries, discussing the impending storm. "Tes blawin' up from the south," he observed. "Seen the long black swell, 'ave ee?"

Lily looked up at Clay when he didn't answer. His face was colorless. "Clay?" she faltered. "What's wrong? Are you ill?"

He didn't hear. He was staring at Cobb, the whites of his wide eyes glimmering in the sickly gray-green air. "You," he rasped, rising to his feet, clumsy.

Gabriel growled low in his throat; that frightened Lily more than anything. "What's happening?" she asked, gazing back and forth between the two men.

"That's what you said, that night. 'Seen the long black swell?' It was you."

Cobb dropped his hat. "What're ee blatherin' about?" He bared his teeth in a travesty of a grin.

"You tried to kill me."

"Have a care, lad. This is panjandle foolishness."

"Because I found out about the money. You weren't giving it away, you were keeping it. Jesus God, it was you."

"Bleedin' 'ell, Clay, don't be a fool."

Clay grabbed Lily's hand and pulled her up. Without speaking again, he began to walk fast toward the house, towing her along.

She looked back fearfully—and screamed when she saw Cobb, striding after them, pull a long knife from his belt.

Clay whirled. Gabriel closed in, stiff-legged, fangs bared, the sound in his throat deep and feral. Cobb came nearer; Clay dragged Lily behind him. The rest happened with blinding speed. Cobb lunged and Clay shouted, *"No,"* flinging up both hands. A second later Gabriel sprang, hurling himself between them. Clay lurched, stumbled backward, and fell. Lily saw the knife in Cobb's hand, dripping red, and screamed just as the dog launched himself again. She heard a smacking sound, then a hideous snarl of pain and fury, and Gabriel collapsed in the bloody dirt at Cobb's feet.

Cobb still held the knife. He moved toward her slowly, lips gleaming in his fierce beard, black eyes flickering between her face and her great, protruding belly. "Don't," Lily begged, backing away, arms folded around herself. "Please, don't, don't." She saw uncertainty in his face, then consternation. When he shoved the knife into his pocket, she wailed with relief.

"Don't move," Cobb warned as he came toward her, huge hands curled.

"I feel so much better now, Dev, since my little nap. I wish I'd told Clay I'd go with him," said Alice, standing in the library door. Devon nodded, his mind on the column of figures he had been trying to add up for too many minutes. "Oh, but no—look at the sky! I didn't realize." She laughed softly. "Poor Clay, he'll be drenched. Now I'm *delighted* I had the wisdom and foresight to decline the invitation." Perceiving that her companion was listening with less than half an ear, she wandered across the room to the terrace doors, the better to watch the coming storm. "It's amazing how quickly the sky changes in Cornwall," she said in a soft voice, mostly to herself. "The clouds in Devon are hardly ever this dramatic, they're more—Oh, no. Oh my God, Dev—*look.*"

Devon scraped back his chair and crossed the room in four long strides. "What's wrong?"

"That dog—there, on the terrace. He's hurt. Dear God, I think he's dead."

Devon threw the doors open and rushed out. Gabriel lay on his side, half hidden in a bloody bed of ivy, his eyes wide and glassy. A long slash between brisket and belly oozed sluggish blood. Devon rose from his knees slowly, wiping his hands on his breeches. "Lily," he cried, and started around the side of the house for the drive and Cobb's cottage.

"She's not there!" Alice called to him.

He halted, spun around. "Where is she?"

"At least—she might not be there. Clay was going to ask her to go with him on his picnic."

"Where? *Where was he going?*"

"He said the drowning cove. Dev, I'll come with you!"

Without waiting for her, he sprinted for the cliff path at a dead run. The trail was easy to follow; it was speckled with Gabriel's blood. Devon ran as fast as he could, into the wind, panting not so much from exertion as from an ice-cold dread that squeezed his chest in a vise. Minutes later he found Clay not far from the cove, crawling in the path, legs churning pitifully to drag himself along. "Jesus," Devon prayed, touching him gently. His wound looked as bad as Gabriel's.

"He's got Lily, he's killing her." Clay's hands were clamped over his diaphragm, holding himself together. Tears streamed down his face. "It was Cobb—shot me, killed Wiley. Get Lily, Dev."

Devon clutched at his brother's bloody shirt and brought his face close. "I can't leave you!" He shouted it like a curse. Then he remembered. "Alice—Alice is coming."

Clay shook his head frantically. "He's killing her. I'm not bad, it's—just blood." He subsided weakly, but kept his wild-eyed gaze on Devon.

"Alice is coming," he said again, unable to think past that, and Clay groaned in frustration. Great thudding drops of rain began to fall on them. Devon leapt up suddenly and started to move, backwards at first, keeping Clay in sight to the last second. Then he whirled and ran.

He and Cobb saw each other at the same moment—Devon beside the blowing remains of Clay and Lily's picnic, Cobb clambering up the rough face of the clifftop, soaking wet. Devon's heart stopped beating when he read sorrow and regret in Cobb's bleak, black-bearded face. It meant he was too late. He was too late.

He came at Cobb on a wild run, not pausing even when he saw him draw a bloody knife from his pocket in an oddly weary, almost stoical gesture. Beyond thinking, Devon dodged the knife's murderous arc by reflex and closed with Cobb in a ferocious, grappling clinch. Cobb gave ground, and found his feet inches from the cliff's stony edge. They wrestled, neither gaining advantage for long, grueling seconds. Both men were strong, but Devon was half-mad with a killing rage. At last he got a grip on Cobb's wrist and twisted; the knife clattered to the ground. Cobb dove for it at the same moment Devon struck him in the throat with his fist.

Cobb dropped to his knees, wheezing. "I'll kill you," Devon gasped, hitting him again. "I'll kill you." He kicked him in the chest with the flat of his boot, and Cobb fell backwards. When he felt the sharp edge of the headland on his spine, he screamed. But when he thrust up an arm and shouted, "Help me!" Devon reached for him.

Wrong arm. Devon grasped air instead of a hand, and Cobb disappeared over the face of the cliff.

# Twenty-Eight

He heard no scream, no sound of falling. On his knees, he shuffled to the cliff's edge and looked down. Directly below, the waves churned over a jagged line of rocks, gray and grim, back-leaning as if aghast at the violence of the incoming tide. He made out the dun color of Cobb's coat in the wash, just for a moment, and then it was all swirling foam. He closed his eyes, breathing hard. When he opened them, he saw Lily in the trough of an ebbing breaker. She was tied by the wrists to the drowning rock. Before his eyes, the tide swept back and buried her.

He shrieked her name into the roar of the wind. Once, there had been wooden steps curving down to the cove, but they had rotted away, leaving only crude stone outcrops in the cliff face, slimy now with salt spray and rain. He scooped up Cobb's knife and plunged down the outcrops, cursing and praying, abandoning caution in his haste. At the bottom he thanked God he hadn't broken any bones, and plunged out into the roiling surf.

He saw her again in the reflux of the streaming, sucking tide. She gasped a deep chestful of air before the next wave swamped her, beating her back against the drowning rock. He strode toward her, arms flailing, struggling against the malignant power of the swell. At the moment he reached her, another wave hit, submerging them both. He held onto the iron ring under water and slashed through her leather bonds—Cobb's belt—with the knife. The wave receded; they surfaced together, gasping. He caught her around the chest with one arm before the next roller could wash her away, and thrashed through the tide with her toward shore.

Shore was two feet of wet shale at the base of the cliff that the inrushing tide had not yet inundated. He fell to his knees there, Lily in his arms. They couldn't speak. Rain pelted them; the wind blew a steady, brutal assault. They felt nothing but each other's bodies. That she was alive, breathing, arms wound tight around him, filled him with light and awe.

But she was crying. He pulled away to see her face. She sobbed, "Clay's dead," and buried her face in his neck.

"Lily, no, he's not. He's hurt, but he's going to be all right." He was absolutely sure of it.

She wiped her eyes and stared. "He's not dead? But Cobb stabbed him with his knife, I saw it. Gabriel, too. But he couldn't stab me, I think because of the baby." That reminded her. "Dev—"

"Gabriel dragged himself all the way home, darling. Alice found him. That's how I knew to come after you."

"Gabe," she whispered. "Oh God. He's dead, isn't he?"

"I don't know. I'm afraid he might be."

They held each other, trading comfort until, all at once, Lily hunched her shoulders and went rigid, convulsed with sudden pain. Devon bit out a panicky curse. She was clutching her abdomen; helpless, distraught, all he could do was hold her. At last she straightened, for the spasm seemed to have passed. He touched her rock-hard stomach with shaking fingers, searching for a wound. Her arms and hands were scratched and scraped from the rock, her shoulders too where her dress was torn, but otherwise he couldn't see any injuries.

"Dev," she gasped, stilling his hands, panting, leaning back against the wet stone. "The baby's coming."

He gaped at her for a second, then shook his head. "No, it's not. It can't. No, no. It's not."

Lily pushed her dripping hair out of her eyes. "Excuse me, but—"

"No, it's not coming. You're mistaken."

"I'm mistaken?"

"Listen—"

"Devon, I'm having the baby!"

"All right, all right," he said, soothing her. But he still didn't believe it. He stopped staring into her frightened face and looked up through the rain at the solid wall of cold, slick stone hulking above them. "Can you, um—"

"No."

"No. I didn't think so." And he couldn't carry her, not unless he slung her over his shoulder, leaving himself one free hand for climbing. Lily was in no condition just now to be slung over anyone's shoulder. "Well now," he said, with false calm. "Let's see, here." While they had been speaking, their two feet of dry land had diminished to one and a half.

"Oh God, oh God," Lily muttered, teeth chattering. "This can't be happening, it just can't be."

"No, exactly, that's what I was just—"

"Uh!" With a terrible groan she tensed again; she had a bone-breaking grip on his fingers that made him want to groan with her. When the pain faded, she was ghost-pale and shiny with perspiration, and he couldn't deny it any longer: Lily was in labor. "Oh God," she wailed, "what am I going to do? I can't have the baby here!"

"It's all right, sweetheart," he said again, trying to sound confident, "everything's going to be fine. I'm going to take care of you. Don't worry about anything except having the baby."

"*Where?*"

Instead of answering, he gathered her in his arms and lifted her. The tide foamed around his feet. He set his teeth against the wind and started off across the rough shale, moving east, staying as close to the cliff as he could. But sometimes the ground dipped and he was forced to wade through surging, thigh-high water. Lily hugged his neck with all her strength and prayed he wouldn't stumble. They had gone about forty paces when a notion of his destination began to dawn on her.

"A cave—you're taking me to a cave."

"A nice big, airy—"

"Cave."

"Yes. Clay and I used to—"

"Play pirate when you were little."

"Yes. It's the only—"

"I'm not having this baby in a cave!" She clutched him suddenly, gasping, "Oh no," while her whole body tightened to meet a fresh pain. Devon sat down in the surf, Lily on his lap, and rocked her.

"That one was worse," he noted unsteadily when it was over. She only nodded. "Darling, listen, there's nowhere else. It'll be dark and dirty, but at least dry and out of the wind. It's right there. See it? Behind that tree in the crack."

"But we'll drown! The water—"

"Flows in for about twelve feet, and then there are stone steps, sort of, that go up into the cliff. Nice and dry." He stood up, still holding her.

"Sort of?"

"Lily, don't worry."

"What does that mean, Devon?"

"It's going to be all right."

"That cave has bats, doesn't it?"

"No bats."

"And snakes."

"No snakes."

"Spiders, then." When he said nothing to that, she cried, "It does, doesn't it?" in miserable triumph. "Oh, *Judas.*"

"I'll step on them." He set her on her feet at the cave entrance, a narrow, grim-looking aperture in the face of the rock. "Let me go first."

"Go right ahead."

"Keep hold of my hand."

"If you insist."

He put his hands on either side of her face and smiled down into her panicky eyes. "It's going to be all right, sweetheart, I promise."

"But, Dev, I'm going to have a baby in a cave!"

He kissed her forehead, her cheekbones. "We're going to have it together. I won't let anything happen to you."

Another spasm gripped her then; she leaned into him, and the taut, strong touch of his body helped her through it. "You won't leave me?" she whimpered when it finally faded.

"I'll never leave you. Come on, love, the water's rising. Hold my hand."

She noticed then that the waves were breaking above their knees. She had to duck to enter the cave, and almost immediately they were plunged into near-total darkness. "Oh, this is wonderful," she grated. Desperate circumstances, she was learning, drove her to sarcasm.

"It's not pitch black in the cave itself," he said hastily; "there's . . . a little light from the top." Or there used to be, he amended silently. About twenty years ago. "Come on, this way." He hoped.

The rock steps were high and jagged; he had to lift her up to each one. Resting on the fourth, she had another contraction. "They're coming so *fast,*" she breathed, frightened again.

"That's good, though," he told her, surreptitiously wiping perspiration from his forehead; the realization that he was going to have to deliver the baby was just beginning to sink in. "It means it'll be over soon." He liked the bold, self-assured sound of his voice, and wondered if she was persuaded by it.

At the top of the last step he told her to stay put, hold on to the wall right there, and not to move. She assured him that she had no intention of wandering off. Would she be all right? Yes, of course. But when he let go of her hand and disappeared completely into the blackness, a blind, unreasoning panic swamped her. "Dev!"

He was beside her in seconds. "It's all right," he crooned, holding her. "Is it bad this time?"

"It's not—I wasn't—" For a moment she considered telling a tiny little fib. But then she couldn't. "I was just scared," she admitted. "Don't leave me by myself. Can't I go with you? You said it wouldn't be dark!"

"It—takes a minute for the eyes to adjust."

"What's that funny smell?"

"I don't know."

"What's the floor like? All covered with spiders, I don't doubt. And snakes too, if the truth—"

"Lily, for the Lord's sake—"

"This is all your fault, Devon."

"*My* fault?"

"Well, it's your baby, isn't it?"

His hand holding hers squeezed tighter, and she bit her tongue. "Yes, it's mine," he announced, victorious. "You're cutting it pretty close, but I'm glad you finally admitted it before the child gets here."

A million thoughts clouded her brain. "I'm not talking to you about this now."

"There's nothing to talk about."

"You're right, there isn't. This is *my* child, not yours."

She thought he muttered something vulgar as he shuffled along in the dark, she holding on to his coat.

Suddenly he shouted a real oath when his foot struck something metallic, and she couldn't repress a scream of fright. "What? What is it?"

"How the hell do I know? Stand still and don't move." She obeyed while he leaned over to investigate. "God almighty."

"What?"

"It's—I think it's—it is."

*"What?"*

"A lantern. Glory be to God, it's even got oil in it. And, Lily." His voice became soft, reverent. "Next to it is a tinder box."

"Are you joking, Devon? Because if you are—"

"I'm not joking. Sit down here, right here, while I light the lantern."

She did, and presently she heard the scratch of flint and steel. Seconds later the lantern wick sputtered, ignited, and glowed. Lily wrinkled her nose. Pilchard oil. The first thing she noticed was that there were no spiders on the ground, at least not in her vicinity. The second thing she noticed made her breath catch and her eyes go wide with astonishment. "Dev, look."

He was looking. They were not kneeling on the floor of an empty, damp, dirty, spider- and snake-infested boyhood cave. They were in a warehouse. Stacks of boxes and barrels and bales surrounded them on all sides. Scarcely an arm's length away was a gaudy wall of rolled fabrics, silks and satins, brocades and velvets, printed muslins. Abutting it were barrels and ankers of wine and rum and brandy. Another wall was stacked with what looked like Turkish carpets, brightly colored and musky-smelling. There were furs in huge piles, beaver and fox and raccoon, next to a mountain of scroll-like rolls that appeared to be painted Chinese wallpaper. They couldn't see the coffee or the tea, but they could smell them—the pungent aroma they'd noticed before but couldn't identify because it was so incongruous. A long metal box nearby was printed with a neat sign that said "Muskets." But the most amazing thing of all was a plain, unadorned wooden chest in the middle of the cave floor less than six feet away. The heavy lid gaped open on its hinges, and inside gleamed a shiny, slippery fortune of gold and silver coins.

"God save us," Lily whispered. "Where are we, Dev?"

He laughed softly, gazing around. "It's Clay's cache. It must be. He couldn't remember where he'd put it."

"Cobb knew. Dev—what he told me! He was your brother—your half-brother. Your father's son."

He turned to her slowly. "What? Lily, what are you saying?"

"Cobb was your father's bastard! He always knew it, and hated it because he was your servant, yours and Clay's. He said he had a right to steal from you."

Devon's face was stiff with shock; he couldn't speak. She wanted to touch him, but another pain seized her then, and this one seemed to go on and on. She meant to keep quiet, and was dismayed to hear herself cry out before it was over. "Damn it, damn it," she panted. "I wanted to be brave, but oh, this *hurts*."

"Scream all you want. Scream your head off," he advised, and hoped his reassuring smile looked less sickly than it felt. "But first let's get you out of that wet dress. You're having this baby on a nice warm pile of furs, covered with silk. How many women are so lucky?"

She was not cheered. "God, I hate this," she grumbled, and kept it up the whole time he gently stripped off her soggy clothes and wrapped her in a roll of burgundy velvet, soft as butter. He left her sitting on the floor near the chest of treasure, still griping, while he made her a thick bed of rabbit and fox fur. "Use the muslin," she suggested practically when he started to spread pale yellow silk on top of the furs for a cover; "it washes better."

He helped her into her new bed and covered her carefully, even though her laboring body was already warm. She felt better sitting up, she told him, so he fashioned her a thick pillow of beaver pelts, wrapped in satin. He stood back, hands on his hips, and grinned at her.

"What's funny?"

"You look like a pregnant bear. On her way to a ball."

Lily's sense of humor wasn't highly refined at that moment. "Thanks very much," she said stiffly—which only made him laugh. "Do you have any more entertaining observations? If so, let's get them all out at once."

Still chuckling, he sat down beside her and took her hand. "Tell me your life story. Tell me all about Lily Trehearne. What did you look like when you were a little girl?"

She eyed him suspiciously. "I'm not telling you anything. Why do you want to know? You should have asked me such questions a long time ago if you were interested." She winced and drew herself up as the pain struck again, harsh and punishing, and seemingly with no end. In its aftermath she lay panting and perspiring, stunned by the intensity this time, and more afraid than ever. "I don't see how this can be natural," she whispered weakly, "this is just—this is too—" She stopped, seeing his face. Immediately he assumed a mask of calm, but it was too late—she'd already caught a glimpse of his torment. It wrung her heart. "But everything's going to be all right," she said as she reached for his hand and gripped it hard, "I'm sure it is. Meraud said I would have a quick and easy time, and she could tell the future."

"Who is Meraud?"

"She was my friend. I lived with her in her house on the moor. You put the magic stones on her grave after you found me that night. I never thanked you for that. Lie beside me, Dev; it helps if I can feel you."

It helped him too. He stretched out next to her on the fur bed and rubbed her stomach softly while she told him all about Meraud and the moor, the sculptures and the glass wall. As she spoke, the image of her old friend became clearer in her mind; she fancied she could almost feel Meraud's presence with them in the cave. It was a comforting fancy.

Devon talked about Cobb. He remembered that his steward's mother had died in childbirth four years before Devon's birth. Mary Cobb was her name. His father's mistress. "It's not so surprising. My mother wouldn't, or couldn't, share a life with my father, although I never really understood why. He must have needed someone while she was off in Devonshire." His father's will had stipulated that Cobb sons could remain stewards at Darkstone Manor forever, generation after generation—Edward's way of assuaging his guilt, no doubt, for never acknowledging his bastard.

"I wonder if losing his hand to save Clay when they were little made him even angrier as the years went by," said Lily, thinking out loud. She remembered the day she had come upon Cobb drunk in his cottage. "A Darkwell bain't a man for a young girl to rely on," he'd warned her. She realized now that he must have been thinking of his mother. "Why did he leave all this, do you think?" She gestured to the stores of treasure all around them. "Why not take it and escape? He could have gone somewhere far away and lived like a king. For that matter, why didn't he kill Clay? Finish the job, I mean. He must have known that Clay might get his memory back someday."

Devon was silent for a long time, brooding. "Maybe he didn't really want to kill anyone. Maybe he stayed because he had nowhere else to go. After all, Clay and I were the only family he had." He couldn't forget the look of remorse on Cobb's black-bearded face when he'd crawled over the lip of the cliff.

Lily had a different memory—of the cruel, bruising strength of his hands when he'd dragged her, pleading for pity, into the surf and tied her to the drowning rock. She had a compassionate heart, but she could not feel sorry that Cobb was gone.

Time passed. The harrowing pains racked her with increasing frequency; in the diminishing periods of rest between them she told Devon about her father, and what she could remember of her mother, and what her childhood had been like. For his sake, she never cried out again. He listened while he massaged her back and shoulders, her feet, asking questions or talking about himself through the pains to distract her. Neither had forgotten the worst of their shared past, and Lily had not forgiven, but they were embarked on something together that deflated the magnitude of all that, made that terrible time, at least for now, seem far away and trivial.

"Go ahead and yell," he urged when the pains began to come in long, racking waves, but still she kept silent. It seemed more helpful to pant. How many hours had this been going on? She couldn't make her legs stop shaking, and it was almost impossible to concentrate. Between contractions she felt miserable and irritable and frustrated; when he told her how well she was doing, she snapped at him—then apologized, tearfully and profusely, until the next pain hit and he coaxed her through it again.

Just when she was sure she could bear it no longer, when she was fully prepared to get up and leave, with or without him, and forget all about this horrible, unnatural business of childbirth, something changed. "Dev," she breathed as a different kind of pressure seemed to build slowly inside her. "I think it's coming."

"Easy, love," he cautioned, crouched between her legs, gauging her progress. "Go easy now. I can't see anything yet."

The next contractions were almost as satisfying as

they were painful, and the intervals between them were nearly peaceful. She went limp, conserving the last of her strength, while Devon massaged her calves and offered endless encouragement.

"Oh, Lord," he said a little later, "I think I can see it. I can see the head! Can you push, sweetheart?"

Could she push? She couldn't *not* push! She was filled with a wild elation as she bore down, panting and crying, excitement far outstripping the pain. "Can you really see it?"

"I can see it! It's coming, it's coming. It's got a face, and hair—brown hair, I think. Keep pushing!"

She obeyed gladly, and it was as if she were finally doing something, finally contributing to this child's birth. At last she felt one final, terrific contraction. As clearly as if she were watching it happen, she knew when her baby's long, perfect body slipped and slithered out of hers. The sensation made her laugh through the tears of relief and release that streamed down her cheeks. "It's a boy, isn't it? I know it is!"

"Yes, it's a boy. He's beautiful. Look at him, Lily."

"Oh, God." He was the most beautiful baby in the world, wet and red and squalling, and wriggling already. His fingers and toes enchanted her; he had a lovely, handsome nose and his lips were perfect. She was in love with his shoulders; his ears were utterly beguiling. His feet!

She reached for Devon's hand and squeezed it. She was almost too tired to move, and yet a deep, sweet euphoria was rising and rising, ready to overflow. His fingers were warm and strong, enveloping hers, and in his eyes she saw the mirror of her own heady excitement. But what amazed her was that he was crying, freely and without embarrassment.

"Oh, Lily," he kept saying, shaking his head, cradling his tiny son's body in one arm. "He's beautiful, he's so beautiful. He looks exactly like me."

# Twenty-nine

At dawn a light rain glistened and puddled on the jagged rocks dozing at the cliff base. Along the shore everything was gray, a misty, monotonic seascape without shape or perspective. But out to sea, miraculous white clouds bulked and massed on the edge of the horizon, and above them the yellow stars winked out one by one. The day would be fair.

Devon breathed in the salt smell of seaweed and driftwood abandoned on the shale by the storm. There was no sound but the gentle breathing of the sea. Thoughts of his father drifted through his mind, random at first, but persistent, like the steady ebb of the outflowing surf.

Edward Darkwell had been a big, handsome man, tall and strong, with brown hair that had turned white in his forties. Devon remembered him as generous and impulsive, a deeply principled man—but also troubled, torn by passionate extremes, and too sensitive to the inconstancies of his own emotions to enjoy sustained happiness for long.

For years, Devon had thought he was like him. His mother called him "intense;" Clay spoke of Devon's and his father's love of the sea and how it "steadied" them. Devon knew now that they had something else in common as well. Thirty years ago Edward had committed a sin, an act of infidelity. The consequences of that betrayal had devastated a family and caused the deaths of two men, one of them his own son. Sometimes justice was slow, but it was sure. And the lesson was bitter but unavoidable: the sins of the father were, eventually and inevitably, visited on the children.

To the east, beyond a crumbling fortress of rocks half buried by the retreating tide, the pale tip of the sun oozed over the skyline. The waves brightened to purple-green, that peacock color peculiar to the Cornish sea and no other. Devon rested his head against the rough cave wall and felt fatigue wash over him, heavy as the sucking tide. Behind him, inside the cave, Lily and the baby were sleeping, nestled naked side by side under their warm fur blanket. He felt the soft, lulling seduction of his dream, his miracle-hope that he could have them both, live out his life with Lily and his child and be happy. But the dream wavered, flickered. The unmoved voice of his conscience disturbed it, reminding him that an old score was not yet settled. He still owed a debt. A man was not rewarded for stupidity and wrongdoing with the object of his heart's desire. Not, at least, in the world Devon had come to know.

One early gull soared over the quiet cove the sea had clawed out of the granite cliffs. The last star disappeared in the wash of the sun. On this rare May morning, the first day of his son's life, Devon understood that the universe was as orderly as the cycle of the tides, that all actions had consequences, and that his destiny was ineluctable. He rose slowly from his crouch above the foam-wet rocks and climbed the high steps back into the mouth of the cave, moving toward the flickering lantern light.

Lily awoke, empty-headed. A second later, the fierce, sweet excitement rushed back as strong as before, as if she'd never fallen asleep. She opened her eyes and saw Devon in profile, cradling Charlie—wrapped in softest cotton and warmest velvet—and studying the baby's face with a look of rapt intensity. A welter of emotions tumbled inside her. She murmured Devon's name and held her hand out to him.

He looked up, and his face changed to a new expression she couldn't read. Their gazes held as he moved toward her. The baby began to whimper. She stretched out her arms expectantly, smiling, feeling lit up with gladness. An odd moment passed. Her smile wavered. She felt a chilly frisson of fear—just before he bent, placed the infant in her hands, and stepped away.

She forgot her anxiety immediately, forgot everything but the extraordinary feel of her baby in her arms. "Look at him, Dev. Oh, look at him." She adored him. "He has your hair. My chin, I think. I don't know whose nose this is, but isn't it wonderful?" She touched the baby's nose with a fingertip, enchanted, then pulled the furs away to uncover her breasts. "He's already hungry again. There, baby. Yes, sweetheart. Look how he knows exactly what to do. It's so . . ." Words failed her. She closed her eyes, lulled by the soft tug of Charlie's mouth at her nipple. This tiny human being had lived inside her for nine months, and now she was feeding him with her own body. Incredible! It was all too much, too splendid; she felt overwhelmed by the miraculous perfection of everything in creation.

Charlie fell asleep with his mouth open, little fists clenched on either side of his face. "Sweet baby," Lily crooned, kissing him. He squeezed his eyes tight,

smacked his lips, and fell into a deeper sleep. She
arranged him with great care in the crook of her arm,
softly tucking the covers under his chin.

"The tide's running out."

She glanced up. Devon had stepped back from the
warm circle of lamplight; she could barely see him, a
tall shadow against the deeper blackness behind him.
"What time is it, do you think?"

"Early."

"Come closer, Dev, I can't see you."

"They must have looked for us all night; I saw lanterns
just before dawn, above the cliff. I'm going up now, Lily.
Will you be all right for a little while by yourself?"

She nodded, frowning into the murk.

"But I have to tell you something first," he said.

She wanted to touch him, but he seemed so closed up,
so far away. "I can't see you," she said again. He
hesitated, then stepped into the light. She patted the
side of her fur mattress invitingly. After another odd
pause, he moved closer and finally sat down beside her.
She felt so full of joy and relief and quiet happiness that
his gravity bewildered her.

"I've made a decision," he said.

A reflex made her tighten her arm around the baby.
Heat rushed to her face. "About Charlie?" He frowned,
and she said quickly, "I named him that months ago. It
was my father's name."

His eyes lit up briefly; he eked out a faint smile. "It's a
good name. I wish I had known your father."

Resolving to think about that later, Lily forced herself
to ask, "What is the decision you've made?" Dread
returned in a flash, anger too, when he didn't answer
right away. How cruel to tell her this now, when she was
too weak to fight him, too—

"I've wronged you, Lily. From the first day we met.
You were right about me—I set out to seduce you from
the beginning, with no thought for the consequences or
the harm it might do. You gave me—everything, and in

return I offered you money. Later, I refined it to a 'living.'"

"I made that choice," she corrected softly. "You didn't force me into anything I didn't want to do."

"That's not true. But we both know that's not the worst." He girded himself to say it. "I thought you had hurt Clay—tried to kill him for money. I *believed* it. It's astonishing to me now; inconceivable. Abominable. I came so close to hurting you—physically hurting you." His face took on a haggard look, but he went on doggedly. "I tricked you on the eve of your wedding to a decent man. I used you in the basest possible way. I made sure that you were publicly humiliated, and then I abandoned you. I walked away and left you to face whatever would come, knowing it would be hard, something—"

He stopped. Lily had begun to cry. He couldn't look at her now, but he had to finish the harrowing list. "If Dr. Marsh hadn't explained it to me, I would not have looked for you. I'd have left you to your fate. You'd have perished with Gabriel on the moor." He turned away, spoke to the shadows. "Lily, I find . . . I find that I must make amends."

Her eyes swam; she used her wrists to wipe them. "What do you mean, Dev?"

"I have something now that can make up for what I've done." His low voice deepened. "This child. I give him to you. He's yours. Go wherever you like, I won't stop you. You're safe from me. I swear it."

She was pressing her hand to her throat. He took her silence for agreement; but a moment later he found he had to know for certain. "Is the debt paid, Lily? Is it enough?"

She couldn't speak; she could only nod, and finally whisper, "Yes, it's enough."

"Good." He stood up. "Then it's done," he said with hoarse finality. His glance flickered over her breast to the baby sleeping at her side. He tried to smile. "It'll be all right, Lily, for you," he told her softly. "I've come to think we get what we deserve in this world." Then he turned around, stiff-limbed, and disappeared into the darkness.

Quiet drifted back in the wake of his heavy footfalls. The sea was only a fitful whisper, distantly echoing the baby's soft, shallow breathing. Lily's eyes darted from shadow to shadow, scouring the cave walls for purchase, for stability. She moved her legs, restless; a pounding in her skull throbbed in time with her slow, erratic heartbeat. She squeezed her eyes shut tight, fighting against a feeling of rightness, a dark, older, unenlightened justice that said, Yes, this is equal, this loss Devon feels is as deep as my loss was, and it's fair. We are even.

*Be gentle, Lily. Forgive the one who hurt you so bad.*

In the deep stillness, the high, quavery voice was as clear to her as if Meraud were in the cave, sitting beside her. She could almost see her old friend, puffing on her pipe, leathery cheeks billowing, blinking into a pungent peat fire.

*Soften your heart, child.*

But he hurt me so much, she countered in self-defense. He believed the worst of me, Meraud. All the things he said just now—

*Let go o' your pride, lamb. What good is being right if you're alone?*

Charlie drew a deep breath; for a few seconds his whole body quivered. Then he subsided peacefully and relaxed against her. She loved him completely, absolutely. She would die for him without a second's hesitation. Did Devon feel the same? She did not doubt it.

*This child's a gift. He makes a circle, Lily.*

A circle. Yes. She and Devon and Charlie were a circle. She saw that anger and the darkness of betrayal had shackled her to her sick intransigence. Once, her body had known better and defied her, in Devon's arms. Afterward, when she'd thought he'd betrayed her again, she felt ashamed. Now her very shame humbled her. And he had given Charlie to her—*given* him to her. His most precious gift. Lily's heart turned over and she forgave. He loved; she loved. The past was over. She was his, and so was this child.

She was smiling through the tears, but a yawn overtook her. She was so tired. How could she stay awake until he returned? But she had so much to tell him! She gave Charlie's soft temple a kiss and focused her gaze on the darkest of the cave shadows, the place where Devon had disappeared, willing herself to stay alert and to wait.

But a minute later her lids drooped. Her last thought was that she hoped he would bring her something to eat, because she was starving. Then she fell asleep. Still smiling.

"She's coming! She'll be right down." Alice floated out onto the terrace in a gown of powder blue muslin, silk slippers, and a beribboned straw bonnet—her bridesmaid's regalia. "She said she had one more thing to do and then she'd come."

Reaction to the news that the bride would be late was mixed. Clay shrugged and motioned for Alice to come and join him on the settee. Elizabeth went back to cooing nonsense to the infant in her arms. Francis Morgan squared his shoulders and made a stronger effort to engage the groom in light conversation. Reverend Hattie said, "Hmpf." Devon broke a recent promise to his mother and started pacing again.

Everyone said it was a fine day for a wedding. The cerulean sea matched the sky and the noonday sun shone high and bright, as warm as a kiss. Flowers draped and garlanded and crowded the terrace with tiers of heady balsam and tamarisk, purple fuchsias in hanging baskets, fragrant myrtle in great clay pots, geraniums and campions, foxgloves from Devonshire, Falmouth orchids and hydrangeas and sweet-smelling camellias. The men observed that there was hardly enough room for the people; the women nodded and smiled, feeling complimented.

"So, Dev."

The groom stopped pacing. "So. Francis."

"Where are you two going on your honeymoon?"

Devon brightened. "Penzance, just for a night or two. Lily's never been there."

"So short a time?"

"We can't leave Charlie with the wet-nurse for longer than a few days." He smiled. "We'd miss him too much." Francis smiled back. Devon studied him casually. Two weeks ago Clay had remembered why he couldn't stand Francis. He cheated at cards. Or he had, one night at Poltrane's back in '92. Clay had a long memory.

"Will you take a real honeymoon later, then?" Francis wanted to know.

"Yes, when Charlie's older. Greece or Italy, we think." Lily was all for Italy, Devon for Greece. He regretted telling her that he'd heard the Peloponnesus looked like Cornwall; now she mocked him, claiming that was his only reason for wanting to go there. Of course it wasn't; it was just his main one.

Reverend Hattie, a tall, lantern-jawed gentleman in a black bagwig, said, "Hmpf," again. Devon sent his mother a look; she caught it, approached the minister, and set out to divert him. Reverend Hattie was a kind soul, but he was from the old school: he didn't appreciate the charm in the attendance of the happy couple's month-old son at the marriage ceremony. In good conscience, he couldn't condone it; and yet his presence seemed to bless it. The reverend was in a quandary.

Devon unknowingly deserted Francis in the middle of a sentence and set out on a new round of pacing. What could Lily be doing? He glanced at the house. Two round-eyed faces stared back at him from the library window. Seeing him watching, they disappeared at once behind the draperies.

He took the wide terrace steps two at a time and strode into the house. "Galen!" he called to his stable-man, who was rushing out of the room, pulling Lowdy behind him.

They stopped and turned around, guilty-faced. "We was watchin', like," MacLeaf confessed. His gap-toothed grin was charming.

"Well, hell, man, come outside and watch."

"Oh! Well now, edn that—"

"Lowdy, where's Lily?"

"She'm gone to the stables, sir."

"The *stables?* What on earth for?"

"Don't know, sir."

"Well, go and get her. Hurry!"

Lowdy dropped a hasty curtsey and ran out.

Devon went back outside.

"Sit down, why don't you? Relax. Have some punch." Clay toasted him with his glass, grinning at him. "Think she's run off? Got cold feet at the last second?"

Devon ignored him and checked his watch. Twelve-forty.

"Maybe she got a look at that waistcoat," Clay theorized. Alice giggled, which only egged him on. "It's hit her that she can't possibly go through life with a man who would wear such a thing to his own wedding."

Devon looked down at his vest. "What's wrong with it?" But he had to smile, too. Crimson brocade wasn't quite his style; he'd chosen it to brighten up the somber black of his dress coat and breeches. Lily hadn't seen it yet; he had an idea it would make her laugh. He hoped it would. *Where was she?*

"I don't know why you're nervous," Clay continued, enjoying himself. Today was his first day out of bed and he was full of high spirits. "It's not as if you two don't kn-*know* each other pretty well already." He wriggled his eyebrows in a suggestive leer; Alice tsked a reprimand, but then spoiled the stern effect by giggling again.

"I'm going to remember this," Devon promised grimly, "next September when you two get married. Just wait."

Clay and Alice laughed delightedly, Clay holding his side; they were at that stage of infatuation when anything remotely amusing seems, in each other's company, hilarious.

Devon shook his head at them, suppressing a laugh of his own. But where was Lily? This had gone on too long—perhaps something was truly amiss.

Elizabeth sat down, abandoning the reverend, the better to make clown faces at her grandson. Her little dog, Midge, looked put out. Devon walked over to Elizabeth and asked, "How's Charlie?"

"Lovely. But he might be wet."

"Here, I'll take him." She handed the baby over reluctantly. Devon smiled down at his son, feeling the usual swell of pride and joy. Charlie's mother had made him a wedding gown of lemon-yellow flannel, with blue embroidery at the collar as delicate as fine penciling.

*Where was she?*

"I'm going after her," he decided suddenly.

"But, Dev—"

"I'm going." He turned and went around house, arms full of Charlie, and headed for the stables.

He found her with Lowdy in the middle of the hard-packed yard, standing still. The two women had their full-skirted backs to him; he couldn't imagine what they were doing. They heard him and turned, and he saw Gabriel between them, sitting back on his haunches, tongue lolling.

Lily beamed, then her face turned apologetic. "I'm sorry—I'm holding up everything, aren't I?"

"It's all right." He gave the baby to Lowdy, then reached for Lily's hand and kissed it. "You look beautiful." He'd never seen her rose-colored gown of silk damask, elegantly simple, with silver lace tumbling at the sleeves and the low bodice. She was wearing her heavy hair swept up in a pretty French twist. Her tall, graceful figure wasn't a bit less desirable for being temporarily more matronly.

"You look beautiful too," she returned, gray-green eyes twinkling, and he stood up taller in his bright red waistcoat. "Is everyone waiting? I'm sorry—I wanted Gabriel to come." She blushed a little. "To the wedding."

Devon said stoutly, "Of course he should come."

"But I didn't realize how long it would take him to get there. He's resting." They looked down at the panting dog. He thunked his tail and grinned at them.

"Did you tell him Midge is waiting for him? That should get him moving."

Lily clucked her tongue, indignant. "I've told you, Dev, Gabriel is *not* in love with that—*animal* your mother calls a dog."

"Love is blind, my sweet. Which is a very good thing for some of us."

She stepped closer and slid her arms around his neck. "Not for you," she murmured, smiling. "My eyes are wide open."

Devon kissed them closed, whispering something Lowdy couldn't hear, try though she might. Lowdy's own eyes grew wide as the embracing couple began to kiss in earnest. Right there in the stableyard, front to front, arms all wrapped, mouths mashed. It got even better when the master started moving his hands around on the new mistress's waist and what-not—and then that long-nose preacher went and spoiled it.

"Here now, enough of that," boomed Reverend Hattie, striding toward them. Lily and Devon broke apart without much haste and not an ounce of shame. "Turn right around, both of you, and march yourselves into the house." Without ceremony, he took the baby from Lowdy and made shooing motions with his free hand. "March! By heaven, this cub's going to have honest parents within the next ten minutes, or I'll know why not."

Devon shrugged, resigned. "Right you are, Reverend. A man's got to do what a man's got to do, however heavy the task." Laughing, he pulled Lily close and kissed her again when she opened her mouth to object.

"No more of that till you're wed," exhorted the parson, then glanced down at the infant in his arms. "Not that it makes much difference now." Charlie stared back at him, mesmerized.

Gabriel got up carefully and began to walk toward the house, leading the way at a slow, dignified pace. Lily and Devon followed, holding hands.

"Who might you be?" Reverend Hattie inquired, craning his neck behind him.

"Loveday Rostarn, your honor," Lowdy piped. She decided to expand. "Her as who you're marryin' next week wi' Galen MacLeaf."

"You haven't got a baby too, have you?"

"Phaw," scoffed Lowdy, blushing prettily. "Tes them two what can't keep their 'ands off each other," she declared, nodding toward the meandering pair ahead. "Me an' Galen . . ." she trailed off, leery of lying to a man of the cloth.

"Have been lucky so far," Reverend Hattie guessed cannily.

Lowdy grinned. "Well, that's as may be, your reverence, but ee did ought t' be makin' haste after them two."

"Why is that, Miss Rostarn?"

"Bain't it clear as day? Ee've a babe in your arms as tes, an' ee can see what *they're* like." And in fact, the pair in question were already kissing and snuggling again. "Was I in your line o' work, I'd be quickenin' along, your grace, t' make sartin there ain't another early-born thistle shootin' up afore next spring!"